INVITATION TO VIOLENCE

Gerald Hanna, an insurance adjuster, is conservative by nature. But his drive home from the weekly card game changes all that when he finds himself in the middle of a jewel heist shootout. Forced to take one of the criminals with him, he soon finds that he's driving away with a dead man in his car … and a bag full of jewels. So Hanna removes the body and takes the bag of jewels home with him. Now he finds himself playing a game of cat and mouse with the cops, who find out his car matches one seen leaving the crime scene, and the leader of the gang, who wants the jewels. And then there's his suspicious fiancée, who just wants Hanna.

A PARTY TO MURDER

It's the night of the Markey Christmas party. After the party, Patricia Andrews' nude body is found on a hotel room bed with a single bullet hole in it. Detective Goodwin interviews everyone who attended the party. Could the murderer have been her husband Clayton Andrews, an older man who had been forced to accept a number of younger lovers in his wife's bed? Or Joel Siddel, Andrews' best friend, and Pat's latest lover? Or Johnny Creamer, desperately in love with her and jealous of her other lovers? Or Hubert Pringle, a man with a bad gambling habit who has been embezzling from the office for years? Or could it have been Harold Markey himself, head of Markey Publishing Company and the biggest bastard in the business—and another one of Pat's former lovers? All Goodwin knows is that Siddel has gone missing, Creamer seems to want to confess to anything and everything, and Andrews himself is gradually becoming unwound. And they all had a reason to kill Pat.

LIONEL WHITE BIBLIOGRAPHY (1905-1985)

Fiction

Seven Hungry Men (1952; revised as *Run, Killer, Run!,* 1959)

The Snatchers (1953)

To Find a Killer (1954; reprinted as *Before I Die*, 1964)

Clean Break (1955; reprinted as *The Killing*, 1956)

Flight Into Terror (1955)

Love Trap (1955; reprinted in UK as *Right for Murder*, 1957)

The Big Caper (1955)

Operation—Murder (1956)

The House Next Door (1956; first published in *Cosmopolitan*, Aug 1956)

Hostage for a Hood (1957)

Death Takes the Bus (1957)

Invitation to Violence (1958)

Too Young to Die (1958)

Coffin for a Hood (1958)

Rafferty (1959)

Run, Killer, Run! (1959; re-write of *Seven Hungry Men*, 1952)

The Merriweather File (1959)

Lament for a Virgin (1960)

Marilyn K. (1960)

Steal Big (1960)

The Time of Terror (1960)

A Death at Sea (1961)

A Grave Undertaking (1961)

Obsession (1962) [screenplay published as *Pierrot le Fou: A Film*, 1969]

The Money Trap (1963)

The Ransomed Madonna (1964)

The House on K Street (1965)

A Party to Murder (1966)

The Mind Poisoners (1966; as Nick Carter, written with Valerie Moolman)

The Crimshaw Memorandum (1967)

The Night of the Rape (1967; reprinted as *Death of a City*, 1970)

Hijack (1969)

A Rich and Dangerous Game (1974)

Mexico Run (1974)

Jailbreak (1976; reprinted as *The Walled Yard*, 1978)

As L. W. Blanco

Spykill (1966)

Short Stories

Purely Personal (*Bluebook*, May 1953)

Night Riders of the Florida Swamps (*Bluebook*, Jan 1954)

"Sorry—Your Party Doesn't Answer" (*Bluebook*, July 1954)

The Picture Window Murder (*Cosmopolitan*, Aug 1956; condensed version of *The House Next Door*)

To Kill a Wife (*Murder*, Sept 1956)

Invitation to Violence (*Alfred Hitchcock's Mystery Magazine*, May 1957; condensed version of novel)

Death of a City (*Argosy*, Jan 1971; condensed version of novel)

Non-Fiction

Sports Aren't for Sissies! (*Bluebook*, May 1953; article)

Stocks: America's Fastest Growing Sport (*Bluebook*, Nov 1952; article)

Protect Yourself, Your Family, and Your Property in an Unsafe World (1974)

INVITATION TO VIOLENCE
A PARTY TO MURDER

Lionel White

Introduction by
Cullen Gallagher

Stark House Press • Eureka California

INVITATION TO VIOLENCE / A PARTY TO MURDER

Published by Stark House Press
1315 H Street
Eureka, CA 95501, USA
griffinskye3@sbcglobal.net
www.starkhousepress.com

INVITATION TO VIOLENCE
Originally published by E. P. Dutton & Company, Inc., New York, and
copyright © 1958 by Lionel White. Reprinted in paperback by Signet
Books, 1959. Magazine version published May 1957 by *Alfred Hitchcock's
Mystery Magazine*. Copyright renewed August 8, 1986, by Hedy White.

A PARTY TO MURDER
Originally published by Fawcett Gold Medal Books, Greenwich, and
copyright © 1966 by Fawcett Publications, Inc.

Reprinted by permission of the Estate of Lionel White. All rights
reserved under International and Pan-American Copyright Conventions.

"Murder Party: The Violent World of Lionel White"
copyright © 2022 by Cullen Gallagher.

ISBN: 978-1-951473-76-1

Book design by Mark Shepard, shepgraphics.com
Proofreading by Bill Kelly
Cover art by James Heimer, jamesheimer.com.

First Stark House Press Edition: June 2022

MURDER PARTY: THE VIOLENT WORLD OF LIONEL WHITE

Cullen Gallagher

Thanks to Stanley Kubrick's film *The Killing* (1956), based on Lionel White's novel *Clean Break* (1955), White's name has never been completely forgotten. But while Kubrick's film went on to become a staple in the film noir canon, White's reputation was largely reduced to being the author of a book adapted into a better-known movie. As Bill Pronzini and Marcia Muller's *1001 Midnights* states, White "was never adequately appreciated by aficionados of the crime genre."

A suspense stalwart in his day, hardly a year passed between 1952 and 1978 without at least one of White's crime novels hitting the shelves (and for many years, there'd be more than one). Ultimately, he produced 36 novels in 26 years, and yet 35 of them seemed to fade into literary obscurity. During the Black Lizard hardboiled noir renaissance of the 1980s, only *Clean Break* was brought back into print (under the movie's title), and even that didn't make the leap when Black Lizard was acquired by Random House and combined with their Vintage Crime label. Nor was White included in Hard Case Crime's lineup when the imprint launched in 2004. Other than a few unauthorized editions of *The Killing, Steal Big,* and *The Big Caper,* the majority of White's legacy seemed in danger of being forever relegated to the brittle bindings and crumbling pages of musty old books—until Stark House Press stepped in.

Stark House began its heroic initiative to revive the literary works of Lionel White in 2015, and have since brought back into print 12 titles: *The Big Caper* (1955), *Clean Break* (1955), *Coffin for a Hood* (1958), *Hostage for a Hood* (1957), *The House Next Door* (1956), *Love Trap* (1955), *Marilyn K* (1960), *The Merriweather File* (1959), *The Money Trap* (1963), *Operation—Murder* (1956), *The Snatchers* (1953), and *Steal Big* (1960). Now, with the volume you hold in your hands, that number increases to 14: *Invitation to Violence* (1958) and *A Party to Murder* (1966). The reappearance of these works is a welcome reminder that White deserves to be known as more than just the source material for a classic movie, but as one of the major mid-century American crime writers.

Perhaps inspired by his early career experiences as a police reporter and true-crime pulp editor, Lionel White saw the potential for violence in every area of our daily lives. It can happen when you take mass transit (*Death Rides the Bus*) or stumble into the wrong home in a sleepy suburb (*The House Next Door*). In *Invitation to Violence*, violence jumps into the passenger seat of the protagonist's car. Insurance actuary Gerald Hanna is driving home after a late-night poker game, and as he passes through a small Long Island town he unknowingly drives into a crime scene. A jewelry store heist has turned into a shootout with the cops, and one of the wounded thieves stops Hanna and, holding him at gunpoint, orders him to drive. After the thief dies in the car, however, Hanna realizes that he is left holding half a million dollars in stolen jewels. While analyzing risks was what he had to do for a living, Hanna never had to consider a risk quite like this before. Did anyone see his car? Is there any possibility he can be linked to the crime? I'll say no more, as I don't want to spoil the beautiful symphony of suspense that White composed.

If you've only read White's heist novels like *The Big Caper*, *Clean Slate*, or *Steal Big*, then *Invitation to Violence* will be a pleasant surprise. This is a clever inversion of the classic Lionel White scenario. Rather than focusing on the meticulous planning and execution of a crime, White begins with everything planned and the robbery already in motion. Instead, he devotes most of the novel to the chaos that ensues when an unexpected element throws the entire scheme off course. And it's in that chaos that White displays his mastery of the ensemble cast, jumping between characters who are unaware of just how tangled a web they are weaving. It is here that he displays his signature style that readers will recognize, that expert ability to shift between characters and action with the agility and dexterity of a film editor.

In *A Party to Murder*, the setting for violence is even more innocuous than a car ride home. Here, a seemingly mundane Christmas celebration at the office of a Manhattan publisher leads to several crimes: a jewelry wholesaler downstairs is robbed of half a million in gems; a police officer outside is run over; and Patricia Andrews, wife of art director Clayton Andrews, is found nude and murdered in a motel room.

White's *Rashomon, A Party to Murder* takes the author's interest in ensemble narratives to the extreme, telling the story exclusively in first person form through the voices of its characters. There's no omniscient narrator (as White often uses) to give some amount of objectivity to the action. Instead, each chapter switches perspective, giving readers access not only to the private knowledge of the characters, but also their prejudices, long-standing grievances, uncertainties, and even the details they withhold from the police. Everybody saw the party a different way: some overheard a hushed conversation, others saw somebody in the bathroom. The one thing they all have in common is that they're not telling the whole story to Detective Lieutenant William Goodwin: one character plans to blackmail two people (and play both ends against the middle), another blacked out and can't remember whether he pulled the trigger or not, and others line up false alibis to save face for their various indiscretions. In this way, White turns a rather simple plot into a rich tapestry of conflicting narratives, and proves that he is truly a master of literary tension.

A Party to Murder might also come as a surprise to devotees of the author because it shows his capacity for dark comedy. It's hard not to laugh just a little at the hubris and arrogance of many characters, especially publisher Harold Markey, who thinks of himself as a Don Juan and business tycoon who is always one step ahead of his wife, his affairs, and his employees. Little does he realize how much they do know about his shenanigans, and how much they resent and despise him.

The pairing of these two works is particularly appropriate because they both exemplify one of the hallmarks of White's narrative worldview: the widespread reverberations of violence. In White's books, crime is not just limited to the triangle of criminal-victim-law, but it draws in witnesses, passersby, relatives, romantic partners, business colleagues, employees. As Woody Haut describes in his study *Pulp Culture: Hardboiled Fiction and the Cold War*,

> [White] depicts the ease with which desperate and dissimilar individuals can be thrown into a world of crime, and the power relationships that occur. For White's work examines the

dialectic between the individual and the group, co-operatives and dictatorships, criminality and honesty. Here crime…goes awry due to human error, chance, foible and the division of labour.

Though he doesn't single out *Invitation to Violence* or *A Party to Murder*, Haut's comments are so spot-on that he could easily be referring directly to either of these texts. For Lionel White, crime not only occurs within our world, but it also creates a world within itself, and sucks all of us in with it. White's murder parties are not exclusive, and anyone—at any point—could receive an invitation, whether they want it or not.

The great writer Ed Gorman once commented, "While White's people were interesting, it was usually their situations rather than their personalities that drew you in." As usual, Gorman is on the money. So, the next time you're driving home late at night and passing through what looks to be a quiet stretch of downtown, or the next time you're drinking cheap booze at the office holiday party and complaining about the boss with your colleagues, think about how your life could change in just an instant. We've all had those thoughts before—fantasies so dark they verge on nightmares. If you're wondering how those scenarios might work out, dive into these books. Lionel White's already done the planning for you.

—March 2022
Brooklyn, NY

Cullen Gallagher lives in Brooklyn, NY. His critical writing has appeared in the *Los Angeles Review of Books*, *Paris Review*, and *Not Coming to a Theater Near You,* as well as in the anthologies *Cult Cinema: An Arrow Video Companion* (2016) edited by Anthony Nield, *Screen Slate: New York City Cinema 2011-2015* (2017) edited by Jon Dieringer, and *Paperbacks at War: 20th Century Conflict from the Front Lines of Vintage Paperbacks, Pulps and Comics* (2021) edited by Justin Marriott. His fiction has appeared in *Beat to a Pulp, Crime Factory*, and the anthologies *Bourbon & a Good Cigar* (2018) and *Time to Myself* (2018). For more information, visit www.cullengallagher.com, or his blog *Pulp Serenade* (www.pulp-serenade.com).

INVITATION TO VIOLENCE

Lionel White

THIS BOOK IS FOR
TWO HIGH-CLASS
UNHUNG
RASCALS
MISHA REZNIKOFF
AND
FREDDY TURCO

CHAPTER ONE

1

Ignoring the legal aspects of the matter, the question still remains. Is Gerald Hanna a rogue and a criminal? Is he, in fact, a cold-blooded murderer; a man who callously permitted another man to be killed so that he could profit to the tune of a hundred thousand dollars?

Or, as some believe who were intimate with him and thoroughly conversant with the details of the situation, is Gerald Hanna merely a fearless, public-spirited citizen who did his duty as he saw it?

There are a number of opinions on the matter and it is significant that these opinions vary widely. Certainly Sue Dunne, herself deeply involved in the incidents surrounding the case, has her opinion. And so does Miss Maryjane Swiftwater, who, although she really knows nothing of what went on, has been Gerald's fiancée for more years than she cares to remember and certainly knows him well.

It is a coincidence that Fred Slaughter should have shared the opinion held by Detective Lieutenant Hopper, as each man was vitally concerned, but from completely different sides of the fence.

Young Vince Dunne himself might have formed a very firm attitude about the thing, but unfortunately Vince didn't live long enough really to know Gerald Hanna. He met Gerald only once in his life and then but for a few moments. Although the contact was very brief, it was extremely intimate. The thing is that Vince was really in no condition to form any opinions about anything, at the time of their encounter.

One thing is sure. When Vince sneaked away from the small apartment he shared with his sister Sue on that fatal Saturday evening to keep his rendezvous with Dommie and Jake, he had no idea that such a person as Gerald existed, let alone that he would ever meet him.

It is more than probable that any conjecture concerning the matter of Gerald's character would be more or less pointless and without value, unless one were to sit back and, calmly and with dispassion, review the events which actually took place and learn at firsthand exactly what did and what did not happen.

These, then, are the facts.

2

Vince Dunne was the first one to show up at the tavern where they agreed to meet shortly after ten o'clock. He carried the black leather jacket, the gas mask and the peaked cap in a small zipper bag, along with the .38 and the half box of cartridges.

There was something vaguely furtive about his manner as he pushed through the wide, half-curtained door and entered the place. He was aware of this characteristic and it annoyed him. He was nineteen years old, old enough to walk up to any bar and order a drink. But he felt the shyness and the hesitancy he always felt when he went into a barroom, or in fact, any public establishment.

He looked his age, but no more, and he always worried that a bartender would turn him down when he walked to the mahogany counter and ordered a drink. The idea of having to prove his age, in front of a lot of strangers, embarrassed him and as a result, his manner was not only furtive but a little defiant as well. He walked as though he carried a chip on his shoulder and being rather slight and of no more than medium height, this tended to give him a somewhat tough and arrogant manner.

He didn't want to be mistaken for a kid, but if it had to be that way, he wanted people to know that at least he was a tough kid. It was a little unfortunate as actually he was normally a pleasant-looking boy with wide-spaced eyes in an overly sensitive face. He had a slightly snubbed nose, a generous mouth, but a rather weak chin. It may be said that these identical facial characteristics in his sister made her an extremely attractive girl.

Vince didn't look at all like a boy who would be carrying a .38 revolver.

He had left the house a little before he had to, knowing it might be tough getting out. Sue was home and she would, quite naturally, want to know where he was going and why.

Any other night but this particular Friday would have been fine. Sue worked evenings, but this was her night off and she was home. She was home, and as always, she was suspicious. She'd been suspicious about everything he did since they'd let him out on probation.

Sue was nineteen also; his twin sister. Her attitude really burned him up, but Vince was in no position to complain. He was fresh out of the can and Sue was paying the bills.

Vince was the man in the family, but it was Sue who'd been holding things together since the death of their mother. He rebelled against her, but it was a silent sort of rebellion and never flared into open resentment. In his heart Vince knew that Sue really cared for him; really wanted to keep him out of trouble.

So Vince had told her that he wanted to hit a late movie and although she hadn't believed him, she'd let him go and now he was here and waiting. Waiting for Dommie and Jake.

He could count on Dommie being punctual. Dommie was twenty-one and he still lived with his mother and father and he, too, would have trouble getting away from his house. Like Vince, he'd foresee the trouble and make his alibi early. Dommie was a lot more afraid of his father and his mother than he was of the police.

Only Jake would be able to stroll in at exactly the moment he was expected to arrive. Jake was in charge of the job, had even helped plan it with the big wheel who was backing them and who was the real brain; the one who would take the stuff off their hands and dispose of it.

Vince had heard a lot about this man—this big wheel. He didn't know him by name because Jake was a lot too smart to throw names around, but Vince had a pretty good idea who he was. He'd met several of Jake's friends and knew that Jake had important connections. Jake usually introduced them as "Mr. Smith" and there was one particular "Mr. Smith" who'd been taking a lot of interest in Vince lately. He had his own ideas all right, but he'd been much too smart to get nosy. It was one thing he'd learned while doing his stretch—don't get nosy. It didn't pay, not if a guy wanted to get places.

When Dommie came into the place, some fifteen minutes after Vince himself showed, he didn't as much as acknowledge Vince's presence with a nod. He just walked right past him and went up to the bar and ordered a shot, although Jake had warned him against it.

"A beer, nothing else, while you're waiting," Jake had said.

It was no problem as far as Vince was concerned. He didn't like whisky and only took a beer now and then to show that he was grown up. But Dommie liked his booze. Not that he was a lush or anything like that; he just liked a quick shot now and then to give him a lift. Vince couldn't blame him for disobeying Jake's orders. He would very likely need that lift before the night was over.

Dommie had the tricky job. He was the one who would handle the chopper and he had to be on his toes, had to be keen.

As Jake explained it while they'd been making the plans, "You have to have perfect coordination; a submachine gun is a lot different than a sawed-off shotgun or an automatic."

"Not that there's much chance you'll have to use it," Jake said. "But if you do, you gotta be right. There's just twenty shots in each clip and there won't be any chance to change clips once you get into action. With perfect timing, you can limit a burst to five or six shots. That means you get three bursts. Four at the most. Then you are through.

"You gotta remember that and you gotta be absolutely calm and cool. If you do have to use the thing, it's going to mean we're in a jam and that's the one time it isn't easy to be calm. So you have to remember. Three rounds, four at the most. No time to reload if anything goes wrong. If you blow up and hold your finger on the trigger and let all twenty shots go at once, the last ten of them are going to be up in the air because that's the way a chopper works. And you won't be getting any second chances."

Later on they'd driven up to the place in the Catskills, the farm that belonged to one of Jake's "Mr. Smiths," and Jake had taken the machine gun out of the case and had let Dommie get familiar with it. Dommie had shot off one clip, and right away he knew what Jake had been talking about. He'd had to be satisfied with the single clip as Jake didn't want to take any chances on creating curiosity and attracting attention.

Dommie was finishing his drink when Jake walked into the tavern. Jake didn't look at either of them, but went at once to the men's room. Vince turned away from the juke box and went out and climbed into the rear of the Ford sedan standing at the curb a couple of doors down the street. The parking lights were on and the engine was idling.

Dommie got in a moment later, sitting in the front, and then Jake was back behind the steering wheel and they were pulling away from the curb.

"Any trouble about the car?" Vince asked, leaning forward as Jake swung into Northern Boulevard and headed east down the island and away from Corona.

"None. Don't talk."

He's touchy, Vince thought. Edgy. Well, he couldn't blame him. They were all edgy. Hell, who wouldn't be, starting out on a caper like this?

3

It is an ironic coincidence that at this very moment, the moment Jake Riddle, driving east on Long Island, ordered Vince not to talk, Gerald Hanna should have pushed his hand into the discard, yawned widely and said, "There's too much talk."

Gerald leaned back in his chair and looking a little bored and a little amused, shrugged his shoulders and continued.

"I think I'll just call it quits for the night and take off," he said. "Have to be up early, you know. I'm about even and I should be getting ..."

They didn't give him a chance to finish.

"It's early, kid," Herb Potter said. "You can't quit now. We need you. Stick it out for another hour. You'll bust up the game if you leave now. Come on boy, just another hour."

Gerald sighed as the others joined in with Potter, urging him to stay.

Well, what the hell. He might just as well hang on for a little longer. It really didn't matter too much. The game bored him, but so did everything else. Even the idea of leaving and going home and getting the sleep which he wanted and needed, bored him.

"O.K.," he said. "O.K., deal 'em out, boy. If you insist on making me a rich man, what can I do about it?" Gerald laughed and pushed his ante toward the center of the table.

"I guess you're right. It really doesn't make any difference if I leave now or I leave later."

He couldn't, of course, have been more wrong. It made all the difference in the world and to a great many persons, none of whom, with the exception of Maryjane Swiftwater, Gerald's fiancée, he had ever met or even suspected existed.

4

Jake drove at a reasonable speed, careful about stoplights and signs. He tried to concentrate on his driving and think of nothing else, but it was impossible to devote his entire attention to the road, methodically unfolding in front of his headlights. His mind kept going back to Sammy.

My God, Jake thought, in another few years Sammy would be as old as that punk in the back seat. In less than six months the boy would be having his bar mitzvah, and then, if time went as fast as it had been going these last few years, before he knew it, the boy would be a man. A man in body and in heart and in mind.

Well, there was one thing for sure. Sammy wasn't going to turn out like young Dunne, or like Dommie, sitting here beside him. Sammy was going to keep on going to school. To high school and then to college and after that, by God, if he wanted to be a doctor or something, he could still go on learning. Jake was going to make sure of that, if it was the last thing he ever did. Sammy wasn't going to end up like these Irish kids and these Wop kids. He was going to learn something, going to be a gentleman.

Sammy was his and Belle's son, their only child. But it wasn't even that which mattered. If they'd have had ten kids, he'd have felt the same way about it. They would all have the same opportunities, all be brought up right. To have respect for their parents and to be good, decent members of society.

Yeah, if he, Jake Riddle, had to knock off a hundred jewelry stores, if he had to rob and murder or anything else, his kid was going to have the best. Sammy deserved the best. He was a fine boy; a good boy. Smart. A damned sight smarter than his old man, sitting here driving a hot car on a hotter job.

They arrived in Manhasset in just under thirty minutes. The movie theater was in the center of the block, on the right-hand side of the street and someone had just cut out the marquee lights as the last show was already underway and the box office had been closed for the night.

The theater was a segment in a series of buildings recently constructed and the builder, fully conversant with both modern design and modern necessity, had arranged so that a large area in back of the structures could be devoted to a parking area. An alley leading into this parking lot lay between the theater itself and the block of stores next to it on the eastern side. Jake held out his hand and signaled before making the turn and swinging the car down the long ramp.

The lot was still pretty well filled with cars of theater patrons and they found a place to park near the back fence, between a Caddie and a Pontiac station wagon.

Jake cut out the lights and the three of them got out. They left everything in the car. Jake checked to be sure that the right key was on the ring, and then locked the doors after winding up the windows.

A man and a woman were getting into a car in the next aisle and they waited a moment or two, until the man had started his motor and pulled away. Then they walked quickly to the rear of the theater.

Candy was there, where he'd promised to be, next to the door with the dim, red-lighted EXIT sign over it. He was in his uniform and he looked like a frail, black ghost. He was looking down at the luminous dial of his wrist watch and his voice was a thin, nervous whisper.

"O.K." he said. "O.K., snap it up. I been here too long already. They'll be wondering up front."

He stepped aside and they quickly entered. Candy closed the door after them and locked it and then brushed past them, leading the way down the long hall and to the stairs. He went down first, muttering a whispered warning that they watch their step.

He didn't wait once they were in the tiny, unused dressing room, a throwback to the mistaken idea of the ex-manager who had hoped to put on amateur nights.

"No noise," he said, "an' don't smoke. No lights."

He flicked on a cigarette lighter giving them time to find the folding chairs and seat themselves and then stole out of the room like a soft breath of wind.

None of them spoke. They sat there, each silent and buried in his own thoughts.

At least I've told the truth up to this point, was the thought going through Vince Dunne's mind. He smiled secretly to himself. He'd told Sue he was going to the movies and he *was* in the movies. It would be a little tricky, later on, after he got his cut, but he'd figure out something. Give her a song and dance about a job and so be able to account for the money he'd have. But he'd have to be awfully damned careful about it. He was still on parole; a ward of the state until his twenty-first birthday. So—he'd just be careful, that was all.

He began then to think about the next couple of hours and in spite of himself, he could feel the sweat coming out on his forehead. It was going to be big time all right.

Dommie was thinking about girls. He didn't want to think about what they were going to do. He'd been in on other jobs before, but nothing quite like this. Nothing in the real money. It was new to him and he wasn't at all sure of himself, but he didn't have any real worries about it. He knew that everything was planned down to the last detail. Knew that Jake, and that other one, the real big guy, had everything laid out.

The stuff was up there, in the store next door, and all they had to do was go in and get it. The only thing which bothered him at all was the knowledge that the Pinkerton man was up there also. It wasn't as though he was a real cop, but Dommie knew that he carried a gun and had a license to use it. Dommie just hoped that the business with the gas would work out all right.

He shook his head and muttered an oath under his breath. The hell with it; it wouldn't get him anywhere worrying about things. He went back to thinking about girls. Man, this little deal was going to make it a lot simpler. Money, plenty of money, could solve any problem. Especially the girl problem.

Jake, on the other hand, made a conscientious effort to keep his mind off anything but the immediate work in front of them. He didn't want to think about young Sammy or young Sammy's mother. Somehow, sitting here waiting to pull the job, it just didn't seem right to think of your wife and your son.

His mind went to the place next door and what he knew was in that place. And it was there all right. He'd seen the stuff only that morning, soon after the store had opened.

God, a quarter of a million in jewels! And out here in the sticks. It just hadn't seemed possible. But of course it was possible and the stuff was there, just where the newspapers had said it would be. It certainly made an impressive display. And for a lousy little local jewelry store in the center of a shopping center.

Of course it was true that the store was a branch of a big important Fifth Avenue store and the stuff was only there as a sort of publicity stunt during opening week, but still and all. It was really something. No wonder they kept the private cop on duty day and night.

That certainly wasn't a part of the publicity stunt. After all, neighborhood jewelry shops aren't exactly equipped to carry a quarter of a million in ice in their tin safes. And it was a lucky thing they weren't, too. Otherwise he and these punks wouldn't be sitting here waiting around to take it away.

Dommie suddenly spoke, his voice sounding hollow in the confines of the small room.

"Must be at least an hour by now," he said.

"Shut up," Jake quickly growled. "No talking. Hasn't been more'n about fifteen, twenty minutes. Just sit tight and shut up."

Vince coughed and quickly covered his mouth. He knew Jake would be only too well aware of exactly what time it was, watch or no watch. He himself knew that the picture upstairs would be off at around eleven-fifteen; that the place would be cleared out within another ten to fifteen minutes. Candy was the one who would close up. He was the last man out. Candy could be counted on. He'd be down to get them a couple of minutes before he was ready to lock up for the night. And then they'd have exactly five minutes to get out and get the stuff from the car and get back inside again.

Candy returned at exactly twenty minutes to twelve. He knocked very softly on the door and a second later opened it and entered. He waited until he was inside before he switched on the flashlight. He'd changed from his usher's uniform to his street clothes.

"O.K." he said. "Let's go. I wanna get out of here and get home as soon as possible and get my alibi set. I'm the one they're goin' to be questioning an' I gotta be ready."

He used a small pencil flash and they followed him upstairs. Back at the exit door, Vince stayed behind with Candy as Dommie and Jake returned to the car.

Jake was careful to make sure that the parking lot was empty and he breathed a sigh of relief when he saw the Ford sedan sitting alone against the fence.

Quickly they went to the car and Jake unlocked the door and reached in for the suitcase, handing it to Dommie.

"Take this and the guns," he said, "and be careful. Give 'em to Vince and get right back. I can handle the tank alone, but I'll need help with the hose and the tools."

As Dommie left, Jake closed the door and then went around to the front of the car and lifted the hood. He put the brace under it and returned to the rear of the sedan, opening the trunk. By the time Dommie had returned, he'd removed the steel tank and was taking out the coiled-up hose.

He closed the trunk and turned and followed Dommie back to the EXIT door of the theater, carrying the tank carefully in both arms. Dommie had the hose draped over his shoulder.

"You left the hood up," Dommie whispered.

"Sure I left it up," Jake said in a low, irritated voice. "The cops check this lot two or three times a night. Looking for kids who come in here for little parties. They see the car with the hood up, they won't bother it. They'll figure some guy had trouble. Anyway, don't worry. Just get moving."

Back in the theater, Jake waited until Candy had once again closed and locked the doors.

"Grab one of the bags," he said.

Candy quickly shook his head.

"Not me, boy," he said. "I ain't got no gloves on an' I ain't leaving no prints on nothing."

He led the way once more, this time turning halfway down the hall and entering the theater proper from a side door. The others followed him with their burdens. They went up the aisle and just before coming to the end of the long rows of seats, Candy stopped for a second.

"I'm turning off the light now," he said. "We're going into the lobby and anyone going by can see the reflection. You have to work it in the dark."

He went on and they passed through the double doors.

Two red lights over exit doors leading off the lobby, kept burning twenty-four hours a day, cast a dim, eerie light and they could just barely make out each other's shadowy figures.

"You all are on your own," Candy said. Once more he moved off like a disembodied ghost, and a second later they heard the slam of the outside door and then the sharp click of the lock as Candy pulled it tight.

Jake gently put the tank on the floor and took a small spot flashlight from his pocket.

"No talking now," he said. As he spoke he switched on the light aiming it up on the wall to his left where he knew the vent would be. The light was on for only a split second but in that brief moment they all saw it. The grilled vent which led outside, but which they knew was only a few inches from a similar vent leading into the building next door.

"Get the hose attached and then hand me the end of it," Jake said. "Vince, you find a goddamned chair or something I can stand on. And both of you be careful not to hit the valve on that tank. One mistake and they'll find us all laying here when they open up for the matinee tomorrow afternoon."

Five minutes later Jake stepped down from the leather seat of the chair.

"She's in," he said, "in and I got her plugged up around the hose as well as I can. But you better get the gas masks ready, just in case."

He leaned down and fumbled around for a minute and then found the valve on the gas tank. Quickly he turned it on full.

"O.K." he said, "back into the theater now. Get the tools out and have everything set. We got time, but we want everything ready. We'll give it another twenty-five minutes, just to be on the safe side. If that Pinkerton hasn't passed out by then, nothing will ever knock him over."

He turned the flash on his wrist watch.

"At exactly a quarter to one we start breaking through the wall. I figure twenty minutes for that at the most. And be damned sure to keep the masks on."

Once again he flicked on the light and quickly looked at the others.

"Dommie," he said, "get the chopper out. Get out into the lobby and stay right there. Stay where you can watch the street. Anything suspicious, just the two short whistles. If anything happens once we get into the jewelry store, I expect you to stay right there and cover us until we get a chance to get out. Remember one thing, it'll only take us five minutes once we get through the wall."

"A lot can happen in five minutes," Dommie said.

"A hellofa lot can happen," Jake said. "But that's just why you are going to be out there with the chopper. The chopper is the difference. All you have to do is remember that. The difference."

"You think it would be safe to light a butt?" Vince asked. "They can't see nothing in here."

"No," Jake said. "No cigarettes. And keep your voice low. Now Vince, just to review it. Once we get our hands on the stuff, I come back through the wall and pick up Dommie. We go out the way we came in, through the back door. We pick up the heap and drive around in front. You, Vince, come out through the front door of the jewelry store with the stuff. It's a simple snap lock, opening from the inside."

Vince cleared his throat.

"Only thing I don't like is my coming out through that front door," he said. "I still can't see why ..."

"I told you a thousand times," Jake said, irritation in his voice. "I told you. The one really dangerous moment is when we start to drive out of the parking lot. A police cruiser comes along then and stops us and they'd stop us for sure. We'd be blocked in and wouldn't have a hope. They check that parking lot two or three times a night. Looking for kids laying up. If by any chance they happen to hit us as Dommie and I are getting in, we got a chance to make a breakout. If we get caught, at least we ain't got the loot and we can ditch the guns when we see 'em coming.

"But you'll be in the clear and you'll have the stuff. If everything goes all right, all you gotta do is walk out the front door. It's a snap lock and closes behind you. We'll be in front ready to pick you up and then, if the cops should happen by, at least we're not trapped. We're in the open and we got a chance."

Dommie scratched a match to light a cigarette and Jake quickly cursed him and told him to put it out. And so they just sat there then, waiting.

The second time Jake flicked on the light and checked his watch, he grunted and got up from where he was squatting on his heels.

"All right, Dommie," he said. "Out front. This is it. Vince, let me have the sledge. Hold the light and keep it on the wall. This stuff is nothing but plaster and lath and it should go like cheese."

Dommie walked into the lobby, carrying the machine gun under his arm as the first dull blow reverberated throughout the empty theater.

Vince suddenly stopped worrying. Now that they were in action, there was no longer time to worry. Anyway, he felt a quick surge of confidence. It was going to work. It was bound to work.

5

It was odd, odd and just a bit ironic, that he should have been reflecting upon the utter mediocrity of his life when the incident occurred.

The seven of clubs was responsible. That is to say, the seven of clubs which Gerald Hanna had drawn to fill an inside straight during the last hand of the evening had started him thinking about himself and about his life.

Gerald Hanna was not a man to draw to an inside straight. He wouldn't, normally, gamble on any kind of straight, even if it was the last hand. As he pushed the money into the pot and asked for the card, he was subconsciously amazed at his audacity.

The fact that he filled, that he drew a seven to make a ten high run, so completely surprised him that for a moment or two he sat there thoroughly stunned.

Bill Baxter had to ask him twice what he wanted to do after he himself checked the bet.

It was the usual Friday night game, which was always held in Bill's place, Bill being the only one of the regulars who was unmarried, or didn't live with his family, or who had a suitable apartment. Bill worked down at Seaboard Life with Gerald and several of the other players.

Dr. Harry Kline, an examiner for the insurance company, and four or five other men who were regulars, were playing that evening.

It was a friendly kind of game, the sort of thing which happens in a thousand towns and cities where several men get together once a week for a night out. The limits were modest, usually a ten-cent ante and a quarter raise with only two consecutive raises allowed, in keeping with the incomes, and the responsibilities, of the players. They were men in the six to ten thousand dollar a year bracket.

Mostly they would drink a few beers during the evening and the money for this was taken out of the pot a week in advance, although now and then Doc Kline would bring along a bottle of Scotch which he would share with anyone who cared for a drink.

The game started at eight o'clock and broke up sometime after midnight. No one ever got hurt very badly and there was never any ill feeling or anger. The nearest they ever came to it was the time Herb Potter got drunk and insisted on raising the limits after he'd gone for three hours without a hand. Even that was understandable and forgiven as it happened only a couple of weeks after Herb's youngster died of polio and everyone knew that he was still feeling pretty much broken up.

They played a fair brand of poker, considering everything. It was usually straight draw with jacks or better to open, or five card stud and each player pretty much knew every other player's game. Packy Wilson was inclined to bluff and Doc Kline was overly cagey, never staying unless he had a little the best of it before the draw, but all in all they played very evenly and conservatively.

No one, least of all Gerald Hanna, would have dreamed of drawing to an inside straight. But on this particular night Gerald did. And he filled. He raised twice and won over a pair of aces and jacks held by Doc Kline, taking in around four-eighty on the hand, which put him about six dollars ahead for the evening.

While he was pulling in the pot, Gerald told Doc Kline that he'd filled an inside straight and Doc Kline laughed sourly and, in a good-natured way, called him the world's biggest liar.

"Don't kid me," Doc said. "You draw to an inside straight? Boy that's one I'll never believe. I'll bet you haven't left your house on a cloudy day in the last ten years without an umbrella and your rubbers."

The funny thing was that Doc Kline was right. Gerald hadn't.

Bill Baxter's apartment was in the East Seventies and when they broke up, Doc Kline offered to drive Hanna home as he also lived on Long Island. Gerald rented a room and bath in Roslyn from a family who had been friends of his mother.

Gerald explained he'd driven his own car in that morning. He didn't wait around to have the final post-game glass of beer with the others.

"Want to get to bed as soon as I can," he said. "Got to get an early start in the morning and the traffic will probably be lousy, it being Saturday."

They all knew what he meant.

Each weekend, after the Friday night game, Gerald went to his rooms for a few hours' sleep and then got up before dawn on Saturday morning to drive up to Connecticut to spend the weekend with his girl.

They knew all about Gerald's girl. He'd been engaged now for five years. Maryjane lived with her invalid father and worked as a librarian, and Gerald and she had agreed that they wouldn't get married until he was earning enough to continue sending money to his own family and also support her father. It was the sensible thing to do, Gerald would argue, although now and then he began to wonder if he ever was going to get married, or if he actually really wanted to any longer.

In the meantime he saw Maryjane on weekends, and they did simple, inexpensive things together, like swimming and picnicking and going to the movies. Maryjane had become a habit. It was like everything else in his life, he reflected, a trifle bitterly. Dull, safe, respectable and routine.

Gerald left Bill's apartment at ten to one and drove up the Drive to the Triborough Bridge and out to Long Island. Traffic was light when he reached Northern Boulevard and headed east. He obeyed all stoplights and stayed well within the speed limit. He was still thinking about that seven of clubs when he passed through Great Neck and reached the outskirts of Manhasset.

He was thinking of the seven of clubs and he was thinking of the incredible dullness of his own life. Until he was almost parallel to the Gordon-Frost Jewelry store he was completely oblivious of his surroundings, driving through the all too familiar streets by sheer instinct and with his mind a thousand miles away.

6

Jake had been optimistic about the time it would take to smash through the partition separating the theater from the jewelry store. It was closer to a half hour than to twenty minutes. Jake himself handled the heavy sledge hammer, not trusting Vince to use it for fear of his making too much noise.

Vince stood behind the older man, holding the pencil flash and wishing there was something he could do. The inactivity intensified nervousness and try as he might, he was unable to control the shaking of his hands.

For the first time since he had embarked on the venture, he began to have serious misgivings. It couldn't work. They were bound to fail. The wall wouldn't break down and even if it did, they would enter the jewelry store only to find the private detective waiting for them with his gun drawn. He was suddenly sure, now that it was too late, that the entire thing was impossible. Someone was bound to hear the heavy blows of the sledge and set up an alarm.

Vince strained his ears, trying to catch the wail of the police sirens he was positive must be approaching.

For a moment the flashlight wavered in his hands and in that instant, Vince had an irresistible desire to drop it and turn and flee for the rear exit of the theater. He half turned, prepared to put the thought into action, when Jake's quick curse penetrated his mind.

"Jesus, hold that light still," he said in a husky whisper. "How the hell can I see."

Vince quickly refocused the light. But he was unable to keep his mind from wandering.

He would have given anything, at that moment, to be back home in his own bed. Back home with Sue. Sue had been right. She was always right. If he didn't behave himself, sooner or later he would end up in real trouble. God, if he'd only listened to her. But it was too late now, too late to do anything but go ahead. He was trapped; there was no turning back.

Jake was through with the sledge now. He'd broken through the plaster and had encountered the tough wire lathing. Jake had hoped that he'd encounter wood lathing, but he'd taken no chances. The heavy tin shears were in the bag and he lowered the gas mask in order to ask Vince to hand them to him.

Jake's shirt was wet with sweat as he worked and Vince knew that the man's face must be dripping under the gas mask. He could feel the water running down his own face and the plastic goggles kept clouding up with steam. He had to admire the way Jake handled things, the deliberate, steady pace with which he went about making the hole in the wall. Vince envied the other man his coolness under tension. He was feeling anything but calm and cool himself.

And then, before he realized it, they were through the wall and in the jewelry store.

It was just as Jake had said it would be. The Pinkerton man must have been sitting in a chair in the inner office when gas reached him and he had slipped and fallen to the floor.

Jake took a few seconds out to go over and check on him. He was breathing heavily and the two of them dragged him out into the hallway and Jake opened a window to clear out the air after quickly binding the detective's wrists with wire. He didn't bother to gag him; they wouldn't be there long enough to make it necessary.

The safe itself was as simple as Jake had said it would be. It was only necessary to use the sledge to break it open and within minutes of entering the room, Jake was filling the bag with the jewels.

In less than ten minutes they were through. Jake went with him to the front door and handed him the bag. He pulled the gas mask from his face then, to speak.

"Give us five minutes to get the car and get around in front. If we are not there by then, it will mean something has gone wrong. Wait five minutes; no longer. If we're not here, you'll be on your own. Don't use your flashlight to see your watch. Count. Count to five hundred. You'll be able to see the car when we pull up in front."

He slipped the gas mask back over his face and turned and quickly headed back through the store.

Vince began to count, moving his mouth silently.

7

Sergeant Clarence Dillon was driving and he would never in the world have seen it if it hadn't been for young Don Hardy, the probationary cop who was on his first night's tour of regular duty and had been assigned to Dillon for the evening. The Sergeant, who was happily married and the father of three youngsters but who had a dangerous weakness for women, was thinking of the new carhop down at the all-night soft drink and hamburger stop. He was wondering just what his chances of making a successful pass might be if he should stop by when he got off duty.

She was a pretty kid, probably Italian, and she couldn't be more than seventeen or eighteen. But she'd given him that certain look a half hour ago when they'd stopped for coffee and he was wondering about her and so his mind wasn't on his job. He never even noticed the car parked at the curb in front of the new branch of the Gordon-Frost Jewelry Company—the car with its headlights off and its motor softly purring.

Hardy, who did spot the car, knew the motor was running because he could see, in the reflection of their own headlights, the exhaust fumes coming from the tailpipe.

They were almost opposite the car by the time Hardy got his companion's attention and by then it was too late to do anything but pull up several yards in front of the car.

Hardy hadn't seen anyone, but the second he swung out of the door and to the pavement and turned back, he realized what must have happened. The occupants, and there were apparently two of them, had ducked down as the squad car passed. Now the doors of the sedan were opening and a man was getting out from each side.

Probationary Patrolman Hardy reached for his police positive.

In spite of his preoccupation with young women, Sergeant Dillon was a good cop and a thoroughly experienced man in his business.

The situation was obvious. There was a car parked with its engine running, its lights extinguished. The car was in front of a jewelry store. It was very late at night and the neighborhood was deserted.

The Sergeant didn't look back at the car; his eyes went to the front of the store and he was just in time to see the figure leave the shadowy entrance and run toward the curb.

A city cop might have fired first and then yelled. But the Sergeant worked out of Mineola, the county seat, and most of his experience had been with prowlers and petty criminals.

His gun was in his hand as he called out the command.

"Hey, you! Hold it right there!"

In that second, Dommie forgot everything they'd ever rehearsed. He lifted the machine gun and it was pointed directly at Sergeant Dillon. The first finger of his right hand pressed hard on the trigger and stayed that way. Stayed that way while the weapon leaped and chattered and the stream of leaden slugs buried themselves one after another in the Sergeant's body.

Probationary Patrolman Hardy didn't lose his head. His eyes had been on the figure leaving the doorway, but the moment Dommie pressed the trigger of the submachine gun, Hardy swung to face him. His first bullet struck the radiator of the sedan, but the second caught Dommie in the stomach as the last of the bullets left the barrel of the tommy gun.

He swung the revolver then, taking the chance that his shot had gone home, and aimed it at Jake, who was running directly toward him. The two fired in the same instant and each shot was effective. Jake staggered, a bullet in his chest just below the heart, and slowly dropped to the pavement.

But the gunman's shot also found its mark, striking Hardy in the right temple and glancing off without actually penetrating the skull itself. The shock was enough to drop him, and Hardy's gun fell from his hand as he went down. He was unconscious for several seconds.

Vince Dunne never was quite sure what had happened.

He'd been at the door waiting when the sedan swung around and stopped in front of the place. Jake was in the driver's seat and Jake had waved to him as he'd cut the lights.

Vince had to fumble to find the catch on the jewelry store's door and it had taken a second or two and then he had the door open and was starting out when he looked up and saw that Jake was frantically waving him back. It was only then that he spotted the squad car.

It wasn't that he panicked. It was only that he realized if he went back inside he'd be cooked. Wouldn't have a chance. He had to get to the car, cops or no cops. Holding the bag which held the jewels tight and close to his chest, he started across the wide sidewalk to reach the sedan. He was climbing into the back when the fireworks started.

The minute Vince looked up and saw Jake slipping to the sidewalk and heard the staccato rattle of the gunfire, he went into action. He reached for his own gun as he climbed over to the front seat and slipped under the wheel. It wasn't until he shoved his foot down on the pedal and rammed the car into gear that he knew the engine was dead. He never did realize that the first slug from Hardy's gun had smashed into the distributor, shattering it into a thousand parts. All he knew was that when he pushed the starter button, nothing happened.

Frantically he leaped to the street, still clutching the bag and with his own .38 held tight in his other hand.

He hesitated only long enough to fire twice, aiming directly at the prone body of Patrolman Hardy. The body jerked as the bullets smashed into it. Then Vince looked up.

That's when he saw the Chevie convertible drawn up opposite the sedan, a man behind the wheel with his eyes staring and his mouth wide open.

Probationary Patrolman Hardy was unconscious for less than a full minute and once he came to, it took several seconds to orient himself. His outstretched hand found the gun lying next to him on the pavement. He was dying, even then, but of this he wasn't aware.

He still had time to fire the two remaining shots from his service revolver. He couldn't be sure about it at all, later on when he was making his deathbed statement to the inspector in the emergency ward at the hospital, but he felt pretty positive that at least one of the shots had gotten the third gunman who was escaping in the second getaway car. He was also pretty sure the second shot had hit the car.

The shattered windshield glass which they found on the road afterward would seem to bear him out on this.

One thing he was sure about. The second car had been a late model Chevie, a two-tone convertible, black and yellow, and the license plate was a New York issue. The last number on the plate was a "3."

8

It was the sound of the gunfire which brought Gerald Hanna to. He had no idea at all of what was happening, but instinctively pulled to a stop, his eyes wide with shocked surprise and horror as he saw the bodies lying in the street in front of him. He watched as Vince Dunne pumped two shots into the body of the already fallen patrolman.

A moment later the man in the goggles and the cap and black leather jacket jerked open the door of his car and climbed in beside him. Gerald Hanna didn't have to be told what was being shoved into his ribs.

"Get going! Fast!"

He wasn't more than normally quick-witted and he didn't have a great deal of imagination, but for once in his life he didn't need a lot.

Gerald rammed his foot down on the accelerator and the Chevie shot forward. As it did, there was a burst of gunfire and the windshield in front of his face cracked and splintered.

Gerald Hanna's life had ceased being dull.

The man's voice was a mumbled whisper when he spoke. The pressure of the gun in his side had lessened, but Gerald knew it was still there. He half turned his head.

"Take the next right."

He slowed the car, surprised that no one was following him. He made the turn, just north of Roslyn.

It was a little used road and Gerald wasn't familiar with it. They passed a few scattered houses and then there was nothing.

Gerald was about to speak, when he heard the man at his side groan and then a moment later there was no longer any pressure at all from the gun and he heard the thud as it fell to the floor.

He stole a quick glance at his companion as they passed under one of the widely separated street lights. The man's cap had fallen off and the goggles had dropped down on his thin, white face and his eyes were closed. He was slumped low in the seat.

Gerald took a chance and made a right turn at the next intersection. His passenger said nothing. Five minutes later he pulled to a stop in a lonely place in the road.

The map light illuminated the interior of the car as he reached quickly for the fallen gun. A moment later he knew that he wouldn't need it.

The man was dead.

It wasn't, however, the body at his side which held Gerald Hanna in frozen fascination. It was the half-opened bag which lay on the floor of the car. Cascading out of it and lying at his feet was a glittering mass of diamonds and rubies and emeralds. Necklaces, bracelets, earrings and one or two watches.

CHAPTER TWO

1

Sue Dunne clicked off the television set at eleven-fifteen, as soon as the late news was over. She was tired and decided to go to bed, although it was actually very early for her. Friday nights were always like this; the one night of the week when she didn't work and had free time, but the one night when she really enjoyed getting to bed early.

That was the trouble with the job at the cafeteria. Or at least, one of the troubles. There were others, of course. Somehow or other, during the past year while she had worked as a night cashier in the place, her whole life had seemed all topsy-turvy. She still couldn't get used to sleeping during the day and working at night; six nights a week, from six in the evening until three in the morning.

Not that it was hard work. Just tedious. Standing there at the cash register and going through the same inane motions hour after hour, night after night. It was a dull, uninteresting job, but it was a job and the pay wasn't bad.

It wasn't the pay, however, which kept her interested. It was the part about having the afternoons free. Free at least to allow her to go on with her studies. Sue was bound and determined to become a singer and she had few illusions about her potential career. She knew it would take a lot of studying and a lot of practice, along with a certain number of breaks. Having those afternoons free save her the time for studying and practice. There was no one around in the afternoons to complain about her singing and for this she was grateful.

There were, of course, other ways to pursue her career. It had not taken a girl as good-looking as Sue Dunne long to find out these ways. There were the offers of nightclub work and there were the other offers. Offers which had been made to her by various men who would have been only too glad to have helped further her career.

Once or twice, coming home in the early morning dead tired from standing on her feet for hours, discouraged with the little money she was making and the high cost of her music lessons, she had been almost tempted to take up one of those offers. But it had been only a passing thought. Quickly she had smiled, wryly, and dismissed such thoughts from her mind. She'd do it the hard way, no matter how long it took. At least she had plenty of time. At nineteen, you always have plenty of time.

She left the light on in the hallway and checked to see that the door was locked and then she went into the bedroom and closed the door. There was no telling what time Vince would be getting in. Vince slept on a pulled-out couch in the living room of the small apartment and he was always quiet when he came in.

That was one of the things she worried about with Vince. He was too quiet.

She took a warm shower after undressing and then climbed into a pair of men's pajamas and went to the window and raised it wide. For several moments she stood there, looking out over the fire escape at the long row of silhouetted apartment houses which lay to the west. At last she sighed and turned and went to the bed. Before pulling the sheet over her, she reached up and set the alarm clock on the side table. She wanted to be up early, before Vince had a chance to leave the house. She'd made up her mind; she would just have to talk to him in the morning. He wouldn't like it, but she was going to talk to him anyway.

It seemed incredible to her that Vince, who was himself nineteen years old, could be such a baby, such a complete child. You'd think, after the trouble he'd already been in, that he would have learned something. That he'd know enough to stay away from bad companions.

Sue had met Dommie and Jake Riddle and one or two others whom Vince had been running around with. Dommie was bad enough, but at least he was only a boy himself. But Riddle. That was hard to understand. She didn't actually know anything about the older man, but she didn't have to. What was a man of his age hanging around with a kid like Vince for anyway. It couldn't be for anything good.

Riddle was one of the men who hung around the cafeteria in the late evenings. He and a half a dozen others. Bookies and loan sharks. She knew the type all right. You can't be a cashier in an all-night restaurant for a year without picking up a lot of stray information about the types who hang around such places.

Slaughter himself had told her about Riddle and some of the others who patronized the place. He knew them all. He'd warned her not to have anything to do with them.

"No good bums," he had told her. "Operators. Stay clear of them."

The odd thing was that in spite of his advice, Slaughter himself hung around with the very worst of them. In fact, he held a sort of court each night at one of the back tables and they would drift in and sit down and then there would be the whispered conversations, the occasional exchange of money.

Fred Slaughter owned the cafeteria, as well as the bar next door and Lord only knows what else. He was a man of many and varied interests.

Well it was probably one of the reasons he was able to warn her about men like Riddle. He knew them and did some sort of business with them.

At first she had thought that it was only because Slaughter liked her and had a sort of fatherly interest in her. He'd been nice about giving her the job, had seemed to take an interest in both her and Vince, whom he knew all about. But she'd soon learned that his interest was anything but fatherly.

Not that he'd been insistent or anything. Just made his pass, the way most men did sooner or later. Tried to take her out and when she had made her position very clear to him, had been a little nasty. But he hadn't fired her and after a while he'd left her alone.

Slaughter had plenty of women and she guessed that he just hadn't wanted to bother. She was a good cashier, so he left her alone and had gone on about his business.

By this time she had begun to realize that whatever Slaughter's business was, it involved a lot more than just owning a bar and cafeteria.

Thinking about it, her mind once more went back to Vince. It had been very tough after their mother died. She and Vince were seventeen at the time and Vince was in reform school. They'd picked him up in a stolen car and sent him away, and Sue was living alone with her mother at the time. She'd already had to leave school herself and was working.

The authorities had investigated, after the funeral, but when they found that she had a job and was able to support herself they had lost interest and had left her alone.

That job had ended after a year when a new boss came in and made things difficult. She'd quit and that was when she got the job in the cafeteria. Slaughter had learned about Vince and he must have had excellent connections because he'd been able to get him out on parole.

Vince was supposed to go to work as a bus boy in Slaughter's place, but he hadn't lasted long. He'd had a fight with a waiter and the manager had fired him. Slaughter heard about it, but he'd merely shrugged his shoulders.

"The kid will get another job," he said. "In the meantime, don't worry about it. I'll tell the parole officer he's still working here, until he finds something else."

The trouble was, Vince hadn't found anything else. It had been a couple of months now, and Sue slowly began to realize that Vince wasn't even looking. Instead, he was hanging around with Jake and with Dommie and some of the others.

Sue leaned up on her elbow and snapped on the table light. She found a pack of cigarettes and hunched a pillow under her shoulders so that she was half sitting up in bed.

Yes, she would have to talk with Vince in the morning. Vince wasn't the brightest boy in the world, but Sue knew that he wasn't really bad. He had sworn he hadn't known the car was stolen, but the judge hadn't believed him and they'd sent him away. In a sense, it was a tragedy. He'd been a different boy when he'd come back.

She finished the cigarette and stubbed it out and once more turned off the light and settled down in the bed. She was determined to get some sleep. She wanted to talk with Vince the first thing in the morning and she had a date at eleven o'clock at the television station for a commercial tryout. She wanted to be fresh and rested when she got there.

She'd just stop thinking about Vince and worrying about him—at least for the time being. He'd listen to her. There was no use worrying about it now. She just wished, though, that he'd get home. It was dangerous for him to be running around this late at night. If the parole board should find out....

By one-thirty, Sue Dunne had fallen into a restless, fretful sleep. Several times during the night she turned on the narrow bed, moaning slightly. Once she woke up for a moment or two, her eyes wide and frightened and her pretty, heart-shaped face bathed in perspiration. She half sat up, her slender body tense, and then slowly sank back on the bed.

She realized that she'd been having a nightmare and forced herself to again close her eyes. She slept then, the deep, quiet sleep of exhaustion, until sometime after daybreak.

2

When Gerald Hanna made his decision as he sat there in the front seat of the Chevie on that lonesome stretch of deserted road out on Long Island in the early hours of Saturday morning, it was a sharp and a sudden thing.

It was seeing the fortune in stolen jewels glittering on the floor mat of the car in the dim rays cast by the dash light which triggered that decision. What brought it about, however, was a long series of events and circumstances which actually bore no relationship to the jewels or the method by which they had arrived at their present destination.

To understand this decision, it is necessary to know something about and to understand Gerald Hanna himself. Gerald belonged to that class which is loosely and incorrectly referred to as the great middle class. A white-collar worker, employed by an insurance firm as an actuary, his background and upbringing was as normal, as routine, as mediocre, as it would be possible to imagine. He'd graduated from high school, taken two years at a Midwestern state university, and come East. He'd had to find a job but had also wanted to finish his education. The job, as a mechanic in a garage, had enabled him to complete a second two-year course at a business school. Then he had gone to work for the insurance firm which had hired him directly upon his graduation.

His college career had presaged his later business life. His marks had been average, he dabbled without distinction at a few extracurricular sports and activities. He didn't bother much with girls, coming from slightly poverty-stricken but respectable parents who had to strain themselves in order to see him through college at all. He was a normal, rather dull, thoroughly respectable, reliable and very average young man. He had neither unusual vices nor outstanding virtues. He was, in short, the stuff of which the backbone of the nation is made up.

A hernia which bothered him not at all had kept him out of military service, for which he was vaguely grateful.

At thirty, Gerald was a good-looking, medium-built young man who still had all of his hair and almost all of his teeth. He was beginning to believe that his eyes were getting a bit nearsighted and had recently been promising himself to find out if he would be needing glasses, at least for reading. He had normal taste, rather limited ambition (knowing the possibilities of an insurance actuary's career), and a sort of lingering desire to get married and settle down. He had met Maryjane Swiftwater at a house party given by one of the men who worked in his office, and they had been engaged for several years.

He had known, for some time now, that there was something wrong with his life. But he didn't know quite what it was. Didn't know, except that he realized his job was dull, his activities were dull and that even the girl he planned and hoped to marry had herself become just a little dull with the passing of the waiting years.

That evening he had taken a foolish chance when he had drawn to an inside straight. It wasn't a matter of the petty sum of money involved. It was a silly, ridiculous thing to do. As an actuary, he could figure percentages.

But he had taken the chance and drawn to the inside straight and it had paid off.

Now, here, lying at his feet, was a fortune in gems.

Gerald's decision involved a second foolish chance. A chance contrary to every law of percentages. A truly insane chance.

Gerald Hanna flipped off the dashboard light and opened the door at his side of the car. He circled around the front of the car and opened the other door. The boy's body was surprisingly light. It took him only a minute or two to half lift and half drag the mortal remains of Vince Dunne from the front seat and over to the side of the road. He was almost gentle as he laid his burden into the pile of bushes, making only a slight effort to conceal it.

That was the easy part of it. What was a thousand times harder was making the trip back to Roslyn and the house in which he lived; finding the house and opening the garage doors and putting the car away and taking the jewels and the gun and wrapping them in his jacket and carrying them up to his room.

He knew the chance he was taking; knew the percentages. He wasn't sure, of course, if the car had been identified. Wasn't sure that even now the pickup alarm wasn't out. He also knew the chance of a cruising policeman stopping a car with a broken windshield, on general suspicion. Of course, if it happened before he turned into his own street, it would be all right. He'd just tell the truth, tell them that he was on the way to find help.

But it hadn't been necessary; there had been no one to tell. He'd made the house without passing a single car or person. That had been a break and the second break was one which already existed and made it possible for him to put his plan into operation. The second break was the fact that the family from whom he rented his rooms were away for a month's vacation in Bermuda. He had the house to himself and what was more important, he had the garage to himself.

There were neighbors, of course, but no one ever came around and even the milkman had suspended service while the owners were absent.

Sitting there in the small bedroom with the blinds carefully drawn and only the single dim desk light on for illumination, he was looking at more wealth, or potential wealth, than he would normally see if he worked for the rest of his life and saved up every cent he was ever to make.

Until this moment, not once in his entire life had he ever considered doing anything dishonest.

Very suddenly he laughed.

Well, in the purest sense of the word, he still hadn't. A man with a gun in his hand had forced his way into his car. The man had later died, probably of a gunshot wound sustained in a battle with the police and had, conveniently, left a fortune in jewels scattered at his feet.

Gerald had merely removed a body which had intruded on him. He had driven home. One life already had paid for the gems and if Gerald was any sort of judge and his eyes hadn't deceived him, several other lives had been forfeited. Certainly it was too late to do anything about that.

As for the owners of the gems, Gerald was certain they were covered by insurance.

Having spent some of the best years of his life slaving for a surety company which neglected to pay him enough money to get married and live decently, Gerald was not overly sympathetic. After all, that was why they were in business and why they charged very high premiums—to take care of just such losses as this.

Before going to bed, he did two things. He returned to the garage and removed the fragments of glass from the broken windshield. Then he carefully checked the car for bloodstains, wiped it over with a damp rag.

He placed the jewels in a briefcase and put it into his bottom dresser drawer. He knew there would be no point in trying to hide the stuff; he must take a gamble that no one had taken the license number of his car.

It was a calculated risk and one which, in view of the possible rewards, he was perfectly willing to assume.

It was very much like the poker game; he'd already filled his inside straight. Now all he had to do was be sure no one else held a higher hand and he would collect the proper rewards for the rather insane risk he was taking.

Just before falling asleep, Gerald Hanna reminded himself that he must be sure and call Maryjane the first thing in the morning. He must make the proper excuses about the weekend. It would, of course, be perfect if he were only able to run up to Connecticut as he usually did, but that would be impossible. You can't run around in a car without a windshield. Certainly not in a certain Chevie convertible which even now was sitting downstairs in the garage.

The idea of disappointing Maryjane failed to upset him and he had no difficulty in falling asleep almost at once.

After all, Maryjane had been disappointing him for a number of years now.

3

The people who knew Maryjane Swiftwater all agreed on one thing—she was a nice girl. A nice girl and a good girl. Just look at the way she took care of that invalid father of hers. And everyone knows how hard invalids are to get along with.

The expression Maryjane used, however, as she slammed the receiver back on the hook, was anything but nice. In fact, even people who didn't know Maryjane and hadn't as much as thought about her one way or the other, would have been hard put to figure out how anyone who looked as sweetly innocent and demure as Miss Swiftwater, would even *know* such an expression.

Old Horace Swiftwater, however, was neither surprised nor shocked when he overheard his daughter's bitter voice as she hung up. Horace knew his daughter very well indeed.

"What's the trouble, baby," he called, from the front room where he sat in the wheel chair with the afghan over his shrunken legs. "Was that Gerald?"

"It was indeed," his daughter said, striding into the room. She looked over at her father hatefully. "He must be either drunk or insane. He knew very well that I've planned the outing for this afternoon. How he can dare, at the last minute …"

"He's unable to come up?"

For a moment Maryjane stared at him, as though aware for the first time that he was in the room. Her small, sharp face was bitter and the thin mouth was drawn tight as her pale eyes looked him slowly up and down.

"No excuses—nothing," she said. "Just called and said not to expect him this weekend. As though he didn't know that I've been planning for weeks now …"

"Perhaps he's ill," the old man said. "You know how it is sometimes, a man …"

"Oh God, I know all right," Maryjane said. "Don't think I could have been around here for the last dozen years waiting on you hand and foot without knowing. But he isn't ill. There's nothing wrong with Gerald. He just merely called and said he wasn't coming up. And when I very politely asked him why he wasn't, he didn't say a thing for so long that I had to repeat my question. And then do you know what?"

She stopped for a minute as she stared at her father and her eyes narrowed.

"He said that he damned well didn't want to come. Can you imagine? Gerald Hanna—said that he damned well didn't want …"

She sputtered and stopped speaking then, her face suffused with color and her slender, reedy body shaking in anger and frustration.

"The boy must have been drinking," Swiftwater said. "Perhaps …"

"Please don't be a fool, Father," Maryjane said. "Gerald drinking! The very idea is preposterous."

"Well, then maybe he meant what he said," the old man said, taking his eyes away from his daughter and staring out of the window. "Maybe he's finally getting tired of waiting, getting tired of having you postpone …"

She swung toward him swiftly and for a second it looked almost as though she was going to strike him.

"Gerald knows very well why we must wait," she said. "And certainly you, of all people, can't accuse me of postponing or procrastinating. As long as I have you to take care of, and Gerald must send money home to his family, marriage is out of the question. Gerald knows it and he agrees with me."

For a long moment the old man looked at his daughter and then slowly shook his head.

"Baby," he said, his voice tired and old, "baby, you know better than that. Nothing stands in the way of you and Gerald getting married except you yourself. I can manage to get by all right. I've got my pension and I can go to a home ..."

"No father of mine is going to go to a home so long as I can work," Maryjane said. "Just stop talking foolishness. Anyway, Gerald still has to send money home and he makes so pitifully little."

Once more the old man shook his head.

"I won't argue with you, baby," he said. "You know the truth as well as I do. I'd be happier in a home and no matter how little Gerald makes, you two could get along if you really wanted to. You're like your mother—you're afraid. You're afraid of marriage and what marriage means. You want a man but you don't want to give a man what ..."

Maryjane turned and started for the door. She yelled the words in a thin high voice over her shoulder as she left the room.

"You're a filthy-minded old man," she said. "You have a dirty, evil mind. You don't understand; you just don't understand anything ..."

She was crying as she ran up the stairs and slammed the door of her bedroom.

Flinging herself on the white counterpane of the single four-poster bed, she doubled her fists and pounded the mattress at her sides.

"They're all dirty—all men," she said in a high, tight voice. "Vile, lecherous, filthy ..."

The words ended in a hysterical series of sobs as she lay staring up at the ceiling with the tears flowing from her half-closed eyes.

She was remembering the night it had happened, once more reliving every second and every minute. It was like it always was when she remembered. She lay there torn by emotions and she had done it so often that even the shame no longer accompanied her thoughts as she went over the details one by one.

It had been his fault, his fault from the very beginning. The thing itself had taken place about six months after they had become engaged. After they had talked it all out and had agreed that they would have to wait.

He had made it all sound so reasonable. They were both intelligent people. Normal, sensitive and intelligent. At least that had been his argument. And the intelligent thing to do was to wait, of course. But why should they deny themselves the pleasures and the delights of a marital relationship? Why should they suffer from frustrations and inhibitions? Oh, he had made it all sound so logical and sensible—

even moral.

Up until then he'd been satisfied with little gestures of affection, with chaste kisses and swift embraces when they would meet and when they would leave each other. Once or twice when he was kissing and fondling her, his hand had reached for her breast, but she had held him off. She was a virgin and she wanted to remain one, at least until they were properly married. She thought that it would be different then.

She didn't quite know how or why, but she just assumed that once they were man and wife, his masculinity would no longer frighten and shock her.

She never thought of herself as being cold or frigid; she merely thought of herself as decent and proper. She knew all about sex, having read considerable material on the subject, but it was a knowledge obtained solely from books. In fact, she prided herself on her open-mindedness and her intellectual approach to something which she considered to be, after all, a minor part of the relationship between a man and a woman.

But he had grown more and more impatient and more and more demanding. He sought to stretch the kisses and the caresses out, wanted to see her more often alone and in privacy. She was sympathetic, telling him that she could understand and appreciate the driving demands of his body, but that he must use self-control.

It hadn't worked.

She never did know how she'd happened to let him talk her into it. Her first mistake had been in agreeing to spend the weekend at the lodge up in Saratoga. The place was owned by a friend of Gerald's and he told her that his friend and his friend's wife had asked them both up over the weekend. They drove up, leaving on Friday night.

It was a small, weather-beaten shanty, a sort of hunting cabin, up in the mountains above the town and they went up late in the fall when the weather was brisk and clear and very cold at night. He'd been there before and he had no difficulty in finding the place in spite of the lonely back roads leading to it. They arrived near midnight—finding the cabin completely dark.

She hadn't suspected anything at first, had merely assumed that Gerald's friends had tired of waiting for them and retired. Gerald had taken their bags from the car and gone to the front door and let himself in, using a key that he carried. The place was empty and he explained that their hosts were probably late getting away from the city and had not arrived as yet.

There was a fire already laid in the great field-stone fireplace, which covered one wall of the room, and Gerald had lighted it. Then, while she warmed herself and took off her coat, he went into the kitchen and made a pot of hot coffee.

She was chilled through and the steaming coffee was welcome. Immediately she noticed the peculiar taste and Gerald explained that he'd laced it with brandy. She protested, as she almost never drank, but he'd insisted. It was odd the effect the drink had on her. It seemed to go through her veins like fire, warming her and making her pleasantly drowsy. He hadn't had to argue about her taking a second cup.

Later, when she came to think about it, she realized that those two drinks had actually made her half drunk. She would have had to be drunk to do what she did. It was while she was finishing that second cup that Gerald had confessed to her. The people who owned the cabin were not coming up. They would be alone in the place.

The strange thing was that she had argued only feebly. She knew of course that she should have insisted and that they leave at once. She should have been furious at his deception. But the fact was she was very tired from the drive and she hated to face the thought of the long, lonely road back. She hated to leave the warm comfort of the place.

He had pulled the great bear rug from the couch and thrown it on the floor in front of the fireplace and she stretched out on it, half dozing in front of the flickering flames. She was only half conscious of his sitting beside her, holding her head in his lap as he talked with her. She was very drowsy, and the brandy was making her sleepy so she only half listened as he talked.

It was the old argument all over again and she had heard it too often. She didn't want to listen and so she had closed her eyes. She must have fallen asleep because she had no memory of his loosening the zipper on her dress, of his taking off her shoes. It was only when he started to remove the dress itself that she suddenly came to and realized what was happening.

She tried to get up then, but his body was pressing against her and his lips were on her lips. He was holding her tight and hard and she could barely move.

She had waited, waited for the embrace to end, feeling a sudden warm, sensuous contentment and postponing the moment. Her arms were around him and she moved her hands and it was then she felt the bare flesh of his back. Then that she realized he was naked.

She had tried to fight, to resist, but there was no time left.

He was an animal. An untamed beast and she had screamed out and fought him, but it had been useless. There had been the horrible, ghastly pain then and she had lain there in shock and agony.

There had been no words, no sound but her own muffled sobbing as he had stood up and found his clothes and left the room, and the white flesh of his body had seemed vile and obscene in the flickering glow of the wood fire.

It was then that she had decided that she hated him; that she hated all men but especially him.

The strange part of it was the decision she reached the moment she realized it. She would never let him go. She would marry him, as they had planned, sometime in the future. He must belong to her, now and forever. But there must be time, time for her to adjust herself.

He owed her something and he must be made to pay for it. Yes, they would be married, but when the time came, things would be different. It would be a marriage on her terms, not his.

She was the stronger of the two; in spite of what he had done to her, she was the stronger. And it would work out the way she wanted it to. There was no doubt about that in her mind.

Lying on the bed and thinking about the thing which had taken place in the cabin, her thin-lipped mouth formed into a hard thin line and her jaw became resolute and firm. Gerald was like her father and she could handle him the same way she handled her father. If he thought he could callously break dates with her, he'd have another guess coming.

4

It was the sound of the ringing of the bell which awakened Sue, but she didn't open her eyes. Instead her hand instinctively reached out and she fumbled around until she found the small, square clock and pressed the button on the top of it.

The ringing stopped and she started to fall back on the bed again. But just as her head again reached the pillow, the ringing began once more.

"Damn," she said, her voice low and sleepy. This time she opened her eyes and the first thing she noticed, even before again seeking the clock, was the fact that it was barely daylight.

Almost immediately it came to her then. It wasn't the alarm clock at all which had awakened her. The ringing was coming from the other room. She grabbed the dressing gown from the end of the bed as she leaped to her feet and started for the door. It wasn't the telephone. It wasn't that kind of a ring. It must be the doorbell.

Sue Dunne silently cursed whoever it was that was waking up the household at this unearthly hour.

The living room curtains were drawn and the room was in semidarkness, but she had no trouble finding her way to the front door which opened directly into the apartment. The first thing she noticed was that the burglar chain was not in its slot, but the significance of this failed to register. She twisted the knob and when the door didn't at once open, realized that the lock had been snapped. She turned it and opened the door, standing in front of it sleepy-eyed and barely avoiding a wide yawn. With her robe held tight around her and her disheveled hair circling her small sleepy face, she looked very much like a little girl. Which, indeed, she was.

The man didn't open his mouth. Didn't say a word. He waited only a second until the door three-quarters opened and then he suddenly lunged forward and crashed into the room, pushing her roughly aside with one heavy, long arm as he entered. It was then that she saw the gun in his hand.

Sue didn't scream. She did nothing, nothing at all but simply stand there, her mouth agape and her eyes wide and alarmed.

He moved fast, still saying nothing. The hand which was not holding the gun whipped out and found the light switch and the room was suddenly bathed in brilliance. It took him less than a second to see that there was no one in the room except the two of them and before Sue had a chance to find her voice, he passed on into the bedroom. She heard the slam of the bathroom door and then the sound of the closet opening and closing. A moment later and he was back, standing in the doorway between the living room and the bedroom.

"All right, where is he?"

For a long moment she just stood there staring at him. She wasn't frightened; it had been too sudden for that.

Wordlessly she moved and half fell into the big upholstered chair near the window. Quickly she shook her head, getting the sleep out of her mind. She started to open her mouth, to say something, and then suddenly stopped. Her eyes had gone quickly around the room and for the first time she saw that the folding bed hadn't been pulled out. Vince had not returned home from the late movie.

"Vincent Dunne," the man said. "He lives here, doesn't he, sister?"

Sue realized that her dressing gown had fallen open and that the top of her pajamas was unbuttoned. Instinctively she clutched the cloth of the robe close to her bosom.

"Say! Say, just who are you?" she said. Her voice was filled with indignation.

For the first time he looked at her as though she might be human. He didn't smile, but at least he looked a little less like a maniac.

"Sorry," he said. He put the gun in his side pocket and then reached into a second pocket and took out the nickel shield.

"Detective Wilson. Out of Headquarters," he said. "Sorry to bust in like this, miss. But I'm looking for a punk named Vincent Dunne. Understand he lives here. That right?"

"Vincent Dunne is my brother and he lives here all right," Sue said. She was fully awake at last and the fear which had escaped her when the man first burst into the apartment was all too apparent at last. But the fear had nothing to do with the man who stood facing her.

"What is it?" she asked. "What has Vince done? Why are you here? What ..."

"Take it easy, miss," the detective said. "I don't know if he's done anything. I'm just anxious to see him. You say he lives here? Then where ..."

In spite of herself, her eyes went helplessly around the room.

"Yes, he lives here," she said at last, her voice weak. She fought to keep the fear out of it, to keep her chin from quivering. "Please," she said. "Please? Is Vince in some sort of trouble. Has he ..."

"I'm just trying to find him, that's all. Just want to talk to him. You say he lives here? Then how come ..."

Sue stood up and unconsciously went toward the couch which made up into a bed.

"He's not here," she said. "He went out last night, to a movie, and he hasn't come back. Tell me ..."

"Your brother hang around with a guy by the name of Dominic Petri?" Detective Wilson asked. "Kid about twenty-one, twenty-two. Goes by the name Dommie. Does your brother know him?"

Sue looked at the man for a moment and then slowly shook her head.

"I don't know who he knows," she said.

"Or a man named Jake Riddle?"

She couldn't help but start as he mentioned the name. She didn't know what to do, didn't know what to say. All she could do was wonder and worry. Worry where Vince was, what he'd been doing. Why hadn't he come home? Where ...

"I can see that he knows them," Wilson said. "You want to help your brother, you best come clean. Tell me ..."

"I've heard those names," Sue said. "That's all, just heard the names. Vince may have known them, but they weren't friends of his. I'm sure of that. They weren't friends of his. Vince is just a kid. He's a good boy; he doesn't hang out with riffraff. He ..."

"He's fresh out of reform school and on parole. He's a punk. If you don't know it, you should. Now, come on, tell me ..."

This time, when the bell suddenly rang and interrupted his words, Sue didn't have to think to know what it was. There was no doubt about it. It was the phone which stood on the end table next to her and the shrill sound of the ring cut his voice short.

For a second both their eyes went to the instrument and then the detective quickly looked back at her. She could see that he wanted her to answer it and as she leaned over to take the receiver from the hook, he quickly crossed the room, leaning close so that he might overhear the voice at the other end.

"Yes?" Her voice was a bare whisper.

The voice which came through the wires was even lower than her own. A deep, soft, masculine voice.

"Vince there?"

She hesitated a moment and looked up at the detective who stared at her without expression.

"Who's calling?" she asked.

"I want to speak to Vince Dunne. It's important."

"Who is this?" Sue said. "This is Vincent's sister. Who's calling him, please?"

Quickly the detective leaned over and took the telephone from her and put the receiver to his ear. He listened for a second or two and then spoke in a high, disguised voice.

"Vince talking," he said.

He waited a moment or two and then spoke again. "This is Vince," he said. "Who's this?"

There was a sharp sound of a click at the other end of the wire and in a moment Wilson hung up the receiver in disgust.

He turned once more to the girl.

"Better get your clothes on," he said. "There's a man down at Headquarters wants to talk to you. Detective Lieutenant Hopper—of Homicide."

Sue slowly nodded and stood up. She looked sick.

"I suppose I can go inside and get dressed?" she said.

Detective Wilson nodded.

"Sure kid," he said. "Go right ahead. And don't take it so hard. Maybe nothing happened at all. Maybe your brother wasn't mixed up in anything and just stayed out overnight."

He watched her as she crossed the room and entered the bedroom.

Yeah, maybe. But he didn't believe it. Didn't believe it at all.

And neither did Sue Dunne believe it.

5

The house, sitting well back on the half-acre plot, was in one of the older sections of town. It was surrounded by large shade trees and a high privet hedge protected it from the street in front and the neighbors on each side and the rear. It was one of the first split-level houses built, having been constructed to fit the natural slope of the land rather than conform to a popular building fashion. As a result, the three levels conformed with the landscaping naturally, allowing the garage level and basement to follow the contours of the driveway, which came in on the right side as one entered the grounds.

A flagstone walk led from a break in the hedge to the front door, which opened onto the second floor.

Originally the house had been designed for a doctor who planned to practice out of his home. Entering a central hallway, a visitor was confronted by a wide arch, which had been curtained off, and doors on each side. The door to the left led downstairs into the garage and basement; the door on the right led into the main residential part of the house, which consisted of half the second floor and all of the third. The archway itself led into what had originally been planned as the doctor's offices.

When the present owners had purchased the house, they had converted the office section into a separate small apartment. This consisted of a living room, a small bedroom, a bath and a tiny kitchenette. These were the quarters which Gerald Hanna had rented and in which he lived. He paid only a nominal rent as the family which owned the house had been friends of his mother and leased out the apartment more as a personal favor than because of any desire for extra income.

The Sandersons, his mother's friends, were an elderly couple whose children had long ago married and left to establish homes of their own. Carl Sanderson was a retired bank executive and he and his wife spent a good deal of time traveling. At present they were in Bermuda, where they usually spent the spring and part of the summer. They were only too glad to have Gerald as a tenant, liking the idea of someone around the place while they were away.

Gerald had the run of the house, but by preference stayed pretty much to his own quarters. He did, however, keep an eye on things. He saw to it that the gardener, hired for a few days each month, kept the lawn and the hedges trimmed and he also made a point of seeing that the Sandersons' car was maintained in running condition. He checked to see that the tires didn't become deflated from standing idle or the battery run down. There was no telling when the Sandersons might suddenly decide to return and he made it a point to be sure everything would be ready in case they did. In this fashion he partly made up for the low rent which he paid for his own quarters.

The converted doctor's offices made a pleasant and convenient bachelor's apartment; would in fact have been satisfactory for a childless couple. Maryjane Swiftwater, however, on the single occasion when she had visited Gerald, had found it hopelessly inadequate when he had casually suggested that it might make their immediate marriage possible. He hadn't argued; for some odd reason he himself found the idea of sharing the apartment with a wife—or at least with Maryjane—slightly unattractive.

When Gerald returned in the early hours of the morning he had, for one of the few times in his life, neglected to set his alarm clock. As a result he awakened late, or at least late for him. It was well after seven-thirty when he slowly woke up and the sun was already streaming through the sheer curtains of his bedroom window, which faced to the east.

For a moment or two, as he opened his eyes and stretched, the events of the previous night were erased from his mind. He started to leap from the bed, remembering only that he had to hurry if he was to arrive in Connecticut as he had planned. And then, halfway to the bathroom, he stopped dead in his tracks. Connecticut? No, it wasn't to Connecticut that he was going this Saturday.

He turned to the dresser where he had placed the jewels and he was unable to resist the temptation to pull open the drawer and check on them. There they were in all of their loveliness.

His eyes went to the clock as he checked the time. It had been more than five hours since he had left the scene of the robbery and the shooting. He breathed a sigh of sudden relief. He began to feel a little safer. No one could have obtained the number of his car; certainly not one of the policemen who had been lying in the street. They would have checked it and found him by now for sure. His calculated risk was beginning to pay off.

He took his time showering and shaving, having put a pot of coffee on to boil first. And then he dressed, getting into a pair of slacks and an open-necked shirt and putting on a pair of tennis shoes. He fried two eggs and several slices of bacon and made himself a couple of pieces of toast. He ate a leisurely breakfast and took time to clean up after he had finished. Then he returned to the bedroom, made up the bed and put away the clothes he had been wearing the previous evening.

The pattern of Gerald Hanna's thinking may have undergone a radical change, but the habits of a lifetime failed to desert him.

At eight forty-five he put in his call to Maryjane. He had his story all ready, his alibi for not coming up for the weekend.

It was probably the quality of her voice that caused him to do what he did. Somehow or other, he was unable to help himself. There was something about the way she framed the question, something in the tone of her voice as she said, "And just why aren't you coming, Gerald?" that made him say what he did. He couldn't resist it.

"Because I damned well don't want to," Gerald said, and then, quite unconsciously, he laughed. He could hear the gasp at the other end of the wire.

Gerald carefully put the receiver back on the hook. He felt fine, just perfect. It was something he'd been wanting to say to Maryjane for a long, long time now.

Gerald left the telephone and at once went downstairs to the basement where his car sat next to that of the Sandersons' in the double garage. He didn't open the garage doors, but instead turned on the overhead light. He started the engine in his car and then pressed the button, lowering the convertible top. He minutely inspected the car for bloodstains. He found no trace of his unwelcome passenger of the previous night.

He realized almost at once what must have happened. The bullet must have struck the man somewhere in either the back of his head or his neck. The bullet had either completely passed through and gone out the windshield, or have struck a bone and stayed buried in the body. What little blood there was had probably dripped down the inside of the leather jacket.

Finishing his inspection of the inside of the car, Gerald next made an inspection of the windshield. He began removing the last remaining fragments of glass. When he was through, he gathered the broken glass together and wrapped it in newspapers along with the pieces he had already recovered, and then put the parcel in a zipper bag which had been given him as a souvenir by United Airlines. He returned upstairs and retrieved the .38 revolver which Vince Dunne had dropped on the floor of the car, and this too he put in the bag. He placed the bag on the floor of the Sandersons' car next to the briefcase which held the jewels.

Five minutes later, at the wheel of the Sandersons' car, he drove out the driveway, after carefully locking the garage doors behind himself.

Traffic was inordinately light and he made good time getting into New York. He found a parking lot not far from Grand Central Station and after checking the car in, took the zipper bag in one hand and the briefcase under his arm and walked the two or three blocks to the station. He realized that the public locker services had a twenty-four-hour time limit, so he went to the parcel checkroom on the ground floor level. He checked both the zipper bag and the briefcase.

He stopped in the lobby of the Biltmore long enough to obtain an envelope and a couple of sheets of stationery. Then he walked around the corner and over to the post office. Standing at the desk in the lobby, he addressed the envelope to himself, folded the check in two sheets of paper and inserted them. Then he purchased a stamp, sealed the envelope and dropped it into the slot.

Returning to the parking lot, he felt considerably relieved.

It took him only a few minutes to drive directly across town and find the entrance to the Lincoln Tunnel.

A lot of changes had been made during the last seven years, since the last time he'd driven this way, but he had no difficulty in finding the place. It wasn't surprising; he'd made the trip often enough, heaven knows, during the two years he'd worked for the garage while completing his course at college. They'd painted the building, added a wing and the name of the firm had changed, but it was still a glass factory. Parking in front of the place, he sensed a feeling of relief. It was an odd sensation walking inside once again.

A man he had never seen before greeted him at the long counter and he guessed that the place had probably changed hands. He asked for a windshield for a '56 Chevrolet convertible. He had the model number, but the man behind the counter didn't need it. The man had the right size glass in stock. Hanna paid for it in cash.

By one o'clock he was back in Roslyn.

He knew a moment's nervousness as he drove into the driveway and stopped. The place was completely deserted, but he still felt the tension as he opened the garage doors. The Chevie stood where he had left it the previous evening.

It took him longer than he thought it would and once he bruised his knuckles badly, but at last he had the windshield installed. When he was finished, he went out to the drive and picked up a handful of sand and gravel. He rubbed it over the windshield, purposely scratching it. Next he covered the glass with a thin layer of mud and then wiped it off, leaving stray bits around the edges.

At three-thirty he was finished and he went upstairs and washed up. Not until then did he sit down and relax. He picked up the newspapers he had purchased on his way back to Roslyn.

CHAPTER THREE

1

The lieutenant had been very emphatic and Patrolman Hoffman was not a man to disregard a superior officer; especially as the lieutenant was attached to homicide and was a detective. No one was going to pass through the door and get into that room. No one. That is, of course, with the exception of the day and night nurses and the doctor.

Looking down from his six feet four inches of muscle and brawn into the upturned face of the slender man in the immaculate pin-striped suit, Officer Hoffman again repeated himself.

"You heard me," he said. "I made myself very clear. No one. No one at all. Those were my orders and I'm going to follow them."

"You do just that, Officer," Steinberg said. "Go right ahead and follow your orders—and the next thing you know you'll be walking a beat somewhere so far out in the sticks they'll have to fly your relief in by helicopter."

Officer Hoffman very carefully removed the toothpick from the side of his mouth.

"A wise shyster from the city," he said. "You know all the answers, yes? Well let me tell you something, mister. You may be a big shot over in Manhattan, but out here, in Nassau, you ain't nothing. Less than nothing."

"Keep your voice down, Officer," Steinberg said. "This is a hospital after all, you know. And perhaps you would like to look at this," he added, taking a folded piece of paper from his pocket. "That is, of course, if they taught you to read. It happens to be a note from the assistant D.A. It's an order permitting me to see my client. Jake Riddle. I don't give a damn for you or your lieutenant. I happen to be Mr. Riddle's attorney and I have every right to see him. This little paper says so. And I'm going into that room and I'm going to talk to him. Alone."

He handed the paper to the other man.

"The doctor ..."

Steinberg whipped out a second piece of paper.

"His permission," he said. "So just roll over and I'll go on in."

Officer Hoffman carefully read both papers and then handed them back.

"And how do I know you are Leon Steinberg?"

"Oh, my God." The attorney reached into his breast pocket and pulled out a wallet. "Do I look like somebody who's going to go in there and shoot him?" he asked. "Do I …"

"It would be a good thing if you did," Hoffman said. "The dirty cop killer! O.K., go on in. But five minutes. That's what the doc says. Five minutes. And if you can get a word out of that rat in that time, you'll be doing a lot more than we've been able to do."

He reached down and turned the key in the door and then opened it.

Steinberg entered the sterile white room, unconsciously observing the barred window and slightly repelled by the heavy anesthetic atmosphere.

He waited until the officer had closed the door of the room and once more turned the key in the lock. Then he moved over to the high white bed and leaned down, speaking in a low, hoarse voice.

"How is it, Jake?"

Jake opened his eyes and stared at the lawyer.

Looking down at him, Steinberg knew that the Assistant D.A. had been right; knew he'd been telling the truth when he'd said that the man was dying. That he wouldn't even need a mouthpiece.

Steinberg wondered if he'd be able to talk at all.

"Dommie's dead," Steinberg said, "but Vince made it. Only he hasn't turned up yet and Fred's worried. You're going to be all right, boy," he said as Jake again closed his eyes. "You're going to be O.K. and we'll get you out of it. Be sure of that—we'll get you out. But try and tell us what happened to Vince."

Once more Jake opened his eyes.

"I'm dead," he said in a choked whisper. "You know it—I'm dead."

"Don't be a fool," Steinberg said quickly. "You'll be O.K. But try and think now, kid. What happened to Vince?—Fred's gotta know. We gotta find Vince."

Jake groaned and tried to turn away, but quickly fell back on the bed. Five minutes later, when Hoffman opened the door to tell Steinberg his time was up, the little lawyer was still pleading with Jake.

Steinberg picked up a cab a half a block from the hospital and gave the driver the address. It was an apartment hotel in upper Manhattan, and the driver didn't want to make the trip that far out of his territory, but Steinberg slipped him a ten spot and so he drove him. On the way, Steinberg muttered to himself under his breath.

"Fred ain't gonna like it—not one little bit. He just ain't gonna like it."

One thing was good about it, though. Dommie was dead and Jake couldn't last much longer. And Jake hadn't talked. Jake wasn't talking to anyone, not even to his own mouthpiece.

2

Belle Riddle looked across the oilcloth-covered kitchen table at her son and raised the napkin to wipe her eyes.

"Sammy," she said. "Sammy, I want you should eat your food."

"You're not eating, Mom," Sammy said.

"It don't make no matter. Eat. You're a growing boy and you gotta eat. And when you finish, I want you to go over to Grandma's for a while. Maybe for a few days."

Sammy pushed the plate away and his delicate, sensuous lips formed a stubborn line.

"I'm not hungry and I'm not going to Grandma's," he said.

Belle felt the tears starting again, but she made an effort to control herself.

"Sammy," she said. "Sammy, what's got into you anyway? A course you'll go to Grandma's. Just for a few days. Just until Daddy is better and maybe gets outta the hospital."

"Daddy isn't going to get better," Sammy said.

"Of course he's going to get better. What are you saying anyway, Sammy? An auto accident can happen to anyone. What kind of son ..."

"Listen, Mama," Sammy said. "I was downstairs a while ago. I got a tabloid. It was no auto accident. I didn't think so this morning when the cops came 'cause cops, that many cops, don't come around because of an auto accident. So I went downstairs and I could tell the way people looked at me. And I got a tabloid and I read all about it. I know what happened. I know all about it so there ain't no use you're trying to kid me."

He stopped talking suddenly, feeling the tears coming to his own eyes. He gulped a couple of times and then spoke again, his voice suddenly thin and high-pitched.

"Oh God," he said, "how'm I ever going back to school? How'll I ever even go out on the streets again. My old man a thief and a cop killer!"

"Sammy! Don't talk that way, Sammy. Don't dare say those things about your Daddy. He was only doing it for us. Only trying to do things for you and for me. Your Daddy is a good man. A fine ..."

"A good man?" Sammy said through bitter tears. "A good man? He's nothing but a ..."

"Sammy, stop it," his mother cried. "Don't say it, Son. Maybe Jake made a mistake; maybe he did a wrong ..."

"Mama, I read the story in the papers," Sammy said. "It was no mistake. You always said Daddy worked in a restaurant. But it was all a lie. He'd been in jail. He had a record. He was a gambler and bookie. The papers said so and so there's no use kidding ourselves. My old man is a crook and a ..."

"He did it for us, Sammy," Belle said. "Don't talk ill of him now. It was for me and for you ..."

Sammy stood up and shoved the table away. He wasn't crying now and his voice was suddenly deeper and harder.

"Nuts, Mama," he said. "Uncle Merv has four kids and he takes good care of them without robbing and killing. He's no smarter than Daddy. You've said so plenty of times. A lot of men take care of their wives and kids and aren't crooks. But me—my old man's a cop killer. I'm proud of him, Mama—real proud. He always said I should be good and live a decent life so he could be proud of me. Yeah? Good. And so now I should be proud of him because he's a thief and a cop killer, is that it?"

He suddenly turned and ran from the room.

Belle started to get up from the table and then slowly sank back into her chair. She dropped her head into her arms and this time there were no tears. Nothing but dry sobs as her heavy shoulders slowly weaved from side to side.

3

Gerald had bought all of the New York newspapers. A quick look through the morning papers turned up nothing, but there were comparatively complete stories in the early editions of the afternoon sheets.

He had to admit that the police moved fast. They didn't have all of the answers, at least according to what the press had learned, but they did have a lot of them.

The *Tele* gave the case the most complete coverage, handling the story without sensationalism, but playing up the pertinent facts. There was a long statement given out by the Pinkerton man, who had been guarding the jewels and who had been found semiconscious from breathing the gas which had been pumped into the office where he sat.

The guard had had a lucky break; police admitted that the only thing which had saved his life was the fact he had been dragged from the office by the thieves. He was going to be all right after a day or so in the hospital, but the police sergeant was dead and one of the gangsters had been killed outright. The other cop, Hardy, was not expected to live and already had been given last rites.

A second mobster, identified as Jake Riddle, ex-convict and known bookie, forty-four years of age and married, and the father of a teenage son, was also dying. During a moment of consciousness he had been questioned, but had refused to talk. He'd asked to see his wife and child and the request had been refused.

It was believed that a third and fourth member of the gang had made a clean getaway in a second car. One of the mob cars, a Ford sedan stolen twenty-four hours previously from a parking lot in Garden City, had been abandoned at the scene of the shooting after a stray bullet had disabled it. Hardy, the patrolman who was not expected to live, had been able to tell investigating officers that a second car was driven off at the time of the shooting. The newspaper said that he had made a partial identification of the automobile.

Hanna, reading this last, paled slightly. A partial identification? He wondered just what the phrase meant. He realized that when Hardy referred to a fourth member of the gang, he must be referring to himself. He could feel his pulse quicken as the thought struck him.

One of the newspapers devoted several paragraphs to the loot itself, itemizing much of it and mentioning that its total value was well over a quarter of a million dollars. It also added that the gems were fully insured.

The dead bandit was identified as one Dominic Petri, an ex-con in his early twenties, known to officials as strictly a small-timer. Police were believed to know the identity of one of the escaped pair and claimed he was a youth who had served time with young Petri in a state reformatory.

Newsday, a local Long Island paper which Hanna had also picked up as he drove through Roslyn, was the only one to mention that a Miss Sue Dunne, nineteen, of 104-16 Meadow Street, Corona, had been picked up for questioning. Aside from saying that she worked as a night cashier at the G. and S. Cafeteria, no other details were given.

Gerald carefully rechecked every news column, but nowhere did he see anything about the discovery of a young man's body, filled with bullets, somewhere on a lonely road on Long Island's North Shore.

He carefully folded the papers and stacked them on an end table when he was through with them. And then he did something he had never done before in his life.

He opened a bottle of bourbon which had been given to him by Maryjane's father the previous Christmas and taking a water glass from the kitchenette, poured about two and a half ounces into it. He added an ice cube and a little water and returned to his small living room and sat down and lifted the glass to his lips.

Downing the drink with a wry expression, he sat back and as the warmth of the liquor hit his stomach and spread through his veins, he felt fine. Fine and relaxed.

A drink before dinner was a fine idea. He wondered just why in the world he'd never tried it before. There were a lot of things he'd never tried before that he was suddenly determined to try.

He felt a pleasant warm glow throughout his body and suddenly he laughed aloud. He was the new Gerald Hanna. Yes, there were a lot of things he had been missing that he would soon experience. A lot of things.

His mind went to Maryjane Swiftwater then and as he thought of his fiancée, his face took on a rather hard, uncompromising expression and he shook his head ever so slightly. The idea of trying out something new with Maryjane completely failed to entrance him, although in the not too distant past he had frequently contemplated that thought with a great deal of frustrated desire and certainly no degree of distaste.

Things had certainly changed.

It was the sound of the doorbell which suddenly brought Gerald back to reality. As he stood up his eyes went to his wrist watch and he saw that it was exactly six-fifteen. He was expecting no one; he rarely if ever had visitors. For a fleeting moment it occurred to him that Maryjane might have come down from Connecticut, but quickly he dismissed the idea as utterly farfetched. Walking toward the front door, his face assumed a curious, but not alarmed expression.

There were two of them; a long thin man with iron-gray hair and a horselike face who wore old-fashioned pince-nez glasses, and a short, round, surly man with a slightly soiled white shirt under an unpressed, badly fitting suit. The thin man did the talking.

"You Hanna? Gerald Hanna?"

Gerald half blocked the doorway with his body as he answered.

"Yes?"

"Well, are you?"

"Yes."

"Detective Lieutenant Hopper," the thin man said, at the same time turning the palm of his right hand and exposing a gold shield. "May we come in?"

The short man needed no invitation, but pushed through the doorway, not waiting for Gerald's weak, forced smile and for him to move back.

As the fat man brushed past him, Gerald felt suddenly faint. These men were police and there could be only one thing in the world which brought them to his door. Somehow or other they had traced the car to him.

He stepped back and made a conscious effort to control his quaking emotions.

The lieutenant followed the other man into the apartment, shrewd eyes quickly darting around and casing the room. Gerald gestured toward the couch and went himself to the big red-leather chair and slowly sat down. The lieutenant seemed to fold up as he slouched down on the couch, crossing long legs so that his trousers were hitched up to expose several inches of thin, scrawny bare shanks over his shoe tops, where his black socks lay in folded rings unsupported by garters. He removed his battered, gray slouch hat and ran a lean fingered hand through his short hair.

The fat man walked over by the window and just stood there, between Gerald and the door.

"Just what ..."

Gerald hesitated as Hopper took a notebook from his pocket and methodically folded back its imitation-leather cover.

"You home alone, Mr. Hanna?"

"Why yes," Gerald said. "That is, I live here alone. Rent this apartment from people by the name of Sanderson. A Mr. Miles Sanderson and his wife. They are in Bermuda at present."

Hopper nodded.

"I see. You own a car, do you, Mr. Hanna?"

Instantly he knew that he'd been right. It was the car all right; they'd managed to trace it to him somehow. He might have known. His luck had been just too phenomenally good. But even as the thought went through his mind, Gerald was catching his second breath.

So they'd traced the car. Well, he'd expected that they might. He was prepared for that eventuality. Wasn't that why he'd made his preparations; wasn't it a contingency which he had foreseen?

There was no point in getting worried, no point in permitting himself to become confused and upset. Now was the time when he must play it smart; it was the moment he knew must come and the moment he had prepared himself for.

Gerald nodded.

"Chevrolet," he said. "Fifty-six convertible. Why?"

"Just wanted to know. Where's the car now?"

"Why downstairs in the garage," Gerald said. "Or at least it was a few minutes ago. Say, just what's wrong anyway, Lieutenant? Have I done something ..."

"Have you?" Hopper asked, looking up quickly, his face enigmatic and bland.

"Well, I mean, is something ..."

"Where were you last night?" the lieutenant interrupted.

"Last night?"

The fat man moved across the room and stood in front of Gerald. "You don't hear good, do you?" he said.

Hopper raised his eyes but not his voice.

"I'll handle it, Harry," he said. He spoke softly. "Harry—Detective Finn here—feels you should know where you were last night. It's a simple question. Where were you?"

Gerald coughed and took out his handkerchief and wiped his mouth. "Sorry," he said. "Well, I spent the evening playing poker. In New York. A friend's apartment."

"Start with the beginning. What time did the game start, who was there, where was it? You might even start before that. Just what do you do for a living?"

"I work for the Seaboard Life Insurance Company," Gerald said. "Wall Street, New York. I'm an actuary. Been with the firm for seven years. I played poker last night at the apartment of a man named Bill Baxter, on East Seventy-eighth Street, Manhattan. He's a salesman with the same firm I work for. Quit around five-thirty and had dinner with Bill and then went with him to his apartment. Several other men from the office sat in on the game. We started playing around eight o'clock."

"You win?" Finn cut in.

Lieutenant Hopper looked at him and frowned.

"Go on," he said.

"Well, there was Doc Kline, Herb Potter, Shelley ..."

"Never mind the rest of 'em. This Baxter got a phone?"

Gerald gave him the number, as well as Dr. Kline's number and that of Herb Potter and he noticed that Finn, rather than the lieutenant, wrote them down in a little notebook of his own.

"When did the game break up?"

"Sometime after midnight. I can't tell you exactly when, but I know it was pretty late. I was going to leave earlier, but the boys ..."

"Never mind that," Hopper said. "You left after midnight. Then what?"

"I came home and went to bed."

"You came home alone? Did you drive?"

"Yes. I drove and I was alone."

"Just how did you come home?"

"I drove."

"You already said that. I want to know how—what route you took."

"The way I always do after a game. Took the Drive up to the Triborough Bridge, cut over past the airport and picked up the Cross County Highway. Turned off on Northern Boulevard and drove directly out to Roslyn. Turned off the boulevard at ..."

"And you don't remember just what time you got here? That right? Did you stop anywhere along the way? Maybe get a cup of coffee or something?"

"Nowhere. I came directly home, put the car up and went to bed. You see, I had to get up early this morning to go up to Connecticut ..."

Gerald stopped suddenly, realizing what he was saying. It was a slip and he tried to recover.

"That is, I was planning last night to go up to Connecticut—I always go up early on Saturday mornings to spend the weekend—and I wanted to get up early."

"But you didn't go up, huh?" Finn interrupted.

"Now Harry," Lieutenant Hopper said. "All right, did you go up?"

"No. When I woke up this morning I had a splitting headache. So I called my fiancée and told her I thought I'd skip it this week."

"Want to give me her name and address and phone number?"

Gerald gave it to him. For several minutes after Hopper wrote it down in his book, he sat staring at the note paper and saying nothing. At last he again looked at Gerald.

"So, as near as you can remember you got home some time after midnight. You can't say exactly when. Now, did you notice anything, anything at all out of the way while you were driving home? Say during the time you were driving along Northern Boulevard?"

"Nothing—no, nothing that I can recall," Gerald said.

"Say, maybe you can tell me what this is all about? After all, I ..."

"You didn't loan your car to anybody after you got home?"

"Certainly not."

"Anyone else got keys to it? Some friend maybe ..."

"No, I have the only keys. I had an extra set, that came with the car when I bought it, but I wouldn't have the faintest idea where they are now."

Hopper nodded.

"All right," he said. "Now tell me, if you didn't go up to Connecticut this morning, well then, just what did you do?"

"Got up rather late, and made breakfast. Telephoned my fiancée, as I have already explained. Then went for a ride, driving into New York, where I did a little window shopping."

Gerald went on to explain that he had taken the Sanderson's car and why he took it. Explained that they had asked him to use it now and then while they were away so that the battery wouldn't run down.

Hopper asked him how he happened to go into town if he'd been feeling bad, and he explained that around midmorning his head began to clear up. So he'd decided to go into New York and shop. He gave them the address of the parking lot where he'd left the car and he was relieved when neither officer marked it down.

He said that he'd gotten back in the middle of the afternoon and had just been laying around the house taking it easy since.

He was still explaining when Finn again suddenly interrupted.

"When did you see Jake last?" he said.

Gerald looked at him, baffled.

"Jake. That's right," Finn said.

"I don't know anyone named Jake," Gerald said.

"How about Dommie—Dommie Petri, or maybe Vince Dunne— you know either of those boys, maybe?"

Gerald still looked baffled as he slowly shook his head. But his mind was racing. There was no question about it now. No question at all. Jake would be the Jake Riddle mentioned in the papers. And Dommie would be the one who had been killed by the police bullets. But Dunne—who was Dunne?

Suddenly he remembered the single paragraph in one of the afternoon papers. The one which had mentioned that police were questioning a girl named Sue Dunne. This Vince must be some relative and he must have been the third member of the gang. The one whose body Gerald had left beside the road.

"Dommie," Gerald said. "Dommie Petri. The name seems to ring some sort of bell. But I don't know just why. I can't remember ever meeting or knowing anyone with that name, but still ..."

Lieutenant Hopper stood up, looking tired and just a little bored.

"Let's take a look at the Chevie," he said. "Don't mind, do you?"

"Of course not."

The lieutenant followed him out of the room and down the inside stairs to the garage. It wasn't until they had entered the concrete room that Gerald noticed that Finn, his partner, remained upstairs.

Lieutenant Hopper must have been acutely sensitive or perhaps a little psychic.

"He wanted to make a phone call," he said, vaguely waving at the rafters above his head. "Hope you don't mind. Had to call his wife about something or other."

Gerald said he didn't mind. But he didn't believe the wife story. Finn would be calling to check on the poker game. Well, that was fine. He wouldn't have had it any other way.

Hopper walked over to the Chevie and Gerald saw him quickly look at the license plate.

"This yours, eh?"

"That's it."

Hopper nodded. He walked slowly around the car, not touching it.

"Leave your keys in it overnight?" he asked.

Gerald instinctively reached for his pocket and then blushed.

"Why yes," he said. "Sometimes I do. The fact is—" he leaned over to look at the dashboard of the car "—the fact is I did last night. I see they're still in the ignition."

"How about the garage door? That locked?"

"Sometimes, when I think of it. Mostly, though, it's left unlocked. No one around here ever bothers anything."

"I see. Then someone might have taken the car out last night after you got home, used it, and brought it back, assuming the door was left unlocked. It could have happened that way. Right?"

Gerald smiled, a little patronizingly.

"I doubt it," he said. "I doubt it very much. I'm not a very heavy sleeper and I would certainly have heard the car starting. I'd have heard them when they returned. No, I don't think there is much chance ..."

"But it could have happened."

"Well, yes. It's possible. But I certainly don't ..."

"You drink much during that poker session last night?"

"Not much. A couple of beers—maybe three or four."

"Any liquor?"

"One shot of Scotch, early in the evening."

"And nothing after you got home?"

"Nothing."

Hopper grunted. He walked over and opened the door of the car and looked inside. He didn't take long, but Gerald was aware that his eyes missed nothing. He pulled the front seat cushion up and checked under it and then replaced it. He slammed the door and went to the rear of the car and opened the trunk, which was unlocked. There was nothing there but the spare tire and tools for making a road change.

Gerald noticed that he completely ignored the windshield.

They spent a few minutes more as Hopper asked a number of additional questions, none of which seemed to have significance. And then, finally, they returned upstairs.

Finn was seated on the couch and he had removed his hat. He was smoking a cigar and it smelled vile.

"Well, sorry to have bothered you," Lieutenant Hopper said, reaching for his own hat where he had placed it carefully on a side table before going down to the garage. "But you see how it is. As I told you downstairs, we're looking for a Chevie with New York plates which end with the number '3'. You just happen to have one. And we have to check everybody. Sorry to have taken up your time."

The fat man slowly got up from the couch. He spoke without removing the cigar from the corner of his heavy mouth.

"You always get all the New York newspapers?" he asked. He didn't wait for an answer, but went to the door and opened it.

The lieutenant followed him out, also without waiting for Gerald to say anything. He closed the door after himself.

Neither of the officers said a word until they were in the black, unmarked police cruiser which they had left at the curb. Lieutenant Hopper started the engine and Finn slumped back on the cushions.

"Well, what do you think?"

The fat man shrugged.

"Who knows?" he said. "There was nothing at all around the place. Except a big pile of today's newspapers. Nothing else. I got that Baxter guy on the phone and the poker game thing is on the up and up. Of course we'll check with the others, but his story certainly seems to be O.K. Should be easy to check that part out. Only thing is, the game ended a little later than he said. But I guess it's easy enough to miss up on the time, especially during a card game. And when you got no wife home waiting to beat your brains out."

He took the cigar butt from his mouth, looked at it with an expression of mild disgust and then replaced it and scratched a match and relighted it.

"Seems like a clean-cut lad," he said. "How was the car?"

"Windshield O.K.," Hopper said. He hesitated a minute and then released the clutch and pulled away from the curb.

"It's a damned funny coincidence though," he said. "Two Chevies, both with New York plates ending in '3' and both out there on Northern Boulevard around the same time of night. Of course, Hardy could have been wrong about the number on the plates. A guy who's filled with lead ..."

"Hardy could be right, too, and Hanna still be in the clear," Finn said. "He's not the type for this sort of caper. These clean-cut boys—Sunday school boys—hell, they go in for rape and an occasional murder. That's their dish. No, if his background checks out, he won't be our pigeon. We're after someone who's tied in with Riddle and Petri. Dunne's the lad, for my money. And Dunne has disappeared."

"Case of time," Lieutenant Hopper said. "Just a case of time. Punks like Dunne don't stay disappeared for very long."

"They don't stay out of jail very long, either, thank God."

"Only long enough to kill a cop or two," Hopper said, his voice bitter.

4

The little man in the horn-rimmed glasses leaned away from the table and carefully capped his fountain pen before joining it with half a dozen others in his inside breast pocket. He pushed his chair out and stretched and then spoke in a garrulous voice.

"That's it, Mr. Slaughter," he said. "Your total worth is exactly $348,675.24."

Slaughter grunted, reaching for the glass which held the Scotch and water. The ice cube had melted and the glass was still half full.

"And?"

"And, outside of sixty-two thousand in back taxes, seventeen thousand in withholding taxes, your debts are a little more than three hundred and ten thousand."

Irving Wiener took a certain amount of quiet satisfaction in quoting the figures. He liked to be right, exactly right. It gave him a certain feeling of real superiority and he couldn't resist a little shrug of self-complacency as he finished speaking. He was nothing, nothing more or less than a servant to a man like Slaughter. *His* total net worth stood at a mere $4,000—but at least he had no debts. Men like Slaughter, these big shots, well....

"Your bar is making money," Wiener said. "The cafeteria breaks even and most of your concessions are all right. But that night club ..." he threw up his hands.

"The night club is new. It'll pan out," Slaughter said.

"That well may be," Wiener replied. "But these other items—these things which you have listed as a's and b's and c's and so forth. I just can't understand."

"You're not supposed to understand," Slaughter said. "It isn't your business to understand. All I want from you is to know where I stand."

Once more Irving Wiener shrugged.

"It's very simple," he said. "You need money. At once—or at least within the next thirty days. If the tax people take out a lien, and they will, along with the creditors who are beginning to act ..."

"Yeah, I know. I know all about it. So I'll get money. Don't worry about it. I'll get money."

"There's nothing in these figures," Wiener waved at the papers stretched out on the table, "nothing here that tells me where. I certainly wouldn't know ..."

"There's a hell of a lot you wouldn't know," Slaughter said. "A hell of a lot you wouldn't even want to know. Just you do the work I'm paying you for and don't even think about anything else. I'll do all the thinking that's necessary."

He started to push the papers away and as he did the phone on the desk rang and he quickly reached for it. For a moment he listened and then spoke into it quickly.

"Five minutes," he said. "I'll be clear—in just five minutes."

Wiener took the hint. Standing up, he reached for his hat.

"Have to be going now," he said. "But you had better start ..."

"Yeah, yeah," Slaughter said. "Just snap the lock so the door is open as you leave. I'm expecting someone." He didn't bother to stand or to say good-by.

By the time Slaughter had gone to the portable bar and mixed himself a fresh drink, Steinberg had slunk into the apartment noiselessly, relocking the door after himself. Slaughter asked him if he wanted a drink, purposely holding back his impatience.

Steinberg shook his head.

"It's good and bad," he said. He looked around the apartment and sat down nervously. "This place, Fred," he said. "Makes me nervous. How can you tell that it might not be bugged?"

"Don't be a damned fool," Slaughter said. "Who the hell's going to bug me? Nobody's got ..."

"They bug everyone nowadays. Why even ..."

"Christ, stop worrying," Slaughter said. "Let's have it. You saw Jake?"

"That's the good part," the lawyer said. "He's dying. Can't last more than a few more hours. And he hasn't talked. He won't talk."

"I know that," Slaughter said. "Of course he won't talk. Good God, Jake's got that kid of his and he knows. Knows what would happen if he talked. I never worried about Jake. But did he talk to you? What's with the punk? Did he ..."

"Nothing," Steinberg said. "Absolutely nothing. He didn't know a thing."

"Was he conscious; was he able to make sense. Hell, he has to know."

"He was conscious all right. Weak and could hardly speak, but he understood me. The only thing he remembers is the rumble and getting shot. Saw the kid for just a bare moment and the kid had the stuff. He was climbing into the car. That's all he knows. Everything."

Slaughter cursed.

"This second car the police yak about? How about that? Did Jake see any second car?"

"He saw nothing. Nothing but the cops, shooting at him. There was no second car, not that Jake saw anyway."

Slaughter downed his drink in a gulp and again cursed. "I just don't get it," he said. "Of course the newspapers could be wrong. They could have got a bum steer from the cops. But it don't sound like it. The kid had to make a getaway somehow and a second car makes sense as far as that goes. The thing is, he would have had to have it planned and I know damned well that young punk didn't have the brains to be a double-crosser. Nobody could have reached him. He wasn't smart enough. No, I just can't buy that second car thing. On the other hand, where the hell is he? Why hasn't he made a contact?"

"Maybe the cops got him. Maybe ..."

"Don't you believe it," Slaughter said. "Don't you believe it for a minute. Not that they aren't capable of something like that. The papers said they checked the kid sister, but that was only natural. They knew Dunne hung around with Dommie. But they didn't get him. It would have leaked out somehow. No, the insurance company is making too big a stink about the jewels. If they'd have got him, they'd have got the loot."

"Maybe the cops just glommed onto ..."

"Even the cops aren't that stupid. Money—yes. It could happen. But not hot ice. No, the kid got away somehow."

"Well, then maybe he just powdered. Figures on fencing the stuff himself."

Slaughter slowly shook his head.

"I can't see it," he said. "Not that kid. Hell, I know the sister; I know what kind of punk he was. Just smart enough to know that he'd never be able to unload without connections and he had no connections. Somebody else, yes. But not the Dunne kid."

Steinberg shrugged.

"All right, Fred," he said, "then you name it. What *did* happen to the stuff and where is the kid?"

"It could be that the rumble just plain threw him into a frenzy; scared him half silly and he's hiding out someplace. With Riddle and Dommie gone, he may just ..."

"He's got my number," Steinberg said. "That's the one thing we know he's got. Jake drilled it into him; told him if anything happened the first thing he should do is call my office. He wouldn't be afraid to call his lawyer. No, something ..."

"There's nothing to do but sit tight. Sooner or later he's got to call. You got someone on the phones, just in case ..."

"Twenty-four hours a day," Steinberg said. "And the office knows where I am. They'll contact me the very second there's word."

"All right then," Slaughter said. He looked down at his wrist watch.

"Seven-thirty," he said. "Solly's on his way up. Hang around and we'll have some food sent in. We can play a few hands of pinochle and just sit tight and wait it out for a while. There ain't nothing else to do. It just may be that that call will come in."

CHAPTER FOUR

1

The police were nice about it. They brought Sue home in a squad car on Sunday morning and it was just as well that they did. She was dead on her feet.

It wasn't that they were rough with her, or pushed her around or anything like that. They didn't even raise their voices when they questioned her. They were very reasonable about the whole thing. Merely the questions. Only the trouble was the questions went on all Saturday afternoon and Saturday night. It was all quite legal; she was formally held on a short affidavit and they saw to it that there was a matron present at all times while they talked to her.

It wasn't merely that she was Vince Dunne's sister and that Vince was missing. Somehow or other they'd turned up a witness who had seen Vince and Dommie and Jake in the tavern at the same time. It was enough for them.

A representative of the insurance company which covered the loss was present part of the time and he was even worse than the police. He did everything but accuse Sue of being in on the thing. The police themselves didn't harp on that angle; they concentrated on trying to find out where the boy could have gone, who he knew, who had he been hanging around with. They were sure that Vince had the jewels and that there was a fourth man in on the robbery. They wanted to learn the name of this fourth man.

By the time the police were ready to call it quits and let her go, they were convinced that she knew nothing; that she was completely guiltless.

The trouble was, that by then Sue knew a great deal. *She* knew that Vince had been in on the robbery; she knew that he was guilty.

This was no juvenile prank, no simple matter of a stolen car used for a joy ride. It wasn't even a matter of a mere robbery. This was murder. They made it quite clear to her; it didn't matter whether Vince himself had pulled the trigger of the gun which had killed a policeman. He would be equally guilty in any case.

Vince Dunne, nineteen years old, was a murderer. Police throughout the country had been alerted and it would be just a case of time.

Sooner or later they would get him and when they did, he would go to the electric chair. They didn't have to draw a diagram for Sue. She knew what happened to cop killers.

And so they sent her home at last in a squad car and she climbed out in front of her apartment house and slowly entered the building. Her feet felt like lead as she walked through the lobby to the self-service elevator. She wanted to cry, but she had no more tears. She'd already used them up during those long hours at the police station between the questioning sessions.

There was a broad-shouldered, dour-faced man standing near the elevator and he carefully avoided looking at her as she waited for it to answer her ring. She knew that he was a detective, waiting there in case Vince should show up. By this time she'd seen enough detectives to spot one a block away. She'd seen enough detectives to last her a lifetime.

She wasn't hungry, but she knew that she must eat something. They'd offered her food at the station house, but she'd been unable to swallow.

Once in the apartment, she listlessly prepared a pot of coffee and soft-boiled a couple of eggs. She knew that she would have to eat; knew that life would have to go on. There was nothing else, nothing now but her job and her career. She tried to blame herself, but even this she was unable to do. She'd done everything for Vince that she could do. It was no longer in her hands.

The police had been bitter about it, bitter and hard and angry. Could she blame them? No, in all fairness she couldn't. She felt bitter and hard and angry herself. Not about Vince. Vince was nothing but a child. A rather weak child who had been too easily led astray. No, the ones Sue felt angry about were the men who had influenced him, the ones who had brought him in on the thing.

She was glad that Dommie had been killed. He was better off dead. And the other one, the man she knew as Jake. He was supposed to be dying and Sue found herself wishing that he'd live. Live so that he could go to the electric chair. She wondered what kind of man he could be. They'd told her he had a boy of his own, a boy only a few years younger than Vince.

She couldn't understand how a family man and father could have taken boys like Dommie and Vince in on a thing like this. And there were others. The fourth man. The police seemed to feel that in back of the whole thing was an organized mob, a tough, vicious, underworld gang. These were the ones they wanted. Wanted as much as they wanted Vince.

Well, she would never be able to do anything to help them find Vince, but she'd give anything and everything to help them find those others. The men who had brought her brother in on the job and had made a thief and a killer out of him.

There was just one way to find out who they were. Sooner or later Vince would get in touch with her. Of this she was morally certain. No matter where he was or with whom he was hiding out, he was bound to try and reach her sometime or other. And once he did, she knew exactly what she would do. She would find out the names of the people in back of the thing. She wanted to see them brought to justice; wanted it more than anything else in the world. More than her career and even more than she wanted Vince to escape the justice she realized he fully deserved.

There was only one thing to do. Vince would be too smart to try and reach her at the apartment. He would know by now that the police were seeking him. No, if he tried at all, it would be while she was working at the cafeteria. That was the place, the key to the whole thing. It had been through the hangers-on at the place that Vince had met his new companions, met the men who had involved him. And it was there that he'd try and reach her.

Tired and sick as she was, she was determined to go to the place as usual that night to work. That night and every night. And sooner or later some man would come up to the counter and whisper a word or two and she would know where he was and be able to reach him. Be able to learn what she had to find out.

She had no more than climbed into the uniform she wore when the manager of the place came over and spoke to her.

"Mr. Slaughter is in his office," the man said. "He'd like to have a few words with you. I'll take the cash box while you're gone."

He watched her coldly for a moment as she turned to leave the counter.

"You could have at least called and told us you weren't coming in last night," he said, his voice resentful.

Sue felt a sudden sense of relief as she walked to the back of the long building where Slaughter maintained a small private office. Her first thought, when the manager had spoken to her, was that Slaughter must somehow or other have learned about Vince. That he, like the police, would start the series of incessant questions.

But no, it wasn't that. She'd been absent Saturday night and had failed to notify the restaurant. That was what he wanted her for. He'd be sore about it and she'd have to give him some sort of story. She didn't want to tell him the reason she hadn't called was because she was in the police station being questioned about her brother—who was wanted for murder.

If he had paid slightly less for his clothes, and purchased them in either good department stores or from tailors on the east side of Fifth Avenue, Fred Slaughter might very easily have passed for a gentleman. As it was, the handmade shirts were just a trifle too sheer, the gray-worsted suit was cut a trifle too wide in the shoulders and the shoes, although imported and expensive, were not the type to be worn with a business suit.

His clothes were like his jewelry. The watch should have been gold rather than platinum and like the cuff links and rings which he wore on each hand, there was just too much of it. The clothes were like the man; a little too good and a little too ostentatious.

In his late forties, Slaughter had the figure of a college athlete. He took exceptionally good care of himself, visiting his barber daily for a shave and a trim as well as a manicure. His dark hair was always perfectly groomed and no matter what time of the day or night, there was always the faint trace of after-shaving powder on his lean, olive jaw.

His manners, at least in public, were polished. But the giveaway was the voice. He had a voice like gravel and even his overprecision in the choice of words and phrases merely served to emphasize the effort he made to sound like a gentleman.

Any smart cop would have spotted his background in a second. Slaughter was strictly East Side scum; a one-time mobster who'd made money fast and ostensibly turned legitimate. He didn't actually fool anybody and certainly he didn't fool the riffraff with whom he hung out and whom he patronized.

His sharp eyes looked up as Sue entered the office and he smiled thinly.

"Close the door, Sue," he said. "Close the door and come on in and sit down. I want to talk with you."

Sue took the chair next to the desk.

"If it's about last night ..." she began.

He nodded and half raised a hand to interrupt her.

"Yes," he said, "about last night. You were off. What was it, kid?

Vince? Was it about Vince?"

She felt herself go pale. How did he know? Why did he go at once to Vince? Of course he would have read about the robbery, would have learned about Jake, whom he knew. But why did he bring Vince into it?

He was quick to see the way her mind was working.

"I know all about it, kid," he said. "You know I have connections. So the law is looking for your brother. Well, you have to expect that. I guess you know what happened. Know about Dommie and Jake Riddle. The police figure Vince was a pal of theirs and that he might have been mixed up in the thing. I guess you can't blame them for thinking that, can you?"

She stared at him and nodded dumbly.

"Where is Vince?" he said.

She dropped her eyes and slowly shook her head.

"I only wish I knew, Mr. Slaughter," she said. "He left the house on Friday night, around ten o'clock. Said he was going to a movie. And he hasn't been back since."

Slaughter looked at her closely.

"And you haven't seen him? Haven't heard from him?"

"No."

"Have the police been around?"

Sue nodded.

"Yes," she said. "They've been around. That's where I was last night. All night. They questioned me until ..."

"What did you tell them?"

She looked up at him, startled by the suddenness of the question and the hard, cold note in his voice.

"Tell them?"

"Yeah. That's what I said. What did you tell them? Come on ..."

"Why I didn't tell them anything," Sue said. "What could I tell them? He didn't come home; I don't know where he is and ..."

"I know, I know," Slaughter interrupted her hurriedly. "Of course you don't know. Who the hell does? But I mean, what did you tell them? You know. They must have asked you other things. Like who he hangs around with, who he knows. Things like that."

"Yes, of course," Sue said. "They asked. And I told them everything I knew. I told them that he knew Dominic Petri and Jake Riddle. What else could I tell them?"

Slaughter looked angry and Sue vaguely sensed his mood and was puzzled. Why should he be angry?

"About the cafeteria," he said. "And me. Did they ask about me?"

Sue looked at him, perplexed.

"Why should they?" Sue said. "Why should they ask about you? It wasn't me that they were investigating ..."

"Listen," he said, "they know the kid worked here for a time. They know I took an interest in him."

"Did you?" Sue asked.

"Of course I did," Slaughter said, suddenly dropping his voice back to normal. "Remember? I said I'd square things with the parole board when he got fired so that they wouldn't know about it. Remember? Certainly I took an interest."

Sue slowly nodded in agreement. She couldn't help but wonder why he was taking such an interest now. It was impossible that he could think any trouble Vince was in could hurt him in any way.

"Listen Sue," Slaughter said, standing up and walking around the desk and looking down at her. "Listen, Vince is a good kid. Don't you worry yourself about Vince. But we got to find him. See? We gotta find out where he is."

Sue looked up at him and slowly shook her head.

"He isn't a good kid, Mr. Slaughter," she said. "No, Vincent isn't a good kid at all."

"Don't talk like that," Slaughter said. "He's just a boy. Maybe a little wild, but just a kid. Don't forget, he's your own brother. Twin brother, isn't it?"

Sue nodded and dropped her eyes.

"Yes," she said, "twin brother."

"Well listen, we just got to find him. You gotta help me. We gotta get hold of Vince."

Sue pushed back the chair and reached her feet. "And then what?" she asked, slowly.

"Then, why then we get hold of the ..."

Suddenly he stopped talking and stared at her. He moved and crossed the room and stood with his back to her, staring out of the window.

"We get hold of a mouthpiece and if the kid's in any kinda jam, we go to work for him," he said, lamely.

Sue stood watching him with wide eyes. She stood dead still, almost as though she were hypnotized. As though she might be looking at a poisonous reptile.

She knew what he had been about to say when he'd so suddenly interrupted himself. She knew it as well as though he had spoken the words themselves. He'd been going to say, "Why then we get hold of the jewels."

He swung back from the window, reaching into his side pocket for a pack of cigarettes.

"Yeah," he said, "yeah. We have to help the kid. So the second you hear from him, you get hold of me. Right off. Call me at my place—here, I'll give you the number."

He took a pad and pencil from the table and scribbled down two or three lines.

"My apartment number, the phone over in the bar, and the phone here. I'll be one spot or the other. Just don't forget. Call me at once. No one else. Definitely not the police. The cops would grab him and then he wouldn't have a chance. No, you hear from Vince, you get me pronto. We'll take care of him, see that he's protected."

Returning to the cashier's cage a few minutes later, Sue thought: Yes, you'll take care of him all right. There's no doubt about that.

Her face was a sickly dead white and she felt as if she could hardly stand.

She was sure. Very sure. She knew now who had been in back of Vince and Dommie and Jake. Knew for a certainty.

Could Slaughter himself have been the fourth man on the job? No, it didn't seem likely. The fourth man would know what happened to Vince and where he was. Slaughter must have been the mastermind; the brains behind the thing.

As the thought hit her, she experienced a blinding, insane hatred for the man. She turned toward the telephone booth at the side of the cafeteria. She had almost reached the instrument before she slowly stopped and then once more turned toward the front.

The phone? The police? What good would that do? She'd tell them about Slaughter and maybe they'd listen to her and maybe they wouldn't. But what possible good could come of it? She had no proof, no proof at all. Nothing but her own intuition. Her own sure knowledge.

No, what she must do was find Vince. Find Vince and get the truth from him.

As Sue Dunne once more returned to the front of the restaurant and took her place behind the cash register, the small portable radio underneath the counter was just beginning to give the early Sunday evening news broadcast which interrupted the usual all-music programs each hour on the hour.

2

Little Shirley Conzoni walked over and stood in front of the deck chair on which her father sprawled, the Sunday paper fallen across his large lap and his eyes closed as the sun beat down on his dark, leathery face.

"He's still there, Daddy," Shirley said.

Anthony Conzoni grunted.

"Go 'way and play, honey," he said.

"Shirley's talking to you, Tony." Mrs. Conzoni spoke up, taking her eyes from her sewing. "Answer her."

Mr. Conzoni grunted again and opened one eye.

Shirley, quick to follow up this brief victory, spoke quickly.

"I said he's still there, Daddy."

"Who's still there, honey?" her father asked.

"Why the dead man," Shirley said.

Anthony Conzoni opened both eyes.

"Now honey," he said, "you shouldn't speak like that. There's no ..."

"There is so!"

Shirley looked at her father furiously. "There is too a dead man. The one I told you about before. He's still there. Nobody's come for him and he's still there in the bushes."

"An imagination!" Mrs. Conzoni said proudly. "What an imagination the baby's got, Tony. A real ..."

"There's no dead man!" Anthony Conzoni didn't approve of his daughter having so vivid an imagination.

Shirley stepped back a pace and lifted her doubled fists and quickly swung at her father's large stomach.

"There is so a dead man," she screamed, striking him several quick blows. "There is so. See! See this?"

Shirley held out the small square of white handkerchief she had folded in her hand. It was stained a reddish brown.

"Blood," she said. "He had it in his hand. Sally dared me and so I took it. If there's no dead man, then where do you think I got this? And that's blood ..."

Conzoni, with amazing speed for a fat man, reached out and grabbed his eight-year-old, pulling her to him. He took the handkerchief from her.

"Where did you get this?" he asked.

"Like I said, from the dead man."

Mrs. Conzoni had gotten out of her chair and come over and was leaning down. She started to put out an inquiring finger and then suddenly drew it back and paled.

"My God, Tony," she said, "my God ..."

Little Shirley started to scream as her father began pulling her across the lawn.

"Come on," he said, "come on now. I want to see this here dead man. You take me to ..."

Five minutes later Detective Lieutenant Hopper was sitting in the front seat of the black police car as it screamed away from headquarters in Mineola. A uniformed policeman was driving and Finn was in the back seat, cleaning his nails with the unburnt end of a match.

They arrived at the deserted stretch of road simultaneously with a car from State Trooper headquarters. A county patrol cruiser, empty, was pulled alongside of the road and the uniformed driver was attempting to keep the rapidly collecting crowd away from the bushes at one side, where his partner was leaning down over what appeared to be a crumpled mass of old clothes.

Hopper made a quick search as they waited for the lab men and the photographers. He was careful not to disturb the body, but he didn't have to worry about footprints or tire markings. The crowd of curious had already very competently eliminated any possibility of identifying either.

It took Hopper less than a minute to find the wallet in the rear trouser pocket of the dead man. The only identification was a Social Security card, but it was enough for the lieutenant, at least for the moment. That and a quick look at the corpse. There was no doubt at all in his mind. Vince Dunne had turned up.

It took another three minutes for Hopper to reach his second conclusion.

Vince had turned up, but the jewels had not. The jewels were still missing.

The lieutenant waited only until after the man from the medical examiner's office showed up to make a preliminary examination.

Then, wishing to duck the reporters who were beginning to appear, he took Finn by the arm and left.

"One bullet," he said, when they were back in the car, "through the back of the neck. Doc said he might have lived for half an hour, no more. I feel a little better about Dillon and Hardy."

"Maybe it wasn't Dillon or Hardy who got him," Finn said. "Maybe it was his own mob."

Hopper half shook his head.

"The bullet's still in his skull somewhere," he said. "It will tell the story. But I think it was our boys. The guy who was driving the getaway car wouldn't have shot him in the back of the neck. Anyway, that's three down and one to go."

"One—and the jewels," Finn said.

"I'll settle for the fourth one," Hopper said. "The jewels can be replaced but you can't replace a couple of dead policemen. The services are tomorrow," he added. "It will be a joint service and I want every available man on the force to show up. It's the least we can do."

"By the way," Finn said, "how did that guy Hanna check out?"

Hopper hesitated several moments before answering. "Well," he said at last, "he seems in the clear. The trouble is, he's almost too good to be true. I've been trying to get hold of that girl of his, his fiancée up in Connecticut. Probably won't mean anything, but it is a little odd that he suddenly postponed his visit up there. I understand from his friends he's been making that trip once each week religiously for the past several years. And then suddenly, he cancels out at the last minute. Seems a little strange."

"No one's talked with her?"

"The local men talked with her father. The girl herself has been out. But I have a call in for her and she's supposed to be back this evening."

Hopper looked over at the clock on the dashboard. "Should be able to reach her by the time we get back to the station," he said.

3

Sunday was probably the most miserable day Gerald Hanna had spent in his entire life.

By now the reaction had set in. Had there been something for him to do, could he have kept busy, it might have been better. But instead, there was nothing, nothing but the idle hours in which to worry.

For the first time he began to wonder what insane caprice of mentality had motivated him, began to wonder if he hadn't temporarily lost his mind. As the full implication of his actions came to him, he was suddenly convinced that he couldn't possibly win. The police were bound to find him out, bound to discover his part in the thing.

He didn't leave the house except to run down to the corner and pick up the newspapers. And then he found that he was unable to concentrate long enough to read them. He just sat there in the apartment waiting, waiting for the police to come once more, thoroughly convinced that it was merely a matter of time until they did.

He had orange juice and coffee for breakfast and skipped lunch altogether. By six o'clock, still not hungry, he decided that he must get something into his stomach. He would have gone out, but for some reason he was afraid to leave the apartment.

He had to be there, in case the police did come. It was a strange thing, but he was deathly afraid that they would return, and at the same time, the thought of their arriving and his not being there filled him with an even greater fear.

At seven-thirty he decided to telephone Maryjane. By this time he was suffering a hundred regrets and nameless fears. Among them was a feeling of guilt for the way he had acted to his fiancée over the telephone. It was inexcusable. He had to admit it. He had been a boor and had behaved like a stupid idiot. No wonder she had been speechless with indignation.

He put the call in and then, when at last she answered, he was overcome with a sudden dumbness.

"Gerald," he said. "This is Gerald." And then, for some reason, he seemed utterly incapable of uttering another word.

"Where are you?"

Her voice was cold and distant.

"Home," he said, at last. "I'm home and I just thought I would call and see if everything is all right."

For a long moment there was no answer.

"Gerald?" Maryjane said, at last. "Gerald? What's the matter? What's wrong? You don't sound right. Please tell me what is going on? I want to know."

She was no longer angry, no longer bitter. She was perplexed, unable to understand what was happening.

"I'm all right," Gerald said. "Yes, I'm all right. I just wanted to call and apologize ..."

"There's something wrong. I just know that there's something wrong," Maryjane said. "Please tell me ..."

"It's nothing dear," he said. "Just that I wasn't feeling well, and ... well, I just ..." his voice trailed off.

"Gerald Hanna," she said, "Gerald Hanna, you tell me this minute exactly ..."

And then, once again just as it had on Saturday morning, it came over him again. He felt that peculiar feeling of cold aloofness. A sensation of almost utter distaste.

"I'm all right, I tell you." His voice was frozen and tight. "Sorry I bothered—just wanted to tell you that everything is fine. I'll see you next weekend as usual. Good-by."

He hung up without waiting for an answer.

Leaving the phone, he quickly crossed the room and snapped on the radio. And then he went to the kitchen and got the bottle of whisky and poured himself a drink.

It was almost like magic. Suddenly he felt fine. Felt just as he had been feeling Saturday night. What in the hell had gotten into him anyway? What had he been stewing around about and worrying for? Everything was going just as he had planned it. Everything was fine.

All it had taken was that phone call to Maryjane to straighten him out. He'd been a fool to sit around and worry.

He downed the drink and replaced the bottle and then returned to the living room and sunk down in the big upholstered chair. He took a cigarette from a box on the table at his side and then reached over and played around with the dials on the radio set until he found a band playing calypso.

At nine o'clock the program was interrupted for five minutes of spot news. It was then that Gerald learned that police had found and identified Vince Dunne's body.

Maryjane Swiftwater was not among the several hundred thousand persons who heard that newscast. In the first place, Maryjane never listened to either the radio or television, considering both mediums vulgar and boring. And in the second place, at the moment the announcer was telling the world about the discovery of Dunne's body, Maryjane herself was having a completely baffling conversation over the telephone with a man who had described himself as Detective Lieutenant Hopper of the Nassau County Police Department.

The lieutenant, from what she could gather, was for some absolutely bizarre reason, interested in her engagement to Gerald Hanna. He refused to say why he was interested and his questions completely confused her.

It never occurred to Maryjane to ask if Gerald were in some sort of trouble. Gerald wasn't the sort of person ever to be in trouble. And it couldn't be that he had had an accident. Why she'd been talking to him herself less than half an hour or so ago. And so she was utterly bewildered.

The man wanted to know how long they'd known each other, how long they'd been engaged. He even wanted to know why Gerald had failed to keep his weekend appointment with her, although to save her life she couldn't understand how he even knew about the appointment.

Five minutes after she had talked with the man, Maryjane made her decision.

There was just no doubt about it any longer. There was something very, very wrong. Something that she didn't know about and couldn't possibly understand. And so there was only one thing to do. There would be no point in calling Gerald back on the telephone. No point at all. The last two calls had been sufficiently unsatisfactory to establish that.

She would go down to New York the next day, on Monday, and see Gerald and have it out with him. If she left her job an hour early, she would have plenty of time to make the two-ten into town and it would get her to New York in time to take a cab to Penn station from Grand Central and get out to Roslyn by the time Gerald himself returned from his office.

It would be best to see Gerald at the apartment; she didn't want to risk having a scene in his office or in some public restaurant.

4

Steinberg was watching a television show at the time and so missed the news broadcast. The oversight, however, was not important; he received the word from one of his ambulance chasers within five minutes of the time the announcer signed off. Within another two minutes he had Slaughter on the phone. He knew at once that Slaughter himself was unaware of the news and he had to be very careful how he broke it to him. Steinberg worried about tapped telephone lines.

It took several minutes and a little double talk, but Slaughter was fast on the pickup and got it almost at once. He told Steinberg to hold the wire a moment and then rushed out into the restaurant.

Sue Dunne had already left. The only thing the manager knew was that she had suddenly gotten sick and said she had to go home.

Slaughter went back into his office and told Steinberg to meet him at the New York apartment as soon as possible. They both arrived within forty-five minutes and took the same elevator up to the floor on which Slaughter maintained his apartment.

"All right, Leo," Slaughter said, the moment they were in the apartment, "let's have it."

"There isn't much," the attorney said. "Maxie said the cops are playing it cagey. But this he does know. Dunne turned up out on the Island, north of Roslyn. Some kid found the body lying in the bushes. Shot. Maxie got there only a minute or two after the cops showed up. Vince didn't have the stuff on him."

Slaughter cursed.

"How does he know?" he asked. "Maybe the law ..."

Steinberg raised a protesting hand.

"Maxie knows," he said. "Hell, they didn't even know it was Vince at first. Maxie was there when the identification was made and he got a verification from a pal at headquarters. No—there were no jewels. Nothing. Looked like the kid got shot and tossed out of a car. At least that rounds that up. We know what happened to him."

"We don't know," Slaughter said. "We don't know nothing. All we know is about Vince and Jake and Dommie. There has to be someone else; someone we don't know nothing about. And there has to be the stuff. We know they got the stuff outta the jewelry store all right."

Steinberg stood up and stretched.

"Listen Fred," he said, "maybe you better forget about that part of it. The boys are taken care of—they're dead. The jewels are missing. Right now, they are about the hottest things this side of hell. Don't forget, two cops died during that rhubarb. Maybe it would be better to just write the whole caper off and stay in the clear while you're still clean."

Slaughter looked hard at the little lawyer and then slowly shook his head.

"No," he said. "No. Not by a damned sight. Some bastard hijacked those gems and I mean to do something about it. For two reasons. I don't like anyone chiseling in on my jobs. But even more important, I've already made the deal to unload the stuff. And I can't miss on it. I have to have the dough. Have to have it."

"But just where do you start ..."

"Well, to begin with," Slaughter said. "There's the girl. We gotta start somewhere and so we might just as well start with her."

"You mean young Dunne's sister?" Steinberg asked. "But why ..."

"I pay you to do my thinking for me," Slaughter said. "Don't make me do all of it. Vince Dunne lived with his sister, didn't he. And she was off work on Friday night. Maybe she got suspicious when he left the house and followed him. I don't say that she did, but just maybe. She could have been worried about him, known something was up. She just possibly could have followed him.

"Someone picked him up, that we know. It seems to me it had to be someone he knew, not someone who just happened to drive by. It could have been arranged in advance, or, in the case of the sister, she could have been there, waiting to see what he was up to. It's a cinch he was picked up and it's a cinch that whoever picked him up, dumped the body when they found he was either dying or dead, and hung on to the loot."

"But the girl, his own sister ..."

"Listen," Slaughter said, "it could have happened. Who the hell else did he know? Who else was close to him? Nobody. If he'd been playing around with someone from another mob, I would have known about it. Sure, it may be farfetched, but we gotta start someplace. Someone has that stuff and I mean to get it. Another thing, I talked with the girl tonight. She acted damned funny, very damned funny, when I asked her about the cops and what they'd asked when they took her in."

"All right," Steinberg said. "So, let's see the girl."

"Tomorrow will be time enough," Slaughter said. "Plenty of time. Right now she's probably waiting down at the morgue to identify her brother. The cops will keep her busy for the rest of the night. But tomorrow—well, we'll see. I'll take care of that end of it. You check with your guy again and make absolutely sure about the stuff. Sure that no one got their hands on it when they picked up Vince."

CHAPTER FIVE

1

Leaving the house early Monday morning, Gerald departed by the front door and looked into the mailbox as he went down to the garage. It was empty, but he expected as much. The mail wouldn't be delivered until sometime in the forenoon and it would bring the envelope he'd mailed himself on Saturday. He would let it stay in the box when it came until he was ready to use its contents. The box would be the safest place. The police might be back; might possibly search him and the apartment. The one spot they would never think of would be the mailbox itself.

He drove the Chevie, leaving it at the railway station parking lot in Manhasset as he usually did on weekdays, and took the train into Penn Station. He arrived at the office at his usual time.

He wanted very much to see either Baxter or one of the other men who had been at the Friday night poker session, but he made an effort to control any temptation to seek them out. The opportunity came, as he expected it would, during the midmorning coffee break. He was at the counter in the drugstore in the lobby of the building, when Bill Baxter entered and spotted him. Baxter moved onto the stool next to his immediately.

"Hi, boy," he said. He laid a heavy hand on Gerald's shoulder. "Say, what were you up to after you left Friday night, anyway?"

"Up to?"

"Yeah," Baxter said. "Don't try and kid me now. What did you do, get picked up for drunken driving or something?" Bill looked at him and laughed but there was a curious expression on his bland face. "The police called me Saturday afternoon—wanted to know all about the poker game and especially wanted to know all about you. Funny thing, the guy who phoned me said he was a detective connected with the Homicide Bureau. Who'd you murder, kid?"

Gerald forced a laugh.

"Oh that," he said. He shook his head, ruefully. "Damnedest thing you can imagine, Bill," he said. "Seems on my way home I passed the scene of a robbery and shooting. Maybe you read about it. Out in Manhasset. Couple of cops and some gunmen had it out after the gunmen were found robbing a jewelry store."

"Jees," Bill said, "don't tell me you were in on that one!"

"Well, I must have just missed it. Anyway, it seems someone spotted a Chevie with a license number somewhat similar to mine and so the cops came around and checked up on me."

"Did you see anything; were you there when …"

"Hell, I missed it," Gerald said. "It was just that I happened to be in the neighborhood at the time or near abouts. I understand the gang got away with a quarter of a million in jewelry."

Bill Baxter whistled.

"You sure you haven't got the loot stashed away, kid? Boy, a quarter of a million."

"I wish I had," Gerald laughed. "By the way," he said, "that stuff was insured according to the papers. It must have been for plenty. I wonder who …"

"They can afford it," Baxter said.

"Who can afford it?"

"Well, without doubt it would be Great Eastern Surety. Used to work for them. They handle all of those big jewelry accounts. And they have more damned money than they know what to do with."

"Eastern, eh?"

"Yeah, a real tight outfit. Incidentally, a pal of mine, Jack Rogers, is probably the man on the account. He takes care of most of the stuff around town here. Know him?"

Gerald shook his head.

"I'm sort of interested in the thing," he said. "You know, what with the cops being by and questioning me and everything."

"Jack can probably give you the low-down. He works pretty close with the police on these things." Baxter hesitated a second. "Tell you what," he said, "I'm tied up this noon, got an appointment at the Downtown Athletic Club. But if you'd like, and really want the story about it, I'll give Jack a buzz and if he's free, I'll set up a lunch date for you."

"Say Bill, that would be great," Gerald said. "You know, with the cops talking to me and everything …"

"I'll give him a buzz," Bill said. "You be in your office all morning?"

"All morning."

Hanna picked Jack Rogers up at the latter's office at twelve-fifteen. He took him to lunch in a Schrafft's restaurant in the neighborhood after a rather embarrassed introduction.

Rogers, a heavyset, middle-aged man with a perpetually worried look, ordered a cold salad and a glass of iced tea and then turned to Gerald as the waitress left.

"Bill said you were interested in the Frost job, out in Manhasset," he said. "Said the police had been around asking you about it or something?" He looked at Gerald with mild curiosity.

Gerald nodded.

"They sure did," he said. "Damnedest thing, I was at a poker session at Bill's Friday night. I left sometime after midnight and drove out to the Island. I live out in Roslyn. Anyway, I must have passed that jewelry store in Manhasset either just before or just after the thing took place."

"It wouldn't be just after," Rogers said. "You'd have seen the police and the ambulances and everything."

"Just before then. Anyway, I was driving a Chevie. And it seems that someone spotted a Chevie at the scene—supposed to be a getaway car or something—and the last number on the license plate was the same as mine. What do you think of that for a coincidence!"

"It happens," Rogers said morosely. "Happens more often than you would suspect."

"Anyway, the police were around the next day. Checking up on me and on my car. They sure asked a million questions."

"They would," Rogers said. "They don't miss much, you know. After all, there was a quarter of a million in jewels lifted. That ain't hay."

"Do you think they'll turn up?" Gerald asked.

"They usually do," Rogers said. "We have offered the usual reward— a hundred thousand dollars in this case. Yes, they usually turn up."

"A hundred thousand!" Gerald whistled.

Rogers shook his head, looking sad.

"The reward won't bring them in this time," he said.

"No?"

"No. You see—this is off the record of course—in most cases like this a deal is made sooner or later. There's a cooling off period and then, sooner or later, someone contacts us. Usually the contact is a perfectly respectable front, either a lawyer or something like that. We pay the reward and we get the jewels."

"You mean the police ..."

"Well, let's put it this way. The police undoubtedly know that a deal is made. Sometimes the mob throws them a fall guy, and sometimes not. But the big thing is getting the stuff back. After they've had their crack at it and if they fail to produce, well, then we go to work on it. Of course we are in on it from the beginning, as far as that goes."

"Then you mean that sooner or later you'll recover the quarter of a million in jewels they got away with?"

Rogers shook his head.

"No," he said. "No, not this time, I'm afraid."

Hanna looked up at him, his head twisted in curiosity.

"Not this time?"

"Not a chance," Rogers said. "You see, this is a little different. This isn't just a simple heist or stickup. Two cops were shot. Shot and killed. As far as the jewels are concerned, we're just as much interested as we'd ever be. But this time it's different. We don't have the freedom to move that we'd have normally. A robbery is one thing. Even a robbery and a murder or two. But not this time. Not when they kill a cop. The police aren't partial to cop killings."

"Then you mean that the thieves ..."

"Well, they got three of them, I understand. But the jewels are missing and that means there are others. Or at least one other. Although I would bet my right arm there's an organized mob in back of it. Anyway, no deals can be made now. Not after they shot those two cops. The police would never stand for that. They don't care about the jewels now. All they want to do is get the guys who are responsible for those two murders."

"And so, you mean, you people get stuck then. That the reward won't bring in ..."

"We still offer the reward of course. There's always the chance that someone may have some knowledge. Maybe one of the mob itself will turn rat. A hundred thousand is a lot of money. But frankly, I wouldn't count on it. We may or may not get the stuff back, but as far as I'm concerned, I don't think the reward will have much to do with it. No, this one will be cracked by the cops themselves. As I say, they don't like to have people going around knocking off their men. They'll go to work on this and they'll stay with it. Sooner or later they'll crack it. They almost always do. When a cop is killed."

They finished their lunch and Gerald asked Rogers if he didn't want a second iced tea. Rogers refused.

"No thanks," he said. "Ate too much as it is," he added, patting his belly and looking sadder than ever.

Gerald insisted on picking up the check. He walked back as far as the door of the building where Rogers had his office.

"Well," he said, "it must be damned interesting work. And thanks a lot for lunching with me. I was really pretty interested, you know, with the police being around and all."

Rogers grunted.

"Not too interesting," he said. "After all, we turn it over to a private detective agency and they really do the investigating from their end. I just sort of keep track of things." He belched and held out his hand.

"Nice to see you," he said. "By the way, is that poker game that you and Bill have every week open to strangers?"

"Glad to have you—any time at all," Gerald said. "But you want to watch the boys; you know how these percentage players are. Especially guys with insurance companies."

"I'll give Bill a ring," Rogers said. "Be seeing you."

Gerald, hurrying through the noonday crowds on his way back to the office, was torn by mixed emotions. A hundred thousand reward. Great. Couldn't be better. But then he remembered what Rogers had told him. This time it would be different. This time two policemen had been murdered. This time it wouldn't be a case of the loot being returned and a hundred thousand dollars being paid over and things allowed to be quietly forgotten. No, this time the police were going to stay right with it. Right up until the end.

As he pushed his way through the streets, he mulled the thing over in his mind. Finally, nearing his office, he slowly nodded, smiling to himself in quiet satisfaction.

He knew what he would have to do. He knew the answer. It was ticklish, devilishly ticklish. But he wasn't licked. Not by a long shot.

At three o'clock that afternoon, Gerald knocked at the door of the private office of his supervisor.

"And so if it's all right," he said, "I'd like to get away a little early. I've got everything pretty much cleared up on my desk and I feel a little bit under the weather. Probably a virus or something," he said.

The supervisor told him to go on home, to take it easy and if he still didn't feel all right in the morning, not to come in. Gerald thanked him and within twenty minutes had left the office.

He had returned to his desk only long enough to type out the note.

He went directly to Penn Station and took the train out to Long Island. In Manhasset he got into his car and drove to Roslyn. The trip, actually, wasn't at all necessary. But he couldn't resist the temptation to stop by at the apartment. He wanted to make sure that the envelope had arrived.

It was in the mailbox and Gerald breathed a sigh of relief when he spotted the white of the paper through the air holes. He didn't open the box but instead returned to the car which he had left at the curb with its engine running. It was probably because he was concentrating on what he was about to do, that he failed to notice the taxi which pulled up behind him as he was putting the Chevie into gear.

2

Maryjane Swiftwater leaned forward on the leather seat and stared through the side window of the taxicab.

"Well!" She took a long breath and slowly expelled it.

"What did you say, miss?" The driver looked over his shoulder.

For a second she stared at him blankly. And then her eyes focused, staring at him in anger.

"That car," she said. "The Chevrolet which just pulled away. I want you to follow it."

"Follow it?"

"Yes. Follow it. That's what I said. I want you to follow that car. I don't want you to let the driver know ..."

"I'm no private detective, miss," the cabbie said. "I don't want to get mixed up in no divorce case or nothin' like that."

If she had had a minute to think about it, she would never have been able to do it. But Maryjane moved without thinking and her hand shot into her bag and she found the tightly rolled-up bills, the money she'd been secretly saving for months now not putting it in her savings account, not letting anyone know about it. The dollar and five-dollar bills which she changed into larger denominations as the sum built up and which she always carried with her. It was her own private hoard, held out from her frugal and careful life. Money she was going to use someday to buy the fur coat she'd always dreamed of and always wanted.

She peeled off a bill at random and waved it over the driver's shoulder.

"Hurry," she said, "just follow that car. It isn't a divorce case or anything like that. Here—" she forced the bill into his hand, where it rested on the wheel. "It's yours," she said, "if you don't lose sight of him."

It wasn't until she leaned back in the seat, jerked to the rear cushion as the car suddenly shot forward, that she realized she had handed the man a twenty-dollar bill. Her shock at the knowledge was almost as great as had been her shock at seeing Gerald Hanna leaving from in front of his house at four-fifteen in the afternoon—a full two hours before he was even due to be home from his office. She couldn't, to save her life, imagine what he was up to. But she was certainly going to find out. Yes, indeed, there were a lot of things she was going to find out about Gerald and his behavior of the last few days.

Gerald, several hundred yards in front of the taxi, drove at a moderate speed, his mind only half on the traffic, which was comparatively light. He wasn't quite sure of the best way to get where he was going, but he knew the general direction. Once in Long Island City, he stopped to ask a traffic officer for directions, checking the address on a slip of paper. The officer told him and five minutes later he was in front of the building which housed the offices of the messenger service.

It was a calculated risk, but one that he knew he would have to take. There was, of course, the chance that the girl wouldn't be home, wouldn't, in fact, return home at all that night. But she had to come sooner or later. It was merely a matter of time. The greater risk was that she would go at once to the police. But this Gerald was inclined to doubt. Sisters of gunmen and killers, didn't, as far as he knew, have any great love for policemen.

But even if she did, even if worse turned to worst, he still had an out. The most they could do would be to convict him of butting into police business. And certainly he had an excuse for being curious.

But Gerald doubted very much that Sue Dunne would go to the police after getting the note. No, she'd be too much interested in seeing him; interested in finding out about her brother.

It took him a little while to make it clear to the manager of the agency just what it was he wanted. The man was suspicious, but then, after Gerald had slipped him the extra five-dollar bill, he apparently was willing enough to overlook it. He assured Gerald that the matter would be taken care of.

Returning to his car, Gerald decided to go directly into New York. He could kill some time driving around Central Park, then stop by the Tavern On The Green and have a drink. It was something he'd always wanted to do.

He might just as well relax. Either she'd come or she wouldn't. It was out of his hands.

He only hoped that the breaks would be with him; only hoped that she'd be alone when she got the note. That it wouldn't fall into the hands of the police before she had a chance to make up her mind.

By six-thirty Gerald was seated at a round iron-topped table slowly sipping a gin and tonic. He had perhaps an hour and a half to kill and he was determined to enjoy himself while he was killing it. His car was parked in the lot a few hundred yards away, and for the moment he was at peace with the world. He felt like a million dollars. Keyed up—yes. But still, fine.

He began to visualize the future. A gin and tonic before dinner, every night. Miami perhaps. Or maybe Bermuda would be pleasant at this time of the year.

The thoughts going through the head of Maryjane Swiftwater, however, were anything but pleasant. She herself was sweltering in the back seat of the taxi where it stood with its motor idling a few yards from the spot where Gerald had parked the Chevie. She'd just returned to the car after walking to the entrance to the tavern for the second time and watching Gerald sitting there over his drink. And she had also just parted with the second twenty-dollar bill to the cab driver, who had the audacity to not only accept it, but to accept it with a whine of protest.

But it was going to be worth it. Worth every cent of it, no matter what it cost her.

Maryjane was no longer perplexed. She was sure. Absolutely sure. Gerald could be sitting there for only one reason. He was waiting for someone; waiting for some other girl.

Much as Maryjane regretted parting with the money, she was determined to sit it out. She just wanted to see this girl. See what sort of bitch....

Gerald drained his drink, smiled complacently, and raised a finger to beckon the waiter.

By seven o'clock the messenger was about ready to call it quits and leave. Hell's bells, he'd been standing here in front of the place for at least an hour and a half. People were beginning to get suspicious of him. That woman, the one on the ground-floor front, had twice opened her window now and stared out at him. It made him damned nervous.

For about the tenth time, he turned and slowly started walking around the block. He'd give it just one more try and then the hell with it. Even if she hadn't shown up by the time he got back, well, an extra couple of bucks or not, he'd just take off. He was due to quit at six-thirty and here already he'd spent an extra half hour overtime. He could just put the damned note in the mailbox and shove off. She'd find it. What could be so Goddamned important about handing it to her personally, anyway?

He passed the tavern again and this time he ducked in and ordered a quick beer. At seven-ten he was back in the lobby of the building and pushing the bell. He was surprised when he heard the answering click of the door lock.

3

At eight-twenty-eight, Maryjane Swiftwater returned to the taxi in the parking lot for the last time and dismissed the driver. She was so mad that she failed to ask for change from the second twenty-dollar bill which she had given the man.

As far as the driver himself was concerned, he didn't waste any time hanging around. He was anxious to get back to Long Island and get home and have his dinner. And he didn't want any more of his present fare, in any case. He knew an irate female when he saw one and there was no doubt in his mind about his latest fare. He was glad to be well out of it. Forty bucks for a few hours' work was all very well and good, but he didn't want to get mixed up in any sort of hassle. Not when a girl with a jaw like that girl had, was involved.

She found a phone booth and it took her several minutes to make it clear to information just what it was she wanted. The stupid girl seemed to think that the only Police Department in the world was in New York. But finally she got it clear and within another minute or two, Maryjane had the right number. She was in luck. This man Hopper, the detective who had called her at her home in Connecticut, was in the office. It took her a couple of minutes to make him understand just who she was.

"Don't you remember," she said, her voice high-pitched in irritation. "Miss Swiftwater, Miss Maryjane Swiftwater. You called me about a Mr. Gerald Hanna."

There was a pause and then the man's voice came back to her.

"Yes, yes of course, Miss Swiftwater. And just what ..."

"You wanted to know all about him. At least you seemed awfully curious about him. Remember, you wanted to know why he broke our appointment. Well! I can certainly tell you. It was because he has another girl. Can you imagine ..."

Hopper cut in with a long-suffering voice.

"I see, Miss Swiftwater. So, he has another girl ..."

"He has. And not a word, not one single blessed word about it to me. I don't know why you were interested in him, but I can certainly tell you this. If ever a man was deceitful, if ever a man was a downright cad and liar ..."

"Of course, Miss Swiftwater," Hopper said. "You mean that when he was supposed to come and visit you, you've discovered he was with this other woman ..."

"I wouldn't know about that," she cut in shortly. "But I can tell you this. He's with her right now. Sitting with her and guzzling ..."

"And where is Mr. Hanna right now?" Hopper asked in a bored voice.

"Some place here in New York. A place called Tavern On The Green. And that woman has just come in and joined him."

"Perhaps a relative ..."

"It certainly is not," Maryjane said in indignation. "I know all of Gerald's relatives and business acquaintances. This girl is a blonde, a painted-up blonde. Her name's Dunne. I heard her give it to the waiter when she came here and asked for him. I heard ..."

"What did you say?" This time the voice at the other end of the line was hard and sharp. "What did you say the girl's name was?"

"Dunne. I heard her very distinctly. She came in a taxi and she told the headwaiter Mr. Hanna was expecting her. She said her name was Dunne. Mr. Hanna is my fiancé and I want ..."

It took Hopper another three minutes to get her off the wire and hang up. It took him a little less than two minutes to reach Detective Finn.

4

They'd been together for more than half an hour now, sitting across from each other at the small, round-topped table in the secluded corner of the terrace. She hadn't touched the Martini which the waiter had brought and put down in front of her and he himself had let the gin and tonic grow lukewarm in the tall glass.

She wore a cheap little cotton suit, but well cut as though she might have made it herself, and her makeup was smeared. Her slender-fingered hands beat an insistent tattoo on the edge of the table and when she spoke there was a note of controlled hysteria in her voice. When she looked at him, the azure eyes were filled with loathing.

But in spite of her expression, he could tell that she was very pretty. Her eyes were really beautiful. He only wished he could see them without the anger. Nothing, of course, could detract from her slender, perfect figure.

Looking at her, Gerald's mind unconsciously went to his fiancée, Maryjane. She would never have approved of this lovely golden girl. Maryjane didn't like women who wore their hair free and careless, who....

She reached across the table suddenly, jerking him by the sleeve of his jacket and interrupting his thoughts.

"You wanted to talk to me, mister," she said, fury in her low, husky voice. "What kind of man are you, anyway? Don't just sit there staring at me. Tell me ..."

"I'm sorry," he said, refocusing his eyes on her.

"I don't understand you," Sue Dunne said. "I don't understand you at all. I have to believe you, but I simply can't understand you. You don't look like a hoodlum—and God knows, I've seen enough of them to know. You don't look like a thief or a crook. Maybe you are an insurance man like you say. Maybe you are legitimate.

"And yet you come here, or rather bring me here, and tell me about my brother. Tell me about his getting into your car. You say that he had the jewels and that now you have them. Or that you know how to get hold of them.

"Why? Why in the name of God do you come to me?"

"It's like I explained," Gerald said. "There was nothing I could have done for your brother. He died within minutes of the time he got into the car. There was nothing I could have done for him. But, I want to know who else is mixed up in the thing. If anyone else was involved in the robbery. I want to know how they planned to get rid of the stuff once they had it."

"But why? Why do you want to know? Say, are you some kind of cop or something? You said you were an insurance man. Is that why ..."

Gerald slowly shook his head.

"No," he said. "No, that isn't why. And I am not any sort of cop or anything like that. It's like I have told you. Five men have already died because of these jewels. One of them was your brother. Nothing can be done about that part of it any longer. But you have to be sensible, be realistic. It doesn't make the jewels any less valuable."

He hesitated a second and watched her closely.

"You see," he said, "I don't know anything about mobs, or gangsters, or fences, or anything like that. I just assumed that maybe you, being the sister of one of the men who took the stuff ..."

She pushed back her chair and angrily got to her feet, leaning down with her hands on the table and staring into his face.

"My brother's dead," she said. "I don't say that he didn't get what was coming to him; I don't even blame the policeman who fired the bullet which killed him. But the very thought of those jewels makes me sick. Makes me want to vomit. Do you understand? I hate the jewels and I hate the men who helped Vincent steal them."

Her slender body suddenly began to shake and Gerald himself leaned forward, taking her by the arms. In a moment she again sat down, half collapsing in the seat.

He leaned forward, still holding her.

"Please," he said. "Please. Just take it easy. I'm not trying to hurt you. I don't want to ..."

She swallowed a sob and looked up at him. The hatred was still there, but there was a difference. He could tell that the hatred had nothing to do with him personally. He was no longer important.

"If there is anything I could do to see that the man who got Vince into this thing was arrested," she said in a low, choked voice, "anything I could do at all, why I'd give my life."

She lifted her eyes again and stared at him intently. "And you expect me to help you contact him? You expect me to help you make money out of the very thing which killed my brother? You must be a fool as well as a scoundrel!"

She leaned back in her seat in sudden tired resignation and he could see the tears forming in the corners of her eyes.

"Vince was weak," she said, her voice soft and barely above a whisper, as though she were speaking to herself and had forgotten his very presence. "Yes, Vince was weak. I always knew that he wasn't much good. But if they'd let him alone, if they'd only left him alone! He could have turned out all right. I would have seen to that. I could have helped him, protected him."

She looked up again and once more her mood changed.

"Yes," she said, bitterly. "Yes, I could have helped him. But they didn't. They didn't leave him alone. They need kids like Vince to do their dirty work—take the chances they are afraid to take themselves."

Suddenly she reached for the Martini and lifting it to her lips, swallowed it in one long draught. She made a wry face as she replaced the glass.

"As far as you're concerned," she said, looking into his face and not bothering to conceal the repugnance in her voice, "as far as you're concerned, if you have the jewels like you say you do, then keep them. Or, if you aren't just a cheap thief, give them back to the people they belong to.

"I wouldn't help you if I could. I don't even know why I'm stupid enough to sit here talking to you. I think maybe you are as bad as Fred Slaughter himself. There's something darned funny about you and I think maybe I should just go to the telephone and ..."

"Slaughter? Was this Fred Slaughter the man—the fence or whatever it is?"

For a long moment she stared at him and then quickly looked away.

"If you are smart," she said, "you'll forget that name. Forget that you ever heard it."

This time when she stood up there was no doubt about what her intentions were.

"I don't know what your angle is, mister," she said. "Maybe you are just a screwball after all. You certainly don't look like a thief and you don't look like a cop. But if you should by any chance know anything about those stolen jewels, I would advise you to get rid of them just as quickly as you can. I'd advise you to go right to the police and tell them everything you know."

She hesitated a moment and for the first time as she looked at him, there was no longer the disgust and the dislike in her expression.

"You are older than Vince was," she said. "You should be a lot smarter. Maybe you are and maybe you're not. Maybe, you too just have to be told what is right and what is wrong."

She moved a step away from the table as he started to stand up.

"I'm going now," she said. "We've had our talk. I'm going home now and I don't think I ever want to see you again."

She swung on her heel and stalked out into the night and Gerald stood there.

Somehow he felt a sudden sadness, a sudden odd sense of loss. It didn't matter how she felt about it. He knew that he himself would want to see her again. Would like to see her soon and often and....

He didn't notice the man several tables away who also sat watching the girl leave. The man himself, for a moment, made as though to get up and follow her. Then, after a moment, he once more sat back and his eyes returned to Gerald.

It was a decision he had to make on the spur of the moment. There was no time to call in and find out which one of the two they wanted him to keep his eye on in case they split up. Well, he couldn't, very obviously, tail both of them. And he guessed that the man would probably be the most important one. The man usually was.

It is more or less of a shame that he reached this particular decision, because, if he hadn't and had decided to follow Sue Dunne instead of stay with Gerald Hanna, he might have been able to do something about what was to happen a few moments later.

At least he would have seen the car which was waiting at the curb, in front of Sue's apartment house when she arrived. He would have seen the man who leaped to the dark street and crossed over and accosted her and a second later threw a strangle hold around her neck and pulled her to the edge of the gutter. He would have seen the other hands reach out and drag her into the machine as it left the curb to speed off into the night.

But instead, this man who had to make the decision stayed on as Gerald sat and finished his warm drink and called the waiter over and asked for his check. He followed him when Gerald went out and got into his car. He was behind him, in his own unmarked police car, all of the way out to Long Island. He was parked across the street, watching, as Gerald closed the garage doors and went on up to his apartment.

5

He wasn't prepared for it. It was funny how that was the first thought that passed through his mind as his hand reached out and he flicked on the wall switch in the living room.

Even before the sense of surprise, of fear, reached his brain, that was the thought. He should have known or at least have guessed. But he hadn't. That was the trouble with having no experience. Experience was always valuable. Gerald could only assume the rule applied to almost any given situation.

A criminal, a man who operated outside the law, would have had that experience and would have known. Would have sensed it the moment he entered the room. But he, Gerald Hanna, was without experience and that is why, as the yellow brilliance filtered through the dark room and he saw the two of them, one on the couch and the other standing by the door, he reacted as he did.

The hand which had found the light switch went to his mouth and his eyes, in the sudden glare of the light, were wide and almost hysterical. He gasped and instinctively he turned and took a step back toward the hallway.

It was the short, fat one, the one called Finn, who spoke. He didn't move and didn't take the dead cigar from between his lips and he didn't raise his voice but spoke in a cool, detached manner.

"Don't leave now, Mr. Hanna," he said. "You just got here. This is your house, you know. Your castle. You may stay."

Detective Lieutenant Hopper merely sat still and relaxed on the couch, his glasses half down on his thin, bony nose and his hat pushed back on his head. He didn't look up. His eyes were on the floor and he seemed to be inspecting the carpet under Gerald's feet.

"Yes, do stay. It wouldn't be polite to leave while you have guests," Finn said, shifting his weight from one foot to the other. He dusted a spot of cigar ash from the unpressed lapel of his dark-gray suit and looked up into Gerald's face, smiling politely.

"You're real cute, Mr. Hanna," he said.

Lieutenant Hopper raised his eyes and sighed. He looked over at the fat man, ignoring Gerald, who still stood half in and half out of the doorway.

"I'll take it, Finn," he said in a tired voice. He transferred his gaze to Gerald.

"Come in and sit down, Mr. Hanna," he said. "We've been waiting for you."

Gerald entered the room, attempting to compose his expression. He took off his hat and carefully placed it on the side table and then moved across the room and pulled a straight-backed chair out from the wall. He straddled it and then just sat there, waiting.

"Where have you been?"

The lieutenant's expression was disinterested as he asked the question in a soft, gentle voice.

"Why—why out," Gerald said. The moment the words left his lips he realized the inane vacuity of them. Realized how silly they sounded. But he still hadn't gotten over his shock at finding the men in his apartment, hadn't adjusted to the reality of their presence.

"He's been out," Finn said, his voice heavy with sarcasm. "I told you he's cute, Lieutenant. Not tricky—nothing cagey or deceitful or reticent about him. Just cute. You ask him where he's been and like a little man he ups and he tells you. He's been out. Simple? Straightforward? Certainly. A man would have to be a Goddamned ingrate not to be satisfied with that sort of answer."

He moved then, moved with amazing swiftness for a man of his bulk. He was halfway across the room when he again spoke.

"Why you dirty little bastard ..."

"Sit down, Finn. I said I'd take it!"

The lieutenant stood up then himself and stared down at Gerald. He began to speak in the same soft, unimpassioned tone of voice, almost apologetically, but his gray eyes were like ice.

"I'd like to explain something to you, Mr. Hanna," he said. He took a step forward, standing in front of Gerald on straddled legs. As he spoke he reached up and pushed his glasses into position.

"I don't believe it's any news to you that we have been working on a robbery. The Gordon-Frost job, to be precise. A quarter of a million dollars in stones and assorted gems. But do you know, in spite of the money involved, in spite of the fact that the thieves got away with the stuff, we aren't really primarily concerned. Interested of course, that more or less being our business, but not hysterical about it or anything.

"On the other hand, it just so happens that two policemen were shot during that particular robbery. One of them was a man a year or so younger than you, but unlike you, he was married. Had a two-year-old baby. His name was Hardy, Don Hardy. I never knew him personally as he was just a rookie when he was shot. He'll never be anything else. He's dead.

"The other one was a man named Dillon. Dillon was a sergeant, an old-timer. Dillon I did know. Knew him, knew his wife, and knew his two sons and his daughter. You'd have liked Dillon—a good solid family man and honest as the day is long. Dillon was the sort of cop who hated to write out a traffic ticket. He wasn't a cop's cop—he was a layman's cop. Everyone liked Dillon. Well, he's dead too. I take his death pretty hard; you see he stood up at my wedding and we were friends.

"But I don't want you to let that influence your reaction to what I am saying to you. A lot of men have friends and a lot of those friends die, sooner or later. Not exactly the way Hardy and Dillon died, of course, but they do die."

Lieutenant Hopper shifted his weight and scratched vaguely at the side of his nose before going on. His voice was softer than ever.

"Around New York," he said, "we take it seriously when someone shoots a cop. We don't like it. Not at all, we don't like it."

Gerald, staring up at the other man, half nodded. He didn't speak.

"Now let's take you," the lieutenant said. "By some amazing coincidence, you just happen to be driving by the scene of a crime at the time or around the time it is taking place. And, through an even more fascinating coincidence, you were driving the same make of car which was driven by one of the men who engineered the getaway.

"Sort of coincidental, eh? But that isn't all of it. Oh no, we have even more and greater surprises in store. Your license plate ends in the same number as the license plate of the getaway car. The truth is really stranger than fiction, isn't it, Mr. Hanna?"

The lieutenant tipped his hat back a bit farther on his head and then took off his glasses. He pulled a linen handkerchief from his breast pocket, carefully polished both lenses and then put the glasses into a leather case and placed the case back in his jacket pocket.

"Now you tell us, Mr. Hanna, that you didn't know anything about that robbery. Didn't know anything about those two policemen who were killed in the line of duty. You tell us further that you didn't know the three men who were known to have been involved in the crime. That you never as much as heard of Vince Dunne, or Dominic Petri or Jake Riddle.

"And yet, tonight, by another one of those utterly fascinating coincidences, you spent a few casual, carefree hours with the sister of one of those men. You met her at a pleasant, restful saloon and the two of you enjoyed the cool of the summer evening over a few drinks. I certainly can't criticize you for that, Mr. Hanna. Having met the young lady, I can only congratulate you on your good taste. I can only envy you your youth and your freedom and your luck. But do you know something, Mr. Hanna? Do you know that I experience another sensation even stronger than envy?"

Suddenly the soft voice was no longer soft, no longer gentle and conciliatory.

"You sonofabitch," the lieutenant said, "start talking! Start talking and make it good. Make it Goddamned good!"

As Lieutenant Hopper finished speaking, Finn moved swiftly across the room. His meaty right hand swung from his hip and the hard side of the palm caught Gerald across the eyes. Twice more, before Gerald could raise his arms in defense, Finn back slapped him, rocking his head from side to side.

"He'll talk," Finn said. "He'll talk until the shit pours out of his mouth."

Gerald talked.

He tried not to lose his head, tried not to panic. Tried to tell them the truth, straight and simple.

Yes, he'd met Sue Dunne and he'd spent an hour or so with her.

They didn't interrupt him as he explained it. He told them that he had read about the robbery in the newspapers and that after that first visit the two had paid him, he'd made the connection and reread the stories in the newspapers. He had realized what it was they had wanted to see him about.

Naturally he had been curious. Who wouldn't be? He'd gone on and followed the case for the last couple of days, reading the papers and tuning in on the news broadcasts. He himself had been fascinated by the coincidences in the thing. The fact that he had a Chevie, that its license ended in the number "3." That he had been near the scene of the crime at the time it had taken place. Who wouldn't be curious?

He'd seen the girl's name in the newspapers and her address as well. There had been a picture of her and he had thought she was enchanting.

At this point Lieutenant Hopper interrupted his story. Finn was back, seated on the couch and the lieutenant still stood, a few feet away.

"Enchanting?" he said. "I'm rather surprised, Mr. Hanna … and you an engaged man. In fact, I believe that you and Miss Swiftwater have been engaged for several years. A nice girl, Miss Swiftwater. Not enchanting, perhaps, but nice. I don't believe, however, that nice as she is, she would quite approve of her fiancé finding Miss Dunne enchanting."

Gerald blushed, but continued.

"I couldn't understand," Gerald said, "how a girl who looked like Miss Dunne could be mixed up with a lot of thugs."

"And is she mixed up with thugs?" the lieutenant asked.

"What I mean to say," Gerald explained, "is how she could be the sister of a thief and a gunman. In any case, curiosity got the better of me, and because I was interested in the case, and because you had questioned me about it, I looked up Miss Dunne and arranged to see her. It was as simple as that."

But it wasn't as simple as that. It wasn't simple at all.

The questioning continued, continued endlessly. A half a dozen times Finn would get up and cross the room and raise his thick hand and slap him. The lieutenant never struck him and he alternated between suaveness and detachment and cold fury. But neither of them shook his story. Neither of them made him admit a thing beyond the bare outlines of his original statement. He had seen the girl's picture and her address, she had interested him, and he had made a date with her.

What had they talked about? Nothing much really. He had offered to help her in any way he could. He had expressed his sympathy over her brother's death.

"It is too bad you didn't sympathize with Hardy's widow or with Dillon's widow," Hopper said. "But then I don't suppose that they tweaked your curiosity. I don't suppose that you found the same 'enchantment' in them."

That was when Finn hit him the hardest.

At one time during the evening the telephone rang and Hopper quickly reached for it. The call was for him and he spoke into the instrument for several moments, mostly in monosyllables. Once or twice he looked across the room curiously at Gerald as he listened to the voice on the other end of the wire. When he hung up, he swung back to Hanna.

"When you left Miss Dunne," he asked, "where did she say she was going?"

"She said she was going back to her apartment."

Hopper nodded.

"You had your car," he said. "Why didn't you drive her back?"

"Perhaps she didn't find Mr. Hanna as enchanting as he found her," Finn said.

The lieutenant turned and stared at his partner for a moment and then returned his attention to Gerald.

"Well?"

"Miss Dunne resented my curiosity," Gerald said. "Also, she was very upset, about her brother, you know. She just wanted to be left alone. I offered to drive her home, but she preferred to leave by herself."

"I can't say I blame her," Finn cut in.

"It couldn't have been because she knew you were mixed up in the robbery, now could it?" Hopper said. "It couldn't be that she just didn't want any part of …"

"I am not mixed up in anything," Gerald interrupted. "The only thing I know about the robbery is what I have read in the papers. I've said it once and I'll say it again. I have absolutely no knowledge …"

They left around five o'clock in the morning. It was the lieutenant who had the last words as they stood in the doorway.

"Brother," he said, "this time we are really going to check you. We're going to find out everything there is to find out. When I get through, I'll know if you ever as much as spit on the sidewalk. I'll know about the time you skipped school when you were in the second grade at P.S. 40. I'll know about the first girl you kissed and the last one you tried to lay. There won't be one Goddamned thing I won't know about you."

He pulled his hat forward on his head and his eyes were deadly.

"And if you are mixed up in this thing," he said, "we'll get you. We'll get you and we'll fry you!"

He didn't bother to close the door as he followed Finn out of the apartment.

Closing the door behind the two detectives, Gerald had an almost irresistible desire to wait for a few moments and then go to the mailbox. He wanted to be absolutely sure that the envelope was there, where it should be. Silently he congratulated himself for having come up from the garage by the inside stairway. Had he locked the garage from the outside and walked around to the front of the house, he would have very likely stopped at the box and removed the letter on his way in. He would have had it in his hand when he was accosted by Hopper and Finn.

Well, thank God, he hadn't made that mistake. And he wouldn't make the mistake now of going to the box. The envelope containing the two baggage checks would be there all right. It had to be there. If Hopper and Finn had taken it out, certainly they would never have walked off and left Gerald free.

Reluctantly, he slowly turned and went in through the bedroom and turned on the light in the bathroom. He'd take a shower before turning in for a couple of hours sleep. He needed a shower, needed to wash off the feel of Finn's heavy hands.

CHAPTER SIX

1

Steinberg walked over to the window and pulled the cord, opening the Venetian blinds halfway and letting the early morning sunshine filter into the room. Then he crossed to the light switch and flicked it. He turned back to face Slaughter, who sat on the couch with the cup of steaming coffee in his hands. Slaughter was in his shirt sleeves and his forehead was wet with perspiration. His hair was messed and there were streaks of dirt down one side of his face.

Four long, raw scratch marks, caked with dried blood, decorated the other side.

"You shouldn't have done it," Steinberg said. "Goddamn it, Fred, you can't do things like that. What the hell are you going to do with her now? You haven't found out a damned thing and now we got her on our hands."

"Oh for Christ's sake shut up," Slaughter said. "What the hell is the matter with you anyway? What do you think I've done to her? Murdered her or something? I just slapped her around. Asked her questions and slapped her around a little. She isn't hurt."

"Sure," Steinberg said. "You just slapped her around. And what do you think she's going to do when she gets out of here, eh? Do you think she'll go out and buy you a nice Father's Day present. Is that it? Fred, don't you know that that kid's going to talk? Going to the cops? She can't be completely stupid, you know. She understands why she was brought here. She knows now that you're mixed up in the thing. So what's she going to do?"

"She ain't going to do nothing," Slaughter said. "She knows what I'd do if she ..."

"You're being stupid, Fred," Steinberg said. "That kid's a square. She isn't like that punk brother of hers. She's on the up and up. It isn't only that she'll be sore about being slapped around—and I hope to God that's all you did do to her—it's that being a square, she's burned up about her brother. And she'll talk. Sooner or later, she'll talk."

Slaughter took a sip of the coffee and put the cup down.

"She'll talk all right," he said. "But it won't be with the cops. No, any talking she'll do will be with me. And don't tell me she don't know nothing. How about that note she had on her when we picked her up? Huh, how about it? She may not know anything, but the guy who sent her that note—the guy she met last night—he knows plenty."

Slaughter took a piece of soiled paper out of his pocket.

"Just listen to this," he said, and read from the slip of paper. 'If you are interested in what happened to your brother, meet me at the Tavern On The Green in Central Park at eight o'clock. Ask the headwaiter to take you to Mr. Hanna's table.' How about that, huh?"

"It doesn't mean ..."

"It means she met him—knows who he is. And if I have to kill her, I'm going to find out. You think I've touched her yet, why ..."

"Work her over any more," Steinberg said, "and you know what you're going to have to do, don't you?"

Slaughter stared up at the little lawyer.

"Are you getting queasy?" he said. "Of course I know what I'm going to have to do. So what?"

Steinberg shrugged.

"The trouble is," he said, "from what you've been telling me all night now, it doesn't matter whether you would hesitate or not. Apparently the tougher you get with her, the more stubborn she gets."

"Well, that's why I'm going to play it your way," Slaughter said. "Or at least give it a try. We'll let her sleep and rest up, give her a breather. Christ, I gotta get some damned sleep myself. But this afternoon she gets her last chance. After she's had a chance to think it over and look at it sensibly. And then—well kid, she'll talk. She'll talk if I have to break every ..."

"O.K., save me the details," Steinberg said. "Do it your way. But realize what you are doing."

Slaughter shrugged. "Go on home and get some sleep. I'm going to turn in for a few hours. You call me later this afternoon. I may have some news for you. In the meantime, maybe you better stay away from the apartment here. The cops know you were representing Jake—I don't want them knowing that you are hanging around here too much."

Steinberg found his hat and walked toward the door.

"One thing," he said. "Keep this in mind. Right now you could probably let her go and you might get away with it. After all, she isn't really hurt. It would be her word against yours. She may suspect a lot about the other thing, but she doesn't know anything and she can't prove anything. Her word against yours. She's the sister of a thief and a cop killer; you're a respectable businessman. I could almost guarantee you that there'd be no trouble. Just get her ginned up and throw her out and you'd be clear. But go one step further ..."

"Christ, will you get outta here and go home?" Slaughter said.

2

Bill Baxter was walking through the lobby of the building shortly after ten o'clock on Tuesday morning, on his way to the restaurant for his coffee break, when he spotted Gerald. He swerved, crossing over to intercept his poker party pal.

Gerald didn't notice him until the other man took him by the arm.

"Hey, kid," Baxter said. "What the hell's the big rush. Not," he added, without waiting for Gerald's answer, "not that you shouldn't be in a rush. Jesus, old Engleman is having kittens. Where the hell have you been? You know how he feels about anyone coming in late."

Gerald stopped, forced a weak smile.

"Overslept," he said. "I ..."

"You better have a better line than that," Baxter said. "The old man is really up in the air. He's been out in the office looking for you about ten times in the last hour. He seems mad enough to ..."

"What the hell's on *his* mind?" Gerald asked. "I've been late before. This isn't the first time anyone ..."

"I don't know," Baxter said. "All I can tell you is that something is in the wind. He's been out about a dozen times and he's sure as hell burned up about something. You haven't been lifting the company funds by any chance, have you, kid?"

He slapped Gerald on the shoulder and laughed.

"Maybe," he said, "you better stop in and have a cup of coffee with me or something stronger. Build up your morale before you have to face the lion in his den."

Gerald shook his head.

"No," he said. "No, I better get on up. The sooner I see him the better."

He moved over to the bank of elevators as Baxter turned once more toward the restaurant. As Hanna got into the empty car, he turned and that's when he again noticed the man. The man in the dark, linen suit and the light-weight felt hat tipped carelessly over his left eyebrow. The man who'd been sitting in the seat behind his own seat on the train into the city. The man who had been across the aisle and down toward the end of the subway car on his way from Penn Station downtown.

There was no doubt about it. The lieutenant was making good his promise. They weren't going to let him out of their sight.

Kitty, the little redhead who sat at the switchboard just off the reception room and who was rumored to have slept with just about every male member of the staff, looked up at Gerald as he passed by her desk. She gave him her usual smile.

"I've been trying to get you out at your place," she said. "For the last half hour or so. Mr. Engleman has been trying to call you. What's up anyway?" she asked, reaching out and taking hold of Gerald's coat. "He's really up in the air. Madder than you know what about something. Things have sure been popping around here this morning," she said.

Gerald smiled back at her and went on.

"Also," Kitty called after him, "you got other calls. A Miss Swift ..."

"I'll check on them later," Gerald called back over his shoulder, not hearing the last of her sentence. "Later. Right now I better get in and see the boss."

He stopped at his own desk only long enough to toss in his hat and nod to the girl whom he shared as secretary with four other actuaries. The girl started to say something to him, but again he said, "Later."

J. Rolland Engleman looked up as Gerald entered the square, spruce-paneled office. He turned to where his middle-aged secretary sat at one corner of the room in front of an electric typewriter.

"You may leave us alone, Miss Goode," he said. "And please close the door."

Miss Goode left them alone.

Mr. Engleman looked up at Gerald, the travesty of a smile on his thin lips. He didn't invite Gerald to sit down and there was nothing humorous about the expression in his pale, washed-out blue eyes which were set close together under all but imperceptible blond eyebrows.

"Late, Mr. Hanna?"

Gerald smiled weakly.

"I'm afraid so, Mr. Engleman," he said. "You see ..."

"I see perfectly," Mr. Engleman said. "I am afraid that I see only too well. But don't let my eyesight concern you. And, also, don't concern yourself too much about being late. You see, we didn't miss you. Not really. We had other visitors. A lot of other visitors."

He hesitated, tapping the ends of his lean fingers together and slowly nodding his head up and down.

"Yes, Mr. Hanna, visitors. Suppose we start with the first one. A policeman, Mr. Hanna."

He looked up expectantly and again smiled thinly. "Yes, Mr. Hanna—a policeman. And do you know—it was about you?"

"About me? What in the world would a policeman ..." Gerald's voice was as innocent as his bland expression.

"That is precisely what I was about to ask you," Engelman said. "Yes—precisely what I was about to ask. Just why, Mr. Hanna, should a policeman invade my office and ask me a hundred questions about one of my actuaries? What have you been up to, Mr. Hanna? As you know, this is a fatherly sort of firm and we take a keen interest in our employees. We pride ourselves in our selection of our personnel and we take a ..."

Gerald held up a hand.

"Oh," he said. He laughed a trifle hollowly. "That. I can explain that all right. It seems that last Friday night ..."

Gerald went on to explain. It took quite a little while, but he made a good story out of it, telling the facts with quiet amusement. The trouble was that Mr. Engleman failed to be amused.

"And you say that you were playing poker before you left for home, eh?" Mr. Engleman said when Gerald stopped for breath.

Gerald nodded.

"Gambling," Mr. Engleman made it sound like the violation of an eleventh commandment.

Gerald nodded sheepishly.

Mr. Engleman stood up.

"I believe you are engaged to be married?" he changed the subject.

Gerald looked up and smiled brightly. Thank God they were on safer ground.

"Yes, sir," he said. "For several years. Miss Swiftwater is a splendid girl and we ..."

"I have had the pleasure of meeting Miss Swiftwater," Engleman said. His expression denied the pleasure. "Yes, Mr. Hanna, I have had that pleasure. Only a few minutes ago. And I should like to inform you that Miss Swiftwater struck me as a very sensible girl. She particularly impressed me when she informed me that she has broken your engagement."

This time Gerald looked at him with legitimate surprise. "Maryjane was here? You mean ..."

"I mean that Miss Swiftwater came to me to find out exactly what has been happening. What you have been up to. She was able to tell me that you are running around with some floozy, that you are hanging out in cheap barrooms, and you seem to have completely lost your mind and that you called her on the telephone to insult her. Frankly, she seemed to feel that perhaps you are suffering from sort of mental ..."

Gerald suddenly held up his hand.

It was the damnedest thing. Exactly like that moment when he had decided to ask for a card to fill an inside straight; like that other moment when he had reached over and opened the door of the Chevrolet and pushed the dead body out into the road. He held up his hand and opened his mouth and he spoke quietly and clearly.

"I am suffering from utter and complete boredom, Mr. Engleman," he said, pronouncing each word as though he were giving a lesson in simple grammar. "I am also suffering from a keen distaste for you and for this stodgy, antiquated, cheap-John firm for which we both work. I am suffering from a frustrated desire to slap your silly tongue into the back of your head and then pick you up and throw you out of the window. And, in fact, if I have to listen to one more word out of that chinless jaw of yours, that is exactly what I shall do."

He took a step forward and Mr. Engleman fell back, leaning against the wall, his mouth wide and his eyes staring. He didn't attempt to speak, but for a second his eyes flitted around the room as though looking for a quick escape route.

Gerald reached over and opened the humidor on Mr. Engleman's desk and took out a long, light-brown cigar. He bit off the end, removing approximately an inch, not having had experience in the past in biting off the ends of cigars. He took the cigarette lighter from the desk and flicked it and touched the flame to the end of the stogy.

"Just so that you will have things straight, Mr. Engleman, when you discuss my firing with *your* boss," Gerald said, "I'll be glad to set your mind at rest. The police were here because I stole approximately a quarter of a million dollars in jewels. A man or two was murdered in the course of it all, of course. And the so-called floozy I am consorting with is everything you could possibly want in a woman—not you of course—but me. She's a cashier in a hash house and has long blonde hair and azure eyes and a build like—" Gerald stopped and stared hard at the other man.

"As for Miss Swiftwater," he said. "It is really fortunate that she has broken our engagement. It will probably save me from cutting her throat. But I recommend Miss Swiftwater to you, Mr. Engleman. You and Miss Swiftwater would go very well together. I can just visualize the offspring. And now ..." Gerald stopped and took a deep lungful of smoke and slowly exhaled it, spoiling the effect somewhat by coughing as he finally emptied his lungs.

"And now I shall go and empty my desk," he said. "I will be leaving at the end of the week, but I don't really think you would like me to spend the last few days around here. Or would you?"

Mr. Engleman's narrow mouth was still formed into a perfect circle as Gerald breezed out of the room, leaving the door wide open. Miss Goode, Mr. Engleman's secretary, was leaning over the water cooler just outside as Gerald passed. He hesitated a moment and then playfully patted her on the fanny.

"Go," he said. "Go at once. He needs you. The master ..."

He looked down into her indignant, startled eyes as she swung around and faced him and then smiled at her sweetly and shrugged his shoulders.

In another minute he was back in his own small cubbyhole of an office. His one-fifth secretary had finished whatever she had been doing at his desk and he slammed the door and fell into his hard, straight-backed chair. He reached for the telephone.

"Kitty," he said, "bring me the telephone book." He waited a moment and then spoke again. "All of them, my sweet," he said. "All of them. Brooklyn, Staten Island, Manhattan, Queens, Kings and anything else you might lay your lovely little hands on. At once."

He replaced the receiver, coughed and looked at the cigar in his hand then casually tossed it out of the opened window at his side.

"A poor thing at best," he said.

3

The Commissioner finished reading the editorial, his face purple and his voice edged with scorn. Carefully he folded the newspaper and laid it down at the side of his desk and then he looked up at the group of men standing in front of the desk.

"Well, you all heard it," he said. "I guess I don't have to tell you what the reaction is going to be. Like the rest of you, I'm a career man myself; I guess some of you can remember back to the time I was wearing a patrolman's uniform. I'm a career man, but I'm also a politician. Otherwise you can bet I wouldn't be sitting here as Commissioner."

He hesitated to let the words sink in, looking down at his wrist watch and noticing that it was just after ten o'clock. He still had fifteen minutes before he had to meet the county chairman and he'd have to make it short and snappy.

"I'm not blaming any of you," he said, "but this sort of publicity, coming before a November election, certainly isn't doing us any good. Two policemen murdered in cold blood, a quarter of a million in jewels taken from under our noses, and nothing being done about it. I don't expect miracles, but if they are necessary, then miracles we will have. I want those jewels found. I want someone, someone who is still alive, for the district attorney."

Lieutenant Hopper was pretty tired, having been up for more than forty hours without sleep, and his temper was anything but complacent.

"Who doesn't?" he asked. "Who doesn't? Nobody wants to crack this one more than I do—or any of the other boys downstairs."

The Commissioner half turned and stared at him. "I don't doubt it," he said. "That's just why we are having this little meeting; why I want to find out what's going on before I see the big boss this morning. And so far, it seems nothing is going on. Why, you've even managed to lose the one possible lead you had. I am referring, as you know, to the Dunne girl."

"There was nothing we could hold her on," Hopper said.

"You couldn't hold her perhaps," the Commissioner answered him, "but by God you could have at least kept track of her. I think we all agreed that there was a good chance she might lead us to something or another. And so what has happened? Well, she has disappeared. We haven't the faintest idea where she is or why."

"We know that she saw that Hanna fellow," Hopper said. "We know that there is some sort of connection there. It was a case of the man tailing one or the other. He chose Hanna. Perhaps he guessed wrong, but there is no telling about that."

The Commissioner shook his head.

"You boys are barking up the wrong tree," he said. "I've gone over the reports. Gone over them very carefully. This man Hanna just doesn't fit. Doesn't fit at all."

"If we brought him in and took him down to the basement for a workout, I'd make him fit, all right," Finn said. "What he needs is a touch of the ..."

The Commissioner raised his hand. "He's not the sort of person you can take down to the basement—you know that, Finn. Not that sort of person at all."

"We're keeping a man on him twenty-four hours a day," Lieutenant Hopper said. "We're watching every move he makes. If he is involved, it's a lot better letting him have his freedom and giving him enough rope to hang himself."

"I quite agree," the Commissioner said. "Well, that's the story. The newspapers are on our backs and we have to do something about it. And damned soon. Those funerals are today and I get sick every time I think of the way the papers will bleed with sensationalism. So let's get moving on this thing. I want to be able to issue a statement for the morning papers that we are definitely solving the thing—and I want to have something in back of that statement."

He stood up, a gesture of dismissal.

"Lieutenant," he said, addressing Hopper, "you look dead on your feet. I think you better get a little rest before you get back to it."

"After the funeral," Hopper said. "I have a cot down in my office and I'll take a few hours out and get some sleep. But I want to be close by just in case anything should break. And we'll turn up the Dunne girl all right, don't worry about that. I've arranged to have her brother's body released and she's bound to show up and claim it."

<h1 style="text-align:center">4</h1>

There were two Fred Slaughters listed in the Manhattan directory, none in Queens, or the other boroughs. One of the Manhattan Slaughters was listed as a CPA and Gerald passed his number up for the second one, whose address was up on Central Park West.

Dialing the number, Gerald thought; another one, another one-card draw to an inside straight. That would be what the odds were, one in a thousand or so. He smiled wryly. Things had certainly changed all right. This business of taking outside chances, playing the long odds, was becoming a habit.

As the sound of the bell at the other end hit to his ear, his mind went back to the scene in Engleman's office. Yes, he was certainly playing the long ones all right, only that hadn't been any gamble. That was a straight and simple matter of burning his bridges behind himself. At the moment he felt fine about it, exhilarated and all keyed up. He wondered if and when the reaction would set in. It isn't every day that a man callously and offhandedly ends a seven-year career as a mere gesture.

But then, of course, it wasn't every day that a man decides to completely change the course of his life, change the very essential pattern of his thinking and planning and living. The job, after all, was a minor thing in comparison to the other factors involved.

The ringing ended suddenly as someone lifted a receiver in the apartment on Central Park West.

"Hello?"

"Is Mr. Slaughter in?"

"Who's this?" It was a hard, uncompromising voice and Gerald detected a slightly Brooklynese accent.

"A business associate," Gerald said. "I'd like to speak with Mr. Slaughter. It is quite important!"

The voice at the other end didn't hesitate.

"You got no name, you ain't important," it said.

"It's important to Mr. Slaughter," Gerald said. "Very important. Mr. Slaughter lost something, lost something very valuable last Friday night. If he is interested, and he should be, you'd better get him to the phone."

There was a long pause and then finally, "Hang on." Two minutes later the second man came on the wire.

"Hello, are you there?"

"I'm here," Gerald said, feeling a sudden sense of excitement. There was an odd quality in that hard, gravelly voice, a quality which at once convinced him that he had the right person.

"What's this about my losing something? Who are ..."

"I'll be in the lobby of the Waldorf at exactly one o'clock, this afternoon," Gerald said, ignoring the other man's question. "The Waldorf at one. Be there. Have Mr. Courtland paged—William Courtland. Come alone. Do it just as I say if you are interested in that little bundle that got away from your friends."

"Say, what the hell ..."

Gerald hung up as the other man stuttered into the telephone.

The trick was going to be in getting out of the building. Gerald didn't know a great deal about police work or procedure, but he knew enough to realize that they would be watching him. They would be watching every move, never letting him out of their sight. As long as he was in the office he was safe. They wouldn't bother him here, not unless they picked him up, and so far they hadn't done that. But what he had to do, he couldn't do from his desk. He had to get out and had to ensure that he'd have freedom of movement. He couldn't have a detective on his tail.

There would be the detective who had followed him that morning. The man would either be in the lobby of the building, waiting for him to leave, or he would be out by the bank of elevators on this particular floor. But there was one thing the man wouldn't know about. He wouldn't know about the private staircase between the two floors occupied by the insurance firm.

The upper floor was used entirely by clerical workers and when he reached it, Gerald walked out into the general room, filled by dozens of girls working at filing systems and IBM business machines. He advanced at once to an unoccupied desk. Out of the corner of his eye he saw Mrs. Wilberton, the office supervisor, approaching. He turned to her.

"Mr. Engleman," he said, "down in the executive offices. His secretary's typewriter went on the bum. Wants to borrow a machine for an hour or so."

Mrs. Wilberton nodded, smiling.

"Why certainly," she said. "I dare say that one will fill the bill." She indicated the typewriter at the unoccupied desk. "Helen, she's one of our girls, is off today. If you will just wait a moment I'll have one of our boys take it down for you."

"Oh that's all right," Gerald said. "I guess I can handle it all right."

"It's mighty heavy," Mrs. Wilberton said. "I think Johnny …"

"I can handle it fine," Gerald said, leaning down and picking up the machine. "I'll just use the freight elevator. If you would be good enough to come over with me and push the button …"

He waited until the operator had closed the door and then spoke.

"All the way to the basement," he said. "This damned thing weighs a ton."

The operator nodded sympathetically. "What are you goin' do, junk it?"

Gerald shook his head.

"Broken," he said. "Taking it over to get it fixed up. I left my car in the alley in back of the building. They told me there's a door from the basement leading into the alley."

"That's right," the elevator man said. "You know," he added, "my kid is learning to use one of them things. I'm sending her to business school. She wanted to go to art school but her mother and me, we think it's a lot smarter she should learn something where she can make a living."

"You're absolutely right," Gerald said.

"Yep, she didn't want to, but she's learning business. I get a little ahead of the game, or if one of my numbers comes in, I'm going to get her one of them machines to practice on at home."

They reached the basement and he brought the elevator to a stop.

"I'll show you the door," he said.

Gerald, carrying the typewriter, followed him to the rear of the building. The man opened the door and Gerald stepped out, noticing at once that there was no one in sight. He sighed and laid the typewriter down at his feet.

"Thanks," he said, starting to walk away.

"Hey. Hey, what about the typewriter? You left the typewriter ..." The man was staring at his retiring back in bewilderment.

"Give it to your daughter," Gerald said over his shoulder. "Consider it a gift from the Seaboard Insurance Company for your loyal and devoted work over the years. She deserves it."

The man stared at him open-mouthed as he turned the corner of the building.

He was in luck. There was a cab at the curb.

5

They sat side by side on a deep couch at the back end of the lobby, speaking in low whispers. They didn't look at each other as they talked.

He'd been very careful in his selection of the spot, seeking out a secluded area, but one from which he could see most of the open space in the large public room. He wanted to be out of the main current of traffic, a place where no one would be able to overhear what they had to say. At the same time, he was careful to select a location that would keep the two of them within sight of other persons. He had no idea of what sort of man this Slaughter would turn out to be and he was taking no chances.

Now, sitting here talking with him, he wondered why he had worried. With the exception of that odd, gravelly voice, Fred Slaughter was merely another run of the mill, middle-aged businessman. He could have been a salesman or an executive, a contractor or a dress manufacturer. There was nothing either sinister or dangerous in his manner or in his attitude.

They'd been talking now for a good half hour.

"Yes," Slaughter said, "you could be telling me the truth. And then again, maybe not. Maybe, instead of being just an innocent passerby—an insurance man you said your racket was, didn't you—well maybe instead of that you are a cop. How do I know? You don't look like a cop, but today, nobody does. What with these college graduates and all."

"I have identification ..." Gerald began, reaching into his pocket for his wallet.

Slaughter put out a hand.

"Don't bother," he said. "Don't bother about showing me anything. Identification would be the very first thing a cop would have." He stopped speaking for a moment and then looked up.

"I'll tell you what," he said. "Lemme make a phone call. I want you to talk to somebody. Let's just get it straightened out for sure whether you are on the up and up. Not, you understand, that I care if you are a cop. You're the one who has been doing the talking. I've just been listening. I haven't said a damned thing. But just so we keep the books right, let's find out."

He stood up and Gerald also stood.

"There's a booth over at the side there. I'll get a number then open the door and you just talk to the party that answers. O.K.?"

"Anything you say," Gerald said. He followed Slaughter over to the booth and Slaughter told him to stand several feet away while he got his party. He concealed the phone with his body as he dialed behind the tightly closed door.

It took him several minutes to get Steinberg and then another minute or two to explain what he wanted. Finally he put a coin in the slot for the third time and then opened the door a crack and signaled Gerald.

"Talk to him," he said when Gerald approached. The two traded places.

The voice at the other end of the wire was very smooth. "Mr. Hanna?"

"That's right."

"Who is the chairman of the board of Seaboard Insurance, Mr. Hanna?"

"Philip Gottlieb," Gerald answered at once.

"And what is the name of the receptionist who would be on duty now?"

"Miss Kitty Donnelly."

The man told Gerald to hold on a second and he could hear him speaking rapidly to someone in the room near him. Gerald knew that he would be checking the names on another telephone.

"All right, Mr. Hanna," he said, "tell me this. If I were to leave seven hundred and fifty thousand dollars to my wife and three kids, and I wanted to set it up so I wouldn't be paying a full inheritance tax, just how would I go about it?"

"Well, you could do it several ways," Gerald said. "Naturally you would be allowed to make a series of gifts over a period of years. Then if you wanted to establish a group of trust funds, the income to go ..."

He went on for several minutes, explaining the thing. Finally the voice at the other end of the wire interrupted him.

"All right, all right," he said. "Just one more thing. What would it cost me a month to amortize a forty-thousand-dollar, twenty-year mortgage at 5 per cent if the mortgage were to carry a life insurance policy for an equal amount and the policy was on an A risk, aged fifty?"

"Roughly five hundred and fifty a month," Gerald said, "Give me a second and I'll give you the ..."

"Never mind, never mind. Put the other party back on the wire."

Gerald beckoned to Slaughter.

"If that guy's a cop," Steinberg said, "he must be one of them quiz kids. No, he's in insurance all right. But what's it all about Fred? What the hell is going on?"

"I'll call you back later," Slaughter said. "Sit tight. I think we got our little problem all cleaned up and solved. Just sit tight."

Once more they returned to the couch where they had first met.

Seated, Slaughter turned and looked closely at his companion.

"All right," he said, "let's say for the sake of an argument that you're on the up and up. That you're telling me the truth. Let's say that you do have the stuff. I can believe it. I'll admit it now—the girl told me you had it. We got that much out of her."

"The girl told you?"

"The Dunne girl. We picked her up; had an idea she might know something and that there was a chance she was in on some kind of deal. We knew that someone had picked up Vince and taken the stuff off of him. We didn't know who, of course, but it had to be someone and we figured maybe she knew something."

Gerald stared at him, saying nothing.

"The thing is," Slaughter said, "I can't quite see why we should buy it back from you."

"I'm not suggesting you buy it back," Gerald said. "I'm merely suggesting you give me the same split you would have had to give the others—your three boys—if they had been successful in getting the stuff to you. This way you get it, and it costs you no more than it would have anyway. As a matter of fact, you should be damned grateful I'm here to offer you the deal. If I hadn't shown up just when I did, the police would have found the jewels when they found young Dunne's body."

Slaughter looked at him curiously.

"How did you get mixed up in it anyway?" he asked. "Was it the girl? Were you working with her and Vince all along?"

"Don't be a fool," Gerald said. "It was the way I've told you it was. I never saw the girl in my life before last night. Never saw her brother until he stuck me up and got into my car. But all of that doesn't matter. I am trying to do business with you. Nobody else matters."

"In that case, it can't matter to you what happens to the girl," Slaughter said. "You see, after you talked with her last night, we picked her up. We sort of felt she might have been double-crossing us, you know. She was Dunne's sister. She could have been getting cute. But what the hell. As long as she's out of the picture, doesn't mean anything to you, we can forget about her."

There was something about the man's voice that sent a cold chill down Gerald's spine. What he said made good sense. It was quite true. The girl was none of his business. She didn't mean a thing to him.

Suddenly he visualized her pretty, heart-shaped face, her angry azure eyes and the determined line of her fine jaw.

"It happens I do care what happens to her," he said suddenly, hardly realizing he was speaking the words. "It happens that she means a great deal to me. So much, in fact, that unless you let her go, at once and unharmed, you can just forget all about the Gordon-Frost jewels."

"You think you are in any position to bargain?" Slaughter asked. "We know who you are now. Maybe the police would like to know."

"Oh certainly," Gerald said, with a slight sneer. "They'd hold me for what? Receiving stolen goods? I'd be out about the time they were turning up the juice for you in Sing Sing."

"All right, all right. We won't argue about it," Slaughter said. "Assuming you got the stuff, I'll make you one and only one proposition. No bargaining and no second guessing. Take it or leave it. Thirty-five thousand in cash for the jewelry."

"Thirty-five?"

"Right."

"And the girl?"

Slaughter shook his head. "The girl will talk," he said.

"Not if you haven't hurt her," Gerald said. "You said that you hadn't ..."

"She's all right," Slaughter said. "But she's bound to spill ..."

"Thirty-five thousand and you release the girl," Gerald interrupted. "I deliver the stuff and guarantee she don't talk. After all, I have plenty to lose too," Gerald said. "I have as much interest as you have in keeping her quiet. But you'll have to let her go. Otherwise—no deal. And—" Gerald hesitated and gave the other man a long look—"and I know now you've got the girl. Just in case something *should* happen to her."

"If you can keep her quiet, you got a deal," Slaughter said. "You're getting a damned good price. That stuff is so hot it sizzles. A fence wouldn't take it as a gift. The stuff will have to be held for months, maybe years."

Gerald nodded. "I know," he said. "All right, about the details."

"We can go up to my apartment ..."

Gerald smiled thinly.

"No," he said. "Hardly. Not that I don't trust you, of course. But I think it will be better if we meet on neutral grounds. Suppose we do it this way. Is the Dunne girl somewhere I can see her within the next half hour or so?"

"Maybe." Slaughter looked at him quizzically.

"All right. Take me to her. Let me talk to her alone, for five minutes. When I finish she'll agree to do as I ask. Then I'll leave, without her. I'll take a room in a midtown hotel. You give me a telephone number where you can be reached and I'll call you at exactly seven-thirty this evening and let you know where I am located. Give you the hotel and the room number. I'll have the stuff with me. You come up. Bring the girl with you and the thirty-five thousand. Just you and the girl. We'll make the switch then."

"And you mean you want to see the girl first, eh. Then leave?"

Slaughter's voice was heavy with doubt.

"What's to keep you from finding out where she is and then calling cops?"

"Good God man," Gerald said. "What's wrong with you? There's plenty to keep me from it. Among other things, the thirty-five thousand bucks. Why do you think I'm here in the first place. Because of the girl? Hell, I didn't even know you had her. No, don't get me wrong. My first interest is the money. It's just that I don't see any reason for the girl to get hurt. You have nothing to lose."

"You didn't want to come to my place at first," Slaughter said. "How come, now you know the girl is there, you've changed ..."

"I didn't want to come with the jewels," Gerald said. "I still don't want to. That's why I suggest the hotel deal. But alone—what the hell. You don't want me—I'm no good unless I have the stuff. Right?"

Slaughter nodded slowly.

"Right," he said at last. "O.K. Let's get going. I'll take you to where you can see her and talk to her. But let me give it to you straight. Get fancy and try anything cute, and you get killed. Very fast you get killed. And after you finish seeing the girl, you'll have a guy with you for the first half hour after you leave. Long enough to give me a chance to move her. So don't get any ideas ..."

"I've told you," Gerald said. "The only ideas I have concern thirty-five thousand dollars in hard cash."

Five minutes later they were in the taxi heading across town.

CHAPTER SEVEN

1

She lay sprawled out on top of the sheet, her eyes filled with hatred as he leaned over and spoke to her.

"I'm taking the gag out of your mouth," he said. "If you yell, or make any trouble, I'll knock your teeth down your throat. Just stay right where you are and be quiet. Someone is coming in to see you for a few minutes."

She fought back the sudden fear, trying to understand. He'd told her that if she didn't talk he'd bring someone in; someone who would do horrible things to her. Someone who would make his own cruelties seem like caresses by comparison.

"You're not going to be hurt," he said. "This man is just going to talk to you." He sensed her fears and spoke quickly. "But remember, no yelling."

She sensed relief then; he must be telling the truth. He wouldn't be taking the gag from her mouth if anyone were going to hurt her. She wondered what would happen next. Wondered what they would eventually do with her. She knew the kind of man he was. She could guess.

Slaughter removed the gag and reached down, lifting her slender body so that she leaned back against the headboard. He turned and left the room, closing the door behind himself. For several minutes she just sat there and then, as she heard the sound of the footsteps approaching, her eyes once more went to the door, wide with fright.

Gerald entered the room and closed the door firmly behind himself. He walked over to the bed and leaned down, sitting on the edge of it. He spoke quickly, before she had a chance to say a word and while the expression on her face was rapidly changing first from fear to utter amazement and then from amazement to bitter amusement.

"Please don't say a word," he said. "I've only got a couple of minutes before he'll be back and you have got to listen to me."

She stared at him, wide-eyed.

"I might have guessed," she began, "might have guessed that you ..."

"Don't guess anything," he said quickly. "You'd be wrong. Just listen. If you are interested in saving your life, just do nothing and listen to me."

"I don't care what they do to me," she said, half hysterically. "Sooner or later the police ..."

"Shut up and listen to me," he said, taking her by the arms and shaking her. "It isn't only your life—it can be mine too. But if you do just as I tell you, we'll both get out of this. We'll not only get out of it, but you'll get what you want."

"You don't know what I want," she said, fiercely, trying to pull away from him.

"I do know what you want," he said. "I know very well what you want. But you simply have to have faith in me. I can't explain, I can't tell you why. I can't tell you anything. I haven't time. But you must do exactly as I tell you."

Watching her as he quickly spoke, he was glad to see her expression gradually change from antagonism to curiosity.

"Some of what I told you last night is true," he said. "But there was a lot I didn't tell you. A lot I didn't know myself. I didn't know that they were going to pick you up. I didn't know ..."

"Are you trying to tell me you aren't in with ..."

"Do please shut up," Gerald said. "Shut up and listen. Don't ask questions. I haven't time to answer them. I've only got another minute. Listen."

He still held her by the arms and he could feel her suddenly relax.

"I've made a deal. They're getting the jewels and they're letting you go free. On the understanding that you keep your mouth shut. That you never breathe a word of what has happened."

"And you," she began.

"Later," he said quickly. "Later, when you are out of here and free, I'll tell you all about myself. Right now please just trust and believe me. Do exactly what I tell you to do and I'll promise that it will work out the way you want it to. You must absolutely convince them that if they let you go you will keep your mouth shut. Later, late today, Slaughter will bring you to a certain place. He'll take the jewels and you'll be released."

"But why ..."

"Look," he said, "dear God, just promise to do what I ask."

For a long moment she looked into his face, this time almost without expression. She half nodded her head.

"And you," she said. "Just what are you going to get out of it?"

For a moment he stared back into her eyes and then he quickly leaned forward on the bed and his lips barely brushed her forehead.

"Me?" he said. "Why I'm going to marry you and live happily ever after."

He stood up, watching her seriously as her mouth fell open in surprise.

"That's right," he said. "And I want you to know that I realize you wouldn't marry a thief or a crook."

Staring at him, she suddenly realized that he was dead serious.

"Why," she said, "why you don't even know me! You must be a little crazy. We don't ..."

His finger went to his lips and he moved toward the door silently.

"I don't even know myself," he said. "But I'm not crazy. Not a bit. I'm completely and beautifully sane—probably for the first time in my life."

He opened the door slightly and called out.

"O.K., Slaughter, we're all through."

2

He made the reservation over the telephone, using a public booth in the rear of a midtown tavern. He hit the right combination on his third try. The desk clerk at the Metropole had exactly what he wanted—two rooms, separated by a bath. He explained that he would be using the suite overnight, sharing it with a business acquaintance. Room 508 he reserved for himself, giving his correct name and address. Room 510 he reserved under the name of Fred Slaughter.

"Mr. Slaughter," Gerald said, "will arrive sometime early this evening. However, I'll stop by within an hour and will pay for both rooms at that time. I'd appreciate it if the maid can have them made up as I'd like an opportunity to arrange my samples."

He wanted to leave the impression with the clerk that he was a salesman.

He took a cab from the tavern to Grand Central. He was vaguely worried by the possibility of being picked up. There was a chance that the police could have found out about his leaving the office and he guessed that the moment he was reported missing, the pickup order would go out.

He hurried into the station and found the checkroom where he had left the briefcase and the zipper bag on Saturday. It only took a minute or so to retrieve them.

The next stop was at a luggage shop in the arcade. Here he purchased a fairly large leather suitcase. He had the clerk remove the price tag and he opened the bag and put both of his other burdens in it.

A door or two away was a haberdashery and he went in and bought several shirts, some socks and underwear. One more stop and he had added a shaving and toilet kit to his luggage. And then he took a cab to the Metropole.

It was a rather small, very respectable semi-residential hotel in the Murray Hill section. The clerk greeted him with a smile when he identified himself. After Gerald had signed the register, he started to reach for his wallet.

"You can take care of it when you are ready to sign out," the desk clerk said.

Gerald nodded and thanked him.

"I'll go on up now," he said, "but I'd like to leave Mr. Slaughter's key for him to pick up himself when he comes in. I'll probably be in and out of my room and I want to be sure ..."

"Certainly. We'll be looking for him."

The bellhop doubled as elevator boy and he stopped the cage at the fifth floor. Gerald followed him down the carpeted hallway to room 508, and stood by as the boy put the bag on the floor while he opened the door. He entered the room and after dropping the bag, opened the closet door and then went to the window and made an unnecessary adjustment to the air-conditioning unit.

As Gerald was reaching in his pocket for a dollar bill, the boy opened the bathroom door.

"I understand you've reserved both rooms," he said. "This door goes into the other part of the suite and you can lock either bathroom door from either side."

Gerald thanked him and handed him the dollar. He shook his head when the boy asked if he wanted ice water.

"Nothing just yet," he said. "Perhaps later. By the way, is there stationery and envelopes?"

"In the drawer over there," the boy said, indicating a writing desk on which the telephone sat. "You want I should come up and get your mail in a while, maybe?"

"It won't be necessary, but thanks," Gerald said.

He waited until he was alone before he carefully inspected the suite.

The rooms were exactly what he had wished for. The windows were closed on the air-conditioning units and they were covered by Venetian blinds and heavy drapes. Neither room was large, but they were adequate.

The bathroom was an old-fashioned and overlarge room. Doors led into each room and they could be locked from the inside to insure privacy. Going into 510, the room he had reserved for Slaughter, Gerald walked over to the radio and turned it on, fairly loud. Then he returned to his own room, carefully closing both bathroom doors.

He nodded his head in satisfaction. No sound from the radio penetrated.

"Perfect," he said, half aloud. It would take the sound of a gunshot to penetrate the double walls.

He opened the suitcase and took out the briefcase and the zipper bag and once more returned to Room 510. He opened the bottom bureau drawer and placed the bags in it. And then once more he returned to his own room. Sitting at the desk, he found the stationery.

For the next half hour he was busy composing the two letters. Finishing them, he addressed the envelopes and sealed them. Then he placed the letters in his inside breast pocket and left the room, turning the key in the lock.

Passing through the lobby, he ignored the postal drop. Once more he took a cab, this time directing the driver to the post office on Lexington Avenue, just north of Grand Central Station. He had the driver wait while he went inside and registered each letter before entrusting it to the mails.

When he returned to the Metropole, he stopped by the newsstand in the lobby and bought the afternoon newspapers and a couple of magazines. He had a little time to kill.

This time, when he returned upstairs, he told the combination elevator boy and bellhop to bring him up a drink from the bar.

"Make it a double Scotch and soda," he said. "In fact, make it two of them."

He might just as well do the thing right. Might just as well relax while he had the opportunity. Another few hours would tell the story. In another few hours, all decisions would have been taken out of his hands. He would either be a wealthy man with the world at his feet, or he would be in jail. There was, also, a fair chance that he might be dead.

Thinking about it as he waited for the whisky to arrive, he smiled a little wistfully. At least he would not be bored.

At six-thirty he checked his watch for the dozenth time and got up from the chair under the reading light and carefully folded the newspaper he had been reading. He slipped into his jacket and then went to the door and carefully checked to see that it was locked.

He looked around the room for a final time and then opened the door into the bathroom. He closed the door between the bathroom and Room 508, not locking it, before entering Room 510. This time he was careful to see that the door between the bath and Slaughter's room was locked, putting the key in his pocket after twisting it.

He had an almost irresistible desire to open the dresser drawer and take out the briefcase and have one last look at the jewels, but he resisted it. Time was pressing now and he had things to do.

Gerald rechecked his watch and then sighed and went to the door of Room 510. Everything was going to hinge on what took place within the next few minutes.

When he left the room this time, he pressed the catch so that the door between the room and the outside hallway remained unlocked.

Back in the lobby, Gerald was pleased to see that the day desk clerk had been replaced by the night man. He went over to the counter and took out the key to Room 508.

"I'm Mr. Hanna," he said. "Expecting a call shortly, but I have to be out for a while. I'd appreciate it if you'd tell the party I'll be back around seven-thirty." He left his key on the desk.

The man nodded.

"Certainly, sir."

The telephone booths were in the mezzanine and Gerald walked up the short flight of stairs. He was glad that they were out of sight of the hotel's desk.

Putting the coin into the slot, he was unable to resist the sudden chill which overcame him. Everything would depend on the success of this call. If his party should fail to answer....

He shuddered, not wanting to think about it.

The number answered on the second ring and he asked for his party. The voice at the other end requested his name.

"The name doesn't matter," Gerald said. "It's a personal matter. But very important."

"I'm sorry, but we have to know who is calling. We can't disturb ..."

"This is about Gerald Hanna and concerns the Gordon-Frost jewel robbery," Gerald said, speaking fast and distinct. I'll call back in exactly fifteen minutes."

He hung up fast. He couldn't take a chance on the call being traced. It was the longest fifteen minutes in his life.

He made the second call from a different booth and this time when he asked for his party, he added, "and if he isn't on the phone within less than half a minute I am hanging up."

He didn't have to wait a half minute. And he recognized the second voice the moment it spoke.

"If you are interested in the whereabouts of Gerald Hanna," he said, "he has checked into the Metropole Hotel in New York City. Got that—the Metropole. Room 508. The Metropole—Room 508."

He slammed the receiver back on the telephone as the voice spluttered at the other end of the wire.

Returning to the booth from which he had placed his original telephone call, Gerald once more closed the door after himself and placed a coin in the slot.

He could detect the nervousness in Slaughter's gravel voice the moment the other man picked up the receiver and spoke.

"You're late," Slaughter said. "Is everything ..."

"Everything is fine," Gerald said. "Now listen. I want you to be at the Metropole Hotel in exactly one hour. Not before and no later. You are registered in Room 510. Under your own name. Get your key at the desk and come directly upstairs. You must have Miss Dunne with you and no one else. You must be prepared to consummate our deal. You have the ..."

"I'll have what I need," Slaughter said. "But wouldn't it be just as well if the lady ..."

"It would not," Gerald said. "She must be with you. In exactly one hour."

Again he didn't wait for an answer, but quickly replaced the receiver on the hook and left the booth.

When he returned to the staircase, instead of going down to the lobby, he turned and started up. He climbed the five flights of stairs and the sweat was soaking his shirt by the time he reached the fifth floor.

This time, walking down the long carpeted hallway, he ignored Room 508 and passed on to 510. He entered through the unlocked door, but was careful to snap the catch so that it clicked behind him. He rechecked the bathroom door to be sure that it was still locked.

Opening the bottom bureau drawer, he removed the zippered bag—

the bag in which he had placed the fragments from his broken windshield and the gun which young Vince Dunne had dropped on the floor of his car. He took out only the gun and then reclosed the bag. He used his handkerchief to remove any possible fingerprints from the weapon. When he was finished, he placed the gun on the bed while he hauled the heavy upholstered chair around so that it half faced the door leading into the room.

Then he picked up the gun, still using the handkerchief, and tucked it down between the cushion and the seat of the chair. The handkerchief remained loosely twisted around the checkered grip.

He was kneeling at the door of the room, some thirty-five minutes later, his ear pressed to the keyhole, when he heard the elevator come to a stop at the end of the hallway.

It wasn't until the footsteps were almost opposite the door that he heard them, softened as they were by the thick carpet. They died out and a moment later he heard the small click of a key in the lock of what he knew must be the door of Room 508. He waited only until he heard the door close and then swiftly got to his feet and crossed to the bathroom door. Once more he knelt, putting his ear to the crack.

There were several moments of silence and then he heard someone enter the bathroom. He heard the sound of voices but was unable to distinguish the words.

A hand tried the knob of the door against which he was standing and it turned but failed to open.

And then all was quiet.

Gerald half smiled, a nervous smile. He looked at his wrist watch and nodded with satisfaction.

3

He tried to remain oblivious of the time, tried to blank his mind, knowing that it would be futile to worry. The die was cast and there was nothing more to be done. It would happen the way he planned it or it wouldn't happen and there was nothing more to do now but sit here in the big leather upholstered chair facing the doorway of the room and wait.

Once, after endless minutes had passed, he became conscious of the ticking of his wrist watch as his right elbow rested on the arm of the chair and his head rested against his hand. He began to count the ticks, counting up to sixty, and checking the minutes on the fingers of his hands—until he suddenly realized that the individual ticks of the watch didn't mark off the seconds but marked off the half seconds.

He was thinking about that, half smiling to himself, when he heard the alien sound; heard the key turning in the lock of the outside door. He knew then for the first time that someone was on the other side of it, someone who had approached on silent footsteps and was standing there at this very moment, preparing to enter.

He sat suddenly stiff and tense in his chair and watched as the knob slowly turned and then the door was quickly opened and Sue Dunne stepped into the room. Slaughter was directly behind her and he followed the girl inside, wordlessly turning and softly closing the door and snapping the night lock.

Gerald Hanna watched the man, but conscious of Sue tense and silent a couple of feet away. Slaughter stood there, his hands thrust deep into the side pockets of his lightweight jacket. He stared at Gerald coldly. Somehow or other he seemed to have lost his suaveness and he no longer appeared to be a small-time businessman or a bank teller or a salesman. He looked hard and dangerous.

"All right," he said, his gravelly voice very low. "All right, where is it? Where's the stuff?"

Gerald jerked his head, indicating Sue.

"Let's wait until Miss Dunne leaves," he said.

Slaughter smiled, without humor.

"She stays," he said. "Right here, until we get through."

Gerald looked at her and saw that she was staring past him, as though he didn't exist. Her face was totally without expression.

"Witnesses," he said. "It's foolish to have ..."

"She stays," Slaughter repeated. "You are the one who guarantees her silence, remember?"

Gerald shrugged, nodded. He looked up again at Sue and this time she was watching him, but he could tell nothing by her expression. Was she trusting him; did she believe in him? He couldn't tell. Couldn't guess.

It wasn't the way he wanted it, with her there in the room, but there was nothing he could do about it. He'd just have to play it that way, take this one additional gamble.

Gerald looked over at the zipper bag sitting on the night table.

"Where's the money?" he asked.

Slaughter ignored the remark and stepped quickly across the room.

He opened the bag and dumped its contents on the white bedspread.

For a moment then the man just stood there, his dark eyes wide and staring as he looked at the collection of broken glass. The blood began to surge up his thick neck and into his beefy face. He swung around with a curse on his mouth.

"What is this," he half yelled. "What kind of lousy joke ..."

"The money," Gerald said. "You were to bring the money. The thirty-five thousand dollars. I haven't seen it yet."

Slaughter stared at him.

"You're cute, aren't you," he said. "Real cute. The fact is, I suspected there was something screwy about this deal. Suspected something like this. Figured you for a phony. So I put the money in an envelope and checked it down at the desk. Now, if you aren't a phony, and you want to play it smart, just show me the stuff and then we can go downstairs together and we pick up the dough."

Gerald smiled thinly at the other man.

"I don't suppose," he said, "that you'd just happen to be carrying a gun in that coat pocket of yours, would you?" he asked, his eyes going to Slaughter's right hand which was still thrust into his jacket pocket.

Slaughter removed his hand, looking at Gerald in disgust.

"Don't be a damned fool," he said. "What do you think, I was going to come up here and stick you up or something? Of course I'm not carrying a gun. You think I'd be crazy enough to shoot anyone in a place like this? I'm no gun-happy desperado."

"I just wanted to make sure," Gerald said.

"All right, now you know. Let's get back to the jewels. Have you got the stuff or haven't you? If you have, then let's see it!"

Gerald nodded his head in the direction of the bureau.

"The bottom drawer," he said. "In the briefcase." He turned to the girl as Slaughter crossed the room in a couple of quick steps.

"Go over and sit in that chair by the window," he said. It wasn't a request; it was an order.

For a long moment her hot, tired eyes looked into his and he was unable to read anything in their depths. She stood as though frozen and he wondered if she had even heard his words. But then slowly she turned and without a word crossed the room and found the chair by the drawn Venetian blinds.

Slaughter had jerked open the drawer and had the briefcase in his hands. He lifted it, almost as though he were mentally weighing it, and then he fumbled with the catch and opened it.

He was staring, fascinated, into the contents of the briefcase as Gerald took the gun from the place where it was half concealed beneath his body at the side of the seat cushion.

As he started to rise from the chair, his finger pressed the trigger.

The bullet crashed into the panel of the bathroom door and even as the sound of the shot reverberated in the confines of the small, closed room, Slaughter dropped the briefcase and swung around.

Sue, in the chair by the window, gasped, but sat still and stiff, as though frozen to the seat.

"You Goddamned insane fool!" Slaughter screamed. "What in the name of God ..."

He was across the room in a single wild leap and slashing down at Gerald's arm with his closed fist. He caught the revolver as it started to fall to the floor, but Gerald held on to the handkerchief which had been wrapped around its stock.

The moment Slaughter's fist struck his arm and he reached for the falling gun, Gerald side-stepped, moving like lightning to Slaughter's right. His hands reached out as he moved and he swung the other man around so that he was momentarily facing the bathroom door.

Gerald was in time to see the door itself bursting inward on its hinges as he made a flying tackle across the room, dropping Sue Dunne to the floor as her straight-backed chair went over backwards, and half falling on top of her. "You double-crossing son ..."

Slaughter was screaming the words as the door gave way. The gun in his hand was half lifted and instinctively he pressed the trigger.

The sound of the explosion blended with that of Lieutenant Hopper's service revolver as the detective fired.

Slaughter never had the opportunity for a second shot. The dark red blood was gushing from twin holes just above his eyes as he crumpled and dropped to the carpeted floor.

Gerald himself had time for only the few brief words as he pressed his mouth close to the girl's ear.

"Remember," he said, "remember what you told me. You'd give anything to get the man who got your brother into it. Keep trusting me. Say nothing—and trust me."

4

Lieutenant Hopper waited until the basket arrived from the morgue and they'd removed the body; until after the chalked outlines on the floor had been photographed and the lab men were all through.

The room was cleared now and there were only the four of them. Gerald Hanna sat as Lieutenant Hopper stalked in front of him. Sue was on the edge of the bed, with Finn next to her chewing his nails and muttering under his breath. The uniformed patrolman was outside the door and all the others had left.

"You certainly have the God damnedest way of turning up," the lieutenant said. "Maybe you are going to try and explain this one away." His voice was thin with sarcasm.

"Nothing to explain," Gerald said. "I'm just glad you took my telephone call seriously and showed up. I was getting a little nervous."

"You will probably be a lot more nervous before it's all over," Hopper said. "Maybe you'd like to tell me about it. It might relieve you and it certainly ..."

"There's nothing to tell."

Gerald looked over at the detective and smiled as he continued.

"You have it all in the registered letter which I mailed you this afternoon," he said. "The letter which you will have in the morning. I said in that letter that if you came here after I called you on the phone, you'd find the loot from the Gordon-Frost robbery. Well, there it is—in that briefcase which your men checked and put over on the dresser."

"So you wrote and explained," Hopper said softly. "How nice of you. And just how do you fit into this thing?"

"That's very simple, Lieutenant," Gerald said. "As you know, I'm in the insurance business. Well, I figured after I read about the robbery, that the stuff must be insured. And I knew that the insurance company would offer a reward for the return of the jewels. Yesterday, through a connection in my office, I found I was right. There's a hundred-thousand-dollar reward. I'm claiming that reward. I sent you a note advising you to come here and pick up the stuff and you did and here it is. I have a receipt for that note.

"To make doubly sure there would be no misunderstanding later on, I mailed a second registered letter to the insurance people, establishing my claim."

Lieutenant Hopper stared at him, his face growing red and congested as Gerald finished speaking.

"That's dandy," he said. "Just downright dandy! So you're going to claim the reward, eh?"

He hesitated, fighting to control his temper.

"And how about the rest of it? How about the two police officers who were killed? By God, don't you remember our little conversation? Don't you remember what I told you about how we feel about things like that? Don't you ..."

"I think I can help you out a little there, too, Lieutenant," Gerald said. Once more he smiled, conciliatorily.

"Yes," he went on. "I believe I can help you. You took a gun out of Slaughter's hand when you broke into this room and after he was shot down. Remember? Well, check that gun down at ballistics, and I'm pretty sure you'll find that it was the same gun which was used to kill your policemen. Slaughter had the jewels and he had the gun. What more do you need?"

The lieutenant looked at him closely for several moments. At last, when he again spoke, his voice was more nearly back to normal and had lost a little of its bitterness.

"All right, just for the sake of argument, we'll assume it was the murder weapon. But how do you plan to prove that Slaughter was in on the job? That he used the gun?"

"That's simple, too," Gerald said. He pointed over to the desk. "Among your other souvenirs," he said, "you have that pile of broken glass which was swept up off the bed. I saw in the newspapers that police found fragments of glass from a shattered windshield at the scene of the robbery. Glass shot from the windshield of the getaway car. I think—in fact I feel absolutely sure—that if you take that glass along with you and match it up with the glass you already have, you'll end up with a complete windshield. So can't we just assume that Slaughter *had* to be in the getaway car in order for him to have the glass in his possession?"

Gerald stood up and yawned, putting his hand delicately to his mouth to cover his social lapse.

"And now," he said, "I'm rather tired and I would appreciate it if you would just let me leave. I'm sure Miss Dunne is tired too and I'd like to take her home."

Gerald's eyes went over to Sue and he smiled, a little weakly, at her.

He noticed then, for the very first time since he had seen her, that the antagonism and the bitterness was gone from her face. That she was looking at him, still wide-eyed and with a trace of amazement in her expression. But there was something else; there was a warmth that had never been there before.

She nodded ever so briefly and half smiled, as her eyes met his.

Lieutenant Hopper was eying Gerald with grim distaste.

"At the very best," he said, "you're a material witness. And so is Miss Dunne. I'm going to hold ..."

"Lieutenant," Gerald said. "You don't want to do anything foolish. The fact is, I'm a sort of hero. I feel quite sure that's what the morning newspapers are going to say. Of course, up until now I have had every intention of explaining to the reporters that I have worked with the police on this and that I am sharing the reward with them—in the hope that their share will be turned over to the widows of the officers slain in the robbery ..."

Detective Lieutenant Hopper shook his head slowly, staring at Gerald as though he were observing some completely new specimen in the Bronx Zoo.

"All right," he said, at last. "All right, Hanna. You'll get the reward, I guess. Maybe you are a hero. But I still don't understand it. I know that I won't be able to make you talk and tell me about it, but in the long run, I am glad to have the thing cleaned up. We'll go over the glass and the gun of course, but I'm satisfied that they'll check out.

"The thing I can't understand, though, is why Slaughter would have the glass with him. Why he'd bring it here to the hotel. It just doesn't make sense."

Gerald looked at the detective and smiled.

"You are so right," he said. "It doesn't make any sense at all. But then so many things haven't made sense. Why don't you just be satisfied that he *did* have the glass with him? After all, that broken glass is the evidence, that if found, would possibly have put him in the electric chair. The same as the jewels would. Well, he had the jewels, so why not the glass? Certainly he wouldn't be leaving it around for someone else to find and possibly use for blackmail, would he? The safest place for it, from his point of view, was with him. After all, he wasn't expecting to be picked up, to be questioned in the case. He was in the clear. But I wouldn't let it bother me. I'd just be satisfied that he did have it."

Hopper nodded, morosely.

"There's one more thing that, for my personal satisfaction, I would like to know," he said. "Since you seem to have all of the answers, perhaps you can satisfy me on this one. If that glass came from the windshield of the getaway car, maybe you can tell me where I can find the car?"

Gerald moved toward the door.

"Miss Dunne is exhausted," Gerald said. "Would it be too much to ask you to give us a lift out to Long Island?"

Hopper nodded, his expression unhappy.

"Glad to," he said. "But about the car? I suppose that's one you wouldn't know ..."

"Listen, Lieutenant," Gerald said, "don't you want me to leave *something* for the police department to do? I've found your hot jewels for you and I've given you your cop killer. You won't even have to prosecute him. And as far as I am concerned, you can share equal billing in credit for solving the case. What more ..."

Lieutenant Hopper grunted and shrugged.

"Oh, I'm happy enough," he said. "Let's get moving. Miss Dunne's tired, Finn's tired, I'm tired ..."

Sue had crossed the room and Gerald felt her slender hand slip into his and as she leaned toward him his arm went around her waist.

"Tired?" he said. "Why I never felt better in my life."

THE END

A PARTY TO MURDER
Lionel White

This book is for
Jean and Danny Hodgeman

PART ONE

1

DETECTIVE LIEUTENANT WILLIAM GOODWIN

Monday morning, December twenty-seventh. I haven't had my clothes off in more than sixty hours, I have had no more than seven- or eight-hours' sleep since I came on duty at midnight on Friday, and what sleep I did get I managed sitting in a chair. I need a shave, I have a foul taste in my mouth. I feel like hell.

Christmas! I celebrated by having a quick sandwich and coffee in the Automat. The kind of good cheer I spread around was breaking the news to my best friend's wife that her husband had been killed by a hit-and-run driver.

I don't like the case I am on. It is a mean and sordid crime and from what I have seen so far, it involves a group of mean and sordid people. The victim—well, no one deserves to be murdered and there is a law against it, but from what I have learned so far, she seems to have given a number of persons sufficient reasons to overlook that law.

For an hour now I have been going over the autopsy report and it makes less and less sense. I can't understand why the people down at Bellevue are unable to draw up these reports so that an average layman, or at least an average cop, can understand what they are trying to say.

In any case, I have attempted to make certain notes and abstract certain basic facts, and I am putting these facts down on paper so that I will have a clear picture.

The subject: Patricia Andrews, age 28, white, married, height five feet two inches, weight 116 pounds, hair natural blonde, eyes blue, skin fair. Body reported discovered nude, spread-eagled on a bed in Suite #73 in the Uptowner Motel at 8:15 a.m., on December 25, 1966.

Autopsy performed in morgue at Bellevue Hospital. Death believed to have taken place between 3 and 6 A.M., December 25. Cause of death: .38 cal. bullet lodged in heart after entering left breast and being deflected by a rib. Death believed instantaneous.

No signs of powder burns on the lips of the wound—it can be assumed that the shot was fired from a distance of several feet. Both upper and lower lips of victim's mouth show bruises and there are contusions on skull just over right ear. Deep scratches on both breasts, insides of upper thighs, and buttocks. Spots of blood discovered on left breast; blood does not match type of dead woman. Fragments of skin and small droplets of blood found under fingernails of right hand; this blood matches foreign blood found on breast.

Contusions on skull could have rendered woman unconscious prior to death, though not necessarily.

Examination shows that victim had sexual intercourse sometime prior to her death—there is semen in vagina.

Rigor mortis had begun shortly before discovery of corpse.

Traces of alcohol and partly digested food found in stomach and a high concentration of alcohol in blood. Heart, lungs, liver, kidneys and major organs indicate victim in perfect health at time of death. No signs of any major operations or diseases in the past, and victim has never borne children.

Official cause of death will be temporarily listed as murder by person or persons unknown. No weapon was reported found in room where body was discovered and there were no powder marks on either hand.

That is about all I get from the autopsy, although the report itself covers more than a dozen closely typed sheets of paper.

I usually don't have to take notes, but as I say, this has been a bad weekend. I didn't have to break the news to Mildred Swendson about Karl, but I wanted to. I didn't want her getting it from a stranger, from someone who didn't really care. My mind keeps going back to Karl and to what happened on that Midtown street. It must have happened at almost the same time that this Andrews woman was getting herself murdered. God, I certainly hope they get the guy who drove that car. It's a damned shame the only witness was a passing drunk who was in such bad shape when he was questioned he didn't make any sense. He's contradicted himself a half-dozen times already, and it is hard to figure just what he did see and didn't see. One thing is sure; he didn't get the number of the car, couldn't even give a halfway decent description of it.

But I can't be thinking about Karl. I have these people waiting to be questioned. I'd better concentrate on the case I am working on ... on these notes I have just finished jotting down.

I don't have to read about where she was found or the position or condition of her body when she was found. Hell, I was the first one on the scene after the patrolman was called to the room by that hysterical maid who had gone in to make up the beds and had discovered the dead girl.

I think of her as a girl, but being twenty-eight, she was certainly officially a woman. Nevertheless, she looked like a young girl lying there naked on that stained white sheet.

Before seeing the dead woman, I stopped at the motel desk—the Uptowner is really a ten-story New York hotel, but because of the basement parking lot they call it a motel—and learned that Mrs. Andrews had checked in alone under her own name. She said her husband would be joining her later. As far as anyone knows he never showed up.

But someone did.

The room was on the seventh floor overlooking Ninth Avenue. The heavy truck traffic is probably the reason no one heard the shot.

She checked in shortly after midnight. I haven't talked with the husband yet. I understand that he is suffering from shock, that he's still incoherent. He's here at the precinct house now.

There certainly was no gun found in that room, or anywhere else in the motel, although we did turn up some pretty sordid and interesting items in the rooms of some other guests who seemed respectable on the surface. I still can't figure why that bullet didn't go right on through her, in spite of hitting a rib. A .38 carries a hell of a lot of velocity. But it didn't.

I spotted those bruised lips and the marks on the body at once and figured right off that it was rape. Of course, the dead woman could have been one of those dames who, for kicks, like to take a beating along with their sex, and that could account for the scratches and the rest of it. And her clothes hadn't been torn off her, either. Her dress was hung over the back of a chair.

A man probably has to be a little corrupt to look at a dead woman and have lewd thoughts, but I must admit, in contemplating the voluptuous body of the dead woman, I found it difficult to confine myself to purely technical curiosity. At the time, I remember thinking that if it were rape, she couldn't have put up too much of a fight. But I must change my mind now in view of this autopsy report. There is the contusion on the skull, which could have rendered her unconscious. Also the business of the stomach contents; the alcohol count in the bloodstream as well as that still found in the stomach and kidneys.

She could have passed out after falling on the bed.

It is far too early to jump to conclusions, but it would be fairly easy to assume that the foreign blood found on her breast and under her fingernails came from the man with whom she had had intercourse. She could have gotten the blood on herself either in fighting him off or in collaborating with him in some sort of perverted sexual orgy. It might be assumed that, having finished with her, the man shot her and then left, taking the murder weapon with him.

On the other hand, he could have left her, and someone else could have entered the room and shot her. The door of the suite was unlocked when the maid opened it and discovered the body.

She could have had a prearranged rendezvous with someone in the motel room. On the other hand, she could have checked in and been expecting her husband, who failed to show up, and been attacked by a complete stranger or one of the motel help. Or the husband could have shown up and killed her and then left.

It's damned sure she didn't shoot herself.

At the moment all is guesswork. The fact that she had checked in at all is not too surprising from what we already know. The Andrewses, who have been married for six years and are childless, live up in northern Westchester and from time to time do stay over in town. On the night she was killed, Mrs. Andrews is known to have attended an office party given by the publishing company where her husband is employed. It is believed that she left the party shortly after midnight and drove directly to the motel. Her car was parked in the motel garage.

This autopsy is far from complete, at least from an investigating officer's point of view. I can assume she was not wearing a diaphragm or it would have said so. Assuming she was having an adulterous affair just before death, could she have been merely careless? The autopsy indicates the man himself used no protective device. Is she one of those women who use anti-pregnancy pills? (At least I can check that out.) Or does the lack of a pregnancy-control device indicate that it really was rape?

There is one big advantage in working with a large law enforcement body. We have the personnel to dig up many facts in a short time. I already know a great deal about the dead woman and some of her friends.

Patricia Andrews was not happily married; her husband is supposed to be extremely jealous and to have had excellent reason for being so.

It is rumored that she had an affair at one time with his boss, a man named Markey. She had a reputation for being promiscuous and is supposed to have been having a long-range love affair with a man named Siddel, an architect and apparently somewhat of a playboy. From what we learn he was tired of the affair and wanted to break it off.

One of the editors at the publishing house is supposed to be hopelessly in love with her and is separated from his wife because of her. The editor is said to have bankrupted himself buying her expensive presents.

A girl who works in her husband's office, and who was at the office party, tells one of our men that Mrs. Andrews was a real slut after she had a few drinks and would lay for anyone, the more crude and unprepossessing the man, the better.

On the other hand, her next-door neighbor in Westchester, who is supposed to be her best friend, says she was a thorough lady and that it is unbelievable that she would let a strange man pick her up. And were she to have an affair on the side she would handle it with utter discretion.

So who knows? But one thing we do know—that office party must have been a real lulu. They usually are around Christmastime, but this was apparently exceptionally wild.

It was probably because of the noise they were making that no one heard the explosion when the safe in that wholesale jewelry firm on the floor below was blown.

And that reminds me that I simply have to find time to telephone Mildred Swendson and see how she is. I'll do it as soon as I have a chance to talk to Andrews, this dead woman's husband.

2

CLAYTON ANDREWS

This homicide detective—Lieutenant Goodwin, I believe he said—is no fool. He strikes me as being an extremely astute and thoughtful man in spite of a certain vagueness and absent-minded expression on his face when he is talking to you. I don't think I pulled the wool over his eyes in the slightest.

God knows, I haven't had to fake a sense of shock or the deep and overwhelming grief that is forcing me to use every ounce of self-control I possess to keep from burying my head in my arms and letting loose the flood of tears I know must come sooner or later to drown my stunned misery.

He recognized the legitimacy of my sorrow, all right, but I feel sure he also knew that I understood his questions and that I was being evasive.

I am sure I have not seen the last of him.

But how in the name of God could I have answered him when he began asking about Pat? Pat is dead. Pat is lying on some cold slab in the morgue, and those grotesque doctors with their scalpels and cruel instruments are slicing and violating her poor body, searching and probing and seeking and tearing the shell of her away, looking for the secrets. Trying to discover what killed her and why she died.

Don't they understand that they will need a lot more than their sorry instruments to find the truth? Don't they understand that no matter how they desecrate the loveliness that was Pat, they will never be able to learn the true reason that she is dead?

The fragile shell of flesh that lies on that slab is only the shadow and the symbol of the substance—and the substance began to die a long time ago.

This policeman, this Lieutenant Goodwin, strikes me as a bright man, and I think he was trying to be kind and humane within the framework of his job. But I could sense the suspicion behind the façade of kindness, the probing intensity of his subtle questions, and I suspect he will be a difficult man to deceive. With his high, wide forehead and those odd, green-gray eyes, the thin arched nose and the sensitive, too full mouth, he does not have the classic face of a policeman. He looks more like a Jesuit. It is an interesting face and I would like to paint it sometime.

He seemed surprised when I told him I am twenty-two years older than Pat, and in spite of his mannered facial control, I could tell he was almost embarrassed when he began asking about our sexual relationship. I am sure he respected my grief and only asked those intimate questions because it was his duty to do so.

But what could I tell him? What could he really have expected? Did he believe for a moment that I would explain to him what our life together was really like?

Yes, the lieutenant is a bright man, but neither is he bright enough to understand, nor am I bright enough to explain that love and hate are Siamese twins and cannot be separated without both dying.

Could I explain to him that I loved her for what she was and that I hated her for what she did? Could I explain to him why she did the things she did, when I myself barely understood the reasons? Could I explain to him that now, knowing she is dead, I am buried under an unbearable sorrow, but that I also feel a sense of relief and freedom which must resemble that experienced by a condemned murderer who has suddenly been granted a full pardon some minutes before the moment of his planned execution?

I did answer his questions, and for the most part I gave him honest and forthright answers, sticking to the letter of the truth.

I told him about our marriage: I explained how and where I had first met Patricia—six years ago, when she had come to me as a model. How we had fallen in love with each other and were married and began living together as man and wife.

I could sense the thoughts passing through his mind as I talked. I could see him wondering about us, wondering what our relationship was really like. I could see him trying to decide in his own mind if she had been in love with me and if so, exactly why. I could almost feel his subconscious appraisal.

I could sense his thoughts; did this girl really love this fifty-year-old man with his slight, rather short body, gray, thinning hair, the sallow cheeks, pale mouth, lined face? As I talked of our first years together I could sense his wondering if she had at first been in love with me because she admired and liked me, because I was something new and novel. And then, perhaps, later on, she had grown bored and tired and, because of familiarity, finally indifferent and contemptuous.

He was very careful in the way he phrased his questions to ask nothing that would have been either offensive or insulting. He didn't actually come out and ask if she had grown disenchanted with the marriage; he never actually brought up the names of other men. But he skirted the question and I could see what he was getting at.

He had heard the stories, the dirt and the filth and the rumors, and he was probing and seeking. But he was very cautious and, in his own way, considerate. He offered me the option of complaining or seeking his sympathy, but in the beginning he avoided coming right out and asking if I knew of Pat's affairs with other men.

I knew, however, that sooner or later he would ask. I could tell when time after time he went back to Harold Markey, my employer. To Joel Siddel, the architect who designed our house and has been my friend for years. Even to Johnny Creamer, one of the younger editors at the office, who has been our guest frequently in the country.

This policeman explained, of course, that it was a murder investigation and he would have to ask a lot of things that might seem irrelevant and unimportant, might have to touch on subjects which could be embarrassing or seemingly none of his business.

But I was really surprised how far afield he frequently went.

He went into infinite detail about the office Christmas party, in spite of the fact that I explained I had stayed for less than an hour after bringing Pat to join the others. I thought he would want all sorts of explanations about why I had left early and alone and how I had spent the remainder of the evening, but he skipped over this in the most desultory manner.

On the other hand, when I casually mentioned getting the diamond bracelet for Pat as a Christmas present, he asked all sorts of pointless questions.

He seemed particularly interested when I told him I had bought it from the wholesale jewelry house on the floor below in our office building. Wanted to know exactly what I had paid for it, what sort of discount I had obtained. Wanted to know how I happened to choose that particular place to make the purchase, and of course I explained I knew the house because I had designed a few little things for them at one time or another on a free-lance basis.

I expressed genuine surprise when he told me the place had been broken into and robbed sometime during the evening of the office party. Apparently the thieves obtained something in the neighborhood of a half-million dollars in uncut diamonds and rare gems.

The sum staggered me, as I'd had no idea Coster and Son carried that sort of inventory. He was a little surprised I hadn't known about the robbery, especially as it has been all over the front pages for the last couple of days.

Well, it isn't unusual, my ignorance of what took place. After all, I learned of Pat's murder Saturday morning, and from that time on I hardly could be expected to be sitting around reading the newspapers.

I guess the only time I really came close to cracking was when he handed me a copy of the autopsy report to read. He at least had the human decency to turn away and not watch my face as I read it.

Christ! It wasn't that there was anything in it that really came as a surprise; anything that deep in my heart I didn't really know. After six years you get used to the blows. They never cease hurting, but somehow or other some atavistic instinct for self-protection begins to take effect and you are better able to absorb them. But seeing it there in cold print....

There is a limit to any man's self-control, a threshold of pain that, once passed, makes it impossible to hold yourself in any longer. I had to leave the room, half gagging as I staggered out. I spent a quarter of an hour in the toilet, throwing up.

He sent out for coffee in two containers, and I sat drained and exhausted and sipped a few mouthfuls before he again began speaking.

"You have no idea who...." he began.

I quickly shook my head. For one flashing moment I was on the verge of telling him that it had been I in that motel room with Patricia. Even dead, I still had an irresistible desire to protect her.

But I knew it would be useless. I knew that my alibi was too tight, that I should never be able to change my story and get away with it. No, Patricia is dead, and I will have to live with the evidence that she has left behind.

"The evidence indicates that your wife was raped some time shortly before she was murdered," he said.

I think he was making a belated effort to be kind. I know he realized as well as I did that the evidence pointed just as strongly to the conclusion that she had voluntarily joined in adulterous intercourse as a willing partner.

"We have to explore all possible avenues," he went on, and this time he didn't look at me as he talked. "Do you believe there is any possibility your wife could have arranged a"—he hesitated for a second out of what I assumed was embarrassment—"arranged a rendezvous with a friend at the motel?"

It was as though a blood vessel burst in my brain. I wanted to get up and hit him. I wanted to scream, "Yes—yes, you son of a bitch, I believe there was every possibility, every probability, that she arranged what you so delicately call a rendezvous with a friend. I believe she left that office party and checked into the Uptowner because she was planning to get laid. That she wanted to take off her clothes and spread herself on that bed and open up her legs and ..."

I reached for the container of coffee, and my hand was shaking so badly I spilled half of it on its way to my lips.

"If you would like to lie down and rest for a few moments," he began.

"It won't be necessary," I said. I looked him directly in the face. "I do not believe my wife arranged a rendezvous with a friend or with anyone else. I knew that she was planning to check into the motel as we had arranged, rather than drive home alone, in case I was to be tied up. As the desk clerk reported, she told him she was expecting me sooner or later. I was just leaving my studio down in the Village, on Saturday morning, when your people found me and gave me the news of what had happened. I was on my way up to the motel at the moment the police arrived. No, my wife had no rendezvous with anyone and could have been expecting no one, except me."

The lieutenant stood up. He started to turn away and then spoke.

"I'm sorry if this has been painful for you," he said. "But you understand that we do have to ask these questions. Just one more thing, Mr. Andrews. You are aware that Mrs. Andrews had deceived you in the past, aren't you?"

I looked at him dumbly for several seconds, and then my eyes dropped.

I said, "Yes," in a whisper.

I knew there would be no point in lying. I knew that he would have heard the stories. Christ, he had probably already heard it directly from the lips of that vicious, rotten bastard, Harold Markey, who is my boss and whom I hate. Markey is the sort who not only takes pleasure in cuckolding a man, but delights in letting the world know about it.

3

HAROLD MARKEY

Well, it was some goddamned party if I say so myself.

Cost me a cool fifteen hundred for the booze and the grub and the extras, but no one can say the Markey Publishing Company isn't willing to go all out to show the hired hands a good time at Christmas. Still and all, I would probably regret the expense if it weren't for the fact that I finally managed to get into that little bitch, Susie, whom we took on as a file clerk last week.

B-r-o-t-h-e-r!

It's really funny that Bertha believed it was Pat Andrews with me when she walked into the office and found us on the couch. She should know me better. Once I've had a woman and wash her out, I'm through for all time. But that Susie was really something.

I knew damned well when Pringle brought her in for me to interview a week or so ago that I was going to have her sooner or later. Said she was twenty, but I'd bet my bottom dollar she isn't a day over seventeen. The second she came through the door, wriggling that little round ass and tossing out her tits, I could tell she could be had. Must admit it took about half a bottle of gin to do the trick and she fought back in the beginning, but when she finally gave in, she didn't hold anything back.

Said she was a virgin, but no one can tell me that kid hasn't been had, and plenty.

She doesn't know it, but when she came in to work this morning and called me Hal, she might as well have handed in her resignation then and there. She's like all these little bitches—you pitch them a lay and they think they have you by the balls. But Hal Markey doesn't run a successful business that way.

I'll let Pringle fire her. He hired her.

Bertha, well, I told her that an office party was no place for the boss's wife. So she just had to come. It's going to be a little hard to square it with her, but she'll get over it. She always has before.

I suppose it will cost me that damned mink stole she's been screaming for. Well, it was worth it.

I really hate to let this Susie kid go, but it would be stupid to keep her now. Maybe I can make some sort of deal, get her an apartment over on the West Side or something.

I must remember to ask Pringle if she's living with her family or what. As long as she isn't working for me, she'll be no problem to handle.

Yeah, it was some party, all right. Went right according to schedule. Someone always gets drunk, insults the boss, and gets fired. Clayton lived up to form. Except he wasn't drunk. Of course, now that this thing has happened to Pat, I'll probably have to change my plans a little.

If I let Clayton go now it would be bound to start talk. But I'm going to get rid of that little bastard just as soon as I can.

I don't know what ever gave him the idea he could talk to me like that and get away with it. After all I've done for him! Jesus, you'd think he'd know the only reason I ever hired him in the first place was because of that damned wife of his. That the only reason I kept him on as long as I have is because she'd lay for me when I wanted her.

What the hell did he think it was? His talent? I can find better art directors in high school. And I don't have to pay them any fifteen thousand a year either. Markey is generous, but he isn't a fool.

I must say he has more guts than I'd given him credit for. Telling me right to my face that I'm a pig. He knows damned well I could break him in two with one hand. And that crack of his about a bonus! I should be giving bonuses when I toss away a fast fifteen hundred clams for a Christmas party! The guy has no appreciation. I let him keep his damned studio downtown, let him take in work on the side, and that's the sort of appreciation I get.

Stands there with one of *my* sandwiches in his hand, *my* drink in his glass, and calls *me* a *pig!*

Boy, they gobbled up that food and swilled down the booze like it was going out of style. Last year I was able to take home a couple of cases at least, but there was no tax-free whiskey for papa left over this time. I think Joel Siddel alone must have gone through a couple of quarts, and he isn't even an employee.

I'd give a lot to know whether it was Bertha or Pat who invited him. I thought that his affair with Pat was over long ago.

I must say Clay is a long-suffering bastard. He must know about Siddel—certainly everyone else in town knows about it.

If the police are looking for a motive for her murder, they won't have any trouble finding one, and that's for sure. On the other hand, if they try to figure out who was shacked up with her at the Uptowner, it will be like looking for a needle in a haystack.

I'm just damned glad I have a foolproof alibi. Bertha may hate my guts, but she won't let me down on anything as important as this. She knows which side her bread is buttered on.

I don't like this cop who is poking around asking questions. He makes me nervous. And I can't figure who's been spilling their guts. My God, he knew all about that business between me and Pat, even knew when we finally broke it off. I suppose he got an earful from Bertha. Or it could have been Clay.

Clay is in a pretty tight spot himself—when it comes to motive, he certainly leads the parade.

I never have been able to figure out Clayton Andrews. You'd think a guy would have more pride. She certainly made no bones about how she felt. Couldn't have cared less and actually seemed to take pleasure in putting the horns on him. But I guess when some guys fall in love, it must be like cancer. Incurable.

I suppose it was only poetic justice that Pat herself flipped over Siddel. He's probably a worse bastard in his own way than she was in hers. He certainly gave her a hard time, but she ate it up. I'll bet Siddel is one guy who's really relieved to know she won't be around anymore.

Patricia Andrews dead should make a lot of people a little happier, especially her husband, assuming he doesn't get unlucky and get life for her murder. I can understand how he might have fallen in love with her in the beginning, but I can't understand how he could stay in love with her after the things she did to him. It's hard for me to imagine what their sex life might have been, the way she sneered at him, despised him and double-crossed him.

God knows she was attractive, even beautiful. But about as frigid as they come. It's a peculiar thing, but I have noticed that these promiscuous broads usually are frigid.

I must admit I went for her hook, line and sinker myself when I first met her. She seemed to promise everything and she was certainly willing. But sex with her was about as much fun as doing push-ups over a live corpse.

I can only figure Clay must be some sort of masochist. That diamond bracelet he bought her for Christmas must have set him back about three months' salary. She couldn't have had it on her wrist for more than twenty-four hours before she hopped into bed at the Uptowner with the boyfriend. Gratitude!

Well, anyway, it was a good party. Mistake, though, having the clerical help and the boys from the shipping and mailing rooms in. Should have had only the editorial and art and business staff as we usually do. Damned trouble was I wanted that little Susie bitch and it wouldn't have looked right if I'd asked just her and not the rest.

That damned lieutenant seemed to think it was strange when I couldn't give him an exact list of just who was here. What the hell does he think I do, take tickets or something at my own party?

Next year I'm going to see to it that no outsiders get in. I don't say we exactly had gate-crashers, although with free booze you can never tell. But there were certainly people there whom I don't remember seeing around the office before.

Yeah, we had too damned many freeloaders.

I better get young Creamer in here and ask him about it. He was supposed to be watching over things for me, keeping things under control. Which reminds me, Bertha said something the other day about Johnny's wife planning a divorce.

I usually don't give a goddamn about my editors' private lives, but when their emotional problems begin to interfere with their work, then it becomes my business. Johnny probably doesn't think I know anything about his affair with Pat Andrews. If you can call it an affair. I am dead sure she didn't give one goddamn about the young punk. Probably just took him for all the traffic would bear and then tossed him over.

It is really strange how these so-called smart boys, intellectuals like Clay and Johnny, can fall for the most obvious dames. You'd think they'd know that if a girl like Pat would double-cross someone else, they'd be next in line for a screwing. Johnny has certainly been around here long enough to know what kind of woman Pat was. Hell, he used to tell me how sorry he felt for Clay. And then he turns right around and falls on his face over her himself.

Well, if it's going to cost him his wife and family, he asked for it. In all fairness, I can't say it has affected his work. But I do know he's all bollixed up financially. In with the loan sharks, and they've got a garnishee on his salary. I guess maybe that's one of the reasons his wife is taking off. He probably spent it all on that bitch.

I better check the books and see if he's dipping his hand in the till. I know damned well he's been selling articles under a phony name, but I better find out if it has gone any further.

I may not be the brightest bastard under the sun, but one thing I know is people. My betting is that a guy like Johnny, essentially a weak guy, will panic when he goes broke and do anything to get his hands on dough. He's been crying for a raise now for months and maybe he's worth it. But what the hell, a few more bucks a month aren't going to solve his problems and there's no point throwing good money away.

Those cops are in talking with Johnny now, but I'll see him as soon as they get through with him. Christ, the way the law has been walking in and out of here this morning, you would think this was the reception room down at police headquarters. I don't know why they should be bothering us about that stupid robbery down on the sixth floor. What the hell have we got to do with Coster and Son, Wholesale Jewelers? The fact that they decided to get themselves robbed the same night we have an office party is no fault of ours. What the hell can we tell them?

The way this joint was jumping, no one would have heard it if they'd set off an atom bomb down there. And that cop wanting to know what I personally was doing between eleven and one. What the hell did he think, I was going to tell him I was putting the blocks to a seventeen-year-old kid on my office couch?

Maybe I better not have Pringle fire Susie right away, after all. With all these police investigations going on and everything, I don't want her getting sore and losing her head or starting to scream. But that doesn't mean she has the right to walk in and start calling me by my first name. I'm *Mister* Markey to her and every other goddamn employee around here, and it doesn't matter whether I give 'em a goose in the hallway or give 'em a fast jump during the lunch hour or anything else. I'm still Mister Markey and they better not forget it.

I suppose I'd better get ready to meet Bertha for lunch. If I stand her up and those cops get back to her when she's sore or something, there's no telling what the hell she might say to them.

It will be best to go over the story again with her. I don't want her getting mixed up and she'd better get it down pat. Exactly what time we left here to go home, what time we arrived there and the rest of it. It's a damned lucky thing that Bertha did go home when she left here and it's even luckier the doorman didn't see her when she got there. I'm a little surprised that she hasn't asked me what I really did do after I left the party. I guess she's getting smart after all these years and figures what she doesn't know won't hurt her. Of course, after seeing me humping that broad on the office couch, she probably got so pee'd off she just didn't give a damn.

Well, I couldn't care less. And what the hell. I don't actually know that she went back to the apartment herself. She said she did, but it wouldn't be the first time she's lied to me. Last I saw her she was talking with Siddel, that road-show Casanova. And somehow or other, I seem to remember them leaving together before I left, or around the same time.

It was peculiar the way that cop kept getting back to him. Seemed to think I would know where the hell he is. Jees, if they can't find him, how the hell would they expect me to be able to?

It was funny, that brush-off Siddel gave Pat during the party. They must have had a fight or something because they certainly were chummy earlier in the evening. Of course, she could have been putting on an act just to get Clay upset. It's the sort of thing she liked to do.

But Joel Siddel is a damn fool if he doesn't show up pretty soon. He must have read the papers. Must know they've been looking for him. I must say he certainly takes a damned funny time to do a disappearing act.

Any way you look at it, this is bound to be a tough week. I'd give anything to duck it, but I know I'm going to have to show up at the funeral services for Patricia Andrews. It wouldn't look right if I didn't, being her husband's boss. And I don't want to do anything right now that could start people thinking. The police already are getting too interested in me.

It would be nice if I knew just when the coroner is going to release the body. These Christians hold their dead forever. Thank God, when I changed my name from Marcus to Markey, I didn't change my religion. At least the Jews have the sense to plant their dead as soon after death as they can.

It's odd, but in a way I'll probably feel a little sad when I see Patricia being put in the ground. After all, she did have something. Maybe it was just the attraction of being a *shiksa*.

Crazy how I still go for the blonde Christian broads every time. But I guess it's natural. The goys always seem to go for our girls and they get the best of it too. Their own women are a hell of a lot harder to make. And when you do make them, the price is a lot higher. Our women give it away more often than not.

One thing I must do, and I better do it right away before I meet Bertha for lunch. I better get this damned tape recorder hooked up and check out the hidden mike. If that cop comes back with more questions, and he sure as hell will, I want a record of what I say to him. Otherwise I can get all the hell and gone mixed up in my stories. You know, I wish I could remember if Bertha and Siddel did actually leave together. I should have asked her. I certainly hope she didn't do anything stupid. Especially now with the cops getting all hot and bothered about not being able to put the finger on Siddel.

I always did figure him for a real weirdo.

4

JOEL SIDDEL

I could take this .38 automatic and hand it over to the police, tell them my story—and Clarence Darrow, Louis Nizer and Sam

Liebowitz combined wouldn't be able to keep me from a life sentence up in Sing Sing.

I am going to lose either way. If I stay here and don't get medical attention, this damned infection is going to get worse and I'll probably be dead within another week or ten days. I can get out of here and try to make a run for it and I could be shot like a sitting duck before I get out of Manhattan.

This simply can't be happening to me. But, my God, it is. I signed my death warrant the day I first met her. I might just as well have gone directly back to my apartment and taken the gas pipe.

They tell me a little knowledge is a dangerous thing. Well, a lot of knowledge can be fatal, and believe me, I've got a lot of knowledge. What I need right now is not knowledge. What I need is a friend, someone I can trust.

I don't know how it's possible for a man to live for forty years, have a highly successful career, a hundred and fifty thousand in securities, membership in a half-dozen clubs, dozens of acquaintances—and still be unable to call on a real friend when he needs one.

I suppose Clayton Andrews is the best friend I have and one of the few men who really likes me and whom I like. Unfortunately, Clay is the very last person I can call on, or have any right to call on. He never came right out and accused me, but I am dead sure Clay has known about me and Pat for a long time now. She may have thought she was getting by with that platonic friendship line, and maybe for a while he was willing to fool himself, but he knows. He has to know.

If only Pat hadn't been so goddamned careless. I guess she just figured he'd stand still for anything. Well, maybe she was right. He certainly took one hell of a lot from her.

Getting herself killed was probably the best favor she has ever done for him.

I'll never forget the time Clay told me that he hadn't found it difficult to stop believing in God, but that when he stopped believing in people, he really suffered. I think it was around then he finally made up his mind about Pat and me. Finally figured out the answers.

It's an ironic coincidence that I should be sitting here now, in this room where Patricia and I had our initial affair. I can still remember the very words I used when I first told her about this place. It was just as we were leaving the cocktail lounge up in Westchester.

"If I were an artist like your husband, I guess I would call it a studio. Actually it is nothing but a rather drafty loft down in the Chelsea district I have fixed up as a sort of hideout when I want to disappear from the office for a few days and get in some honest work. I have fixed it up so it is rather attractive, and it actually has a bath and sort of bar and kitchenette that I am proud to say I built myself. Not even my secretary knows where it is."

She laughed.

"It all sounds rather intriguing," she said. "Are you taking me there to show me your etchings?"

"I am only taking you there because I intend to seduce you," I said. "And the only reason I intend to seduce you, my dear, is that you are the most utterly desirable creature I've come across in years, even if you are the wife of a slightly aging acquaintance of mine."

She turned her pert little head and looked up at me guilelessly.

"And you always seduce the wives of clients you are designing houses for?"

"Only when they are as beautiful as you," I said.

"Well, I am not at all sure that I'll let you seduce me, but I will be thrilled to see this hideaway of yours. I shall justify the trip on the grounds that I am checking your craftsmanship."

"We shall check each other's craftsmanship," I said. "I rather suspected, after you let me kiss you last night...."

I had known I was going to sleep with Patricia Andrews long before she first kissed me, first opened her mouth and let my tongue probe the sweetness of her own mouth. Pressed that lovely body against my body, and the sudden hardness in me.

I had known from almost the moment Clay had taken me to his house to meet his young wife and tell me that they were planning a new home and that he wanted me to design it for them.

That was three years ago.

I have known Clayton Andrews for a good many years, but had seen little of him since the time we both worked for the same firm when I was in my twenties. He is some ten or twelve years older than I am and is really a first-class artist, even if he has preferred to do commercial work rather than devote himself to painting.

Clay looks like anything but an artist. He is a colorless, slight little man with an uninteresting face, but has a rather quick wit and a dry, subtle sense of humor.

I can still remember my shock when he said, "I want you to meet my wife, Pat."

Beautiful, petite, blonde, she looked young enough to be his daughter, and in fact she was young enough. I wondered from the very first what in the world she could have seen in Clay. She was bright, full of life, almost but not quite flirtatious. Her attitude toward Clay was very odd. She seemed to like him, almost be proud of him. But she gave the impression that he completely bored her.

I sensed from the very beginning that she was discontented, looking for something. I believe she was attracted to me immediately, as I was to her. I can say, without undue modesty, that I am a fairly handsome man and certainly, next to Clay Andrews, I could be considered positively glamorous. In any case, an outsider, seeing the three of us together, would have instinctively looked at Pat Andrews and me and said, "What an ideal couple."

Some women are coquettish and don't mean it. But in Patricia Andrews I recognized a woman who was coquettish and did mean it. I don't know how it is you can tell, but you always can. I am not saying she was a nymphomaniac or anything like that. I never believed she was, although I am sure she had affairs with a number of men at one time or another.

It is just that she was one of those women who, through curiosity, boredom or some strange longing to find satisfaction, are forever trying to find their answers in a sexual relationship with a new man. I became that new man in her life the day we first came down here to this so-called hideout of mine.

In thinking back about it, I can't remember what we talked about, or if we really talked much at all. It seems to me we arrived, came into the studio, made up a pitcher of martinis and, before we had drained them, were in bed. There was no shyness, no embarrassment. It was the most natural thing in the world. She came to me without the usual preliminaries, without protest. It was as though we had been lovers for years.

She showed no reluctance as I took off her clothes and slowly undressed her until her small, exquisite body was naked before me.

For some reason, probably because of the complete lack of hesitancy on her part, I assumed she was thoroughly experienced. I was surprised to discover a peculiar lack of sophistication in her sexual techniques. I sensed at once that she was a woman who was used to taking a completely passive part in the act of love. Aside from a sudden tenseness of her body and the tightening of her arms around my naked back, she made no sound at all at the moment of climax, and I guessed that it was only I who had achieved satisfaction.

I wondered if she could be frigid, and I know I speculated on what kind of sexual relationship she could have with her husband. I assumed that because of the difference in their years, their sex relationship must be both infrequent and unsatisfactory.

Later on, after I had gotten to know her much better and we had spent endless hours talking about her and Clay, I understood that although Clay approached his wife far more often than the average husband, she was completely indifferent to him, getting neither pleasure nor sexual gratification from their almost nightly embraces. It was as meaningless to her as though she were scrubbing his back.

In the beginning, before our relationship changed and she told me she was in love with me and wanted to marry me, I would ask her why, feeling the way she did, she continued to be a partner in a marriage that was so completely without meaning to her.

"Oh, Clay is all right," she would say. "He loves me in his own way and he tries his best. I give him what he wants and he gives me a certain security. I can meet his demands without really giving anything of myself, and he isn't too bad to live with. As long as he's satisfied ..."

But I knew that she was either lying to me or was kidding herself. I was soon seeing a great deal of both of them and I knew Clay wasn't satisfied. He either suspected or knew a great deal more about her than she admitted and he lived in a state of constant bitterness, jealousy and frustration. Part of it was undoubtedly because of the one-sidedness of their sexual relationship, but I believe a lot more was because he was honestly in love with her and was unable to find a successful formula to offset her boredom and dissatisfaction with life, her unusual ennui and her constant seeking for something or some goal she didn't even understand herself.

In spite of her usual gaiety—for she was anything but a morbid person—her interest in a wide variety of things, books, the theater, painting and a dozen assorted hobbies, there was this strange restlessness in her. She was certainly not the usual self-centered, bored woman who is forever pursuing trivialities in an effort to escape her own inadequacies. No, it was more subtle than that. I think, perhaps, if it isn't an oversimplification, that her responses to the act of making love might be symbolic. Unable to really give of herself, she found it impossible to really receive.

This was when I first knew her. It changed. Everything about her changed when Pat finally fell in love, probably for the first time in her life. And in falling in love she may have found what she was really looking for. But she didn't find happiness. She found death.

I don't know whether it is because of the fever or because of some more subtle form of psychological block, but at this point my mind refuses to function. I don't want to think about it; I can't think about it. The thing becomes grotesque, and if I am to preserve my sanity as well as my life, I must erase everything but the immediacy of the moment.

Why am I sitting here thinking of Pat Andrews? Pat Andrews no longer exists. There is merely a shell of a body lying down in the morgue, the lead slug from a .38 buried somewhere deep in that once soft and yielding flesh.

The dead have no problems. All problems have been solved irrevocably for them.

But the living have problems and I am still among the living.

I won't be for long unless I get medical attention. I won't be for long if a certain impetuous gentleman discovers this studio of mine on the top floor of this loft building in Chelsea.

I won't be for long if the police beat him to it and find me first.

5

SUSAN FLANNERY

Well, I must say some people have a nerve. Just who does he think he is, anyway, and who does he think he's kidding? Can you imagine? Spends half the night telling me I can call him Hal, and then when I walk in this morning and say, "Hello Hal," he glares at me and says his name is Mister Markey.

Mister Markey! I'll Mister Markey him. Maybe he thinks I have forgotten already about that party. Maybe he thinks he can do what he did with me and just forget all about it. Well, he's got another thought coming. Some men just don't have any respect at all for a girl. And I can tell you one thing, he isn't much of a man. I guess I was a darn fool for ever going into that office with him in the first place.

I knew he had his eye on me right away. And I knew that sooner or later he was going to make a pass. But I certainly didn't know he was going to turn out to be some kind of queer. And not only that, he isn't only a queer, he's *Jewish!* He may fool everyone else, but he isn't fooling me. I *know* he's Jewish.

He probably thought because I took a couple of drinks and I let him kiss me and feel me up, that I would just go along and do whatever he wanted. He doesn't know that if it weren't the Christmas season and the spirit and all, I never would have consented to be in there alone with him. And after all, he is the boss here and so what could I do? And if he thinks I let him feel me and put his greasy hands all over me and slip off my bra and everything, it was because I LIKE him, he's just plain crazy. I must say he was all right when he started out and I guess because of the drinks and everything, I didn't mind too much when he put me down on that couch and everything. I don't like men with fat thick lips but at least he didn't try to kiss me on the mouth.

I should have known right then there was something fishy about him.

So he just wanted to lie on top of me. Ha! I knew right off that that's ALL HE COULD DO. The big slob. If he weren't the boss, I would have walked right out then and I'm sorry now I didn't.

I know darn well Joe didn't believe me when I told him those red marks all over me were where the cat had licked me. Why, if I were to tell Joe what he did and what he wanted me to do to him, Joe would come right up here and kill him. What kind of a girl does this *Mister* Markey think I am anyway? I certainly feel sorry for his wife.

He didn't even seem embarrassed when she walked in on us, can you imagine? Of course he still had his clothes mostly on, but she musta known. Or maybe she's just used to walking in and finding her husband making indecent proposals to a girl.

Handing me that whip and asking me to beat him. I'll beat him, all right, if he ever tries anything like that again with me. I'll beat him with an empty Coke bottle. The dirty queer.

Joe said these office parties always end up in a mess, and he was certainly right. I never should have gone in the first place. I wouldn't have minded just a little smooching around and everything, and since it was the boss and all, I would have gone ahead and done it with him, but how was I to know he's some sort of pervert who can't get it up?

Another thing, he didn't have to use those dirty words. If there is one thing I can't stand, it's a man who uses filthy language. Mr. Pringle is real nice and I'll say for him that even if he was drunk and did want to take me into the file room, he was a gentleman about it. I'm sort of sorry now I didn't let him, but my God he is ugly, and if there is anything I can't stand it's an ugly man. But he is a real gentleman. Didn't come right out and say let's screw, or I wanta lay you or anything like that.

He said he would enjoy having an affair with me. Well, so would a lot of other guys, and if I were to roll over for every jerk who wants to go to bed …

That Mr. Siddel was a nice man and I would have done it with him if he'd asked, but he didn't even give me a tumble. I don't know why it is, but it's always the dogs who are after me. Some of the guys around here would turn your hair gray. As a matter of fact, what with all these policemen around and everything, this is hardly a place for a decent girl to be working, and I wouldn't be surprised if I just up and quit this week.

What's a job more or less?

In a way, it really wasn't too bad a party and that Santa Claus was really a scream. I still can't figure out who he was. I thought I'd die when he came into the boss's office and found us there half dressed. But Mister Markey didn't think it was funny at all.

A few minutes later, when I ran into him again, it wasn't funny at all. It just goes to show you, it never pays to make snap judgments about people.

I sure had plenty to drink and I guess I got home all right, but Joe was sure mad when I came in. Somebody put me in a cab, but I can't for the world imagine who.

God, it's really terrible about poor Mrs. Andrews. She was really nice and you could tell right off she was a first-class lady. Some sex fiend must have followed her to that motel and killed her. Just to think, I spent all that time talking with her, and only an hour or so later she was murdered. It gives me the creeps.

I never did have a chance to thank her for being so nice and taking me downstairs to the ladies' john when I got sick and had to throw up. I can't see why they have a ladies' can downstairs and a men's on this floor. This must be a pretty cheap building if they can't afford one of each on every floor.

And that was real weird running into that fellow down there in the women's room. I guess he must have gotten lost or something. He certainly hightailed it out of there when we came in. He didn't seem drunk either.

Maybe he's some kind of pervert too, hanging around women's

johns. Of course, he could have been a stranger and just didn't know his way around. But it still wouldn't explain what he was doing in the ladies' can. Oh well, it takes all kinds to make a world.

They didn't really have any right asking me to contribute for the flowers for Mrs. Andrews' funeral, me being here only such a short time and all. But I am kind of glad I did give them something. She was a real lady and she was nice to me and I am sorry she had to go and get herself killed.

I feel sorry for her husband. I think he's just about the only man in this whole office who hasn't tried to give me a feel or proposition me since I been here.

Maybe he's some kind of a queer or pervert too.

Well, I better get back to work and stop thinking about it. Anyway, when I go to confession this week, I'll tell Father O'Connell what I did, or what I let Mister Markey do to me. If you do something wrong it's always best to confess. But I won't tell him that Mister Markey is a Jew. Mr. Pringle is ugly enough to be a Jewish man, but I don't think he is. He's a real gentleman, and even if he did ask if he could have an affair with me, I think it just shows he has good taste.

6

HUBERT PRINGLE

I have just finished talking with that police lieutenant and I am absolutely sure that he didn't believe a word I said. He was very polite, very courteous. It was hard for me to realize that he actually was a policeman. At no time did he pressure me or try to bulldoze me. He never so much as indicated by a raised eyebrow that he questioned any of my answers.

But I know. I know that behind that soft, sympathetic voice and the understanding warm eyes is a keen skeptical mind and that he was insidiously leading me on so that I would contradict myself time and again.

The whole thing is incredible. How, after twenty years as a loyal and faithful employee, a good husband and father, a decent citizen, can a man's whole world suddenly collapse? Suddenly come to an end?

Where did it all begin? Where did I start going wrong? At what fatal moment did I first make the initial mistake that has resulted in my life suddenly becoming a shambles and a disaster?

Was it twenty years ago when, my heart filled with gratitude, seething with ambition, I heard Harold Markey tell me he was taking me on as a bookkeeper with Markey Publications? God, I can still remember how I rushed home to tell Martha the great news. It was in this very room, in front of this very desk at which I now sit. It was Markey's desk then and Markey's office. I never dreamed that twenty years later it would be my desk and my office and that I would be general manager of the firm.

When I thanked him, I know there were tears in my eyes. I thought he was the kindest, most generous and decent person I had ever met. He knew about my record, knew that I was on probation. Knew all about the thing I had done. The money I had taken to squander at the race track. He had even talked to my previous employer, who had not only refused to give me a recommendation, but had advised against hiring me.

Yes, I thought Harold Markey was the most understanding and Christian human being I had ever met. I remember that night, before I fell asleep, I literally asked God to bless him.

Twenty years. It seems like yesterday, they have gone so fast. And how could I have been so wrong?

Harold Markey is without doubt one of the world's worst bastards. How I hate and despise that man! For twenty years I have been doing his dirty work, covering up for him, paying off his cheap women, pandering, bribing, conniving and committing every low and indecent act in the book for him. I have paid my debt of gratitude in full and I have sold my very soul in doing so.

Yes, that was the mistake. When I took this job just twenty years ago.

There have been exactly two persons in the forty-six years of my life I really have hated. Harold Markey is one of them and the other is Marty Feathers, my brother-in-law. God knows that Martha, my wife, is far from perfect. She is careless and slovenly. She is not a good mother and she whines and complains incessantly. She is wildly extravagant and thinks less than nothing of lying. But with all her faults it is hard to realize she could be of the same flesh and blood as her brother Marty. Hard to believe the same mother and father could have brought both of them into the world and raised them.

Yes, Martha has her faults, but she is not a criminal, not a double-crosser. She has some basic sense of loyalty and decency.

It is odd that during the entire hour and a half I spent with the policeman, those were the two I had to lie for and cover up for. The man to whom I was once so grateful for the opportunity he gave me to remake my life, and the man who gave me his sister in marriage. The two men whom I have learned to hate so bitterly. The two men for whom, at one time, I would have laid down my life. Well, perhaps before this is all over with I will have laid down my life. But it won't be because I want to.

I have always hated these office parties. I particularly dislike Christmas parties because of the essential hypocrisy behind them.

Doesn't Markey realize he is fooling no one? Is the man so blind and callous he doesn't realize that even the most naïve of his employees knows the only reason he gives the Christmas party is to avoid paying a decent bonus at the end of the year? Can he be so stupid that he fails to understand that there isn't a person in this office who wouldn't rather receive even a small bit of money to help him through the holiday than a few drinks of inferior liquor and some indigestible canapes?

Yes, he may realize it. But that would make no difference to Markey. Markey isn't a man given to considering the feelings of others, considering their preferences.

He isn't fooling me in the slightest. I know what is in that twisted mind of his. He *uses* the parties. He uses them first to satisfy his own evil, lecherous desires. This year was like every other year. There is always some young girl. Some new file clerk or secretary or assistant editor or researcher. Always some fresh bit of goods he manages to seduce into that office of his so he may commit his obscenities upon her body while she is drugged and stupefied by the liquor he has poured down her throat.

He uses the parties as a sort of grim espionage device so he can learn what is really in the minds of the people who work for him. He knows that with the combination of the booze he supplies and the general feeling of freedom and festivity because of the season, inhibitions will be let down and his people will talk out and give away their feelings. Little feuds will come out into the open, office politics will be made public.

It always ends up the same way. The same little girl—except that each year it is a fresh one—goes into that office to be violated, and the week after the party two or three employees who have made the mistake of being too frank are summarily fired.

This year was no exception. Markey took this new girl, Susan, into his office. He has already told me to give notice to young Ronson, in photography, who made the mistake of complaining in a loud voice about his salary.

But this year is different from the other years in one respect. This year it was more than merely the seduction of an innocent girl and the firing of an employee or so. This year it ended in a real tragedy. For I am absolutely sure that Patricia Andrews' murder is linked in some way with this Christmas party.

I am sure this Lieutenant Goodwin also thinks so. Otherwise, why in questioning me would he have constantly harked back to the party? To last Friday night when Markey Publications made its one great, noble gesture of the year.

I will have to leave Markey Publications. That is definite. I will have to leave a lot more than that. The way things look, it appears that I shall have to completely disappear. This is a tragedy in more than one way.

Everyone says that I have no sense of humor. Because I don't happen to like dirty jokes, because I have never been able to see anything amusing in sadistic horseplay and that sort of thing, I am considered a dry, humorless stick. But they are wrong. I think if people realized that even now while I am facing financial, moral and social bankruptcy, the basic reason I consider the entire thing a tragedy is because of the watch, they would know I do have a sense of humor.

It is because of the watch, more than any other reason, that I hate leaving Markey Publications. For ten years now I have been waiting, planning exactly what I was going to do on that day, five years hence, when Harold Markey would present me with the gold watch in appreciation of twenty-five years of loyal and faithful service to the firm.

Markey doesn't retire an employee at sixty or sixty-five or anything like that. You retire at the end of twenty-five years of service, no matter what your age. And you retire without a pension or a bonus. You just plain retire. Die.

But there is the dinner and there is the watch.

It is a damned shame I shall never be able to give the little speech on which I have worked so hard. I was going to make that speech with misty eyes.

Standing on the dais, facing my benefactor, amidst the silence of that roomful of Markey employees, I would hold the gold watch in my quaking hand and, with tears dimming my eyes I would look at Harold Markey, and say, "Mister Markey, for the rest of the days and the years of my life I shall ever hold this moment precious. Mister Markey, I want you to take this gold watch and shove it up your big, fat ass."

And then before the stunned and mute admiration of that entire roomful of Markey Publications employees, I would let Harold Markey have it right in the teeth, as hard as I could hit him, still holding the fine token of appreciation in my closed fist.

Yes, that is the moment I dreamed and planned for. But it is a moment that will never happen. Because there is not the most remote chance I shall be here in another five years.

If it hadn't been for that party, for what happened to Patricia Andrews, I am sure I could have straightened things out. I know I could. But now it is too late. The fat's in the fire, as they say, and there is nothing I can do. Nothing except try to save my own skin any way I can.

I had a premonition about that party right from the very beginning. I don't know whether I am psychic or not, but somehow I always seem to know. It's like this Susan Flannery. I absolutely knew the very minute I brought her into Markey's office for his OK that he was going to make her. Perhaps it was the way he looked at her, perhaps it was just that I knew him so well, but I could tell.

Normally, I would never have hired the girl. She is a mediocre typist at best, she barely knows how to speak English, she certainly has no ambitions as far as the publishing business is concerned. But when you pay the kind of wages we pay here, you cannot be selective.

Of course, I wasn't kidding myself a bit. I was sure she would cause a certain amount of stir around the place and I was sure that every married man in the office would be after her within a week. In her case I figured even the single ones would be making a try. I was right, of course. But I was desperate and I am always shorthanded with the tight budget under which I must operate. So I brought her in to the boss and he said hire her and I did.

When Markey told me that we would have the clerical help and the shipping room people at the party this year I should have had sense enough to know what was in the back of his mind. Susan was in the back of his mind.

Perhaps I am nothing but a hypocrite myself. Or perhaps I am only human after all. But when I saw the way she was flirting and carrying on, I broke down and made a pass myself. God knows I try to be a decent man, but when some little sexpot like that all but shoves it in your face, what can you do? At least I didn't try to rape her or to take advantage of my position here. I just asked her outright. And she told me outright. She hesitated and for a moment I thought I was in. But then she just laughed and shook her head.

I suppose it is because I am so damned ugly. But I can't help the way God made me. I guess it just takes an unusual sort of woman to see behind the façade of my physical repulsiveness and understand what I am really like. And Susan is anything but an unusual woman.

It is odd that Marty should have noticed her. Getting Marty to come to the party was a real mistake. But again, I was powerless.

Markey himself told me that he didn't want one of the employees to play Santa Claus this year. He told me to get some outsider to do it, but with the money he gave me to cover all the expenses, I just couldn't stretch it far enough to buy what he wanted and still shell out to hire an actor.

I know damned well why he didn't want to use one of the staff. This phony Santa Claus gives out the presents—not actually presents but just a lot of cheap favors, ballpoint pens, trick hats, that sort of thing. Last year when young Creamer played Santa Claus and gave them out, Markey was burned up. He said Creamer acted as though he, Creamer, were the giver rather than Harold Markey and Markey Publications. And he didn't want any employee thinking he was responsible for the magnificent and generous gestures being made.

So I brought in Marty Feathers, my brother-in-law. I knew Marty would be willing to do it for the free drinks and the food and he jumped at the chance. It was a little odd, too, the way he accepted. I first asked him more than a month back and he stalled me off and was hesitant, and then about two weeks ago he came to me and reminded me about it and said he would like to do it. I guess he probably had had something lined up for that Friday night earlier and it fell through. Free booze and grub were better than nothing.

It is an evil coincidence that the robbery had to take place downstairs Friday night. Marty blames me for that, which just goes to show how really stupid and ungrateful he can be. How in the world was I to know Coster and Son would have their safe broken into? How was I to know the thieves would get away with a half-million dollars in uncut gems?

Of course I had to lie to Lieutenant Goodwin. Could I tell him Marty was here that night? Could I tell him anything about Marty? I know how the police mentality works. I know how they figure. God knows, I've had my own experience to guide me.

Give a man a criminal record and he's marked forever. Hounded forever. If anything happens within a mile of him, he's at once suspect. And with Marty out of a state penitentiary less than a year, even if he was only sentenced for forgery, I know exactly what would have happened if I'd told the truth.

It would be enough to tell them Marty was my brother-in-law. It would start them digging, and in no time at all they would learn about that old trouble I was in. It is easy enough to guess what would happen. We would at once be prime suspects in that robbery downstairs.

I don't say the police frame innocent men, but if a man has a criminal record, the burden of proof is on him. Even if he can prove his innocence, other things come out during the investigation and he can be destroyed.

I am probably tilting at windmills. Lieutenant Goodwin is investigating a murder, not a robbery. I never left the party and there are a hundred people who can swear to that.

No, they couldn't have proved a thing. But that isn't the point. Once they found out about Marty's record, and my own past mistake, it would be enough. It wouldn't make any difference to Marty, of course. God knows he is used to being taken down to headquarters and questioned. He couldn't care less. But they would start in on me, and the next step they'd begin looking into the books here, and then they would know.

They would find out what I have been doing these last three years.

It would be the end and there would be nothing I could do to cover up. I could certainly expect no mercy from Harold Markey. Even under normal conditions he's a vindictive man. Give him just the slightest real excuse and ...

The funny thing is, I am absolutely sure Markey has known for some time that I've been doctoring the books. I don't know how he knows or how he found out, but I am quite positive. Call it another one of my premonitions.

I can't understand why he has let it go on, why he hasn't already done something about it. Is it because he enjoys playing some sort of sadistic cat-and-mouse game? Is it because he is merely sitting back and giving me enough rope to really hang myself? Or is it because he has some sinister plot in mind? Some idea of letting me get in so deep that I can't possibly get out and then using his knowledge as an instrument to force me to collaborate in some evil plan he himself might have?

I don't know.

I suspect it is the last. That day a few weeks back when he saw me out at the track on Saturday afternoon and pretended he didn't see me gave me a sort of clue. And little things he has said.

God, if I only had time! I know that I could get the money and make restitution. But I don't have any time now. No time at all.

I can't imagine what ever possessed me to take Marty into my confidence and tell him about my troubles. I guess in sheer desperation I just wanted to share my problems with anyone at all, and Marty is probably the only person I know who at least would have some sympathetic understanding. After the trouble he's been in and the times I have helped him out, he should have. Also, I was sure that he suspected something was up. He saw me around the house several times while I was figuring out the scratch sheet and he knows what always happens when I go crazy and start believing I can beat the horses. And of course it was my bad luck he had to be the one who picked up the phone that time the bookie called up and threatened me.

Well, what has happened has happened. I guess that's just another of the reasons I have for hating the idea of Marty living with us. Or better yet, I should say on us.

It is really fantastic the lengths a man will go to when he is pushed against the wall. What an intrinsically honest man is forced to stoop to when the pressure becomes too great.

In a way I am honestly glad Clayton Andrews was not in his Greenwich Village studio when I arrived early last Saturday morning after the Christmas party. Clayton is a decent man and has always been a friend of mine. I don't know how I could have been so goddamned low as to even try and do what I planned.

Low? It was worse than that. Can anything be more cheap and sordid than to sell a man information that will make him divorce his wife? Even now when I think of it, I blush. I really wonder, had Clayton actually been there and had he let me in, would I have gone through with it?

Of course I was tight and I was desperate and probably about half out of my mind with worry. But what a thing to do! To tell a man his wife is cheating on him and then offer to sell him the proof of it. God, how I despise myself at times.

The fact that Clayton wasn't there and that I didn't do it is no excuse. I was going to. I thought at the time it was the only way in the world I could get enough money to partially reimburse the company and stall things off for a while longer. I guess in a pinch a desperate man will stoop to almost anything to save himself and his family.

Well, it's too late for all that now. There is no hope in the world that I can stall off the disaster. Nothing I can do to avoid the disgrace and the scandal. I can't save Martha and I can't save my job. The only thing I can do now is try to salvage a few of the broken fragments, try to make a getaway. The catastrophe has already occurred and the one thing I might still be able to do is physically divorce myself from it. Make a break and simply disappear.

It is ironic that I should have such scruples about what I didn't do to Clayton Andrews and yet—have absolutely none about what I am about to do to Bertha Markey and her husband. I don't even flinch at out-and-out blackmail; I don't flinch at something which is even worse.

I have no hesitation about blackmailing Harold Markey to keep certain information out of his wife's hands and then turning right around and selling Bertha Markey that same information. I could probably obtain enough money from either one of them for my purposes. Enough money to get away and lose myself in a new identity and make a new start somewhere else. But I am not going to be satisfied with that. I am going to compound the felony.

I once read somewhere that misdemeanors lead to felonies and felonies lead to murder, and I guess it's true.

I have, of course, an alternate plan. It is both safer and a great deal surer of success. I am probably the only person in the world who knows Clayton Andrews was not in his studio down in the Village as he told the police he was, during the time his wife was being murdered. And because of the information concerning Patricia Andrews and her adulteries, I am very, very sure Clayton had every reason in the world for killing her.

If the police knew what I know, Clayton would be as good as in the death house. Clayton would pay a great deal of money to keep them from having this information. But I will not blackmail Clayton Andrews. God knows that man has already suffered enough.

I can't imagine how that policeman learned I left the office party long before it broke up. Left just before Patricia Andrews herself departed for her fatal rendezvous at the Uptowner Motel.

He was really very subtle, very tricky when he questioned me. Maybe he thought he was fooling me when he switched the tenor of his questions and wanted to know if I had seen anything in connection with that patrolman who was run down by a hit-and-run driver in front of the building. Of course, he knew I could have seen nothing of the actual accident or I would have reported it at once. But those odd questions about my possibly having seen a body lying in the gutter near the entrance. "Like it might have been some drunk who'd passed out, you know," is the way he put it, I believe.

I know damned well he was just trying to get me off stride. Trying to switch the mood so that when he sprang the questions about where I had gone and what I had done during the next couple of hours, I would be unprepared.

It was most unusual that he didn't question my story about the all-night movie. He seemed to think it was perfectly logical that I could have been feeling a little drunk and woozy and just wanted to get away by myself and sober up before getting the car out of the garage and driving home to Long Island.

Thank the Lord I had already seen the picture and remembered it. And it was a real break that I actually had seen it at the theater where I said I went, up in Times Square. Seen it only three nights before when I really had been feeling woozy and wanted to sit back for a few minutes and relax and forget my worries. Of course, I hadn't been drunk then, just too upset to go home immediately and hear all of Martha's petty little problems. Yes, it was lucky, because he certainly asked enough questions. About what scene was on when I came in and all the rest of it.

He wasn't surprised either when the girl at the box office failed to remember me. Naturally she can't be expected to remember every single person who buys a ticket. But she did say I seemed somehow familiar and I guess that was because of having seen me several nights previously.

My alibi is certainly good enough and at least I don't have that to worry about. I just hope Clayton can come up with as good a one. He's going to need it. Everyone who attended that ghastly party is going to need one before this is all over and finished. Even Markey and his wife.

Which reminds me, I had better make a telephone call and arrange to see her. I am afraid Bertha Markey is going to come in for a rather unpleasant little surprise.

On the other hand, it actually should be rather pleasant. She certainly can't be under any illusions about her husband, and at least I will be giving her good value for money received. I'll give her enough so that she can get a divorce settlement that will strip him right down to his nasty eyeteeth.

7

BERTHA MARKEY

My mother used to say to me, "Bertha, there is one thing I don't want you to ever forget. You're a Roth and your family goes straight back to the de Rothschilds. No man is too good for you."

Well, Mama picked out Harold Marcus and maybe she thought he was good enough, but for once Mama made a mistake. I have been married to Harold Marcus, or Hal Markey as he calls himself now, for some twenty-two years, and I can tell you one thing. My husband is a louse.

Mama died of a stroke while we were still in Europe on our honeymoon and I only thank God she didn't live long enough to know what her son-in-law really was like. It didn't take me any twenty-two years either to find out. I got a pretty good idea on the very first night of our honeymoon, and I have been improving my knowledge ever since.

A good provider, yes. That he is. But Mama should have known that it was only because of the hundred thousand dollars she gave him when we were married that he was able to pull his crummy little publishing business out of the red and get it really started. She should have known about the other seventy-five thousand that I inherited when she died and that he actually stole from me to weather himself through that second year.

He's made it since, I admit. Made it big, and if I have managed to put away a nice tidy piece of it over the years, it has certainly been my due.

He's always throwing up to me everything he has given me, but let me tell you one thing—any woman who could go to bed with Hal Markey, night after night, month after month, for twenty-two years, deserves every dollar of the eight hundred thousand dollars I have put away in good safe blue-chip securities.

When I think of the things I have done for that man, the things I have had to stand for and the things I have covered up for and how I have swallowed my pride and protected him ...

I lied to that detective. Lied to him deliberately and I thought I made it convincing, but somehow I have the feeling he didn't believe me. But I couldn't care less. There is no way he can really know. Hal knows and this time Hal is really going to pay. This time he has managed to get himself into something he isn't going to find so easy to get out of.

You would think, with all the experience he has had with women—and God only knows he's chased after every kind there is—you would think he'd have learned something. But not my Hal. No, you can count on my Hal making a complete damned fool of himself every time.

I tried to warn him about that Andrews woman. I knew she was after something. What in the world would a good-looking girl like that—and I must admit she was good-looking even if I don't myself see what is so attractive about those washed-out skinny blonde types—anyway, what would a good-looking girl like Patricia Andrews be doing making up to an ugly fat slob like Harold Markey unless she was out to get something from him?

Well, I guess he found out all right. She must have really taken him for plenty. And I guess she had the goods on him, all right. He should have known she had a certain amount of class and that he couldn't get away with his usual thing and just hand her a few dollars or a sealskin jacket and dump her. She must have had her hooks into him good.

I tried to warn him he was playing with fire, but when did he ever listen to me? He thought I was warning him because of Clayton, but I knew he wouldn't have any trouble with Clayton. That mousy little man wouldn't hurt a fly. I know very well that Clayton knew about Hal and Patricia. Who didn't know, in fact?

But Clayton wasn't going to do anything about it. Clayton is one of those soft, I guess you would say artistic, types, who just sit around and break their hearts and don't do anything but try to understand what is as clear as glass to anyone else. No, Hal wouldn't listen to me. And so now he's in trouble.

Mama always used to tell me I had a sort of second sight about things and I really think that I do. I had a feeling about the party. Of course, when Hal acted the way he did, as though he didn't want me to come to it, I made up my mind right then I would go. I had a feeling he was up to something.

He's always telling me I don't take an interest in his business, but how can I when he never tells me anything? Anyway, who wants to hang around a dingy office with a lot of dingy people? I thought he was up to something, so I decided I would just show up and see what was what. I guess he was considerably surprised when I walked in just as they were getting ready to give out the favors.

I must say, considering how tight Hal is about buying liquor for the house, I was a little more than surprised to see the way the booze was flowing. He can certainly spread it out when it's for something he wants or for something away from home.

The very first person I ran into was Patricia Andrews and I spotted that bracelet on her wrist right off. Hal denies it, but I would bet my life he bought it for her. It was probably a part of the payoff he's been making. I am as sure as I am breathing that she has been blackmailing Hal for at least a year or so now.

She told me her husband gave it to her for Christmas, but I have a good eye for that sort of thing, and that bracelet cost four or five thousand dollars if it cost a red cent. I can't see a man who makes the kind of money Clayton Andrews makes buying his wife a five-thousand-dollar Christmas present. At least not a wife like Patricia Andrews, who was not only playing around with Hal, which most people knew about, but had fallen head over heels in love with Joel Siddel, which everyone and their brother knew about.

Of course, Joel could have given her the bracelet just to get rid of her, and God only knows he was all through with her, but I don't think Joel is the kind to go around buying ex-mistresses expensive presents.

Yes, I had a feeling in my bones about that party. I was dead certain Hal had some new little tart lined up, and as usual I was right. I must admit when I walked into his office and found him with that girl I thought at first it was Patricia. It would have been just like Hal to take Patricia in for a fast lay while her husband was outside celebrating Christmas and his own wife was in the next room.

It's the sort of thing he likes to do.

I was wrong, of course. But I must say I think he has finally blown his top. That child couldn't have been more than sixteen or seventeen and you'd think that after all his troubles with young girls he'd have learned something about statutory rape. It still burns me up when I remember what he had to pay off to the Klosman girl's family that time he took her up to Grossinger's for the weekend. Well, maybe he can afford it. It's a sure thing I can't.

Sometimes I wonder what kind of a maniac I'm married to anyway. It was bad enough, having that young girl on his couch, you might almost say right in front of his whole office staff, but then what does he do? He takes off before his own party is finished and doesn't get home until after daylight the next morning and has the gall, the unmitigated gall, to ask me to alibi for him to the police.

Well, I lied for him but it's the last time. I lied for him, but it wasn't to save his lousy skin. I'm not going to let his damned stupidities spoil everything for me at this stage of the game. And Hal may not know it, but I am absolutely certain that that police lieutenant, that man Goodwin, knows all about his affair with Pat. I am sure he has already figured out Pat was blackmailing him for every nickel she could get. And I am sure he has figured that Hal Markey probably had a better motive than almost anyone else for shooting her.

I am certainly no eavesdropper and even my worst enemy wouldn't accuse me of having an interest in anyone else's business, but I can't help it if people don't lower their voices when they speak. When I saw Joel and Patricia arguing over in that corner, naturally I wanted to know what they were saying, because after all Joel was really my friend. Wasn't it I who commissioned him to do our summer place up in the Adirondacks?

I wasn't the only one who heard them, either. I know for sure that Clayton must have listened in on part of it, because when I walked closer because the record player was making so much noise, he stalked out from in back of the partition they were talking behind, and from the look on his face he could have chewed nails. Clayton looked mad enough to kill.

Clayton left the party then and didn't come back, and I went to where he had been standing and really got an earful. They were having at it hot and furious. I remember hearing Patricia tell him that if he stood her up again he would regret it as long as he lived. I gathered they had arranged for some kind of private date after the party and Joel was trying to get out of it.

You would certainly think a woman would have more pride. Couldn't she understand he was through with her? That it was all over and done with? I will admit Joel Siddel is a darned attractive man, and I should certainly know. But even I am smart enough to understand his kind. Joel Siddel is not the marrying kind and he certainly isn't a fellow to want any long-lasting relationship.

The dumbest little bunny understands men like Joel. Great company, charming as they come, he dresses beautifully and makes a woman feel like a million dollars. But reliable? I could laugh. He makes a woman feel like a million dollars all right, but he makes *every* woman feel like a million dollars.

Joel Siddel can get any woman he wants and I may not be smart about men, but one thing I do know. With men like Joel, the minute a woman breaks down and gives in, he loses interest. Anyway, I don't think Joel really gives a damn about women, in spite of being such a wolf. I think he gets his real kicks by taking a woman away from some other man. I think he just likes to see if he can do it. And once he's got her, he couldn't care less.

If anyone was going to get himself killed, I would have said it would have been Joel. I can think of half a dozen husbands around town who would be perfectly willing to shoot him on sight. In fact, I can think of several women who wouldn't hesitate for a second to put a few drops of arsenic in his martini.

I would have liked to stay there long enough to know how the argument did end up and if Joel really did keep his date with Patricia. But that stupid husband of mine had to take that particular moment to come staggering out of his office, still buttoning up his fly, and I could see the lipstick smeared all over his face and I just didn't want him to look a bigger fool than he usually does, so I had to go over and tell him to go into the men's john and straighten himself out.

From what the papers said and from the stories going around, someone certainly kept a date over at the motel with Patricia. It might have been the one who killed her or it might not have, the police say, but someone was in that bed with her, you can bet. It could very well have been Joel, but from the way they were fighting, it doesn't seem to me that he would have ended up in her bed.

One thing I am sure of. Joel Siddel didn't kill her. He isn't the kind who uses a gun to kill his discarded women. He does it even worse; he just coldly tells them to go to hell and walks off and breaks their hearts for them. It's like what he was telling Patricia when I overheard them by accident.

She was saying, "How can you do this to me, Joel, after all we have meant to each other? After what I have given you and the way I have loved you?"

And him saying, "How could you do what you have done to your husband after all you meant to him and all he gave you and the way he loved you?"

He certainly had her in a spot there all right.

It really is surprising, to me at least, that anyone who has played around as much as Pat has could be so stupid.

It's a lucky thing for Hal that Joel has apparently panicked and is hiding out somewhere. He must be a bigger fool than I figured him for. When the police asked me about him I had to tell them what I knew. Had to tell them about that conversation I overheard. They would have found out anyway that Joel was going to see Patricia after the party was over. If he's in trouble he certainly asked for it. Anyway, as long as the police are interested in Joel Siddel, they won't spend too much time wondering about Hal or checking up on where he actually did spend the night.

That Lieutenant Goodwin said he would be talking to me again and I guess it wouldn't hurt to sort of put a bug in his ear. I don't particularly want Joel to get in trouble, but if someone has to, it's a lot better that it be he than my husband.

I simply can't understand why Hubert Pringle wants to talk to me. He certainly sounded as though it was something important. He had plenty of opportunity to talk to me the night of the party and he never came near me.

I have never liked that man and I have told Hal a dozen times I couldn't understand why he keeps him on.

Twenty percent of the stock of Markey Publications is in my name and you'd think I would have something to say about how the business is run. Of course if it was up to me, I'd go down there and fire about half the people Hal has working for him. Pringle would be the first to go, and I would get rid of that dumb, empty-headed girl who is on the switchboard. She never yet got a message right, and I don't like the way she always tells me she "will see if Mr. Markey is in." She knows damned well he's in when she says that. I wonder who she thinks she's kidding?

That Creamer man is another one I'd fire right off. He didn't hear one thing I was saying when I was talking to him about that article he ran in *THE HOMEMAKER* last month. He not only didn't hear me, he was downright rude. After all, I am the boss's wife and I think he owes me a certain amount of respect. I can understand pretty well why his wife left him if he treats her the way he treats other women. He was really drunk before the party was half over.

The way he was following Patricia Andrews around all night was positively disgusting. It's bad enough that he should fall head over heels in love with another man's wife, but he doesn't have to let the world know about it.

8

JOHNNY CREAMER

I honestly believe I am going insane.

If I could only remember. This isn't the first time I've gotten stoned and drawn a blank. It's happened before, but my God, I have always been able to put the pieces together somehow afterward.

Lieutenant Goodwin said he could understand, but I wonder if he really does? I know I had the gun and there was simply no point in denying it. Whoever the hell it was who let me cry on his shoulder certainly knew about the gun because I remember taking it out and showing it to him. But whether I went to the Uptowner Motel that night after the party or not, I simply do not know.

Could I have killed her? It doesn't seem possible. I simply can't believe I did it. God only knows I loved her enough. I've been mad with jealousy and I've lost all control and just about every ounce of sense I ever had, but I can't believe I would have hurt her. Maybe I was shooting at Joel Siddel, if I did go there and found them together, and maybe the bullet hit her. But if that's what happened, then why in the name of Christ hasn't Joel showed up and said something about it? Why would he just simply disappear?

And someone would have seen me. Someone would have known. And how did I ever end up at that god-awful dive down on the Bowery? How did I get there? Did someone take me?

They tell me I arrived around four o'clock on Saturday morning, dead drunk. Well, they were right about that part of it, anyway. I was drunk all right. So blind drunk I don't even remember leaving the party. Don't remember one damned thing except the business in the office when I was telling my troubles to ...

To whom? That's the part I don't remember. I can't understand why whoever it was hasn't come out and said something.

Well, Mary Ann was right about one thing. She said I was heading for trouble and I have sure enough arrived. If she wants her divorce now, she won't have any trouble getting it. I can't blame her, God knows.

It is impossible for me to really believe that Pat is dead. But she is dead and I simply can't understand my own feelings about it.

When I told her that if I couldn't have her, no one else was going to, I never dreamed it would turn out like this. I know in my heart I did think I would rather see her dead than with someone like Joel, but I also know now I wasn't telling myself the truth.

No matter what she did or who she did it with, I didn't want her to die. And I wouldn't have hurt her. I would never have hurt her in any way at all.

I knew damned well I shouldn't have taken that first drink. Knew what would happen if I did. I guess it was only when I heard her making a date to meet Joel at the motel that I lost control. He'll never know how close he came to getting killed right then and there.

Actually, when I went into my office, I went to get the gun, and it is a lucky thing the flask was in the drawer next to it. Because I think if it hadn't been there, I would have used that gun. But I stopped and took the drink and then I just sat there, crying. I finished the bottle and by that time I was so stoned I just wanted somebody to talk to and to listen to my problems. And that's when that guy who was doing the Santa Claus routine came in and ...

Hell, he must have been the one I was telling my troubles to. Funny, it's coming back to me now. I remember thinking at the time he was a complete stranger and how peculiar it was to be telling a man I had never seen before all about my love life and everything else. I don't think I could have told it to anyone I really knew or who knew Pat. I am pretty sure I didn't actually mention her name or let him know whom I was talking about, but again, I don't know. I can't be sure. I can't remember.

I wish to God I knew who he was. He would probably remember whether I had the gun with me when I left the party. I just vaguely recall his saying something to me about not doing anything foolish. Could I have given him the gun?

If I didn't give it to him I must have given it to somebody else, or someone could have taken it away from me. One thing is sure, the gun is gone. Can it be sheer coincidence that Pat was killed by a .38 caliber bullet and that my gun was a .38?

If the damned gun would just turn up, I would know.

The lieutenant seemed to feel pretty sure the gun would show up.

He said they usually do, sooner or later. Well, I hope he is right. Even if it's the gun which killed her, even if somehow or other I actually fired the fatal bullet, I still hope he is right. I want to know. Anything is better than not knowing.

God only knows I don't care what happens, any longer. I don't care whether I go on living or not. But I must know. I must find out.

I think Hubert Pringle is a damned liar. When I asked him who the guy was who played Santa Claus, he said it was just some bum he'd picked up off the street.

Well if that's so, why hasn't that bum shown up? He must be able to read the papers. Must listen to the radio.

I can't understand why Pringle would lie about it, but I feel sure that he was lying. What is Pringle trying to cover up? He certainly could have nothing to do with Pat. I guess he's probably the only guy who attended the goddamned party who didn't have any kind of connection with her, any motive for killing her.

Clayton could have killed her. He had plenty of motive, but Clayton isn't my picture of a killer. In his own way, I guess he was as much in love with her as I was. And she didn't give any more of a damn about him than she did about me.

That bastard Siddel could have killed her. But he wouldn't have killed her because he was in love with her. He would just have wanted to get rid of her.

Hal Markey. Could Markey have come in and taken the gun after I passed out? Could he have followed Joel and Pat to the motel, assuming that Siddel was the man with her when she checked in? Markey certainly had an affair with her at one time or another. That swine.

No, he's too goddamned selfish. Markey isn't capable of enough feeling to do anything to jeopardize his precious hide. Murder isn't his bit; he just likes to destroy people in other ways. Markey is a man I could cheerfully shoot down.

I am really surprised they haven't arrested me. They know I had the gun. I admitted it. And I can't explain where I was or what I was doing when Pat was killed. I don't know how they found out, but they seem to know I was crazy about her also.

Somebody should horsewhip the bastard who wrote that story in the paper this morning. How could he have written those things about her? God, isn't it bad enough the things men did to her while she was alive? Do they have to completely destroy her reputation now that she's dead?

I think I am the only person in the world who really knew and understood her. Knew why she did the things she did, acted the way she did. Slept with the men she slept with. It's a goddamned bit of irony that I'm about the only man who didn't sleep with her and I am the only one who was really in love with her. The only one who really understood what a truly beautiful person she was.

Why is it she couldn't understand? Wouldn't listen to me? Why did it have to happen to her?

I can't do anything for Pat now, but there is one thing I can do. I can try to find out who killed her. Even if that person should turn out to be me, I want to know.

I have to start somewhere and I have to know what happened after I began getting drunk.

I simply have to find that guy who was playing Santa Claus.

PART TWO

1

DETECTIVE LIEUTENANT WILLIAM GOODWIN

There are times when I hate New York, hate the millions of rushing, nervous, self-centered people who make up its teeming masses. An innocent person can be brutally murdered in front of half a hundred witnesses and no one will raise a hand to go to his defense or even call in an alarm.

I wonder if this could have happened in the case of Karl Swendson.

One thing is certain, at least a score of people passed within a few feet of where his shattered body lay in the gutter and not one of them bothered to see how badly he might be hurt or if he were alive or dead. Not one of them bothered to phone in a report to the police. And at least one man, this derelict they are holding down at the Tombs, actually saw him killed. He was drunk of course, but he wasn't so drunk that he doesn't remember something of it. Could others also have been present when that hit-and-run driver smashed the patrolman's body into a bloody, broken corpse?

I talked with Conrad Fairman this morning. That is the man who saw Swendson run down. This isn't my case but I am interested for two reasons, one personal and one official.

Swendson was my friend and that is the personal reason. I'd like to see his killer apprehended and made to pay for his crime. The other reason is the time and place the incident occurred. It happened some time early last Saturday morning, almost directly in front of the office building which houses the Markey Publishing Company. I know very well that at least a dozen or more persons left the party and left the office building sometime after Swendson was struck and before the accident was reported. Several of them have admitted seeing his body lying there in the gutter. They claim they thought it was just another drunk who had passed out from too much booze.

They also saw this derelict, Conrad Fairman, who was sitting in a doorway with a bottle in his hand, half passed out. They figured the two men must have been together. No one bothered to investigate. It wasn't their business.

Of course they didn't realize Swendson was an officer of the law. He was not in uniform because he was off duty and on his way home.

Fairman remembers very little, but persistent questioning has brought to light certain facts. He tells us he was sitting in the doorway where he was eventually picked up for several hours. He vaguely remembers a car parked in front of the building. A man got into the car, and someone crossed the street and hailed the car, as though he wanted to question the driver. And then the car shot out from the curb and struck the man. It makes us believe that Swendson must have seen something suspicious about either the car or the driver that drew his attention.

Swendson couldn't have known about the robbery of the safe in the jewelry firm, so it couldn't have been that. So what was it? Was there something about the driver himself?

But what interests me officially is the possibility that someone from the office party saw the accident. Left the building at the time it took place. It is very possible. And if someone did, why is he keeping silent about it?

Our derelict doesn't remember any particular person who left the building that night, which is a double disappointment. I want to find someone who may have seen Mrs. Andrews leaving. Her car was also parked on the street near the entrance. I want to find out if she was alone when she left, and if not, who was with her.

These people I am talking to are infuriating. This whole Andrews case is infuriating. The man I most want to talk to, Joel Siddel, has completely disappeared. The witnesses I do talk to are either evasive or are outright liars. I don't believe one single person has told the complete truth.

The business with Susan Flannery earlier this morning was typical. I was waiting for her at nine o'clock in her office when she telephoned in to say she was quitting her job. Before I could get to the telephone, she had hung up. So I drove out to Brooklyn to see her and discovered she has left home and that her mother, with whom she lives, hasn't the faintest idea where she is, where she has gone, when she expects to return. She could only tell me her daughter had returned home last night, apparently very upset, and said she would be going away for a few days.

We've put out a wanted on her.

Mary Flannery is a fat, blowsy woman, the janitress in the apartment house in which they live. She is a hard-working woman, a good Catholic, not particularly intelligent, but I think honest. The trouble is she has what so many first-generation Irish have, an instinctive distrust and fear of authority. Especially of the police. I could sense the antagonism at once when I knocked on her door and she answered, carefully keeping the burglar chain in place. I asked for her daughter and it wasn't until I identified myself and showed her my badge that she was willing to talk at all. She let me in grudgingly and the only reason she did is that she didn't want the tenants to know a policeman was around asking questions.

It took me the best part of fifteen minutes to even find out that Susan was no longer home, that she had left the previous evening, taking nothing with her but an overnight bag.

"Mrs. Flannery," I said, "isn't it a little unusual, your daughter just taking off for apparently no reason at all?"

She shook her head.

"Maybe she had her reasons. Anyway, what do you want with her? Susan is in no trouble. She's a good girl, though maybe a trifle wild. But Susan would have no trouble with the police. Why you want to bother a good girl …"

"We don't want to bother your daughter, Mrs. Flannery," I said. "We merely want to ask her some questions."

"But I tell you, Susan …"

"Mrs. Flannery, Susan is in no trouble. She has done nothing wrong. But she attended a party, a party at her office, a few nights ago. A woman who was at that party was murdered later in the evening. We know Susan talked to her at one time or another and we are anxious to learn …"

"But I tell you my girl knows nothing." Mrs. Flannery, who had not asked me to sit down, stood in front of me, her raw, red hands on her great hips, and glared.

I was getting nowhere and I knew I would not get anywhere trying to use reason and logic. I hate to bulldoze a witness but sometimes it is necessary. I changed my tactics.

"We can pick up your daughter and hold her as a material witness, Mrs. Flannery," I said. "Hold her under high bail. I don't want to have to do this, but if she makes herself unavailable for questioning I am going to have to. Now why don't you just tell me where she is. It will make it a lot easier for her, believe me. All I want is to find her and ask her a few questions."

"I tell you I don't know where she is. I have no idea."

"You knew she quit her job this morning?"

"Yes, I knew. She told me so last night after she got the phone call."

"The phone call? What phone call? Did she get it before she said she wanted to go away for a few days?"

"Sit down, mister," Mrs. Flannery said. She moved over herself to a straight-backed chair and dropped her heavy bulk on it, sitting on the very edge, her body still tense and alert.

I sat at the table across from her.

"If I tell you what I know, you promise you won't arrest her? Hold her in jail as a witness like you said?"

"I promise that if when we find her she agrees to keep herself available until this case is settled and is willing to give us any information she might have, we won't hold her."

She thought for several minutes and at last nodded, but still looked grim and antagonistic.

"Well, about eight o'clock last night the phone rang. I didn't answer it so I don't know whether it was a man or a woman. Susan took down the receiver. I heard her say, 'Yes, this is Susan Flannery,' and that was every word she did say. She listened for several minutes, maybe two or three. And then she just put the receiver back on the hook. She didn't say a word to me and I didn't ask her nothing. These young girls today, you just don't ask them about their private affairs anymore."

"And then what did she do?"

"She didn't do nothing. We was sitting down to supper and had just started and we just sat and finished supper. But she was sort of thoughtful and didn't hear me a couple of times when I spoke to her. We don't talk much anyway when we're having supper. We're both tired and we just don't talk much.

"After supper she went to her room and came out in about twenty minutes. She said she'd decided that she wanted to go away for a few days. She seemed kind of tense and excited but when I started to question her, she just shut me up. After all, she earns her own living and it's been a long time since I've been able to tell her anything."

"Do you think she was meeting anyone ..."

Mrs. Flannery jerked up her head and her chin came out.

"I'll have you know my Susan is a good girl," she said. "She's not the kind to be meeting anyone. Anyway, she's got a boyfriend, and when Joe gets a promotion they are planning on being married and Susan isn't the kind ..."

"Could she have been meeting this Joe?" I asked.

Mrs. Flannery shook her head.

"No. Joe called about ten o'clock, a half hour maybe after she left. He didn't know nothin' about it."

"Well, do you know of any relatives or perhaps a close girl friend ..."

Mrs. Flannery shook her head emphatically.

"She just said she wanted to go off by herself for a couple days. Said she'd call me sometime tonight and tell me where she was."

I talked to her for another fifteen or twenty minutes and I am pretty sure she was telling the truth. I don't think she knows where her daughter is or why she left. I don't know myself. But I am certainly going to try to find out.

So that's the way my day starts out. I lose a witness. I stop down at the Tombs to see this bum they have finally dried out so he can stop shaking long enough to talk and make a little sense and I learn nothing. I am back now at Clayton Andrews' studio apartment down in Greenwich Village and he's in the bathroom getting his clothes on.

He was in his bathrobe and slippers when he answered the door and said he'd been working all night. He looks like hell and maybe he was working or maybe he wasn't, but it's a cinch he didn't get a lot of sleep. I feel sorry for him—I guess he's taking it pretty hard—but I am going to have to put him through the wringer anyway. There are a lot of things he's told me which don't seem to iron out. And he has one of these alibis I hate. There is no way of either proving it or disproving it.

My eyes keep wandering around the walls of the studio as we talk. There must be at least a dozen or more oils of Patricia Andrews. Some are completed and in frames, most are not. There are other paintings, so I think he must use this place mostly for the serious work he does on the side. There are a number of nudes, but most of the paintings are portraits. I don't know whether any of the nudes are his wife or not. They all seem to be the same body, but in every case, he has painted the girl with her head turned so that the face doesn't show.

He is very nervous, smokes incessantly and lights one cigarette from the butt of the previous one. He hates every second of this conversation, hates my questions. But he is answering the questions and even if he resents them, I can see that he has his emotions under control. But I have the feeling he may crack at any second.

"You strike me as a man who was very much in love with his wife, Mr. Andrews. One thing puzzles me. We know—you have said as much yourself—that your wife was unfaithful to you. And yet you deny that you resented it, that you were jealous. That you felt any desire to retaliate or punish her."

He looked up at me and blinked rapidly.

"You don't understand about Pat," he said. "Sex didn't mean anything to her. With me or anyone else. She was a good, a kind person. She never learned how to say no. And because it never really meant anything, sex didn't actually have anything to do with her real feelings and emotions. She just went along and did foolish things."

"But it must have meant something to you?"

He was quiet for a long time, evading my eyes and staring blindly down at the floor. Finally he spoke, and his voice was very low.

"You have to try to understand about love," he said. "Suppose—well let us suppose you had a wife, or perhaps a son, who drank. Who was a drunkard. Who was sick and couldn't stop or could not control himself. Would it make you stop loving him and trying to take care of him? I don't think so, not if you really loved him. No matter how much it hurt you. And you wouldn't in your heart really blame him. You would try to cure him."

"And if the cure didn't work?"

"You would keep on loving him."

I nodded.

"This is true," I said. "It is true if you can look at sex and promiscuity as a disease. But let us say that sex became something else. Suppose that sex, instead of being merely a meaningless and pointless thing, became something else. Suppose your wife were to have fallen in love. In love with another man. And that sex did take on a meaning for her. How would you have felt then?"

He spoke up very sharply, and this time he stared me in the face and his eyes were hard and unfriendly.

"My wife was in love with no other man," he said.

"I am sorry, Mr. Andrews. Sorry to have to say this. But from what I have learned, I believe you are wrong. I think your wife was in love with Joel Siddel. This architect who has disappeared."

He stood up, and for a moment I thought he was going to hit me. His right hand tightened into a fist and the blood left his face. He lifted his arm and took a step forward. He stuttered when he spoke.

"You're a stupid fool," he said. "A stupid fool. My wife was in love with no one. Joel Siddel—Joel Siddel is one of my best friends. One of Pat's and my best friends."

"Sit down, Mr. Andrews. Sit down. Certainly it is not news to you that your wife and this Siddel, this best friend of yours, were having an affair. Had been having an affair for more than two years now."

The blood came rushing back to his face and when he again spoke his voice was a whisper. A whisper filled with endless misery.

"I knew about it," he said. He looked up quickly. "But it was like the others. It was meaningless. It was only that Pat was lonely. In many ways I failed her. I am older, I have other interests. Things she didn't care about. And Siddel is a charming man and he liked her and paid attention to her. But it didn't mean anything. It was like the others."

"But this man was a good friend of yours, your best friend. Are you trying to tell me you didn't resent the fact he was sleeping with your wife, whether it meant anything to her or not?"

He stood up and crossed the room, and perhaps it was unconscious and perhaps not, but when he spoke his voice was almost a whisper and he avoided looking at me. Instead he stared at one of the portraits of his dead wife.

"I hated the son of a bitch," he said.

"Why did you let it go on for so long?"

"At first I simply didn't believe it. I knew she had slept with other men and God knows that bothered me enough. But I didn't believe it about Pat and Joel. I couldn't believe it. I thought it was the way she said it was. That she liked him and admired him. That they had a platonic friendship and just enjoyed being with each other and talking with each other. But finally I knew."

"And when you finally knew, was it your wife who told you?"

Andrews shook his head.

"She never told me and I never asked her."

"Why?"

"Because if she had admitted it to me we would have left each other. She would have left me or I would have left her. And I didn't want to lose her. No matter what, I didn't want to lose her. I knew that so long as we could pretend, so long as I didn't actually face her with it, that sooner or later it would be over with. I was afraid to bring it into the open."

"I think I understand," I said. "But Mr. Andrews, there is one thing you still are not being honest with me about. You knew that with Siddel it wasn't just another casual, meaningless affair. You knew she had fallen deeply in love with the man, didn't you?"

He turned to me now and the way he looked at me, I could see he was begging me to believe him and to understand.

"She was infatuated with him," he said. "Infatuated—like a schoolgirl. She would have gotten over it. It was just something she had to get out of her system."

I was tearing his guts out, but I couldn't stop. I had to go on. I had to learn the truth.

"Why, if she was in love with him, would she have gotten over it?"

"Because Joel was not in love with her. He was never in love with anyone but himself. He was incapable of love. He didn't know what the word meant. Sooner or later, she would have known and understood. Understood that he had merely used her when it suited his convenience to do so. And she would have gotten over it."

"And you insist you forgave her? That this time, this one time when she really did fall in love with the man, you forgave her?"

"I forgave her. You see"—and he looked at me almost pleadingly—"you see, that's what love really is. Understanding and forgiving. Pat fell in love with Siddel, whether he was worthy of that love or not. Whether he returned that love or not. And I was in love with Pat—whether or not she was worthy of that love and whether or not she returned it. Do you understand?"

"Yes. I think I understand."

I stood up and reached for my hat. At the door I turned.

"And Siddel?" I asked. "How about Siddel? Have you forgiven him?"

"If I knew where he was, I would find him and kill him," Andrews said. "I would kill him because he took her without loving her."

I hesitated one minute more.

"You would kill Siddel because he didn't love your wife," I said. "Let me ask you just one more thing. Do you think Joel Siddel could have killed your wife because she did love him and he wanted to get rid of her?"

Andrews looked at me and slowly shook his head. He wore the travesty of a smile.

"I would be happy to put that bastard in the electric chair," he said, "whether he's guilty or not. I'd even try to do it if I thought there was a chance in hell it would work. But Joel didn't kill Pat. It wasn't his hand that held the gun that put the bullet in her heart. That isn't his style. Joel Siddel is far too selfish ever to take a chance like that. He doesn't kill the women he drops; he just uses them and leaves them. No, if Joel has disappeared, is hiding out, it is just because he's a coward. He may think the police believe he did it. Or it may be he was there and saw who did it and is frightened and has panicked. Is waiting for the killer to be picked up and put behind bars before he dares show his face.

"There is one other thing. Siddel knows that now Pat is dead, I blame him no matter who pulled the trigger. He knows the second I see him I am going to kill him if it's the last thing I ever do."

"You had better think that over a long time, Mr. Andrews," I said. "Killing Siddel won't bring your wife back. It will solve nothing. It will merely smudge and dirty her reputation. If you still love her, you'll do nothing to besmirch her memory. And there does happen to be a law against murder. Even justifiable homicide. You still have your own life to live. The only vengeance you should seek is vengeance on the person who did murder your wife. And this vengeance the state will take care of."

"Perhaps. Perhaps the state will. But you have to find your murderer first, Lieutenant," Andrews said.

Businessmen are forever accusing government employees and officers of every crime in the book. Negligence, malfeasance in office, stupidity, incompetence, bribery, corruption and God-only-knows-what. Public servants are supposedly totally unrealistic, hopelessly inadequate for their particular work. But frankly, when I see an outfit like this Markey Publishing Company, I don't know where they get a leg to stand on.

If the police commissioner ran his department like Harold Markey runs his publishing business, he'd be tossed out of office overnight and the whole damned city would fall to pieces. Maybe the people at Markey know something about getting out magazines and making a fast dollar, but it is damned sure they don't know anything about integrity, or honesty or even human decency. The last certainly goes for Harold Markey himself. He seems to be uniformly hated by the people who work under him, and after four days of seeing too much of him, I can certainly sympathize with them.

The Flannery girl has been missing for two days now. Siddel, the architect, still hasn't shown up. And I wouldn't be a damned bit surprised if a couple of more Markey employees were very shortly among the missing.

My bet is that young Creamer is just about ready to flip his top. Pringle, who I found out has been stealing consistently from the firm for a couple of years now, is either on the verge of being fired or will panic and try to make a break for it before he is indicted for larceny.

From what Mrs. Markey has told me of what happened a couple of days ago (and *that* marriage is certainly one where each of them deserves the other), Pringle will probably be facing a blackmail charge as well.

Creamer surprised me. When I suggested he take a lie detector test, I really thought he was lying about drawing a blank the night of the party when he drank himself into a stupor. But he was only too willing. It didn't mean, of course, that he failed to remember what he did. It just meant he was pretty sure either that he didn't do anything which could incriminate him, or that he thought he could get away with the test without trouble.

Well, the test proved one thing and one thing only. It proved he very likely doesn't remember what happened. Because, when it came down to cases, it was just about the most unsatisfactory test we have ever given. Any question asked concerning those key hours, from eleven o'clock Friday night until four o'clock the following Saturday morning, came up just about as blank as Creamer says his mind was during the interlude.

So we are right back where we started. He could have taken the gun—we feel there is a strong possibility it was his .38 automatic that was the murder weapon—and shot Patricia Andrews to death, could have been so drunk he doesn't remember a thing about it. And the lie detector would never be able to do us the least bit of good. Or he could be completely innocent and still have drawn a blank, and again the lie detector would do us no good at all.

As to what he has done and what he does remember, he has been far and away the most cooperative witness we have had so far. Damned near too cooperative. Half the time it is almost as though he is disappointed that he can't break right down and confess to us he committed the murder. It doesn't quite seem natural somehow.

Certainly he had no reticence in telling us he was in love with the woman. He even seems proud of the fact that he broke up his own marriage over her, that he squandered his money buying her presents, that he made a complete fool out of himself for a love which apparently was not even partially reciprocated. He admits he was mad with jealousy, wanted to kill any man who came near her. He says when he took that gun out of his desk drawer he was seriously thinking of killing Joel Siddel or killing himself. He has even gone so far as to confess he had considered killing Patricia Andrews and then taking his own life. In fact, the damned little fool seems almost obsessed with the idea of railroading himself into the electric chair.

There is only one thing which really makes me wonder. Is this all just one great big act? Is there a chance that he did, coolly and deliberately, kill her, that he knows he did and is putting on this act to throw us off the trail?

Does he realize and understand at this point, that on the strength of the evidence he has given us, none of which would really stand up in court, we don't actually have a case against him? At least not one on which we could obtain a conviction. And that as long as he sticks to this "drunk and don't remember" act, it is going to be almost impossible for us to get a clear-cut case against him—assuming he is guilty. Can he be this subtle? This clever? I wonder.

Creamer keeps harking back to that hour or so he spent in his office when he was crying his heart out on Santa Claus's shoulder. Again I wonder why. And I think it damned odd he could talk to some guy for an hour or more and not have any idea who the guy was. And there's another thing. Hubert Pringle and Markey both deny they know who played the part of Santa Claus at the party. Pringle hired him and Markey paid him and it isn't like Markey, from what I have seen of him, to give money without knowing whom he is giving it to.

Pringle's story about picking up some bum off the street could be true. God knows, at this time of year there are literally hundreds of men working in department stores and other places playing Santa Claus, and it is quite reasonable that one of them would be willing to put in a few extra hours at night to pick up a few extra dollars. Pringle could, as he claims, have just seen him on the street in the Santa costume and hired him for the night. Given him a ten-spot to come in for a few hours. But somehow I get the impression Pringle is lying about it.

Of course, if Pringle is telling the truth, we'll dig up our Santa Claus sooner or later. We're checking the stores in the neighborhood, checking the employment agencies. I don't think it is going to make a lot of difference when we do turn him up, but it's a loose end and I don't like loose ends. In any case, it may take a load off young Creamer's mind. Creamer seems to think he showed this Santa Claus the gun and told him what he was planning to do with it. Or was it someone else he showed the gun and talked with? He was pretty drunk.

One thing which makes us feel very sure the gun was used in the killing is the fact it has disappeared. This phony Santa Claus could have taken it, of course, but it doesn't seem too likely. Guns aren't hockable, at least in New York State. Especially this kind of gun, unless there are a damned lot of questions asked.

Guys who are willing to work half the night dressed up in a Santa Claus costume for a lousy ten-spot aren't usually the ones who go around stealing anything as hot as a .38 automatic. But the killer could have taken it. If Creamer had it lying out there on his desk when he passed out, just about anyone could have walked in and grabbed it.

One thing does baffle me. If the gun was taken for the premeditated purpose of murdering Patricia Andrews, why wouldn't the slayer leave it at the scene of the crime? It would have been a perfect way to frame young Creamer. Or is the killer keeping the gun to use in a second murder?

It has been a theory of mine for years that all criminals are essentially stupid. A man who is reduced to crime in order to solve his problems has to be stupid to some extent or other.

I think Hubert Pringle is a perfect example. If Pringle had not been so utterly stupid as to try to bribe or blackmail Bertha Markey, it is very possible we would not have learned about his stealing from the publishing firm. At least not for a while in any case. Nor would we have learned about that old record of his. I'm afraid it's a case of once a thief, always a thief.

Pringle didn't strike me at first as a stupid man. But then again, he didn't strike me as a thief. He has turned out to be both. Could he be a murderer? He doesn't strike me as that either.

I rather doubt the last, of course. Small-time office workers who steal from their companies very rarely go in for the more violent types of crime. Blackmail, forgery, that sort of thing, yes. But not armed robbery, not assault and certainly, very rarely murder.

No, I think Pringle is merely a stupid, second-class larcenist who happens to be caught up because of bad timing and a bad break. If Patricia Andrews hadn't managed to get herself killed after that office party, he probably wouldn't have been exposed for some time to come. But sooner or later he would have slipped, and so as far as he's concerned, it doesn't really matter too much.

It is very possible that Pringle knows something about what has happened to the Flannery girl. He certainly has been evasive when we have brought her name up.

This man Pringle has surprised me all the way through. I have just had a telephone conversation with Detective Sergeant George Maidens, who has been working on the Coster and Sons jewel robbery. I talked with him after I learned Pringle was frantically in need of money. I had a sort of wild thought that Pringle might have been involved in that burglary, which took place the night of the Markey office party.

When I learned Pringle was desperate for money and had a criminal record dating back some twenty years, we checked him out very thoroughly. It didn't take us long to learn that his brother-in-law, who lives with him, has recently been released from the penitentiary. For a moment it looked as though we were about to wind up the Coster case, even if we were getting nowhere on the Andrews woman's murder.

Maidens went out to the Pringle house and talked with Pringle's wife, and he was disappointed to learn from her that this Marty Feathers, her brother, never left the house Friday night. She swears to it, and she is the sort of woman whose testimony would stand up in front of any jury.

Maidens called to tell me that Feathers has purchased an airline ticket in Pringle's name. A ticket for a flight to Brazil which is leaving in another forty-eight hours. Is it possible Pringle did rob the jewelry firm and is planning to fence the gems through his brother-in-law? Is it possible that that is the real reason he is planning to leave the country, rather than because he is about to be exposed for stealing from his company?

There is only one fault to the theory. Why, if Pringle robbed the jewelry company, would he have been trying to blackmail Markey? If he had gotten away with several hundred thousand in jewels, he wouldn't be interested in a small-time blackmail attempt.

No, it simply doesn't add up.

It is a shame they haven't been able to more accurately pinpoint the time of that robbery. All we know is that it occurred sometime between eight o'clock Friday night and nine o'clock on Saturday morning, when Coster's bookkeeper came in and discovered the safe blown open.

But one thing is sure. We must not let either Pringle or his brother-in-law out of our sight. Sergeant Maidens still thinks Pringle is an excellent suspect, but he bases his entire theory on Pringle's desperate need for money and his record of pilfering from his employers.

We could, of course, arrest Pringle and hold him on a larceny charge, but to do so might alert his brother-in-law if the two acted in conspiracy in the robbery. After all, we can always pick him up, and at the moment he might well be of more value to us out of jail than in.

Once you start stirring up one of these mare's nests, it's amazing the things you find out about people. Markey is the president and principal owner of a very prosperous publishing business and apparently as solid as gold. But we have learned he has been playing the market on the side and has taken a terrific beating during the last few months. On his own level, it is very possible that Markey is as desperate for cash as Pringle is on his. From what I have seen of Markey, he would stop at nothing to solve his problems.

But I can't waste my time worrying about a jewel theft; I am working on a murder investigation. The way my witnesses keep disappearing, I may be working on a couple more murders before I am through.

If this man Joel Siddel fails to show up within a very short time, the district attorney will undoubtedly take out a warrant for his arrest, charging him with murder. We have, at this time, enough circumstantial evidence to justify such an action.

There is no doubt at all that Siddel and the Andrews woman made plans to meet at the Uptowner Motel. We have at least two witnesses who overheard them discussing it. We know Siddel left the office party shortly after Patricia Andrews left. We have shown a photograph of him to the desk clerk at the Uptowner and he is positive he saw the man in the lobby some time during the early hours of Saturday morning.

Siddel could very easily have picked up the .38 automatic which young Creamer had on the desk in his office. The one weak point in the case against him is a lack of sufficient motive. It is true they had been having a romance and that he'd tired of it, but would that be a strong enough reason to have inspired him to kill the woman? It doesn't seem reasonable. On the other hand, they could have had a fight and he could have lost his temper. There is always the possibility he may have had a motive of which, at this time, we are utterly unaware.

But the main thing is, he is missing. People do not simply disappear for no reason at all.

On the other hand, there is the Flannery girl, who has also disappeared for no logical or known reason. One thing is certain; we can eliminate her as a possible suspect. But somehow or other, she must be involved. Is it remotely possible, if Siddel killed Patricia Andrews, that Susan Flannery might have knowledge of the crime and have presented a threat to him? Could he have tracked her down and destroyed her as well?

It appears that not just Siddel knew Patricia Andrews was planning to check into the Uptowner; several other persons were also aware of the fact. Certainly her husband knew. Mrs. Markey knew, and if we can believe her, young Creamer also heard the argument between Siddel and Mrs. Andrews. Could Mrs. Markey have told her husband about it?

The one person who apparently didn't know was Pringle. On the other hand, Pringle is also one of the few persons who had no motive for committing the crime.

But almost anyone at the party could have picked up Creamer's gun. Could have used it. As well as Creamer himself.

If Siddel had also been found dead in that room with her, I could solve this case in five minutes. I wouldn't be talking with Clayton Andrews, I would be placing him under arrest. Had Clayton Andrews walked into that motel room and found Siddel in bed with his wife, he wouldn't have killed his wife, he would have shot Siddel. He might, of course, have killed them both, but he would have been sure to get the man who was cuckolding him.

The same would be true of Creamer, whether he was drunk or sober. After all, aside from her husband, Creamer had perhaps the strongest motive of all for committing the crime. Unless blackmail can be considered a motive, and in that case, Markey himself is far from in the clear.

If it was Markey who followed her to her room in the motel, he would have waited until Siddel, or whoever else was sleeping with her, had left, and then committed the crime. There is no real reason to believe it didn't happen that way in any case.

But at the moment, Joel Siddel seems our best and most obvious suspect. We must find him and find him as soon as possible. We must also find Susan Flannery, very possibly to save her before our killer finds her. I can't help but believe that she is in danger.

2

SUSAN FLANNERY

Oh God, have I been a damn fool.

I never should have listened to them, that subway guard and those others. The fat man with the briefcase who said he was a doctor, the people standing around, the motorman on the subway train. They tried to tell me I was hysterical, that I was in a state of shock or something like that. Told me it was an accident and it could have happened to anybody and instead of worrying about it, I should thank my stars I was lucky and that the colored boy had the guts to jump down on the tracks and pull me over under the platform. Not but what I didn't damn near die of fright anyway.

Yes, they told me it was an accident and because I wanted to believe them, I did. But I know better now. I know it was no accident. Somebody pushed me. Somebody tried to kill me.

I'm nineteen years old (even if I don't look it because of the good care I take of myself) and I have been around a lot and I thought I knew everything. But what's happened these last couple a days, well as they say in books, I've lived a couple of lifetimes. Also I have almost died, too. Been murdered like that Mrs. Andrews. Someone tried to kill me, someone wants to kill me.

I never thought there was anything in this world I would ever be afraid of, unless something like Ma dying and me being out of work at the same time. Well, Ma isn't dead, but I am out of work and I am scared stiff. I'm scared it's me that may do the dying.

Joe was right about one thing. He said I shouldn't go to the office party last Friday night. He said no good would come of it. Somebody should have told me how much bad would come.

I never should have taken a job with Markey Publishing Company in the first place. From the very beginning I had a feeling there was something creepy with that outfit.

I don't know what this is all about. I don't know why somebody pushed me off that subway platform on my way home Monday night, don't know why I got the money in the mail, don't know why I got those phone calls.

All I am sure of is one thing. It started when I went to that office party.

For hours now I've been sitting here in this hotel room trying to figure it out, trying to make some kind of sense out of the whole thing, and the more I think about it the less sense it makes. I have been to plenty of parties before, a lot better ones and a lot worse ones.

That business with Mister Markey. It was very disgusting, but I've been through worse. I got pretty boiled, and on the way home I had to ask the cab driver to stop while I leaned my head out the window and all. But I've thrown up my cookies before. Had hangovers before. Outside of Mister Markey, I danced around a little and I guess more than one guy didn't want to dance so much as he wanted a free field day, but that isn't unusual, especially at a party.

So I don't know what it was, but I am sure the thing started last Friday night when I went there. Mrs. Andrews went to that party and she ended up dead. Of course I didn't do what she did and leave the party to go to a motel with some guy—although more than one asked me—but I still think these things that have been happening, the reason I am sitting here in this room afraid to move out of it and afraid to let anyone know where I am, are tied up with something that happened at the party.

The first thing was after Joe picked me up for our usual Saturday night. I knew right away the way he acted he was spoiling for trouble. Instead of taking me to the Chinese place where I like to go, Joe insisted on that crummy Italian restaurant, and he knows I hate the smell of garlic, even if I do eat a pizza now and then.

He started right off with the cracks about me being used to champagne and all those fancy drinks they probably served at the party last night, I probably would find the dago red a little disgusting, so I knew he just wanted to start a fight of some kind.

Joe is an Italian, but I know he doesn't like that kind of food, so he was just doing it for spite. That's the way the evening started.

I could tell the way he didn't ask me anything about the party, but kept telling me I looked like I got no sleep and all, what was on his mind. I finally said to him, "Mr. Prado"—he hates me to call him that even if it is his name—"Mr. Prado, if you think I look so bad you are ashamed to be seen in a public place with me, maybe you had just better take me back to my residence and spend the evening with somebody who you may think looks better."

He didn't say anything and we finished dinner, which was very greasy and didn't make my stomach feel any better, and then he asked me what show I would care to see. Well, sometimes on Saturday night we do go to a movie but more often than not we go up to Joe's apartment, which he shares with his sister who is always out on Saturday night until all hours.

I knew when Joe suggested the movie, instead of me, he was really taking a burn because Joe is the one who always wants to go right back to his place after dinner. We usually just sit around and play records and do some smooching, because being engaged and all and just waiting until Joe gets a little more money until we get married, I have insisted I am not the kind of a girl to go all the way with a man until we walk down the aisle.

I felt that if he wanted to be like that it was all right with me, so I said yes, I would like to see a picture and I suggested we go into Manhattan to the Palace because I know he hates to go all the way in when pictures just as good are playing in Brooklyn.

Joe had his sister's Chevy, and we started for Manhattan and that's when he got the idea this car was following us. I thought he was kidding because he said it was probably one of my secret admirers or some boyfriend I had on the side, but after what's happened Joe could have been right. Somebody could have been following us.

We went to the Palace and the picture was lousy, and afterward, because Joe seemed to be feeling a little more friendly, I agreed to go back to his place for an hour or so. When we went into his apartment, he left the lights off and started right in on me.

I must say I was surprised and it wasn't like Joe, because usually we just sit on the couch and he kisses me and loves me up and I may let him put his hand down my front and feel my breasts, but nothing else.

This time he just threw me on the couch there in the dark and tried to start right in and when I told him what was what, he said something about like I let other guys so why shouldn't he, especially as he's going to be my husband when he gets more money.

Well, I didn't like that crack about other guys because Joe knows darn well that I am a virgin, or anyway, I know he doesn't really know and he is sure I am a virgin, which is why I never let him really do anything. So I shook him off and got up and turned on the lights and said, "What's got into you anyway? Have you gone a little nuts or something? What kind of a girl do you think I am, and is this any way to act toward your fiancée?"

I guess I put him to shame, because he did calm down then and the rest of the evening went all right and in fact because he seemed so sorry for everything and acting like an animal, I did let him go a little further, and I let him put his hand on my leg and move it up.

Lately I have been thinking a lot about when Joe and I get married and if he really would be able to tell that I wasn't exactly what I said I was, on account of I understand men can tell and nobody believes those horseback-riding stories anymore, so I sort of figured I would take advantage of the situation and let him do something to me with his hand.

I did, and I guess he got pretty excited too. It is a lucky thing his sister came in just when she did or I guess maybe Joe wouldn't be marrying a real virgin after all.

At least that is the one good thing that happened, because now I don't think when we get married Joe will be able to tell that I have been letting I don't know how many different guys go to bed with me ever since I was fourteen years old, and I did it the first time with my uncle Tim because he said he'd buy me a fur coat.

Joe got me home at five o'clock, and I was so pooped I stayed in bed all day Sunday and Ma was sore because I didn't make mass. Monday I went to work as usual and all those cops were around asking questions and it was Monday night after I left the office that the thing happened in the subway.

That five-fifteen crowd on the IRT is always murder, which is another reason I never should have taken the job at Markey Publishing because there are plenty of jobs for a girl which will let her out at a quarter to five so she can miss the real worst of the jam. But I went over to Grand Central and did my usual pushing to get toward the third car of the local, which isn't quite as bad as the others.

There were a million people crowding and shoving as usual and I was way up near the front of the platform, which is probably what saved my life.

The train was coming in and I could feel somebody right in back of me, but I thought it was just another fresh guy trying to get his free kicks by getting too close, when all of a sudden somebody put a hand in the middle of my back and pushed.

I was already on the edge of the platform and the train was slowing down. But it wasn't just a push. I didn't even have a chance to barely open my mouth to really tell the louse off—I guess I had just started to turn my head when I felt myself go. They say I really did scream then.

I don't even remember falling or hitting the track, but I must have because of this lump on my head.

Things happened so fast then that I don't even remember exactly what did happen. I know one thing though. It's going to be a long time before I walk into a subway again without my heart going into my throat and the sweat breaking out.

The only thing I really remember is lying there half under the platform with this colored boy covering me with his body, except of course I didn't realize he was colored right then. Although frankly, I wouldn't have minded if he'd been a Jewish Chinaman. And hearing the sound of the iron wheels on the tracks as they screeched to a halt with all the brakes on.

I guess it must have shook up those people on the train, coming to a stop like that.

Later, I found out that if that colored boy hadn't leaped down on the tracks when I fell—when I was pushed—and rolled me under that platform, they would have been picking up pieces of me from under the second car.

I got this nasty cut on my head and I was bruised up a lot, but I wasn't really hurt bad. The subway guard insisted I go to a hospital and get an examination anyway. I guess they were afraid of what I would do when I saw a lawyer or something.

There was a policeman and he asked about a million questions and wrote it all down in a little black notebook. When I told him I thought someone had pushed me off that platform, he just laughed and wanted to know if I had been drinking. It sure burned me up. He said I was pushed all right, but that it was an accident. Everybody gets pushed in subways. I could see whose side he was on, all right. I should have known better than even to talk to him. Policemen aren't interested in poor people. They only protect the rich and big companies that own things like subways.

I'm smarter than they think I am and I wasn't going to any hospital. I told them I would have my own doctor examine me so they called a cab and one of the men who worked for the subway insisted on taking me home all the way to Brooklyn.

It was just as well Ma wasn't in when we got there because I was pretty shook up, but I'd made up my mind not to tell her anything about it. I still wasn't really convinced that it was anything but an accident, but I was beginning to worry about it.

If it wasn't for the telephone call maybe I never would have known.

The call came while I was deciding whether I should try to call a doctor, just to be sure nothing really was wrong with me. It was a man's voice and he said, "Is this Susie?"

There was something funny about it, I don't just know what, but all at once I seemed to know there was something wrong.

"This happens to be Miss Susan Flannery," I said. "And who is speaking?"

For a minute or so all I could hear was a kind of heavy breathing and then he spoke again.

"You were very lucky, Susie," he said. "But I am going to give you some advice. Stay out of subways—you may not be so lucky next time. And stop talking to policemen. They won't believe you anyway."

Well, you know I honestly didn't get it at first. I started to say something like, "Now say, just who is this?" or something, but all of a sudden it hit me, and my hand began shaking so much I could hardly hold the receiver. I don't think I could have spoken then if my life depended on it, and while I was still sitting there shaking and trying to catch my breath I heard the receiver being hung up on the other end of the line.

Ma didn't get home for another half hour and I was in bed when she came in. She knew something was wrong but she didn't ask me anything after I told her I had a cold and didn't feel well, and I guess she just thought Joe and I had had a fight or something.

But I didn't go into work the next day. I wouldn't have taken a subway into New York for a million dollars.

The mail came at eleven o'clock the next morning and again I was lucky because Ma was out getting some things at the grocery. There was just the one letter and it was addressed to me. I almost fainted when I opened it and found the three one-hundred-dollar bills.

No letter, nothing. Just the money. I was still trying to figure it out when the second phone call came. This time when he said, "Is this Susie?" again, I knew the voice at once and I just gasped.

"I want you to take a two-week vacation, Susie. Leave tomorrow. And when you get back, take another job."

By now I was so shook up I hardly knew what I was doing. I only knew one thing. I didn't want to be there when Ma got back. She'd know something was wrong and she'd start deviling me and I just couldn't take that. So I got my clothes on and I left her a note and said I had decided to go into work after all since I was feeling better, and then I left the house.

I just had to try to figure it all out.

Until that envelope with the money came, I thought someone was trying to frighten me, or maybe even trying to kill me for some crazy reason or other. But why would anyone who was trying to frighten me or kill me send me away on a vacation with three hundred dollars? It just didn't make any sense at all.

I left the house and went to a movie because I can always think better when I'm watching a movie.

It suddenly occurred to me that maybe Mr. Markey was back of it all. Maybe he got scared about what he did at the party and was afraid I would talk or something. Maybe that's why I was told to get another job. Maybe that's why I was told to stay out of subways and not go to work.

The more I thought about it, the more sense it seemed to make. Except why would someone have pushed me off that subway platform? Mr. Markey would have had enough sense to know that I would be only too glad to have a vacation for free. He wouldn't have to go around pushing me off subway platforms.

On the other hand, the way he acted in that office the night of the party, he certainly seemed like some sort of nut and you can never tell what a kook will do.

The more I thought about it, the sorer I got, until after a while I forgot to even be frightened anymore, I was getting so mad. I decided that if he was so worried, it should be worth a little more than a vacation and a lousy three hundred dollars, and that's when I decided I would just make a telephone call and find out a thing or two.

It's lucky for Mr. Markey he wasn't in or I would certainly have told him a few things. When I left the phone booth in the lobby of the theater I went back in and saw the picture over again. Then I went on home and I must have still been sort of upset because I could tell the way Ma looked at me she knew something was wrong. She didn't ask any questions though and I guess she still thought Joe and I had been having a fight.

We were sitting down to eat when the last phone call came and this time I just listened. It was the same voice, but it didn't sound like Mr. Markey, although I have never heard his voice over the phone.

I'm in this hotel room now and I am scared to death and it was that last phone call which finally did it. Just what he said and the way he said it.

"If you are not gone by tomorrow, Susie," the voice said, "you will never be alive to have another chance for a vacation." And he hung up.

Maybe I should have told Ma then what it was all about, or maybe I should have called Joe or something. I don't know. I only know that after that last phone call I really started getting scared. I was scared to go anywhere and I was scared to stay where I was.

I thought about going to the police, but then I remembered they hadn't believed me when I told them I was pushed in front of that subway train. They certainly wouldn't believe some nut sent me three hundred dollars through the mails. All they'd do is take the money. I decided the best thing to do was just disappear for a while until I could figure what it was all about.

I finished dinner, and then I went into my room and packed a bag and told Ma I was going away for a few days. I would have called a cab, but I didn't want Ma to know anything, so instead I went down to the candy store on the corner and called one from there.

I went to this hotel over in Manhattan on Eighth Avenue, which I remembered from the time about four months ago when the man I was working for took me there, so I checked in there and didn't use my own name.

I sat down then and began to think things over. I was glad I'd decided to quit my job. I'd had all I wanted with Markey Publications. The more I thought about things, the surer I was that it was Mr. Markey who'd sent me the money. I guess he started worrying about what he'd done to me the night of the party. He was probably afraid I'd talk and get him in trouble. But my God, he didn't have to go shoving me in front of a subway. I thought again about going to the police, but I knew it wouldn't make any sense. They would never believe me and I had no proof it was Mr. Markey who'd tried to get rid of me. They'd take his word instead of mine.

I began to get mad all over again. If he thought he could get by just paying me off with a lousy three hundred dollars, I was going to have a surprise for him.

The next morning I tried to get him on the phone again a couple of times but I didn't have any luck. They wanted to know who was calling, but I just said a friend. I wasn't going to give anyone my name.

I sat in that hotel room all day and all night and I can tell you I was worried. Worried and frightened. The money wasn't going to last forever. One thing I finally decided. I had to get some more money, and there was only one way I could figure to do it. I had to get it from Mr. Markey, whether he was the one who tried to kill me and sent me that three hundred dollars or not.

I went down to the lobby and got a paper and read that they were having the funeral for Mrs. Andrews Friday. That's the woman who was murdered the night of the party. It gave me the shivers.

I tried Mr. Markey again today but I was smart and gave the girl a phony name when she asked who was calling. This time I did get him. When I told him it was Miss Flannery, he pretended he didn't know who I was and then I explained I was the girl he did things to at the office party.

He knew then, all right.

He didn't sound at all like the man who called me at the house and threatened me, but that doesn't mean anything. I can change my voice over the phone when I want to.

When I said I wanted to see him, he said he was busy. I told him I would come in the next day and he told me he wasn't going to be around. He had to go to a funeral. He was half nasty and then he got nice and wanted to know if I could come up and meet him in his office after dinner that night.

Well, I was too smart for that. I sure wasn't going to take any chances on seeing him alone, in his office or anywhere else.

"After what you did to me in your office and tried to do in the subway," I said, "don't think three hundred dollars is going to square it."

He didn't say anything for so long I thought he'd hung up on me. And then he yelled like a bear.

"You're nuts," he said. "What the hell you mean, three hundred? You must be out of your mind."

He hung up.

He's not going to get away with it. I'll see him, all right. And not in his office, either. Not alone. The safest place will be out at the funeral tomorrow. If he's trying to hurt me, he wouldn't dare do anything in broad daylight and especially in a cemetery. I'm going out to Woodlawn tomorrow and see Mr. Markey and he's going to have to get some real money up.

In the meantime I'm staying right here in this hotel. I'm not going down any more subway stairs and I'm not going to go back home or anywhere else where anyone will know where I am at.

I still think someone is trying to kill me. Maybe I should go to the police after all. But if I do, I sure won't get any more money.

Maybe it isn't Mr. Markey at all. Maybe it's someone else.

3

HAROLD MARKEY

One thing I am absolutely sure of is that the only reason Bertha called Manny Gottlieb in when I had that attack of acute indigestion after dinner tonight is because she was trying to scare me to death. Manny Gottlieb may be on the staff of Flower Fifth Avenue and he may have graduated at the top of his class at Cornell, but he's a hell of a poor doctor if he can't tell the difference between a simple gut ache and a heart condition.

I'm going to take his advice and check in for a cardiogram and a general physical checkup after I get back from the funeral tomorrow afternoon, but it isn't because I think he knows what he's talking about. Nobody can tell me that a man of my age, in my shape and as strong as I am, can suddenly have a heart condition without having had some previous warning of it.

I'm paying him, so I'll do what he wants me to, but he is barking up the wrong tree.

A nervous stomach, yes. And why not, after what I've been going through these last few days? But a heart condition? Don't make me laugh. The only thing wrong with my heart is probably that it's too big. Even Bertha had to admit that closing the office tomorrow because of Pat Andrews' funeral is a lot of damned foolishness and a lot more than I really should have to do.

A couple of people around this place are going to find out damned soon that Hal Markey doesn't have quite as big a heart as they think he does. That Hal Markey isn't as big a sucker as they have taken him for.

Monday morning young Creamer gets fired. I don't give a damn how good an editor he is, he's through. And Pringle? Pringle I am going to send back to prison, where he belongs. Send him back where I got him from, the goddamned ingrate. I'll teach him to steal from the man who picked him out of the gutter and tried to make something out of him.

There are going to be several surprises around this place when we open up again on Monday morning. I may be in a little trouble myself, but a lot of other people are going to be in even more trouble.

At least there is one bum I am not going to have to fire in order to see that he gets what he's been asking for, and that's Clayton Andrews. I wouldn't be a bit surprised if Andrews is under arrest for the murder of his wife before the weekend is over.

The thing that always amazes me about people is how really stupid they are. Take Creamer, now. Did he think I wouldn't find out about those things he told that detective lieutenant? Did he really think I wouldn't find out? He's supposed to be smart, but if he was half as smart as he thinks he is, he could have guessed that I had a reason when I offered to let the police use my office while they were interviewing the hired hands. He could have guessed I would have a tape recorder take it all down.

But compared to Pringle, Creamer is a positive genius. Doesn't Pringle think I know about the money he's been stealing the last few years? Is he so incredibly stupid he doesn't realize I have purposely let him get away with it? He should have been satisfied to have a good thing going and let it go at that. But then he turns right around and tries to sell me down the river to my own wife. Good God!

He's going to be a little surprised to know that I've come back to the office tonight and that I am going over the books, getting the evidence that is going to put him behind bars until he's an old man.

That girl who called up. I suggest she come up here to meet me and she starts talking about three hundred dollars. She must have been either drunk or crazy. Probably drunk. She was muttering some nonsense about a subway.

Three hundred dollars. Good Christ, what does she think she has anyway? She was smart to quit before I bounced her. If she calls back again, I'll offer her three dollars and she'll probably grab for it.

I'll give Bertha credit for just one thing. She was bright enough not to pay off Pringle. But it wasn't loyalty. It's just because she thinks she has enough on me that she doesn't have to buy anything else.

I guess Bertha is going to get the biggest surprise of them all. Loyalty. Jesus! I think I resent her lack of loyalty more than anyone else's. I guess I never will really understand women. She thinks I have a heart attack and goes to the trouble of calling a doctor. And then, ten minutes after he leaves, she reminds me that she's my alibi for the time Pat Andrews is killed and asks me to turn over another thousand shares in the company.

When this Andrews business is all over and Clayton is indicted for the murder of his wife, Bertha is really going to get a little shock. I'm going to let her know about that power of attorney she signed when she thought she was just signing a routine insurance form. And I'm going to let her know what happened to that stock she's already sucked me in for over the past ten years.

The nice part is there won't be one single damned thing she can do about it. Maybe she would have been smarter to make a deal with Pringle.

This place is certainly lonely this late at night. Even the damned cleaning women have left. I've gone through Pringle's desk and from some of the stuff I have found, I'm beginning to think it might be a good idea to do a little checking on some of the other people around this place. It's almost midnight, but I'm not really tired. This damned indigestion has come back and I think I'll take a few minutes off and have a small Scotch and soda.

I can't say I look forward to tomorrow. If there is one damned thing I hate, it's going to funerals. But it wouldn't look right if I didn't show up for Pat's.

I can't understand how that cop was so sure we had an affair. It's a damned cinch Clayton wouldn't have said anything, even assuming he suspected. Bertha probably guessed, all right, but she has too much pride to mention it, and I can't guess who else might have known.

It's a cinch I never told anyone and I doubt like hell if Pat did, unless maybe she talked to Siddel. On the other hand, the cops themselves haven't been able to turn him up, so how could the police be so sure about it? It really doesn't matter, however. They can't arrest you for screwing somebody, even if that somebody does go out and get herself killed.

It's a funny thing, but somehow or other I do feel sorry about her. I suppose in a lot of ways I'm a son of a bitch, but I did really like her. At least she wasn't a phony. She never made any pretense about caring for me. Made no bones about the fact the only reason she let me lay her was because of Clayton. That she was paying off for his job.

Well, in this world when you want something, you gotta pay for it, and I guess in the long run she did care about him. She was certainly willing to pay.

That was one relationship I never will be able to figure out. She double-crossed the guy up and down the line and yet she was willing to go all out to advance his career. Of course, as I say, I never will understand women.

Pat's mistake was Siddel. How a smart broad like that could flip for one of those phony collar-ad boys is something I will never understand. I guess it was some sort of poetic justice she should make as big a fool of herself as a lot of guys made of themselves over her. At least no one can say she hasn't paid the price for it.

I could have sworn I just heard the outside office door open, but I must be imagining things. Who the hell would be walking into Markey Publications at this time of night? Christ, I'm lucky if I can get the bums who work around here to show up in the daytime.

That drink really did some good. Better for indigestion than a dozen Dr. Gottliebs. If one is good, as the man says, two should be twice as good, so I guess I'll have another short one and then go back into Pringle's office and go through that last set of books. When I talk to the D.A. I want to have all my facts. The way I figure it, he's probably taken something like ten or twelve thousand in the last two years alone, and you can bet your life the bookies got most of it.

What with his old record it should be enough to earn him a nice ten-to twenty-year rap.

I'll teach the little ingrate to steal from Hal Markey and then turn around and try to sell him down the river.

I think it must have been Pringle who tipped off the police about the licking I have been taking in the market these last few months. They sure as hell know about it. Pringle probably thinks I am in trouble and I am damned sure Bertha thinks so. But are they all going to get a surprise when they suddenly discover that I am as solid as a dollar!

Sure, I've been hurt, and hurt plenty. But I can afford it now. Markey will do what he has always done. Come out on top. Come up smelling like a rose.

Damn it, there is someone in this office. This time I am not imagining it. That was a door slamming and no one can tell me different.

Now who in the hell can be hanging around this office this time of night? It's a cinch no one was here when I came in.

I better knock this drink off and see who it is.

4

JOEL SIDDEL

I am going to have to do something before I pass out again. This fever is worse—if I read the thermometer right, I am running a little over a hundred and two. I am afraid if I fall into a state of unconsciousness once more, I won't come out of it. I won't be able to do anything, not even get to the telephone and try to get help.

According to the radio, it is half past one, Friday morning. I think I heard the announcer correctly, but I can't be sure. I can't be sure of anything, except that I am a very sick man. I undoubtedly have blood poisoning because of this infected wound and I wouldn't be surprised if I am dying. What a stupid way to die, and for an incredibly stupid reason.

My entire right arm now has become so swollen and sore that I can no longer even close my hand. The pain is almost unbearable and my whole body feels as though it were on fire. It is strange that although I am burning up, the sweat is pouring out of me, and this dirty sheet on which I lie is drenched.

There is only one thing left to do. I must manage to get to the telephone and call this detective who is in charge of the investigation into Pat's murder. I must call him and have him come here and bring an ambulance so I can be taken to a hospital. It still may not be too late if I can only get proper medical attention.

But if he comes I must have my story straight. I must remember everything, every little detail. I must have my story absolutely clear in my mind. There will be no point in getting to a hospital so the doctors can save me, if it will only be to end up facing a murder charge. So I must go over everything, from the beginning. Must remember exactly what took place from the very moment I left that office party until I arrived here a week ago. I must remember in particular what took place in that motel room.

If only I had been able to go out and get the newspapers so I might know what has been going on. But I guess it wouldn't really matter. The papers are little better than the radio, and the police never really let anyone know what they are doing, what they have found out. There is no way of knowing what they have learned, no way of really protecting myself. The only thing I can do is try to remember and then try to make what I have to say fit in with the truth as closely as possible.

That radio commentator said tonight—or was it last night—I really can't remember—anyway, he said the police are seeking me as the missing key witness and that once they find me, they will be able to say exactly what did happen.

Perhaps they are right, but I really suspect that the reason they want to find me is not so much to learn the truth as it is to have someone to lay the blame on. Someone to hand over to the district attorney.

One thing I will have no trouble at all in convincing them of: I was in that motel room with Pat Andrews when she was murdered.

God, I am thirsty! It seems all I want to do is drink gallons and gallons of water. Why in the name of God didn't I bring a glass back with me the last time I went over to the sink? I just can't seem to think straight anymore.

I don't think I will be able to climb out of this bed and make it across the room to the kitchenette again. If I do I won't be able to get back here, and the phone is here next to the bed and if I want to live, I have to be able to use it to call this detective and get help.

I'll have to let the drink go and use my strength to think and get my story straight. I have to have the story right, so that even if I am semiconscious when they question me, I'll get everything straight.

Oh God, why did I ever go to Markey's office party in the first place? I knew Pat would be there and I guess, to be honest with myself, that's why I went. I wanted to see her and have it out with her once and for all. To break it up for good. Stupidly enough, I thought it would be easier to do at the party, with other people around.

I am a coward and I was afraid of a scene.

I knew she would want to see me alone afterward and I just didn't have the guts to turn her down. It wasn't because I was afraid to be alone with her, wasn't because I thought I would weaken. I've known for a long time it was no good anymore. That it was getting neither of us anywhere.

What in the hell is wrong with women, anyway? Don't they understand that everything runs its course? That there always comes the time to end it? That no romance goes on forever?

I was honest with her. Honest from the very beginning. I told her I wasn't the type to get married and, even if I was, I wasn't about to break up someone else's marriage. She knew her husband and I were old friends. And she was willing to keep things on that basis in the beginning. Willing to settle for a small love affair on the side. No one getting involve, no one getting hurt.

God damn women anyway. They can never leave well enough alone. Never settle for what they have. They always want more.

I have to admit that during the first couple of years she was great. It couldn't have been better. But then she had to spoil everything. How many damned husbands does a woman need, anyway?

Damn this pain. It's getting worse. I'd like to take my temperature again, but somehow I can't seem to see very well and I doubt if I could make out the scale on that thermometer. It would only worry me, anyway.

I really should telephone now and not put it off. But I have to get this story straight in my mind. I can't have the policeman come here and start questioning me and just go on rambling about what Pat and I were to each other during those first two years when things were fine. I've got to tell him about what happened the night of the party and what happened afterward.

I just wish I could concentrate a little better and that my mind would stop rambling around.

The hell with those first two years and what we meant to each other. They'll want to know about this last year, the last night that we were together.

I can explain why I agreed to meet her at the motel. They'll understand that. Even policemen are human beings and they know what happens between a man and a woman when one of them decides to break off an illicit romance. They'll know why I agreed to meet her that one last time. That I didn't want trouble or any hysteria or anything that would upset the apple cart.

But dear God, did that apple cart get upset!

Christ, I wish I could get warm. These blankets don't seem to help at all. They just make me sweat more.

Where was I? Pat. That's right, Pat. We met at the party. But I won't tell them it was prearranged and that she called and asked me to meet her there. I'll just explain it was one of those accidental things. We both happened to be at the same place at the same time.

So we ran into each other and we started talking. She told me she was checking into the motel and asked me to meet her there after the party.

That was natural enough. We'd been having an affair. There won't be any use in denying it. Too many people know about it. The police are bound to have found out. I'll be very frank and come right out at once and admit it.

Perhaps it would be best to not even mention anything about wanting to break off the relationship, to end it. Not tell them that was the only reason I agreed to see her after the party. They might think I would go to any ends to finish the relationship. No, I'll just say I planned to meet her for the same reasons we had met each other in secret places so many times during these last three years.

That's best. It sounds logical. And they'll know I am not hesitating to be frank and tell the truth as it is. Lying is always bad, but in this case I think it will be necessary.

The police know she went there to meet someone. They know someone was in bed with her either before she was shot or when she was shot. They are sure to have figured out that I was that someone. I made no effort to sneak into the place. Somebody, a desk clerk or a bellhop or someone, is sure to have seen me. It will be best to come right out and admit it. Simply explain that I went to the Uptowner and went up to her room as we had arranged. Went in and took off my clothes and climbed into bed with her.

Be honest and aboveboard about it. They will understand that I am only trying to tell the truth, bad as it may look.

They will believe me. The police are always ready to believe the worst. I know how they work, how they operate. They'll want a blow-by-blow description. Every single detail. That's how they catch you if you are lying. And that's why I have to have everything down pat. Everything down Pat.

Good God, I must be losing my mind, making puns at a time like this. I guess I really am a little bit out of my head.

Details. They will want every last one. How did I get into the room? Did I have a key? Did I phone up from downstairs? No. She gave me the room number and I just took the elevator and went on up. She came to the door when I knocked. Did she have her clothes on? Was she ...

God, I can't even remember. But it won't matter. No one can remember now except Pat herself and she's dead. Like I am going to be if I don't get on that phone and get an ambulance soon.

So she came to the door when I knocked and she was fully dressed. I went in, and we sat down and had a drink.

No. We didn't have a drink. As I remember, we didn't. We just took off our clothes and got into bed. This part I am sure about because she wanted to talk first, but I knew that if I once got her in bed, she would calm down and after it was over I might get tears, but there wouldn't be the anger. I remember thinking that.

So we took off our clothes and got into bed.

Did we turn off the light? I'll be damned if I can remember, but it won't make any difference. I know that the light next to the bed was on when I left. It was probably on all the time. Just how much detail should I remember? How involved shall I make the story?

Good God, do these damned police have to know everything? Every little sordid fact? What positions we assumed? What ...

Yes, everything. I must explain things right down to the last tiny action. With this wound of mine, and the fact that I still have the gun, which they will find when they come for me, I shall have to be absolutely explicit.

We undressed—the light was on—and naked we climbed into the bed. Under the covers, not on top of them. Every little tiniest detail.

We started to make love. Wild, violent, passionate love. After all, we were not in a hurry. It was to be our last time together.

Damn it all, I'm forgetting. I am not to tell them that. Not to tell them it was a final rendezvous. We just made love. But wild and violent and passionate love, because I had been drinking and it took a long, long time.

I have to be extremely careful here. Have to go into the most intimate sort of detail. Have to make them thoroughly understand, so they will know how it was possible for someone to open the door and enter the room without either of us so much as being aware of it.

I believe it is possible even a policeman will understand that during a moment of extreme sexual pleasure, two persons can be utterly unaware of anything except each other. It should be simple enough for even the dullest mind to follow. We lay there, eyes closed, writhing in an ecstasy of sexual delight, our ears closed to all but the moans escaping from each other's lips.

Naturally we didn't hear the door open, heard no soft footsteps as he entered the semi-darkened room.

Here is where I must be extremely careful. Must explain each second.

He was already in the room. He closed the door behind him softly so that neither of us heard it.

But I must remember. I didn't know that yet. I only realized it later on, when he opened it once more to leave.

These are the small, inconsequential details that can catch one up most easily. The seemingly unimportant. A little thing like the closing of a door. Of course, I could not have known then.

I didn't hear him enter, didn't know he was there. I didn't know when he crossed the room and stood over us, looking down at our bodies on the bed, writhing in a final acrobatic erotic dance.

I must be sure to remember to say that she always kept her eyes closed. And of course, lying on top of her, face buried in her soft neck, hands deep under her and fingers pressing into her rounded buttocks, I could see nothing, know nothing. Know nothing at all until that moment when, spent and exhausted, my breath coming in short gasps, I heard the click as he cocked the trigger of the gun.

The sudden quick movement of my body then as I released her buttocks from my cupped hands and tried to rise and twist. How else can I explain the bullet passing through my shoulder as he aimed at her heart?

And then, simultaneously with the crash of the explosion and the bullet striking me and passing through me and smashing into her, my rolling from her body and half falling   to the floor. A second later, before I could turn, the sound of the deadly second click.

I won't try to say I realized that the gun misfired on his second shot. I wouldn't have been able to know that then. Wouldn't have known until I examined the weapon later.

And there again I must be extremely cautious. Thank God, this long gash on the side of my head will bear me out when I explain that before I could even turn and see who the assassin was, he raised the barrel and brought it slashing down across the side of my skull.

I sank to the floor but did not completely lose consciousness. I could hear his footsteps as he turned and rushed to the door and threw it open. Slammed it behind him as he left.

Shock? Yes, I was in a state of complete shock for several minutes. Until long after the time I could have given an effective alarm. At last I got to my knees, and the first thing I was aware of was Pat lying on the bed with her eyes wide open, the blood welling out of the hole just above her left breast. I too had been shot, by the same bullet which had pierced her body after passing through mine. I had been struck on the head and was in a semi-coma.

My slow trek to the bathroom, the stanching of my wound with a towel. Bathing my face and head in cold water to bring me to. And then the slow return of my full senses. The realization that I was still alive and able to command my body.

My return from the bedroom. The realization that Pat was dead.

I must be careful there as well. How did I know? She didn't seem to be breathing. She didn't answer my frantic questions. I leaned down and felt for the pulse in her wrist and then I put my cheek close to her lips to see if she was breathing.

It will be essential that I convince them I was sure she was beyond all human assistance.

That is where I must be most convincing. That will be the most difficult part of all to explain. To make them believe.

A girl had been killed, brutally murdered. A girl I must have had some feeling for. Hadn't I just finished having a love affair with her?

I myself had been shot. The girl was beyond medical attention, but I needed help. Needed it badly. A killer was on the loose, possibly still in the building.

Why didn't I at once spread the alarm?

I must make these policemen believe two facts.

Pat was dead. Nothing could any longer help her. The capture of her killer, all the medical science in the universe—nothing. That is the first thing.

The second is my sure conviction that my own wounds were superficial. That I was in no danger, either from the lead slug which passed through my shoulder, or from the blow with the barrel of the gun, which undoubtedly had given me a concussion.

Perhaps I can also convince them that because of this concussion, I was not able to think with logic and clarity.

Next came my panic. The realization that someone had killed Pat and tried to kill me. A man who saw and without doubt recognized me, but whom I did not see. A man who will still want to kill me, if for no other reason than because he may believe I recognized him and can be a witness against him in Pat's murder.

They may believe this. They must believe it.

But then why did I do what I did next?

Why did I carefully get dressed, pick up the gun from the floor, conceal it, and then leave the room? Leave the motel and come down here to my hideout in Chelsea and say nothing of what happened to anyone? Why did I do this?

I can have but one answer. Only one.

I was afraid. I am a craven, rotten coward. An adulterer and a coward.

I recognized this .38 automatic. I know whom it belongs to. It belongs to young Johnny Creamer and I saw it the very night of the Christmas party in his office where he was sitting at his desk in a drunken stupor. My prints were all over this gun from picking it up and examining it. What could convince the police that I myself didn't take it from Creamer and follow Pat to the motel and kill her? I said there was another man, but where is the man? Who is he?

Is that man Clayton Andrews, the deceived husband? If so, then isn't it true that he had every moral, if not legal, right to slay the woman who had been deceiving him for years? And shoot down the best friend, who has cuckolded him?

Or could the man be young Creamer, who owns the murder weapon? Could I make that stick? Not if it turns out Creamer had a perfect alibi, something I have no way of knowing.

No, in that moment of panic, while I was hesitating, immersed in my own feeling of guilt, I was suddenly convinced the police would never believe my story and would take the easy way out and make me the killer.

I was on the scene, I had not yet spread the alarm. The gun was available to me. Even now my prints are on it and if I wipe them off, things will look even worse for me.

I would be made to order for them. Who could have a better motive? I know we were overheard fighting at the party. A dozen people would be willing to swear I had been trying to break off our affair. I am probably the one person whom they can be sure was in the room with her when she was killed. I could have shot her, then put this bullet in myself and substituted a fresh cartridge for the empty one.

If they want a perfect circumstantial case, they would have to look no further.

And so I panicked and ran. I ran for a double reason. I was afraid I would be framed for the murder of Pat Andrews. I was also in mortal fear the killer would again make an attempt against my own life. This anonymous killer who knows who I am but who is able to work within the freedom of his very anonymity.

I panicked and I fled. First I stanched the blood from my wound and, tearing up my shirt, arranged a makeshift bandage. I washed and cleaned the wound on my head which had fortunately stopped bleeding. I dressed and then, leaving the room exactly as it was when the killer himself fled, I too departed.

I was weak from shock and in pain, but I was able to make my way downstairs and leave the motel. I flagged down a cruising taxi, which dropped me off at Thirty-fourth Street and Eighth Avenue. From there I took a subway down to Twenty-third street. I staggered up the steps and finally arrived at this studio of mine which no one knows about, aside from Pat.

And Pat is dead.

I needed time to think. Time to recover and plan what to do. I couldn't let this terrible thing which had happened spoil my whole life. As yet I was not too worried about this gunshot wound. It didn't at first seem too serious.

I thought if I had time, perhaps the police would find another victim. Find a man who they could prove committed the murder. Perhaps I would not have to be involved at all. Perhaps it would not even come out that I was the one who was sleeping with her in the motel, and Clayton Andrews would never learn that his wife and his best friend ...

Dear Jesus, but I really must be suffering hallucinations. Why am I worrying about Clayton Andrews or what he will think? Why am I lying here procrastinating?

I was wrong about the wound. An infection has set in and I am sure I have contracted blood poisoning. I need medical attention if I am to live at all. I can wait no longer. Even now it is going to be almost impossible to pick up that receiver from the telephone at the side of this bed and make the call.

It seems to me that man on the radio said Pat's funeral is tomorrow. Or rather today, because the funeral is for Friday afternoon and even now I can see the first signs of the dawn through the east skylight and so already it must be Friday morning.

I would like to have been able to go to Pat's funeral because, although I didn't love her, I had a very definite and strong feeling about her. She was able to make me very happy, very often. Someone who really liked her should be at her funeral. I wonder how many who hated her will be there.

This damned phone seems a million miles away.

My eyes are really going on me and I shall never be able to see a number in the phone book. Years ago I remember seeing the telephone number of the police headquarters. SPring something or other. But it doesn't matter.

You just ask for the operator. Or dial the operator. The last hole in the dial.

"Operator? Is this you, operator? The police. Get me the police ...!"

5

BERTHA MARKEY

"I wish to speak to Lieutenant Goodwin. Detective Lieutenant William Goodwin."

"Who's calling, please?"

"It doesn't matter who's calling. I just want to speak to ...!"

"We have to know who is calling, ma'am. Your name, please?"

"Well, if you must know, this is Mrs. Markey. Mrs. Bertha Markey. And I'd like to speak ..."

"Who do you wish to speak to, ma'am?"

"I already told you once. Lieutenant William Goodwin."

"I'm sorry, ma'am, Lieutenant Goodwin isn't in the office at the moment. If you would tell me what it is in relation to ..."

"You just ring me through to Lieutenant Goodwin. I said this is Bertha Markey and it's important and I am sure the lieutenant ..."

"The lieutenant is out of the office at the moment, ma'am. If you would tell me what you want the ..."

"You policemen keep hours like bankers. Well, anyway, it's about my husband."

"Your husband, ma'am?"

"That's right. My husband. Harold Markey. The publisher."

"What about Mr. Markey, ma'am?"

"Well, he didn't get home last night again and I ..."

"I'll transfer you to Missing Persons, ma'am. If you'll just hold the line a moment ..."

"I don't want Missing Persons. I told you I want to talk to Lieutenant Goodwin. Detective Lieutenant William Goodwin."

"I'm sorry, ma'am. Lieutenant Goodwin is not in the office at the moment, but if you would care to tell me ..."

"Oh, for God's sake. I already did tell you. It's about my husband. About Mr. Markey. He's the publisher and he didn't get home last night and ..."

"We'll be glad to relay a report to Missing Persons, Mrs. Markey, if you will just give us ..."

"Say, are you stupid or something? I didn't say my husband was missing. Mr. Markey is no more missing today than he's ever been missing when he goes to some cat house or something and stays out all night. But this time I am fed up with it. I've had it. If that louse thinks he ..."

"We can't help you find your husband, ma'am, unless you make an official Missing Persons ..."

"For God's sake, I don't want to find him. I just hope he gets lost and stays lost. But I'm tired of lying for him and covering up and this time he's gone too far. So if you will just get me Lieutenant Goodwin ..."

"If you want your husband to get lost, ma'am, I'm afraid that is out of the province of the Police Department. However ..."

"Get lost yourself. You and your Lieutenant Goodwin. I'll go directly to the district attorney and the hell with all of you ..."

"You can reach the district attorney's office at REctor—"

Bang!

Did I slam that receiver down on the hook! It's no wonder the police in this city never solve a crime. Until you've tried to have dealings with them, you simply wouldn't believe that the Civil Service or whatever it is could find such a completely stupid and incompetent collection of idiots. Here I am, trying to do their work for them and give them the essential clue that will solve a crime that for an entire week has completely baffled them, and I can't even get hold of the man who has been in charge of the investigation.

Well, if the police don't want to get the credit for solving a murder they would never be able to solve themselves, they can go straight to hell. And I won't go to any district attorney, either. I'll go right down to the *Daily News* and I'll tell them what I know and let them print it, and then we'll see who's sorry.

Missing Persons, bah! We'll see who's missing before I get through talking and telling them what I know.

I've warned Hal. Told him for years that someday he would go just one step too far. Someday there'd be the straw that breaks the camel's back. And this time he's put that straw on my back.

God only knows I've taken plenty and I might have taken plenty more, but this time he went just one step too far.

When I think how I rushed to telephone Dr. Gottlieb last night after he made a pig of himself at the table and ended up with indigestion. It's like it's always been. He does something wrong and I do the worrying. Trying my best to be a good wife and take care of him.

He can laugh all he wants but you can't tell me he didn't think it was a heart attack when he got those pains. But I should have saved my worries. He wasn't so sick he couldn't make an excuse to get out, once the doctor gave him the pills and the pains went away. He wasn't so sick—he lied to me and never went near the office and just used it as an excuse to stay out again all night.

Maybe he thinks I'm stupid or something and wouldn't check up. But I did. As soon as I felt up to it after Pringle left, as soon as I got over the shock of what he came to tell me, I called the office, even if it was after midnight, and as usual he lied. He wasn't there. No one was there.

It's lucky for him he wasn't. I would have told him plenty.

Well, Mister Harold Markey is going to have one great big surprise waiting for him when he does show up again. This time he can read about it in the newspapers. He may have one of his tall stories for me about where he was last night, but I couldn't care less. What he'd better do is figure out a story to tell Lieutenant Goodwin and the police about where he was and what he was doing a week ago after he left the office party.

He's going to find that the police are a lot harder to fool than a simple-minded wife.

When I think how I was all prepared to lie and perjure myself for that man—after what he's done to me—it makes my blood boil!

I am certainly glad he did go out last night. If he'd stayed home, maybe Pringle wouldn't have come here and told me about that power of attorney Hal had me sign under false pretenses. Wouldn't have told me about Hal's transferring that stock of mine back into his own name. Wouldn't have told me about his selling it later to pay those gambling debts of his, because he was so stupid he managed to lose money when everyone else in the world was making money in the stock market.

Remembering how Pringle tried to shake me down for information about Hal the other day, at first I just didn't believe it. But then, when he told me he didn't want money anymore and was just telling me so I would know what kind of man I was married to, then I had to believe him. And after I went to the safe-deposit box at the bank this morning, I knew it was true.

Wife or no wife, those stocks were mine and belonged to me and when he tricked me and took them it was stealing, and he isn't going to get away with it.

I may not get those stocks back, but Hal Markey is going to pay dearly for taking them.

I know there is some law that says a wife can't be forced to testify against her husband, but there is nothing that says she can't if she *wants* to. And there certainly isn't any law that says she has to lie to protect him.

If Hal made me lie to Lieutenant Goodwin about his coming home with me after that party, there has to be a good reason for it. He's covering up something. I can put two and two together as well as the next one, and I think the police are going to be pretty interested in a couple of other things besides his not coming home with me and not getting in until after daylight the next morning.

They'll be interested to know that I told him I overheard Pat Andrews giving Joel Siddel the room number and the name of the motel where she was found murdered. And I told Hal that Siddel came right out and said he wasn't going to keep his date with her. That should interest them.

He's going to have a lot of explaining to do. He's going to have to explain what he was doing in Johnny Creamer's office after Johnny passed out. Creamer has already said somebody came in and took that gun away. I don't honestly think Hal could be so stupid as to follow her to the motel and kill her, but with that man you never know. Maybe he just wanted to get back that piece of jewelry I am sure he gave her, even if she did say it came from her husband. Who knows? They could have had a fight over it.

Anyway, whether he did shoot her or not, he's going to have a lot of explaining to do, and this time it isn't going to be a simple thing like telling his wife of twenty years a lot of lies. He'll be up against a lot tougher competition when he faces those policemen.

One thing I'm sorry I didn't do. I should have had Hubert Pringle sign a sworn statement about Hal making me sign that phony power of attorney. I'd go down and see him at the office this morning and try to get it from him, but the office is closed because of the funeral.

In any case, I guess Pringle is all through with Markey Publications. He didn't seem very shook up when I told him right out last night that I had informed the police he tried to sell me information about Hal's infidelities, and he must know that by now the police have told Hal about it. And Hal will know soon enough that it was Pringle who told me about the power of attorney and how my own husband swindled me out of my stock.

But I have enough troubles without worrying about Pringle or what's going to happen to him.

I wanted to go to Pat Andrews' funeral today but I am going to have to miss it. After all, I did contribute the flowers.

I'll make one more try and see if I can't reach Lieutenant Goodwin, and if he's still out, I am going right down to the *Daily News.*

They'll be happy enough to hear what I have to say.

6

JOHNNY CREAMER

"What did you want to see me about, Creamer?"

I looked at the lieutenant and then my eyes went to the uniformed patrolman who was typing at a desk under the window. I nodded toward him, said, "I'd rather tell you in private."

Lieutenant Goodwin looked at me oddly for a moment, his head bent over his desk, merely raising his eyes so that the whites showed under the iris.

He gave a half grunt, turned to the other man and cocked his head toward the door. The patrolman got up and left the room, carefully closing the door.

"I came in because I heard the report over the radio," I said.

"The report?"

"About Joel Siddel. I understand he has given himself up."

Lieutenant Goodwin nodded.

"Has he admitted the murder?"

Again I got that curious look.

"Why should he?"

"Well, I understand that when he was picked up he was in possession of the murder weapon," I said. "That was the report on the radio."

"You can't believe everything you hear on the radio," the Lieutenant said. "He is merely being held for questioning."

"It is probably an unusual request," I said, "but I wonder if you would be able to do something for me. I'd like very much to talk to Mr. Siddel."

This time the lieutenant took his attention from the papers on his desk and looked me straight in the face. He put his head on one side and said softly, "Why? Why do you want to talk with Siddel? Is it because you think he is in trouble and needs help? Because you are good friends?"

I shook my head.

"We are not friends at all," I said. "It is because of the gun. The radio said that the police found a .38 automatic on him."

"And?"

"And I think it is just possible the gun may be the one that belonged to me."

The lieutenant nodded, understandingly.

"I see," he said. "Unfortunately, Mr. Siddel is not available at the moment."

"Not available?"

"Mr. Siddel is in Bellevue Hospital, under heavy sedation."

"But when he comes out of it, will he be able to receive visitors?"

"He is in the prison ward, under guard."

He was watching me closely for a reaction. The radio had said nothing about his being ill, nothing about his being in the hospital. The report had merely said he had given himself up and come in for questioning.

I started to stand up.

The lieutenant made no move. He waited until I had turned toward the door. "What makes you think it might be your gun?"

I stopped. Already I was sorry that I had come in to talk with him. It merely goes to show how upset I have been. How utterly unable I am to think straight, to act with reason.

"Well—as you know, I had a .38, and on the night of the office party the gun disappeared. Something must have happened to it. Perhaps if I were to see the gun that was found with Siddel, I would be able to identify it."

Lieutenant Goodwin nodded. He looked down at a paper on his desk and read it for a moment. I am sure he didn't have to read to know what it said.

"We can set your mind at rest, Mr. Creamer," he said. "It is the gun that you owned and that you say someone took from your desk. You see, we checked back when you told us about having the gun. You said you bought it from a sporting goods house in Nevada, and they had a record of the sale. Of course, you know it was a violation of the New York State Sullivan Law for you to have the gun?"

"I know," I said. "You already told me that. But I knew it anyway. I wondered why I wasn't arrested because of it before this."

"We didn't have the gun as evidence," Goodwin said dryly. "We only had your word that you still possessed it."

"Am I going to be arrested now?"

The lieutenant smiled thinly. "Not at the moment," he said. "However, you can expect that charges will be made sooner or later. The fact that you confessed to owning the gun, have been completely frank about it, is in your favor. That is, of course, if you weren't the one who used it."

"Are you saying it was my gun that killed Pat Andrews?" I asked. "Would that make me something like an accessory before the fact?"

He ignored the first part of the question. He said, "The only way you could be an accessory before the fact would be by giving someone the gun when you had knowledge of his intention to use it to commit murder. You have already told us you didn't know who took the gun. Can I assume that you also had no knowledge that a gun was going to be used?"

I blushed, annoyed. I didn't think it was any time for facetiousness.

"Sit down again for a moment, Mr. Creamer."

I returned to my seat and he in turn stood up and began to walk back and forth as he talked.

"Let me see if I have it straight, if I remember exactly what you did tell us about that gun. As I recall, you told me that on the night of the office party you were upset, emotionally disturbed. That you became quite drunk and were feeling sick and somewhere around ten o'clock went into your office. Drank from a bottle you had in your desk drawer. The gun was lying there and you took it out. As I remember, you said you were in a very deep state of depression and for a moment or so considered the possibility of using the gun to commit suicide. Is that right?"

I nodded, not looking at him.

"And why were you so depressed?"

"I think I told you," I said. "My wife and I have recently split up. I haven't been feeling well. I have been drinking too much lately and can't seem to control it. My finances are in pretty bad shape. I told you all about it."

"And there were no other reasons?"

This time I did look at him. I knew what he was getting at.

"I don't believe I care to discuss my personal life," I said. "I was depressed. That should be sufficient."

"And are you still depressed?"

I didn't say anything.

"Mrs. Andrews' funeral is this afternoon," he said.

I gritted my teeth but again I kept still.

His voice again changed, and it was as though he hadn't thrown in the remark.

"And as I remember, you told us that sometime during the evening one or more persons came into your office while you had the gun on your desk and you remember vaguely talking to them."

"That is right."

"But you haven't been able to remember exactly who they were?"

I nodded my head. No.

"Could one of them have been Joel Siddel?"

"I have already told you I don't remember. When I get drunk, very drunk, I simply don't remember things."

"Could one of those persons have been Mrs. Andrews? I am sure that if she came in you would remember."

"Yes," I said, "I probably would remember. But I don't think she came into the office."

"Why would you have remembered her, and not someone else?"

I wished to God he'd stop talking about Pat. I was sorry I was insane enough to have come here in the first place.

I was having another of those ghastly headaches and nothing seemed to make any sense at all. I didn't know what was wrong with me. I really did think I was losing my mind.

I stood up.

"I don't know what possessed me to come here," I said. "I am not feeling well and I think I had better leave."

"What possessed you to come here? Why, you came because you were interested in Mr. Siddel."

"That's right. So I was. You said Siddel was under heavy sedation. In the hospital. What is wrong with him? Is he ill?"

He spoke very casually when he answered.

"Quite ill," he said. "You see, an infection set in and he didn't take care of it."

"An infection? What sort of an infection?"

"Why, from the wound," the lieutenant said, as though he were surprised at my not knowing. "An infection from the bullet wound he received when the .38 slug went into him."

My eyes grew wide and I fell back into the chair. For a moment I was dizzy and thought I was going to faint.

"Don't take it so hard." The lieutenant's words barely reached me. "After all, you have just explained that you were not friends. And by the way, you asked before if your gun was the one used in killing Mrs. Andrews. I forgot to answer. It was."

But I was no longer listening, no longer hearing him,

I suddenly realized that I wouldn't be going to Pat Andrews' funeral this afternoon. I wouldn't be going anywhere at all.

For a week I had been living in a state of semi-shock. I had been surviving in a living hell. Trying to think back, trying to remember. I thought perhaps because I drew a complete blank during that time on Friday night and Saturday morning while I was dead drunk, that if I were to get drunk all over again, it might come back to me. But nothing came back and the drinking did no good. I even found it hard to get drunk. The liquor gave me no solace, not even when I finally passed out each night. Because when I came to again in the morning, it started all over again and each time it was worse.

I had this terrible sense of impending disaster, completely illogical, because the disaster had already occurred. It started when my wife asked me for a divorce, it reached a climax when I finally realized I meant less than nothing to Pat, the only woman I have really ever loved. It came to an end when I learned that she was dead. So why didn't it go away? Nothing could happen any longer that would touch me in the slightest.

I had this sense of guilt. A sense of guilt that was a lot stronger than the normal feeling of guilt experienced by everyone who has been drinking heavily.

God, I was sorry I hadn't had the courage to take that gun last Friday night while I sat there in the office and put it to my temple and pull the trigger. One thing was sure: if I had, Pat would have still been alive. I was sure of this.

Until a moment before, I really hadn't known. Hadn't known what had actually happened. But then I knew. Then at last I was sure. Then I understood why my conscious mind had refused to remember. I hadn't dared remember.

I know very little about modern psychology, but a few things I do understand. I knew why I had this sense of guilt. Because I was guilty. I knew why I couldn't remember. I simply couldn't face, with my conscious mind, what I must have done.

The facts were irrefutable. And I think I must have known it all along. It was my gun, the gun that killed her, the gun that shot Joel Siddel. If ever a man wanted to kill another man, I wanted to kill him when I heard Pat arranging to meet him that night after the office party at the Uptowner Motel. Perhaps in my insane jealousy, I too wanted to kill her. I know that at one time I told her if I couldn't have her, no one would. I must have really meant it.

I couldn't remember where I was late that Friday night and early Saturday morning and there was a good reason I couldn't remember. I couldn't remember because I was unable to face the things I must have done during those hours.

I told this Lieutenant Goodwin a few minutes ago I didn't really know why I came here this noon. But I did know. I must have wanted to confess. I must have subconsciously been driven to coming here and telling the truth at last.

For some reason my headache miraculously cleared up. My mind was functioning perfectly for the first time in days. I was feeling ...

"Are you sure you are feeling all right, Mr. Creamer?"

I looked up and I suddenly realized that I had pushed his hand away and the glass of water had spilled on my trousers.

"Yes. Yes, I am all right now."

"Can I get anything ..."

"Get a police stenographer. I want to make a statement. I want to confess the murder of Pat Andrews."

7

HUBERT PRINGLE

It's a damned funny thing how the habits of twenty years hang on. The minute I walked into the office and saw all the lights on, the first thing I thought about was bawling the janitor out on Monday morning. It's his responsibility if the cleaning women don't turn off the lights when they finish up for the evening.

I am afraid I really do have the soul of a bookkeeper. Eighty-nine one-hundred-watt bulbs—I counted them once—from seven in the evening until nine in the morning, seven nights a week, three hundred and sixty-five nights a year, at six and a half cents a kilowatt hour, would come to ...

And who gives a damn. I had to laugh as I suddenly realized what was going through my mind. I am probably the very last person in the civilized world to care if Hal Markey is out a few dollars because a cleaning woman forgot to turn off the lights.

I walked down the hallway and went into my office for the last time. I wanted to clean out my desk before I left.

I had thought I would have plenty of time, but since finding out the police are having me followed, I realize that time is running out on me. I wasn't sure at first and thought it was only in my mind, but since leaving Bertha Markey a short time ago, I now realize the man I have been seeing these last few hours and who was waiting for me outside of the apartment house is one of the detectives working with Lieutenant Goodwin.

When I leave here, I must be absolutely sure to shake him before I meet Marty in the men's room in that dismal little bar on Eighth Avenue at twelve noon tomorrow. I will be safe enough here for a while, perhaps even through the rest of the night and tomorrow morning, as no one will be in in the morning, with the office closed because of the funeral. But I don't think it is a good idea to just wait around.

If the police are already having me followed, it must mean they plan to make an arrest, and I can't take a chance on that happening before I see Marty and pick up the Pan Am ticket he has for me, and the money.

I never really believed that Marty Feathers, my brother-in-law, would come through in a pinch, but perhaps Martha has been right all along. Perhaps this brother of hers really does have a spark of decency and loyalty in him somewhere. Perhaps the leopard does change his spots.

On the other hand, it is more than possible it isn't pure altruism that has inspired him to come up with the money and the ticket. Maybe he merely figures it is worth it to get me out of the house for good. What is truly surprising is that he was able to get his hands on the money. He must have had a private little nest egg put away all along.

In all fairness to Marty, I must admit he's always been crazy about Martha and it is very possible he is only thinking that the disgrace of my arrest and trial would probably half kill her.

Still and all, I am surprised he is willing to help me out of this jam. But I mustn't look a gift horse in the mouth. It's enough that he is doing it for me.

I can't waste time worrying about it now. I've got to get on with things, get this desk cleaned out and then think about how I am going to shake that cop downstairs. It will never do to have him on my tail when I meet Marty.

It must be almost midnight, and it has taken me less time than I thought it would. It is amazing how a man can spend twenty years on a job and then, in something less than half an hour, clean out his desk and prepare to leave an office in which he has spent so much of his life, leaving no trace behind him.

Is it possible I am having regrets, now that it is all over and I shall never again sit in the chair, behind this desk, in this office?

It is going to be awfully hard to start all over again.

South America! God, I don't even know the language. I'll have almost no money. I won't even have a proper identity and I won't know a single soul. I don't really know how I will manage. But anything will be better than being behind bars. I'll simply have to play it by ear and try to get by some way or other. It won't be easy.

If I only had a little more time, a little more cash. I should have made more of an effort to get money from either Bertha or Hal Markey. My tragedy is that I am not even a competent crook.

Marty said once I located in South America, he would try to send me a little to help out, but I can't count on him.

I'm afraid that from now on, the only person I will ever be able to count on will be myself. So I had better get on with it. Had better go into Hal Markey's office now and break into his desk and take the few hundred dollars I know he always keeps in the locked right-hand top drawer. It should be easy enough to jimmy it open.

I never dreamed I would stoop to common burglary.

But I have no option. I must get hold of every cent I can lay my hands on.

So if I must do it, I better get started. If I wait I may lose my courage.

I still can't understand why all these lights are on. At midnight on Thursday.

The larger hand of my wristwatch is pointing directly at twelve. The small hand points to three.

I have been back here in my own office for almost three hours. I have been sitting here trying to gather my wits, trying to think what to do. Trying to understand what happened and how it could have happened.

But all I can think about is what is down the hallway in that office I left just after midnight. All I can think about is Hal Markey's gross body, lying here on the floor, the blood welling from the cut on his forehead and spilling down across his dead face and staining his shirt and jacket.

The telephone is ringing again, but again I shall let it ring and not answer it. Exactly as I didn't answer when it rang the first time, almost three hours ago, within minutes of the time I walked into Markey's office and saw him sitting there at his desk, a glass of whiskey in his hand.

I don't know which one of us was the most surprised when I softly opened the door of his office and faced him. I believe he was just beginning to stand up from behind his large flat-topped mahogany desk, which faces the door as one enters.

For one brief moment I stood there frozen and speechless, rooted to the thick pile of the wall-to-wall carpeting that covered the wide expanse of floor between us.

It is a large rectangular room, with a huge red leather couch, red leather armchairs, a large portable bar and rather elaborate furniture. The room has indirect lighting and a fireplace that doesn't work.

It looks more like a gentleman's private den than a business office.

His desk is at the far end of the long room, between two huge windows that are concealed behind heavy velvet draw curtains. There is a second door along one side of the room that leads to a private bathroom. The door through which I entered is activated by a pneumatic closing device and the door gently closed behind me as I stood there motionless, my eyes wide with surprise, my face suddenly losing all color and my mouth half agape.

Yes, he must have been just starting to get up from behind his desk, because for a split second he didn't see me. Wasn't conscious of me until I was already in the room.

He held the almost empty glass in one hand, the other hand on the desk, helping him rise. And as he started to straighten, his eyes lifted and looked straight into mine.

For an endless moment we stood staring at each other and then he slowly sank back into his seat. "Why, come right on in, Pringle," he said, his tone almost sugary.

For twenty years now I have always called him Mr. Markey. He has never called me anything but Pringle. Never Mr. Pringle and never my first name, Hubert. I think this, more than any other thing, has annoyed me most. It is probably rather petty, but that subtle distinction, that small blow to my dignity and pride, has irritated me more than anything else in our relationship.

Until he spoke, I had been overcome with a sense of guilt and embarrassment. But the moment he said "Pringle," I regained my composure and my sense of anger.

I did something I had never done in all of the hundreds and thousands of times I had entered that office. I walked over and dropped into one of the large red upholstered chairs without being asked.

Markey frowned but quickly changed his expression, smiling suddenly with a flash of friendliness that fooled me not at all. I could see he was getting ready to play his usual cat-and-mouse game. He knew I had no right entering his office unbidden and he knew that I knew it as well.

"An odd hour for a visit," he said in his too-smooth voice, "but I am always glad to see you, Pringle. Perhaps you will be kind enough to tell me what brings you here? Is it because, as a loyal and faithful employee, you feel that you must get your work done no matter how many hours you devote to the job? But no, it couldn't be just that. You don't, as I recall, do your work in my private office, do you?"

I said nothing; there was nothing I could say.

But my silence didn't bother him. He wasn't anxious for me to speak. He was too fascinated with the sound of his own voice. Too anxious to pursue the cat-and-mouse game. It was a favorite trick of his, asking questions to which he well knew there was no logical or reasonable answer.

He sat back in his chair and put the fingers of his pudgy hands together so that they formed a tent, and he smiled, half nodding his head.

"On the other hand," he said, "perhaps you aren't paying this little visit tonight merely because you are a loyal and hard-working employee. Perhaps it is because the sort of thing you do best is done after dark. After everyone else has left the offices. Correct me if I am wrong, but I do understand thieves always work best at night. Am I right? Am I correct in this? Is that why you are here, Pringle? Because you are a thief and this is the proper hour for you to do your work?"

I could feel the flush coming to my cheeks and when I spoke I know my voice quivered, and it infuriated me almost as much as his words did.

"Is that why *you* are also here, Mr. Markey?" I said. "Because you too are a thief and prefer to work at night?"

I expected the remark to infuriate him. I was trying to infuriate him. For a second there was again the faint trace of a frown, but he quickly recovered, and I knew that my remark had been childish and inadequate and that I was merely playing into his hands.

He leaned back and roared with sudden laughter.

"Well, well," he said. "So I am a thief, too. That is good, Pringle. Really very good. And just whom have I stolen from?"

"You have stolen dignity and pride from everyone you have ever had working for you," I began, but he roared again with laughter and quickly interrupted me.

"You'll have to do better than that, Pringle. Men like you have no dignity or pride. Men like you are common sneaks and thieves. No, I am afraid I am in a different class altogether. They don't put a man in jail for stealing dignity and pride, as you call it. Although I really can't see that you have either for me to steal, even if I wanted to. But what you steal is money. You steal money from your benefactor and employer."

He stopped smiling now and stared at me coldly. The stare he had always used with such total effectiveness in bulldozing those who worked for him and depended on him for their livelihood.

"And you, Mr. Markey, steal from the woman you are married to. I can see little difference."

He leaned suddenly forward with his heavy arms on the desk and his tiny reddish eyes half closed as he sucked in a long breath of air. There was no trace of a smile now on his flushed face. He spoke in a tight voice.

"Just what do you mean by that?"

"I think you know what I mean. I am talking about that phony power of attorney you had Mrs. Markey sign. I am talking about that stock of hers you took out of the vault and transferred to your own name and later sold to pay off your stock market losses."

He stood up then, leaning hard on the desk and glaring at me.

"Be very careful, Pringle," he said. "Very careful. I don't often lose my temper."

For some reason I was not afraid. I knew that he had a capacity for violence. Knew that he was capable of physically attacking me and that I would never be able to defend myself against his brute strength.

I also stood up.

"For twenty years I have been taking your insults and listening to your snide insinuations," I said. "And for twenty years I have been wanting to tell you exactly what sort of swine you really are. The time has arrived ..."

He began to move around the edge of the desk and I could see that his mouth was twitching as he attempted to get out the words that were choking him. His face was beet red and he looked like a man about to have a stroke.

I backed up toward the side of the room where the phony fireplace was and my hand instinctively reached out and rested on the iron poker that was there strictly as a decoration.

"Why you—you goddamned little pipsqueak! I'll break every bone in your thieving body."

He started toward me then and I half raised the poker.

"Don't you come near me," I said. I am afraid my voice changed then to a falsetto.

I backed up a step, but he came on.

"If you dare raise that poker," he began and then he choked on his words and his hands reached out to grab me by the lapels of my jacket.

I struck then, hitting him on the forehead with the poker, and he stopped dead in his tracks.

It seemed to me that we held the tableau for minutes on end. He just stood there, hands half raised, eyes staring at me in wild disbelief.

I saw the blood suddenly breaking through the skin where the poker had struck him. I stood frozen, waiting in a state of complete paralysis for his huge, ham-like hands to reach out and take hold of me. I was unable to move.

His eyes seemed suddenly to lose focus, and his chin dropped. I think he started to say something, then, as the saliva drooled from the corners of his mouth, he lurched forward. My own eyes closed and I could feel my body weaving.

There was a sudden crash as he rolled over on his side, and when I opened my eyes he was lying at my feet, his hands spread out in front of him. I could see the shudder go through his huge frame, and then his mouth emitted an odd, rattling sound and he was still.

It was a full two minutes before I was able to make my way over to the bar and find the opened bottle of Scotch and pour myself a drink.

I swallowed it, choked. And then I filled the glass half full and went back to where he lay stretched out on the floor. Stooping down, I put one hand under his head to raise it so that I might pour the liquid down his throat.

There was blood on my hand, and I believe I started to say something. It took me several seconds to realize he was not conscious. That he couldn't hear me. I was surprised because I believed the blow from the poker wasn't that hard. My arm had been only partly raised, and the end of the wrought iron instrument had traveled but a few inches.

It took me seconds to realize he was not conscious; it took me several minutes to realize he was dead.

It was while I was rising to my feet after listening in vain for a heartbeat that the telephone began to ring. I looked over at the desk and then, with my eyes filled with horror, slowly backed to the door and turning, twisted the knob.

And now it is three o'clock and I have been sitting at my desk for hours, adjusting my mind to the reality that I am a murderer.

I have been trying to get up the courage to return to that office down the hallway and break into the desk drawer and get the money I am now going to need more than ever. But I know at last that I shall never be able to do it. Nothing in this world could force me back into Hal Markey's private office. Nothing could force me to ever again look into the dead face of that man whom I have hated for so many years.

I have been tempted to call the police and explain exactly what happened. That the whole thing is some sort of nightmarish accident. That I lifted that poker in self-defense and only meant to stop him from attacking me. That finding him suddenly dead at my feet was a complete and utter surprise and that I had no intention of killing him.

But who would believe it?

I am not even going to return to wipe my fingerprints from the handle of the poker. It would be a waste of time. The detective who followed me all evening saw me enter the building and knows I am up here. There is no hope of merely running away and hoping no one will find out.

Hal Markey has played his final and dirtiest trick on me. There is nothing left to do but go through with my plans. I must get away from this building and somehow or other get rid of the detective who is waiting downstairs for me. I must stay out of sight until noon and then I must go to meet Marty and get the airplane ticket and the money from him. If I am lucky, very, very lucky, they won't find the body until I am already on the plane and well on my way.

It was easier than I thought it would be.

Sitting here in the darkened security of this Forty-second Street movie house, I am amazed at both my audacity and the success of my maneuver. Is it possible that I have the talents of a professional criminal after all?

It was after four o'clock before I finally got up the courage to leave the offices of the Markey Publishing Company. And by then I had figured out a method by which I could get away from the building without that detective seeing me. It was really quite simple.

Instead of taking the elevator downstairs and going through the lobby, it occurred to me I could walk down the stairs, and when I arrived at the main floor, merely keep on going down to the basement. I would have to be careful about running into the night watchman, but he didn't worry me too much. I knew his habits. He made his rounds every hour and he always took the elevator, going from floor to floor, to make his periodic checks. I only had to wait until I heard the sound of the elevator going through the shaft to know he would be on his rounds, and then I could go on down the stairway without meeting him.

At the rear of the building that houses our offices is a narrow alley, and a short ramp leads from the basement up to this alley. I know it well because this is where office furniture and all sorts of things are delivered to the tenants of the building. It would be a simple matter to go down the stairs to the basement, walk through it and then up the ramp and find myself in the alley.

I almost made the fatal mistake of following this course. But at the last minute I changed my mind. Instead, I purposely left the Markey offices and took the regular passenger elevator to the lobby of the building, let myself out through the main doors and onto the street.

My hunch had been right. As I started west toward Fifth Avenue, I saw out of the corner of my eye the man who left the shadows of a doorway across the street and began following me.

I gave a sigh of relief.

What made me change my plan at the last minute was a matter of simple logic. I suddenly realized if I were to leave the building without being seen, sooner or later this detective would come looking for me. And although he would not find me, he would find the body of Hal Markey, and the alarm would be out.

It was well after five o'clock when I checked into the small residential hotel on West Forty-fourth Street. I had selected the place with a great deal of care. I wanted a thoroughly respectable hotel of the second or third class. A quiet place with little transient business. A small place with not too many rooms. A place where I would have to ring a bell to raise the night desk clerk, who would not be too used to guests checking in at such late hours.

A sleepy-eyed, pimply-faced youth finally came to the desk from somewhere behind a partition, after I had rung several times.

I took a room and bath on the third floor and paid in advance. And I told him I wanted to leave a call for twelve o'clock noon. I emphasized it and explained I was very tired and that even under normal conditions I was a heavy sleeper; they must be sure to ring until I answered, as I had an important appointment at noontime.

I went up to my room then and carefully locked the door behind me, first leaving a DO NOT DISTURB sign on the outside doorknob. I lay down on the bed without removing my clothes.

I waited a full hour before getting up and silently opening the door, gliding down the hallway to the stairs that lay behind a steel door with a red exit sign over it.

The lobby was deserted as I passed through on my way to the street. There was no sign of anyone following and I was sure my hunch had been right. My shadow had talked with the desk clerk after I checked in. He was sure that I was settled for at least the next six or seven hours. He had probably called the station house for instructions and had been told to go home and get some rest himself.

And so now I am in this second-rate grind house and am about to see the same dismal Western epic for the second—or is it the third?—time. I have just lighted a match so I can see the face of my watch.

In exactly an hour and twenty minutes I am due to meet Marty in the men's room at the back of that tavern.

It is going to be very hard not to tell Marty what I have been doing. What has happened during these past eight or ten hours. He has always accused me of lacking imagination and guts. He refers to me in front of Martha as the "gutless wonder." I wonder what he would think if I were to tell him how cleverly I got rid of that detective who was following me.

I wonder what his expression would be if he knew that a certain man is lying dead in his own blood on his own office floor because I killed him.

Marty Feathers, this petty little criminal and blowhard, who gets his kicks out of dressing up like Santa Claus—what would he think if I were to let him know that his brother-in-law is capable of cold-blooded murder?

I am meeting him in a little more than an hour, but I won't tell him. I'll just take the ticket and the money and I'll tell him nothing. I'll let him go on living in his little world of illusion and fantasy.

I got here ten minutes early and it is just as well I did, for two reasons. I needed that double bourbon and soda I had at the bar. I am very nervous. I would say I am frightened except I don't quite know what it is I have to fear. Everything is working out just the way I planned it. But still, the drink came in handy. It quieted me down a little bit at least.

And I had a chance to talk to the bartender for a moment or so. I had a feeling Marty would be a few minutes late. He always is. And so I took advantage of my talk with the bartender to explain to him I have been suffering a great deal lately from a severe case of constipation. It will set his mind at rest as to why I have been sitting here on this toilet seat for so long.

Thank God, I just heard the outside door of this men's room opening and someone is coming in. There is a foul odor in this place and I find it hard to avoid nausea.

From where I am sitting on this toilet seat, I can see a space opposite me through the louvers of the swinging door. The twin sinks and the large cracked wall mirror are directly across the room. Further along the wall, near the outside door, is the urinal. I am unable to see that from where I sit, but whoever came in is using it.

He is through now and is walking toward the washbasins.

Damn! It isn't Marty. Where in God's name can Marty be?

From his back, this man looks vaguely familiar. He is lifting his face now and looking into the mirror.

Dear God, did he give me a fright! He looks exactly like that detective who was following me last night. But I must be wrong. I am sure I shook him. It is just a case of nerves. This man is obviously a stranger. He is combing his hair now.

The door has opened again and someone else is entering. I never should have chosen this place to meet Marty. I didn't think anyone ever came here.

This man who looks like my detective has moved away now and I think he is putting a coin into the machine at the entrance that gives back a squirt of perfume for a dime.

Marty is now in front of the mirror, washing his hands. Won't that other man ever leave?

The door slammed again and Marty is looking up. I can see that he knows I am in here waiting. I guess he just wants to be absolutely sure we are alone.

He has turned now and is looking directly at the door of the toilet, and he just whispered my name.

I reply, also in a whisper, "It's me, Hubert, Marty." He is smiling and I feel a terrible sense of relief.

His hand has gone into his breast pocket and he is reaching for the ticket and the money that are going to spell freedom for me.

I knew that Marty would come through. I knew he wouldn't let me down.

Oh Christ! Christ Almighty!

What is Marty doing with that knife in his hand?

Why...

No, No, No-o-o-o

8

CLAYTON ANDREWS

I am going to telephone Lieutenant Goodwin now. He has struck me all along as a sensitive and understanding man. I shall explain everything to him and I think he will understand why I had to kill her.

Someone must perform the duties of a nonexistent God.

The moment I woke up early this morning and realized it was Friday, I knew it would be a terrible day. The most terrible day of my life.

The three Demerols which I took late last night made me sleep like a dead man. Turning my head slightly on my pillow, I could see the alarm clock on the table next to my bed. It was almost eleven o'clock.

I must hurry and get up and shower and shave and dress. Dark suit and black shoes and socks. White shirt and a deep maroon tie, because I have no black tie. I must dress carefully and try to look my best. It wouldn't be right to go to Pat's funeral and not look my best.

I will put a pot of coffee on to percolate while I am getting dressed, but I don't think I am going to be up to eating anything. I don't feel as if I shall ever want to eat again.

I must try to be more careful. That was a nasty nick I gave myself on the chin with the razor. My hands seem to shake incessantly and apparently that long, deathlike sleep has failed to actually rest me or relieve this nervous tension under which I have been suffering all week.

I don't know how I am ever going to be able to get through the funeral, but I must make the effort. Thank God, no one interfered with my plans, and it will be simple and quick. Merely the barest ceremony in the private chapel out at the cemetery, and I requested the smallest of their rooms because I want as few people as possible present. No actual service, just a few moments of silence. And then the burial.

That will be the worst moment, when they are lowering her coffin into the grave.

It looks very cold outside, overcast. I certainly hope we don't get snow. I must drive out to Woodlawn, and snow would make it extremely difficult. On the other hand it might serve to keep some of the sordid sensation-seekers away.

I hope no one shows up. I could kill Hal Markey for closing the office so the staff could attend. As though any of them actually ever really cared for Pat. God, the lengths people will go to to get a macabre thrill.

This studio depresses me terribly, so I think I will go down to the restaurant on the corner for my cup of coffee. I have a little time to spare and I would like to take my mind off what I have to do this afternoon.

I'll buy an early edition of the afternoon paper and spend a few minutes over the coffee. It may settle my nerves.

That fat waitress gave me the oddest look. Of course she knows who I am. I've been coming in here for several years now. There can be no doubt that she knows all about this thing that has happened. But still, I wonder why she looked at me like that.

It is just as well I am having this second cup of coffee. I must be careful not to show any expression, not to let any of these people who keep staring at me realize what I am feeling. I am sorry now I bought the paper.

That story of Joel Siddel giving himself up to the police was quite a shock. It told me nothing really. Merely that he is being held for investigation and that he is in the prison ward at Bellevue. I wonder how ill he actually is.

So they have the gun. I wonder what they make of that. If they believe Siddel is guilty, they are bigger fools than I would have thought. At least there is one good thing about Siddel being in custody. He won't be able to attend the funeral this afternoon.

The coincidence of Hal Markey being found dead in his office early this morning is almost unbelievable. Who would ever have guessed that he had a bad heart?

I can't understand why the newspapers are unable to give more complete information. Just the fact that the superintendent noticed the lights left on, and knowing the offices were to be closed, went in to turn them off and found Markey lying on the floor dead. They did discover that he had had a mild heart attack last night in his home but had thought it merely acute indigestion.

From what I gather, he returned to his office to catch up with some work and, sometime during the night, started drinking. When he fell after the fatal attack his head struck the poker in front of his fireplace, so I dare say he was crossing the room to refill his glass.

The man always was a swine, about eating and drinking and everything else. It seems almost like poetic justice that he should have died while he was satiating himself.

Thank God, that's another one who won't be at the funeral.

Markey dead and Siddel apparently critically ill and in a prison ward. And both on the day of her funeral. If I believed in God I would almost be inclined to think there is some justice in the world after all.

I had better leave now and get the car out of the garage. I don't want to be late. After this is all over, I shall sell the car. I won't be needing it anymore because I will also sell the house in the country. I know I will never be able to return to that house again. I never want to see or touch any of the things we shared. I can't even bear the thought of returning to the office, because it was from there she left just a week ago to go to her death.

I don't know, nor do I much care, what I will do with the rest of my life. I only know I shall never go back. There is no place to go back to.

Damn. I almost hit that car coming out of the side street. I must pay more attention now. I can't let anything happen until I have finished out at the cemetery and have seen the last earthly remains of the woman I once loved so much laid to final rest.

It seems utterly incredible Pat has been dead only a week. That last time I saw her, as I was leaving the office party Friday night, seems like something which happened years ago.

These policemen who have been haunting me and ferreting around into the secrets of her life will never solve the puzzle of her death. No more than I was able to solve the enigma of her life while she still existed.

They would do better to forget about the whole thing.

This drive out to Woodlawn is interminable. I am almost sorry now I didn't hire a private car or take a cab. I find it very hard to concentrate on my driving. Perhaps if I turn on the radio ...

God Almighty, can't I ever escape? It would almost seem as though I am being pursued by a private army of personal devils. First I open a newspaper and read about Siddel and Markey and then I turn on the radio and hear the newscast about young Creamer.

I have thought for a long time he was cracking up, but who could have guessed he would have gone stark raving mad? What sort of insanity ever led him to go into a police station and confess that it was he who pulled the trigger which sent the leaden death into her heart?

At least the police seem to be showing some small iota of intelligence. The announcer said they are holding him for a mental examination, and well they might.

I have heard of certain psychotic types who confess to having committed this or that sensational crime, either in a search for publicity or to satisfy some megalomanic inner craving, but I never would have dreamed that Creamer would do such a thing. I have long known that he is neither bright nor very stable, but what an odd thing for him to do. Does he actually expect anyone to believe him?

It is quite true that no matter how well one thinks he knows another man, he can never be utterly sure in making a judgment. I was certainly wrong about Siddel. Nevertheless, I would stake my life that that callow, romantic idiot Creamer would no more be capable of committing murder than I—well than I would be capable of flying.

Thank the Lord I am here at last. I didn't think that fool outside would ever tell me where to park my car.

I am early, but I am still surprised there are not more people in this small private chapel. The casket is on the dais up there a few yards away and I have noticed several people go up and hesitate in front of it for a moment before taking a seat.

I am very glad I ordered the undertaker to keep the lid closed tight. That I refused to have any flowers at all.

I have seen no one from my office, which surprises me. On the other hand, I have seen almost no one at all whom I know. Several have come by and said a few words to me, but I am not at all sure who they are.

The Unitarian minister who is to conduct this brief service has just arrived and has nodded to me. He will ask us to bow our heads in a moment of silent prayer and contemplation and that is the single concession I have made to a religious service.

I wonder who that young girl is who keeps looking around the room as though she is looking for someone. She seems somehow familiar, and when I caught her eye, she gave me the slightest sort of nod. I wonder what ever possessed her to wear a sweater and scarf and a short pleated skirt to a funeral service.

I am sure she has no brassiere on under that awful-looking garment.

I am not surprised that Bertha Markey didn't show up. She has her own dead to concern her this day.

Hubert Pringle should be here. He was a friend of mine. Pat and I were about the only two people I know connected with Markey Publications who ever showed him any kindness. He could at least have come and paid his final respects.

The minister is on the dais now, standing beside the coffin, and the moment has almost arrived. I can see people already beginning to bow their heads.

That young girl's face haunts me. I am sure I have seen her somewhere before. I would like to paint her face. It is so utterly vulgar, which is odd, because if I look at it feature by feature, it is really a beautiful face, in a classic peasant sense.

That incongruous apparel she is wearing shows her figure off and I can see that she must have a truly lovely body.

I would like to do a nude of her.

My mind must be slipping. I came here to think of Pat for the last time and instead I am thinking of painting a common little girl who couldn't interest me less. It must be the fetid, overheated atmosphere of this small room.

I do feel slightly faint. I wish they would get this part of it over and done with.

"There will be cars outside to accommodate any of you who wish to follow the casket to the grave."

It is over now and done with. It wasn't quite as simple as I would have wished, because the minister did say a few words and offer up a prayer after the moment of silent contemplation. But at least that part is finished. I am deeply gratified that so many of my friends and associates observed my wishes and permitted these services to be completely private. That they stayed away.

That girl looks exactly the way I feel. Bewildered, lost. As though she doesn't quite know what to do next. It is very odd.

I am sure I have seen her somewhere before. I do believe she is coming over to speak to me. I could swear she is about to cry.

I wonder why it is there always seems to be something so forlornly tragic about tears in the eyes of a truly stupid person. Certainly her face expresses nothing if not vacuity and stupidity.

I do remember her now. She worked in the office a week or so but I think the only time I ever spoke to was at the office party last Friday, a week ago.

It was nice of her to have come. I didn't know that she had ever met Pat.

She is trying to say something to me, but she can't seem to find the words.

I must help her; she was nice to come here today. She is the only person from the office I have seen.

"Would you like to ride out to the grave with me?"

It is all over, finished, done with. She no longer exists, except in my mind, and she will be there forever.

The last clod of earth will have been tossed and those men, whose grim task it is to finish up the final details, will have carefully raked the dirt over the slight mound and have scattered the grass seeds so that the winter snows will cover them and the sod will come up in the spring to make green the grave where she lies deep in the ground.

I have returned to the city, to this studio of mine down in the Village. I am not alone. Across the room is the girl. Her name is Susan and she came back with me, sitting next to me in the car, mute and sullen-eyed.

She has told me that on that one night she met my wife, Pat was kind to her and that is why she came out to the funeral.

She told me that she sensed I was alone and bitter and lost and unhappy, and she felt I needed someone to be with me. Perhaps she was telling the truth. It is hard for me to know, because in her I also sensed someone who was alone and helpless and lost.

We have almost no words at all, but when I offered to drive her back, she came along willingly.

I stopped and purchased two quarts of whiskey at the liquor store and it seemed the most natural thing in the world that she should come up here to the studio with me.

She is sitting across the room now, on the couch, a glass in her hand.

She has taken the scarf from her head, dropped her coat on a chair and kicked off her slippers, which were soaking wet from walking through the snow which finally fell. She keeps sneaking odd, furtive glances at me, glances which seem composed equally of curiosity and a sort of vague sympathy.

Twice more she has told me that she thought my wife was a real lady and that my wife was kind to her. She has also told me she thinks that when someone is heart-broken, he should not be alone.

She strikes me as being unbelievably vulgar and sentimental. She also strikes me as being utterly sincere.

I am going to refill her glass. She is getting just a little bit drunk, and I am feeling this whiskey myself. I am glad that she is here and I am glad that she is satisfied not to talk.

"Can I do anything for you, Mr. Andrews?"

"Do anything?"

"If a person is sick and unhappy, it is sometimes good to just forget everything. Isn't that why you are drinking?"

I got up and crossed the studio and stood in front of a canvas that was standing on an easel. It was a nude, not fully completed. An oil I had started doing of Pat some years back and had never finished. I looked at it for several minutes, saying nothing, and then I picked it up and turned it around and replaced it on the easel.

I went back and got the bottle and I poured a straight shot into her glass and one into my own.

I wanted to thank her. Thank her for showing an understanding I hadn't believed her capable of. Instead I said, "Yes, yes, you can do something for me."

She took a drink from the glass and made a face.

"What can I do?"

"You can take that sweater off. And the skirt. And anything else you might be wearing. I would like to see if your body is as beautiful as I believe it to be."

For several seconds she stared at me and then, without a word, stood up and began to remove her clothes.

I had almost forgotten how desirable a really beautiful woman's body can be.

I am back in the studio again and I have just finished the last of the first quart of whiskey. I am alone.

She is still in the bedroom, lying prone on the bed, spent and exhausted from our labors. It was done without words and it was only after it was over that she began to talk.

Her story is almost beyond belief. At times I had difficulty following her, because of her ghastly Brooklyn accent as well as because of the way her mind rambles. But I had to believe what she told me.

Without doubt she exaggerates here and there; without doubt she is unable to put various events in their proper context. But there is no doubt of her fear, no doubt that someone has been trying to get rid of her.

For some weird reason, she seems to feel that the entire course of events is somehow related to Pat and to the party at the office last Friday evening.

This liquor is making me quite drunk, but my mind is absolutely lucid and clear.

I haven't actually questioned her yet. I have only listened. In a moment or so, as soon as I am up to moving again, I shall return to the bedroom. I want her again. I want to feel the wild straining movements of her lithe, superb body. I want to crush my mouth against her vulgar red, parted lips, feel the nails of her hands across my back. Feel the strength of her young legs as they twine over my own legs. I want to hear her breath come in short agonizing gasps.

And I want to ask her questions.

I will bring her another drink from this fresh bottle. The whiskey will make her talk. I have this feeling that somehow she is right. Somehow these things that have been happening to her are connected in some way with Pat and with what happened to Pat.

I am sure that she has the facts but I am equally sure she is not bright enough to fit them all together so they will make sense.

It is quite strange that when I am with her, holding her, joining her in an erotic series of acrobatics, I seem to forget who she is and believe that I am once more with the woman who was my wife and whom I buried this afternoon.

This time, at the moment of climax, I was sure she was Pat and I used Pat's name as my body rose and fell. She cried out sharply and I suddenly realized I was hurting her.

I have brought her another drink and now she is lying naked on the bed and I am sitting next to her.

"You say that my wife was kind to you?" I said. "When? Where? How was she kind?"

"When we went downstairs to the bathroom."

It wasn't making sense. Or perhaps I have been drinking too much and I am not hearing clearly.

"The bathroom?"

"When I was frightened."

It still didn't make sense.

"Because of Santa Claus," she said.

"You are making no sense at all," I said. "What in the name of God are you talking about?"

She looked at me, annoyed.

"Don't you understand? It is like I told you. After that disgusting experience with Mr. Markey—at the Christmas party—I was feeling a little sick. So I went downstairs to the ladies' room. And that's when I saw him."

"You saw who?"

"Why, the man in the bathroom. The man dressed up like Santa Claus. He was in the ladies' room."

"You must have dreamed it," I said. "What in the name of God would he be doing downstairs in the ladies' room? The men's room is upstairs and ..."

She was annoyed that I doubted her word, and she pouted.

"Well, all I can tell you is that he was there. In the ladies' john. He seemed to be hiding or something and if you don't believe me—well, your wife saw him too. I musta screamed or something, because he ran out, right past your wife, and she saw him too. That's when she was nice to me."

"And you have never mentioned this to anyone? This business of seeing 'Santa Claus' in the ladies' room down on that floor?"

"No. I didn't mention it because I was embarrassed. Being in the ladies' john with a man."

I looked over at her naked body lying there on the bed. I remembered what she had told me about Hal Markey. I thought— embarrassed? Good God in heaven!

I stood up and started for the studio. I wanted another drink. My mind was very clear now. I was remembering something. I was remembering the jewelry robbery which had taken place on the floor below the offices of the Markey Publications on that night of the office party.

I was remembering something else that had also happened sometime on that same evening. I was remembering a policeman, dressed in plain clothes, who had been deliberately run down by a hit-and-run driver. I was remembering the testimony of a dimwitted alcoholic drifter who had been half passed out in front of the building and had vaguely recalled seeing a man cross the street to question someone sitting behind the wheel of a car.

Why would a man disguised as Santa Claus be hiding in a ladies' room a couple of doors away from the office of a wholesale jewelry firm around the time it was burglarized?

If I were a policeman—an alert policeman—and I saw a man disguised as Santa Claus climb behind the wheel of a parked car, is it possible I would cross over to question him?

Two women had been on that floor and seen this fraudulent Santa Claus where he was not supposed to be. One was dead; one's life had been threatened.

A policeman was dead.

The thoughts kept rushing around in my head as I reached for the bottle and took another long drink. I noticed that this second bottle was now less than half filled.

Things were getting a little mixed up. I wanted to return to the bedroom. This girl, this girl whose body reminded me so much of the body of my wife, was lying there. Naked, waiting.

I'll take the rest of the bottle in with me this time. I don't know whether the liquor makes me think clearly or actually only serves to confuse me more. I keep wanting this woman in the other room because her body reminds me so much of Pat. So much that each time I have her, there comes that one wild, insane moment when I think that she really is Pat. That's when I have hurt her.

The phone is just across the room and I should really go over first and put in a phone call to this Lieutenant Goodwin. Tell him what I know. What I have learned.

I'll do it as soon as I come back. I want to go inside and see Pat ...

What am I saying? I want to go inside to this rather vulgar girl, with her soft, compliant body. Finish off this bottle and have her once more.

9

DETECTIVE LIEUTENANT WILLIAM GOODWIN

It seems this day will never end.

The truth of the matter is, it is actually another day and within a few minutes it will be six o'clock. Six o'clock on Saturday morning.

Very shortly, daybreak will be lighting up the windows in this studio of Clayton Andrews, where I am now sitting. I have been here for almost an hour. I came as soon as I received his telephone call—within minutes of the time our man had signed the confession and we had taken him down and booked him. I had thought it was all over and I could go home at last and get some rest.

But then the telephone call came, and so I am here instead.

Andrews is sitting across from me, still in his dressing gown. Still with that dazed expression on his face. I know that he is very drunk, but it is strange how he seems to come to every now and then. When he is doing the talking, he makes very good sense and even pronounces his words quite clearly. But then when I try to tell him something, he seems to fade away and I feel quite sure that not a word I have said has gotten through to him.

I wish I could make him understand, because, when he comes to sometime later in the day, he is sure to want to know exactly what took place.

He will want to know about Pringle and how we found him slumped down on the toilet seat, already dead, within seconds of the time that his brother-in-law, Marty Feathers, stabbed him.

It was a bad break that our man was unable to get back into that room in time. But how were we to know? How were we to guess that Feathers, that mad-dog killer, was out to erase any possible witness?

In a perverse way it is lucky for us, of course, that we caught him red-handed. Once he realized we had him for murder, he knew that there would no longer be any reason for him not to make a full confession. As he said himself, we can only hang him once.

He won't hang, of course, but he will do at least three life sentences, and I feel sure that they will not run concurrently.

There is a certain irony in the fact that Pringle, who was covering for his brother-in-law—innocently or otherwise—should have died by his hand. One thing that really surprised me is that Feathers should have hung onto that Santa Claus uniform. That he should have hidden it, along with the jewels that he took from Coster's safe, in his sister's home. Sooner or later we would have searched the place, but perhaps he hoped to be gone by then. Certainly the airline ticket he purchased for this weekend indicated as much.

If Andrews would only stop falling asleep, I would like to explain to him how closely his theory fits into the facts. That Feathers' confession bears him out completely.

Feathers, having been seen in the washroom by the Flannery girl, realized the threat she presented. He had to either kill her or get her out of town until he could make his own getaway.

The only thing that really saved her was Pat Andrews seeing him as he left the building just before he ran down Patrolman Swendson. She saw him, but of course she didn't realize the danger. Of course, when he put the car into gear to follow her, he couldn't stop. He couldn't wait for Patrolman Swendson to question him. So he ran him down in cold blood and then followed her car to the motel.

Siddel was lucky—or unlucky, according to how you look at it. If Feathers had followed her upstairs at once and killed her, Siddel would never have been shot. But Feathers already had heard her tell Siddel what room she had checked into, so he thought he had plenty of time. He wanted to duck the Santa Claus uniform first since it would make him too conspicuous.

And then later, he returned.

Siddel will never know how lucky he was that the automatic jammed on that second shot. That is, he will be lucky if he pulls through.

The Flannery girl was lucky. Lucky in the subway and lucky she decided to hide out.

I see that Andrews' eyes are closed and I believe he has finally passed out. In a way I am glad.

It is just as well that he is not awake and alert when the ambulance gets here and they bring the basket up and get that body in the other room.

I am absolutely sure he still has no idea that he murdered her. That he twisted the sheet around her neck and pulled the ends tight and held them until the last breath of life escaped from her tortured throat.

I wonder if he will ever really know why he killed her. He seemed to be so sincerely grateful for the information she gave him.

I have only one theory and it is probably too farfetched, too bizarre for even Andrews' own defense attorneys to use at his trial.

I think it is quite possible Andrews, far back in his subconscious mind, wanted to murder his wife all along. And some time a few hours ago, in his highly emotional condition, drugged by alcohol, he made a mistake in identity and confused this girl he was sleeping with with the wife who had already been murdered.

The ambulance should be arriving any minute now.

I am going to hate to have to awaken this man, Clayton Andrews. For the first time during this week I have known him, his face has lost that tortured expression and he is relaxed. He seems to be at peace with himself.

I can hear a siren somewhere in the distance.

It has been a long night. A long, long week.

Thank God for the New Year.

THE END

www.ingramcontent.com/pod-product-compliance
Lightning Source LLC
Chambersburg PA
CBHW070922190726
48292CB00004B/1062